ONE BROTHER SHY

Also by Terry Fallis

The Best Laid Plans

The High Road

Up and Down

No Relation

Poles Apart

ONE BROTHER SHY

A NOVEL

TERRY FALLIS

McClelland & Stewart

Library and Archives Canada Cataloguing in Publication is available upon request

ISBN: 978-0-7710-5072-5
ebook ISBN: 978-0-7710-5073-2

Typeset in Electra by McClelland & Stewart
Book design by Five Seventeen
Cover image © procurator / Getty Images
Printed and bound in the United States of America

McClelland & Stewart,
a division of Penguin Random House Canada Limited,
a Penguin Random House Company
www.penguinrandomhouse.ca

1 2 3 4 5 21 20 19 18 17

For my identical twin brother, Tim.

(Had I known I was going to write this novel next,

I wouldn't have dedicated No Relation *to you!)*

PART ONE

I was silent throughout. I had no choice.

CHAPTER 1

She died before she could tell me. That's my theory, anyway. She thought she had more time. I thought she had more time – perhaps not much, but some. Clearly, neither of us really had a handle on it. Then again, even if we'd known, you're never really ready, are you? No. You think you are. You hope you are. But you never are.

But the timing was out of my hands, and apparently out of hers, too.

I'd left for work that Monday morning as I always did, turning Mom's care over to the wonderful Malaya, Saint Malaya. Mom wasn't awake when I left. Hell, I wasn't awake when I left. But lately, Mom had been sleeping more – deeper and longer – often for a good part of the day. It was somehow easier for her to breathe when she slept. Or perhaps when she slept, she simply was not conscious of how difficult it was to breathe.

Malaya arrived at the apartment, as she did every weekday morning, at eight, and left each night whenever I made it home from the office, usually before six. That's really all I did, and all I'd done for the preceding two years. Work. Take care of Mom. Shop for groceries. And see my therapist. My sessions with Dr. Weaver were Mondays and Thursdays at noon so I didn't miss any time in the office. And trust me, I didn't want to provoke my bellicose beast of a boss with extended lunch hours. On the positive side of the ledger, skipping lunch two days each week helped keep my weight steady at 170 pounds.

I certainly didn't begrudge my lot in life, though I suppose many might. For my mother, I'd have gladly carried on with this routine for ten years or longer. She had taken care of me for, well, for all of my life. Even at the end, she was still caring for me, even as I cared for her.

I am Alex MacAskill. When this started to play out, I was twenty-four, a software engineer, and I wrote beautiful, pristine code for Facetech, a company developing an advanced facial recognition program. Given my academic credentials, I really shouldn't have still been writing code, though I can't deny I was good at it – still am – modesty aside. I should have, at the very least, been leading a team of coders rather than toiling among them. But I wasn't. I'd not yet become the person I was supposed to be. I was fifteen years old when it happened, nearly ten years earlier, but I was still not yet back on the rails, not yet ready, not yet whole – hence Dr. Weaver, Mondays and

Thursdays, at noon. Over the years, Mom had always believed Gabriel was to blame. She was probably right. Who am I kidding? Of course she was right. But maybe, just maybe, there was more to it.

Facetech's corporate headquarters and much of senior management were in Vancouver. But the software development team was based in Kanata, about a half-hour drive from our Ottawa apartment in Sandy Hill. The company occupied two floors of a garden-variety suburban glass office tower. My own office was on the ninth floor. When I say office, I don't really mean office. I mean cubicle. When I say cubicle, I don't really mean cubicle. I mean a desk with one lame fabric partition separating me from my nearest colleague, Abby, whose desk abutted mine. There were sixteen other coders on the floor, and another ten one floor below, all stationed in makeshift two-desk units that masqueraded badly as legitimate cubicles. They weren't legit at all. Even at 8:35 a.m., there was a sort of low-level buzz running through the space. Whispering voices, clacking keyboards, and the heavy sighing of less than fulfilled employees coming together to provide the white-noise soundtrack for my working days.

When she heard me settle in to my squeaky chair, Abby popped her head up above her side of the partition with slightly more explosive force than a highly strung jack-in-the-box.

"Alex man, welcome to your week!" she said in a voice just loud enough for everyone on the floor to hear.

I dropped back into my chair from an unknown altitude, my hand on my chest quelling what I'm sure qualified as a bona fide "cardiac event."

"Oh, sorry," she said. "Did I startle you?"

Not at all. What gave you that idea? When you greet me like that, I always launch myself from my chair just by flexing my buttocks.

"A little," I replied, trying to breathe normally.

"Sorry. Did you have a good weekend?"

Well, if you call shopping for groceries, filling prescriptions, emptying catheter bags, cooking and serving meals, cleaning up the kitchen, changing oxygen tanks, and then doing heaps of laundry, a good weekend, then yes, mine was just awesome, thank you.

"Yes," I replied as I watched my MacBook Pro boot up. "Thanks."

"Hello? Eyes up here, please."

I don't know about you, but I don't actually listen with my eyes. I'm hearing you loud and clear, as is everyone else on the floor.

I sighed, looked up at her, and managed the formative stages of a smile.

"Better," Abby conceded. "Now, again, did you have a good weekend?"

"Yes. Fine," I said, holding her eyes before turning back to my computer.

"Okay, just calm down, Alex. I mean it. I just can't handle your incessant chatter this early on a Monday morning. It tires me out. So please, lay off the caffeine and try to contain yourself," she said. "And by the way, yes, my weekend was just fine, thanks for asking."

I was almost going to ask, really, but you sucked all the air out of the room and it left me a little light-headed. Besides, my heart rate is only now returning to normal.

She sighed, too, and disappeared back behind the partition.

Abby Potts. Another hot-shot coder. She's a pistol, usually with a bullet in the chamber and the safety off. A curly mop of brown hair, dressed more like a student than a nine-to-fiver, she's smart, cute, and cool. But she scares me. Most people scare me, but she does, in particular, in her own special way. Then again, she does make an effort. I've suspected for a while now that I might be her office project.

Above me, Abby hove into view once more.

"Hey, how is your mother doing?" she asked with a note of concern.

Not good. Not good at all. I think we're in the final stages. Weeks now. Maybe a month. But it means a lot that you asked.

"About the same, thanks," I replied, making sure I was looking at her when I said it, my fingers hovering over my keyboard.

She gave me a long look of pure, unadulterated sympathy, before slowly lowering herself behind the partition like she was riding an elevator.

There was one real office, with walls, albeit glass ones, in the sun-soaked southeastern corner of the floor. Relative to the real estate the rest of us enjoyed, it seemed the size of a small principality, though squash court is likely a better comparison. The palatial enclave belonged to Genghis Khan. Sorry, force of habit. The palatial enclave belonged to, as she frequently put it, *the boss of all of you*, Simone Ashe. And no, I'm not sure what I'd done to deserve a desk in her line of sight. With better luck, I might have been isolated in a distant desk-pod one floor below. Just my good fortune. Perhaps I was paying for habitually pulling wings off flies in an earlier life.

Simone knew nothing about software or the strings of code that align to make it work. She was a lawyer and had started in Vancouver as Facetech's in-house counsel. I figured she got bored pushing paper and asked – more likely demanded – to be given a bit more range. Then, through the power of a loud voice, a fierce countenance, a wicked temper, too much confidence, and not enough competence, she cut a swath through upper management and wound up coming east to lead what is arguably the most important unit in the company. (I can easily see why her senior colleagues happily promoted her right out of the Vancouver office.) You see, we were the team creating what just might propel Facetech to the promised land of the initial public offering, or, better still, an acquisition by some Silicon Valley Goliath. We were building the next generation of facial recognition software – a significant leap beyond current platforms. The commercial applications were virtually limitless (read, the potential profits were virtually limitless). And my precious code was right at the heart of it all. No pressure.

I swivelled in my chair to find Abby standing right beside me. After jerking my arms in surprise and embedding my pencil in our partition, I closed my eyes and tried to slow my breathing.

"Again? I startled you again? Sorry man, but you really need to work on your fooking peripheral vision," she said, iPad in hand.

Fooking?

"Sorry, what kind of peripheral vision?"

"Fooking," she replied. "It's a word that looms large in my personal profanity reduction program."

Ah, I see. Your PPRP. Got it.

"Oh," I said.

"It's time," she said with a heavy, anxiety-freighted sigh. "You ready?"

Abby, whether or not I'm ready is a moot point. Until Simone Ashe actually arrives in the boardroom, often like a grizzly with an inflamed hemorrhoid, only angrier, we have no fooking idea what's coming our way.

I took two deep breaths and nodded. Then I stood, grabbed my notebook, and followed her through the maze of two-desk stations. Our Monday morning staff meetings were like a big old box of bon-bombs. Something was going to explode. We just never knew what or when.

It was a big boardroom. Windows along the outside edge, glass along the inside, and pressed up against the transparent end wall of Simone's office as if it were her personal boardroom – and in her mind, it was. The usual protocol played out. Two floors of coders arrived on time and sat in silence for the 9:00 a.m. meeting. We, of course, could see Simone through the glass at her desk next door, apparently deeply engaged in something critical on her laptop screen – my money was on Minesweeper, but there was also some action on Scrabble. She was sneaking glances at all of us waiting for her. She wore yet another Chanel suit. This one was red. Sorry, Simone once referred to the colour as Pomegranate Spritz. And no, I wouldn't know a Chanel suit from a safari suit, but Abby provided weekly F-bomb-laced reports on our boss's wardrobe.

Simone just sat at her desk. She understood that one very simple demonstration of power was the control over our time. At 9:15, she checked her watch, rose from her desk, and walked, empty-handed, out of her office and into the boardroom. Tension followed her in and draped itself over the assembly. She slid into the very chair you would expect her to assume. It was at the head of the table. It was plusher, bigger, and higher than every other chair in the room. And it swivelled. The rest of us sat in plastic stacking chairs. She looked down on us like the captain of a slave ship about to demand we row faster so she could water-ski.

"Hello, my little pretties," she started with a smile. "I hope you all had good weekends. No, that's not really true. I don't actually care. But I am trying."

Yes, very trying. But wait, there's more. You're also an egomaniacal, megalomaniacal, bombastic, and malevolent tyrant. But thanks for trying.

"Anyway, on to more important matters. You promised me we

could have Facetech Gold in beta by October 16. Are we on track to meet that deadline?"

Well, we might make that deadline if you'd stop humiliating and abusing your team. With three coders on stress leave and two with physician-diagnosed post-traumatic stress disorder it's a tad difficult to stay on schedule. Oh yeah, and it's not that great for morale either. Just sayin'.

Of course, no one responded.

"I distinctly remember asking a question just now. Who'll provide me with an answer?" she continued, scanning the room.

Twenty-seven coders looked in forty-two different directions, and none of our eyes came anywhere close to the creature on the throne at the head of the board table.

"Answer me!" she shrieked, leaning forward in her chair and banging both hands on the table. Several coders flinched. Okay, I was one of them, but clearly my flinch featured more artistry than the others.

"MacAskill! Are we on schedule or not?"

I forced myself to look at her. I didn't really have much choice.

"Yes" was all I said.

"Yes what?" she demanded.

Yes, omnipotent nimrod?

"Yes, we'll make the deadline," I replied.

"Fuckin' right we will. Not only that, HQ has just told me we now have to deliver the beta by October 9, or my ass will be detached from my body. And trust me, you don't want to know what'll happen around here if my ass is detached from my body."

Oh I don't know. It would be something to see. Your Chanel suits wouldn't fit quite as well, but still, it might be worth it.

I looked up just as Abby stood up. Uh-oh.

"Simone, some of what we're doing just can't be compressed any more," she said. "It's a process that has to run its course. Not every step can be accelerated. We're making software here. I don't think we can make the ninth."

I thought I knew what true silence was. I'd already experienced it a few times in my life. Remembrance Day, of course. And during the pause I strategically placed in the middle of performing, not reciting, performing, one of Macbeth's famous soliloquies, in grade nine English class. (Incidentally, it was a tour de force.) And several years ago when my mother told me she'd been diagnosed with idiopathic pulmonary fibrosis. But I was wrong. The silence that greeted Abby's pronouncement was so much more, um, *silent*, than anything I'd ever heard. (Or is it *hadn't heard*?) If a pin had dropped on the carpeted floor, it would have sounded like a car accident.

Abby realized what she'd done and looked a little queasy as she lowered herself back into the chair. Simone just stared at her, agape. No sound emerged from her open mouth. We sat there for what seemed like minutes – probably because it actually was minutes. Then she slowly reared up on her hind legs. Her next words were issued in what can best be described as a cross between a growl and a snarl.

"It's Abby, right?"

Abby nodded.

"Well, Abby, I don't need your insolence and insubordination when I'm trying to keep this ship off the rocks and still get us into port a week early."

Then she paused, presumably to consider her next salvo. She didn't consider it for long.

"You've been quite the little smartass since you landed here in your too tight jeans that really aren't office-appropriate, and I'm getting tired of it. But I'm told you write good code and we need all hands on deck, even the mutineers. So just watch yourself, Abby whatever your name is."

It was quite amazing how well Simone was able to enunciate through gritted teeth.

Abby could not disguise the shock and anger that were plastered all over her face. In fact, I don't think she was even trying to disguise it. Not a good move.

That's when Simone detonated. I know. You thought she'd already detonated. Nope. Discretion and decorum prevent me from reporting on the rest of Simone's vitriolic and venomous invective. It went on for quite a while and got ever more nasty and personal. No, I didn't think that was possible, either. At the zenith of her tirade, I suddenly stood up. I didn't mean to, but I seemed unable to control myself. I just couldn't stay seated any more.

"Please." My almost whiny, one-word entreaty somehow slipped conveniently into a moment of silence as Simone refilled her lungs to continue her attack.

She snapped her eyes to mine.

"Please, what, MacAskill?" she said, turning towards me.

Again, was I not clear? Obviously I meant please continue tearing strips off Abby until there's nothing left of her. She'll be so much better equipped to help us meet this asinine deadline if you just carry on with the flaying.

"Please, stop," I clarified. "We've got so much work to do."

"Wow! Now that was impressive," Simone said, standing and applauding. "Sticking up for Ally and all. How quaint."

"Abby," I said not quite quietly enough.

"I know her fucking name! I was just choosing not to use it," she shrieked.

Then she sat back down, still breathing heavily from her exertions. I seemed to have momentarily knocked her berating bully function offline. I sat down, too. Then she spoke very calmly and quietly. It was quite unsettling.

"MacAskill, I need you to update the weekly status deck so I can present it to the senior management team at one this afternoon on our weekly call. I'll need the new graphics in there as well as the code status summary and rollout plan. PowerPoint, even if you have to skip lunch to get it done."

I frowned. Again, I didn't mean to frown. It was unplanned and involuntary. It kind of just happened.

"What's with the sad face, MacAskill?" she said, pouting. "You got something more important going on right now – and think carefully before answering."

To be honest, right now, trimming my nose hair is more important to me, but whatever.

"It's Monday," I said.

"Oh my, congratulations! Aren't we doing well on the days of the week? Before you know it, you'll know all the months, too. Oh, they grow up so fast," she sneered.

"I have my lunch-hour appointment every Monday and Thursday. I can't change it this late," I replied.

She rolled her eyes.

"Jesus, can't you skip just one session to do your goddamn job, or is lying on a couch for an hour twice a week really all that important?"

I felt my face grow hot and red. I said nothing. Abby saved me.

"Simone, I'm sorry about my tone earlier," she said almost in a whisper. "It's only 9:30 now. Alex and I can work on the deck together until he has to leave, and then I can finish it up and make it look pretty over lunch. You'll have it by 12:45. We'll get it done. Promise."

Simone just stared at her.

"Not one minute later," Simone snapped before wheeling out of the boardroom and slamming her office door.

The rest of us slunk back to our crucibles, er, cubicles. Soon after, Simone left the office, likely to have a smoke. When she'd gone, Abby came around to my side.

"That was fucking unbelievable," she said. "She is absolutely, certifiably, psycho bat-shit crazy."

I nodded and opened PowerPoint to start mapping out the update presentation.

Abby put her hand on my shoulder.

"Thanks for at least trying to come to my rescue. That was fecking nice of you," Abby said.

I have no idea how that happened or why I stood up. And I didn't exactly turn the tide, now did I?

"It's okay," I replied.

"Eye contact, Alex. Eye contact."

I turned to look at her.

"Better," she said. "I thought you were either brave or a little unhinged in there, but I'm grateful."

I think "unhinged" is a reasonably good approximation.

I turned back to my laptop.

She said nothing for a minute but watched as my fingers moved around my keyboard creating section header slides to give the presentation some logical flow and format.

"Hey, you're an engineer?" she said, surprised, pointing to my pinky ring. "What flavour?"

"Software engineer."

"Right. Now I know why your code is so tight and elegant. You should be running this joint," she said.

Maybe on paper, but I'd Hindenburg fast if they pushed me into management. It would be uppercase UGLY *in a hurry. Trust me. Surely you can see that.*

"Um, it's not really my thing," I replied. "Anyway, thanks for bailing me out on this presentation."

"Hey, that might be the longest sentence you've ever spoken to me," she said. "Anyway, it makes sense. After all, our desks are stuck together. I figure that's a sign we should stick together, too."

I'm not exactly sure what you mean by that, but let's see where it takes us.

I nodded and she pulled her chair around so we could both see my laptop screen. We worked for the next two hours and by the time I had to leave, we had the presentation pretty well cooked. We agreed it was thoughtful, logical, and comprehensive. It also showed in the work plan at the end that we could deliver the beta by October 9, even though neither of us truly believed it was possible. I left Abby to work her design magic – which she insisted she possessed – on the slides.

As I made the seven-minute drive to my appointment, I gnawed on baby carrots. I liked Wendy Weaver. I liked her a lot. She wasn't exactly warm and friendly, but after nearly nine years together, I knew she really cared about my situation. With Dr. Weaver, my reticence evaporated. My inner voice was actually outside and audible. Or as she would put it, "We've succeeded in achieving an 'inside-out' relationship." The goal was to overcome my chronic shyness and build more and more inside-out relationships. Right now, I'm up to three: my mother, Dr. Wendy Weaver, and in the last year, Malaya Matiyaga, even though she's very quiet. I'm almost completely relaxed with all of them, but with no one else. With others, I still cling almost unconsciously to my invisibility strategy. Head down. Just blend in. Don't draw attention to yourself. Fade into the background. Transparent. Invisible.

"Are you close to going inside-out with anyone else?" Dr. Weaver asked after I'd settled into the chair opposite her.

"Well, I think I can see moving towards that with Abby in the office," I replied. "But it's going to take a while. She's a little intimidating. Then again, I still find Smurfs a little intimidating."

Dr. Weaver smiled and flipped back in her notes.

"Abby. Abby Potts. Your desk-mate, right?"

I nodded.

"Are you continuing to formulate your conversational responses to people you meet in everyday encounters, even if you're not saying them out loud?"

"Yep. It's kind of become a habit now. I think I'm getting pretty good at it, and quicker, too."

"But you never say your lines out loud?" she asked.

"Hardly ever, unless I have no choice. I'd certainly say them out loud if I were with you or my mother. In fact, sometimes, at the end of the day, I even re-enact the conversations I should have had for my mom. Of course, I play both parts."

"And what does your mother think of this?"

"She thinks I'm funny and pithy, and that I should stop performing them for her and actually do it live when the opportunity presents itself. She thinks it's been long enough, that I should just go full inside-out," I said. "But I'm not ready for that. I'm not there yet."

"But at least we're all in agreement on the long-term goal," she said.

I nodded.

"You loved acting when you were growing up," she said. "Both you and your mother told me you were very good at it."

"Well, I was good at it until, you know . . ." I added.

"But why were you good at it? Why did you succeed at acting?"

"I just felt comfortable slipping into someone else's shoes and inhabiting their character. It was fun shedding all of my own instincts, beliefs, and mannerisms, and becoming someone else. It was a challenge. I just liked it. Loved it."

"What about now? Do you still like to act?"

"I do have fun when I'm performing some of my crazy scenes from work for my mother. She says I'm very convincing as my delusional and deranged boss."

"But you feel comfortable doing it?"

"Well, for my mother, yes."

"Have you ever acted for anyone else?"

"Not since that night," I replied. "Not since Gabriel."

"Hmmmm. I wonder how you'd feel now if you were acting in front of others?" she mused.

"Well, I have difficulty speaking at staff meetings, so I'm pretty sure I'd be terrified if I were actually acting."

"Really? Interesting. When you try to muster the courage to speak at a meeting, you're being yourself. If you were acting, you'd be somebody else, as you said, inhabiting a different character. Those are two different scenarios," she said.

"I guess. Maybe, but I'm not sure I see the relevance of it."

"Let's just park that thought and perhaps come back to it sometime," she suggested. "Have you given any more thought to the 'closure therapy' I put on the table a couple of weeks ago?"

"I'm not ready."

"Not ready to think about it, or not ready to pursue it?"

"Both. I'm just not feeling it. I don't think I could do it. I'm not ready."

"Just to clarify. Do you mean you're frightened of it, or you just don't think it would accomplish anything?"

"I don't know," I replied. "I'm just not there yet."

Our session unfolded as it usually did. Wendy asked questions. I tried to answer them. She'd prod and probe. I'd think harder and talk some more. It was comforting and, I assume, therapeutic for me. I felt safe in her office.

"Okay, I'm watching the clock here. I don't want your boss to have a meltdown," Dr. Weaver said, closing my file in front of her. "Any more Gabriel dreams?"

"Plenty. And sometimes I don't even remember having them."

"How do you know you've had them?"

"I'm not sure. I know it sounds weird but I think I can somehow sense Gabriel. It's just a feeling sometimes when I wake up. But it's there."

I slipped back into the office at 1:02 and was relieved to see that Simone was at her sleek desk bent over her computer with her headset on. The senior management team call had obviously started. I could just make out a rather colourful PowerPoint slide on her screen. I sat down in my chair, gathered myself, then, before I lost my nerve, popped up so I could see Abby over top of the partition.

"Um, hi. How's it going?" I said, affecting nonchalance and immediately regretting the somewhat unlimited scope of my inquiry.

She looked at me and kind of grinned in a tired, put-upon way.

"How's it going? How's it going, you ask? Well, lunch? Didn't get one. These new jeans? Too tight. I put vanity before comfort. My hair? No time this morning, as you can see. I put coffee before vanity. This white shirt? Just noticed this stain on the arm. Clearly I put coffee, well, I put coffee on my sleeve. These shoes? Well, they're killer comfortable, but Simone said they look like really bad bowling shoes. Other than that, it's going okay. Thanks."

She continued to smile up at me. Despite the harsh fluorescent lighting and anarchic hair, her face at that up-tilt angle was really quite beautiful.

Wow, you've had quite a day so far. Hey, here's an idea. In honour of those funky but comfy shoes, why not click your heels together three times and we'll skip out for the p.m. and go bowling?

"I kind of meant the PowerPoint for Simone," I said.

"I know. The PowerPoint. The deck is just fine. I made your coding update and work plan look screamin' pretty and I even put a few builds into the slides. Simone is easily impressed by furking bright shiny objects, and by bullet points that fade in and out. But I stopped short of sound effects. She had it in her little Tyrannosaurus claws with plenty of time to spare."

"Thank you. I really appreciate it," I said, and lowered myself back down behind my padded wall.

"No worries" came drifting over the partition.

I entered our apartment just as Malaya was folding a tea towel and slipping it over the oven door handle. She stepped towards me offering an open palm. I swung my open palm to meet hers.

"Tag," she said and smiled.

"Tag," I replied.

It's a thing we did every morning and every night that had its roots in the TV tag team wrestling I would sometimes watch as a kid. It was shift change in the MacAskill hospice.

"Everything cool?" I asked.

"She's a little tired, but in good spirits. The oxygen tank will need to be changed before she sleeps. Don't forget."

"Right," I said, looking around the spotless living/dining room area. "Malaya, the place looks, well, spotless again. You know you don't have to do housekeeping. Right? That's my job."

"I know, but your mother is sleeping a lot and I get bored. It's no trouble."

"Saint Malaya."

She grabbed her coat, stuck her head into Mom's room to say goodnight, and then slipped out the door.

I washed my hands in the kitchen sink with antibacterial soap I'd bought at the medical supply store. It smelled rather clinical but was recommended by one of Mom's many doctors. I towelled my hands dry.

IPF is a bitch, a real bitch. Idiopathic pulmonary fibrosis. To break it down, *idiopathic* means the cause is unknown. *Pulmonary*, as you might expect, relates to the lungs. And *fibrosis* is a fancy word for scar tissue. In other words, for no apparent reason, my mother's lung tissue began thickening about four years ago. Scar tissue formed, severely compromising her lung function. And inexorably, unrelentingly, it got worse. To be clear, and perhaps a little crass, my mother has been slowly but steadily suffocating for the last four years. Most IPF patients don't live beyond four or five years after diagnosis. I can't think of a worse way to go than to have your breath taken away from you. Breathtaking and heartbreaking at the same time.

My mother had always been immensely practical. She accepted her very short-straw diagnosis with stoic dignity, good humour, and clear eyes. It was amazing to witness. There was no self-pity, no "it's not fair," no "why me?", no deep depression. None of that. Just a resolute acceptance, a stalwart dedication to her treatment plan – in all its ultimate futility – and a pragmatic approach to her inevitable demise. All the plans were in place. She'd insisted.

"Hi, Mom," I said as I entered her bedroom.

I could hear the very faint hiss of oxygen as it pushed its way into her recalcitrant lungs. She'd been on oxygen for so long by that stage that I barely noticed the tube crossing her face, or the prongs in her nostrils.

"Alex," she said, looking up from the book she probably wasn't really reading. "How are you? How was your day, honey?"

The same banal questions that families around the world ask one another in the evenings, yet if the doctors were right, I'd only need two digits to count the days till this nightly ritual stopped.

"It was fine, Mom. How are you feeling?" I sat down in the familiar bedside chair and squeezed her hand.

"Never better," she wheezed. This was her standard response. Then right on cue, following her script, she continued, "Any prospects?"

"Well, now that you mention it, I'm starting to get to know my desk-mate, Abby. She's really quite unusual. She's brash and bold, and routinely scares the . . . scares me. But I find myself liking her."

"Ask her out," Mom replied, again on cue.

"Mom, I'm not on the market right now. You know I'm still searching for . . . you know."

My mother stirred and turned slightly so she could hold my

eyes with hers. It was either a stare or a glare. I'm not sure which, until I was sure which. Okay, it was a glare.

"Alex, you've tried to find her. You've looked for years. You don't know who she is. You don't know her name. You don't know where she is. You don't even know if she's alive. And you have no way of finding her. Time to let go, honey. Ask out the scary one."

"Mom, she was there. She helped me make it through. It was in her eyes. Pure empathy. In that short trip from drama to trauma, I think we somehow bonded that night in a way that was, I don't know, unusual. I could feel it. It was different. She never looked away. Not once. She was with me all the way down. I can't forget that." I paused and my mother waited for me. "So I'm still looking. I actually have a few Facebook leads that I'm running down."

"Alex. It's time to move on and find someone to love. You know what's happening here with me, right? Please find somebody."

"Mom, I hear you. I understand. But you are my focus right now. I've tried to tell you, finding a girlfriend is just not a priority for me right now."

"Well, make it a priority," she said, trying hard to keep her eyes open. "What about calling up Cyndy? You two were good together."

"Mom, please. That ended a very long time ago. I can't go back there."

She carefully slipped her hand under her pillow, sighed in the laboured way an oxygen-deprived person sighs, and brought her hand back into view. She opened her eyes and looked at me again.

"Alex. I need to talk to you about something else. Something important. Very important. But I just don't have the strength or the air to do it now," she said.

"It's fine, Mom, it'll keep."

"Not for long, it won't. Promise me you'll wake me up in the morning. It has to be done, before you go." She was whispering now.

Just before I left her, I changed the oxygen tank and made sure the hose was delivering a steady stream of oxygen. She nodded that it was working. She held out her hand. I slipped mine into hers. It felt thin, fragile, and cool.

"Tomorrow morning. Promise me," she said, her grip relaxing.

"Promise."

It was dark. Pitch black. I was cold, uncomfortable, scared, but calm, resigned.

CHAPTER 2

When I opened my eyes the next morning, I instantly knew I'd just had the dream again. I had no true, vivid memory of it, just its now familiar residual sensation. I knew by how I felt in that instant my consciousness flickered to life for the day. It always but briefly left me a little undone. But I'm used to it now. Nearly ten years is a long time to be haunted by the same dream.

When I opened my eyes, I immediately noticed what I'd not seen the night before. My clean laundry was folded and stacked neatly on my desk. Saint Malaya. We really struck it rich when she showed up three years ago. She'd served as the only personal support worker Mom ever had. Malaya has told me more than once that providing end-of-life care is the greatest honour and privilege she can imagine. She'd grown very close to Mom. It was a special hybrid relationship where employee becomes friend.

Like so many other Filipino women, Malaya had come to Canada for her family. Not *with* her family, *for* her family. Staunchly Roman Catholic, she often had her rosary beads woven through her fingers as she worked. Every two weeks she sent a significant share of her less than generous paycheque from the agency back to the Philippines to support her husband, Benji, and their two kids, a girl, Divina, eight years old, and a boy, Danilo, six. The goal had always been to save enough money to bring Benji and their kids to Canada. She'd worked very hard, scrimped, saved, and sacrificed, all for the Canadian dream. It wouldn't be long now. On those rare occasions when I'd seen her eating her lunch at our kitchen table, she'd always pull the photo of her husband and kids from her wallet and set it down next to her plate so she could stare and smile at them until it was time to resume her duties. It was a ritual that did little to bridge the distance between them, but she claimed it helped a little.

Malaya is the sunniest and kindest person I know. I very seldom ever saw her without a smile. It was as if the resting position of her face was a grin. Asleep? Smile. Headache? Smile. Coma? Smile. The word "Malaya" apparently means free or independent. She told me she was not yet "free" but would be when her family had joined her. Her surname, Matiyaga, means patience. When she shared this, she laughed and said that she not only had patience but served patients, too. She thought that was quite clever, and so did I. We were very lucky to have her.

By 7:20, I'd showered and shaved and was about to make myself a bowl of instant oatmeal when I remembered my promise. I opened Mom's door and moved to the window. Mom didn't stir. I opened the curtains to let in the early morning light. It looked like it was going to be a nice day. Mom was not in her usual sleeping position.

And I knew. In an instant, a nanosecond, even less, I knew.

I didn't know when in the night she had died, but her skin was cool to the touch. I checked the oxygen line to make sure it had been working. The oxygen was still flowing. I removed the hose from around Mom's face and turned off the tank. I smoothed out the sheets and blankets. I don't know why I did that. Her eyes were closed and mouth was open. She didn't really look quite like my mother any more, so I pulled the bedspread over her head as I'd seen in countless films. It seemed the appropriate and respectful thing to do. I stopped for a moment to try to take in what had happened. The sun was nearly up now. I could see cars and people on the street below behaving as if it were just another day. But I felt nothing, nothing except perhaps gratitude that we'd talked last night and I'd held her hand.

Perhaps to keep reality at bay, I switched into practical mode, which is exactly what my mother would have done. I reached for the file folder that was always in the top drawer of her nightstand. The single page of lined paper inside bore an itemized list in my mother's hand. While the title at the top was no more specific than the two innocent, harmless little words "To Do," it was a list we'd worked on together, of tasks to be done upon her death.

I started at the top, took several deep breaths, and called the funeral home. I spoke to the after-hours person on duty. Trained to be or not, she couldn't have been nicer or more sensitive. She suggested I leave my mother's room and close the door. She dispatched a team from the funeral home to take away Mom's body. By this time, it was 7:45 a.m. I started to dial Malaya's number to tell her not to come in, but realized she'd be on the bus by then for the final leg of her daily commute and would be here in a matter of minutes.

I then found the Facetech staff list on my iPhone and dialed Abby's mobile before I lost my nerve – and I had very little nerve to lose. I'd never called her before. I don't call many people.

"Alex, is that you?" Abby said when she answered. "Alex?"

"Yes."

"What's wrong?" She paused waiting for me to say something, but I didn't, or couldn't. "Oh no, Alex. Is it your mother? Is she, well, is she all right?"

"No. She's gone."

"Ah, Alex. I'm so sorry. That sucks so hard. Ah geez. Fruck man, that so bites. What can I do?"

"Well."

"Should I come over? Do you need help? Where do you live?"

"No. I have a list. Thanks. Can you just tell Simone I won't be in for a few days?"

"Of course. I'll take care of it. Don't worry about anything going on here. Focus on what you've got to do there," she said. "And I can come, you know, if you need me," she added.

"Thanks. But I'm okay. I've got some help."

"So sorry, man. I'm here for you."

"Thanks."

Just when I put the phone down, I could actually hear Malaya's footsteps coming down the corridor. It was a familiar sound. After three years of morning tags, I knew the cadence of her walk. She knocked and turned the key in the lock at the same time, as she always did. She came in with her open palm already raised to tag me, as she always did. Then she stopped when she saw me, lowered her hand, and burst into tears.

I'd kept myself on an even keel so far. It had been easier when I was alone. But seeing Malaya pushed me over the edge. I wasn't expecting that. Then again, I was new at this. We sat with one another on the couch and engaged in what amounted to mutual catharsis. Then it passed. It wasn't gone, but we both just put it in a different place, at least temporarily.

"I'm not supposed to cry. My supervisor always tells me that," she said, wiping her eyes. "I don't like my supervisor."

That actually made me laugh a little.

Malaya sighed, stood up, and headed for Mom's room. I rose to follow her, but she held up her hand.

"Please, Alex. Stay here. I will go in," she almost whispered. "It's what I'm supposed to do."

I sat down again. Malaya entered the bedroom and closed the door behind her. I could hear her moving around the room, sniffling and crying softly. I assumed she was tidying up, dealing with the medical equipment, and preparing the room for the arrival of the funeral home folks.

They arrived about two minutes later, while Malaya was still in with my mother. It was two young women who were soft-spoken, respectful, gentle, and kind. I guess they do this kind of thing often, but they do it well. They had a stretcher of sorts and a black zip-up bag. I knew what it was and tried not to look at it. They told me a doctor was on the way to confirm and certify the passing. Apparently this was standard. Only a doctor can sign a death certificate. Malaya came out to greet the two women and take them into the bedroom. Again, Malaya asked me to stay in the living room. I suppose I could have overruled her and gone into the bedroom. But I didn't want to.

When Malaya emerged again and closed the door behind her, she came to me and held both my hands. She looked me in the eyes and told me to go out for some fresh air, walk to Starbucks down the block.

"I'll call you when you can come back," she said.

Part of me thought I should stay to deal with the doctor. But a larger part of me suddenly wanted very much to be outside.

"Thank you for being here, Malaya. I'm not sure what I'd have done if you weren't here."

She squeezed my hands, then released them. I grabbed Mom's handwritten "To Do" list and slipped out into the corridor. I stepped out of the elevator and made my way through the lobby to the door. These very familiar surroundings suddenly looked a little different, slightly off kilter. I had reached the sidewalk when my iPhone chirped. Abby's name appeared on my screen.

"Hi, Abby."

"She is such an asshole!" she opened. "I could just kick the flacking shit out of her right now."

"Who? Why?"

"Simone Ashe-wipe," Abby said. "She says she has to hear from you directly. Apparently, having me tell her about your poor mother isn't good enough. You have to call her. I'm really sorry. I tried to reason with her but she threatened to fire me again. That's twice in two days. A new record for me."

"Thanks for trying, Abby. Don't worry. I'll call her."

I walked to our local Starbucks. It had a large and generally underused seating area one floor above. I took my Tall Flat White and yogurt and granola upstairs and sat down in the far corner. I wasn't hungry in the least, but Malaya had instructed me to eat something, anything. It was going to be a long day. There was only one other person in the room seated at the other end talking on his phone with the newspaper opened on his lap. I pulled out my iPhone, steeled myself, and dialed.

"Ashe."

Hole.

"Hi, Simone. Abby said I should call you."

"Who is this?"

You're kidding. Who do you think it is? Has that much happened in your world in the last seven minutes that you can't remember your conversation with Abby? Congratulations, you just won the gold medal for self-absorption.

"Alex MacAskill."

"Oh right, Alex. Sorry about your father."

Thank you. Yes, it was hard growing up without a father, but this morning we're actually dealing with my mother's death. Do try to keep up.

"It was my mother, but thank you."

"Right, mother. Sorry. Yeah, Abby said you wouldn't be coming in for a little while and I just wanted to chat with you about that."

"Well, I have to deal with, you know, the funeral arrangements and the will and all that stuff."

"Of course, and you should take as many hours as you think all of that will take," she said. "And how many hours do you think you will require? I'm just trying to get a handle on what this means for the Gold beta rollout."

No, you did not just ask me that. As detached from reality as you are, even you could not have just asked me to calibrate my grief in hours. Maybe I could work on the beta during my mother's burial? Would that help? It's kind of dead time anyway. Everyone just stands around looking uncomfortable. It would probably put others at ease if I were occupied with something else while the coffin is lowered into the grave.

"I don't know. The Gold beta is on track. My part is essentially done. It's over to design and UX now," I replied, clenching and unclenching my right hand and various other parts of my anatomy.

"What's UX again?" she asked.

It means you are a serious moron. Unbelievable.

"User Experience. UX is short for User Experience. The code is done. The software works. The UX team, sorry, the User Experience team, now needs to work with the graphic design team on the interface, sorry, on what it's like to use the software," I explained, speaking very slowly.

"Oh, that UX," she replied.

"Yes. That UX," I confirmed. "Abby can guide it from here."

"So when will we see you? Maybe later in the week?"

When will you be a normal human being? Maybe never in your life? Sixty-three minutes ago I discovered my mother had died in her sleep. So, thinking it all through and balancing all the competing priorities, it occurs to me that I have no fucking idea when I'll be back in the office.

"I don't know. I'll call you."

"Please do. And again, sorry about your father."

And I'm sorry about your stunted cerebral function.

"Thanks."

I ended the call and tried very hard not to hurl my iPhone against the wall. Breathe. Just breathe. I sipped my coffee. It was good. I unfolded my "To Do" list. Seeing Mom's handwriting again did something to my throat, but I swallowed a few times and was back in business. I uncapped the ballpoint in my pocket and put a check mark next to "Call Funeral Home." I moved to the next item and slowly worked my way through the list.

I really didn't like making phone calls to strangers – frankly, I didn't like making calls to anyone – but this was one task I could not and would not escape. I called my mother's respirologist first. She'd been very supportive through Mom's illness and was sorry, though not surprised, to hear the news. She asked me a few questions that I tried my best to answer. I thanked her for all she'd done for my mother and me. I then called Mom's palliative care physician. I didn't reach him directly, but left a message with his office. The receptionist I spoke to was very nice. I suspect it was not her first such call. Another check mark.

I dialed Mom's estate lawyer.

"Melany Franken," said the voice.

"Um, Melany, it's Alex MacAskill, Lee MacAskill's son."

"Yes, Alex, we've met. How are you?"

"Well . . ."

"Oh no. I'm sorry, Alex. Has it happened?" she asked.

"Yes."

"I'm so sorry, Alex. How can I help?"

"I'm not really sure. I just wanted to let you know so you can commence whatever process needs to be started."

"Yes, of course," she replied. "I'll need a copy of the death certificate. The funeral home should give you several copies. The will is very straightforward. With Lee as a single parent and you as the only next of kin, it's a simple procedure. I'll get started."

"Thank you."

Malaya called then, so I drained what was left of my coffee and headed back. Apparently the coast was clear. As I turned off the sidewalk and up the concrete path to the front door of the building, I could see the funeral home's dark van still parked at the loading dock at the back of the apartment block. One of the women was just sitting in the driver's seat chatting away on her cellphone. Her colleague was waiting for me when I entered our apartment. Malaya retreated to Mom's bedroom to give us some privacy.

It took no longer than two or three minutes. The doctor had already been in and out. I guess it really didn't take too long to confirm that one is no longer among the living. There are, after all, some indisputable indicators. She gave me several copies of the official death certificate, along with a folder with the burial arrangements all outlined in more detail than I thought possible, let alone necessary. Then she walked me through the process of drafting an obituary to run in the *Ottawa Citizen*. She had blank forms I could have used, but I told her I'd submit it online. Eventually, she moved to the front door. She held my hand in both of hers when she said goodbye. Check mark.

Almost noon now. Malaya had the vacuum cleaner going in the bedroom. Even though the door was still closed, I could smell the unmistakable scent of Mr. Clean. I wrote the obituary in about fifteen minutes. I'd written it in my mind over and over again, so it wasn't that difficult. I did have to stop a couple of times when my eyes welled up, but I got it done and uploaded to the *Citizen*. I'd included a shout-out to Malaya in the obit. I'm not sure "shout-out" is the appropriate term when referring to an obituary, but that's how I thought of it. Malaya deserved it. As per my mother's instructions, there was no photo attached to the obit. Check mark.

I returned to my list and dialed the Cordon Bleu Culinary Arts Institute over on Laurier, just a short walk from the apartment. I asked to be put through to the Human Resources director. A man answered.

"François Meilleur."

"Hello, it's Alex MacAskill calling about my mother, Lee MacAskill."

"How is Lee? We really miss her here," he said in a French accent. "It's not the same without her. And the customers ask about her every day."

"I see. Thank you. Well, I'm sorry to tell you that she passed away this morning."

"*Mon dieu!* I'm so terribly sorry. And there I go spouting off before you had a chance to tell me. I'm so sorry."

"Thank you. It was not unexpected. We just thought . . . well, we thought we might have a bit more time."

My mother had worked at the Cordon Bleu Culinary Arts Institute for twenty-seven years. She was the hostess at the Signatures restaurant housed in the ground floor of the institute. She loved her job there, and everyone she met loved her, too. She came to know all of her regular customers, their names, habits, culinary preferences, still or bubbly water, dessert or just coffee. She was as much a fixture there as the crème caramel.

"The staff will be devastated. I wish your call had been bearing better news," he said.

"I'm sorry. She wanted me to thank you for all your support over the years."

"That's just like her to worry about that when she was so ill. Is there anything we can do to help in this difficult time?"

"I wondered what happens to her pension now that she has passed away?"

"I'm sorry? Pension?"

"Yes, her pension."

"Alex, we are a simple cooking school and restaurant. We only have twenty-four full-time employees. We have no pension. We've never had a pension. I hope there's no confusion."

Actually, there's loads of confusion. Weird.

"Oh, I see. I must have misunderstood my mother. Thank you for clarifying," I said. "I'll let you know when the burial is happening. Thank you again."

Strange. Mom had always said that our rent, groceries, and whatever part of Malaya's salary that wasn't paid by the province was covered by her "pension." That's what she'd always called it, her pension. And she wasn't talking about her old age pension. She was too young for that.

I walked out onto the balcony and leaned on the railing looking at nothing in particular. Living on a high floor yielded a great view of this part of the city. My eyes sought, then found, the Cordon Bleu Culinary Arts Institute a few blocks away. As I watched, the

Canadian and French flags on the front lawn lowered to half-mast. I felt like I ought to be saluting or cuing a bugler. I was not aware of any other recent tragic news involving France, Canada, or the culinary world that might have prompted the lowering of the flags, particularly at that precise moment. I knew my mother was well liked at the institute, but I was not ready for such a formal expression of their feelings for her.

By the time Malaya left at around 4:00 p.m., the apartment was so sterile, open-heart surgery could have been performed in the kitchen with no fear of infection, though our overhead lighting wasn't quite up to OR standards. She'd washed all the sheets that had come with the rented hospital bed and folded them neatly. I'd phoned the medical supply company earlier, giving me yet another check mark, and the bed and linen were picked up at about 3:30. By then, Mom's bedroom was nearly empty. With my blessing, Malaya had worked her way through Mom's dresser and closet, packed up her clothes in green garbage bags, and piled them near the front door. The good folks from the Canadian Diabetes Association clothes drive were going to pick them up the next day from the loading dock at the back of the building. Check mark. I carried the bags down and left them near the back door with a sign so no one would toss them into the big steel garbage bin.

It was a busy afternoon. It was good to be busy. It kept me from experiencing what it would be like *not* to be busy. And I wasn't quite ready for that. Not yet. Did it feel strange moving so quickly to cleanse my mother's own room of her presence? Yes. Yes, it did. But I was following her explicit instructions. This is what she'd asked me to do. I was working my way through *her* "To Do" list. She also wanted me to move into her bedroom. I understood her reasoning. Her room was larger and offered a better view. But I couldn't put a check mark in that box. Not yet.

Just before she left, Malaya, her eyes still red and puffy, pulled a pan of lasagna from the freezer, reminding me that I hadn't eaten anything since my morning trip to Starbucks. I wasn't hungry, but she turned on the oven, shoved in the pan, and set the timer. Then she grabbed something from the kitchen counter and walked to where I sat on the living room couch.

"Alex, I found this under your mother's pillow this morning," she said, handing me an envelope.

One word was written on the envelope in the most frail and feeble version of my mother's hand I'd ever seen. "Alex."

"She hasn't been out of her bed for three weeks. Where did she get an envelope?" I asked.

"I'm not sure. All I know is that she asked me to bring her a purse from the shelf in the front hall closet yesterday. I gave it to her and then went out to the store for more dish soap. When I came back, she said I could put the purse back in the closet."

"Did you look in the purse?" I asked.

"No, no. I would never do that. I just put it back on the shelf."

"Which purse was it?" I asked. "She keeps a few up there."

Malaya retrieved the purse and handed it to me. It was a very old, very shiny black leather purse with sharp edges.

"She hasn't used that in years."

I put the purse and the envelope on the coffee table. I couldn't bring myself to open either of them.

"I'm going to drive you home," I said, standing up and grabbing the car keys from the pegboard near the front door. I needed to be doing something.

"No, no, Alex," she protested. "I'll just take the . . ."

"Malaya," I interrupted. "I'm driving you home."

We didn't say much in the car. She lived with two other PSWs in a clean but lower-market apartment building near Carleton University. When I stopped in the parking circle at her front door, she slowly raised her hand toward me. I smiled at least a little, raised mine, too. When we tagged, she held onto my hand. Tears were streaming down her cheeks. I performed another full-body clench-up but held it together.

"Alex, I'm coming tomorrow," she started.

"Malaya, you don't need to. Take the day off. You deserve it."

"Alex, I'm coming tomorrow. You don't need to pay me. But I'm coming tomorrow. I need to come tomorrow."

I nodded and gave her hand a final squeeze.

"Of course we'll pay you, um, I'll pay you. That's not a problem," I said. "You can come as long as you like."

"Thank you. There's still lots I can do around the apartment till you get settled."

"Thank you for all you did today," I replied. "I couldn't have managed without you."

She stepped out of the car.

"Don't forget to eat the lasagna," she said as she closed the door.

While I knew there really wasn't much for Malaya to do at the apartment, I was glad she was coming back the next day.

I wasn't hungry until I stepped into the apartment and smelled the lasagna. Then I was ravenous. I devoured at least a third of the pan before I looked up from the kitchen table. I suddenly realized it was the first time I'd been alone in the apartment for more than a year. I looked at the closed door to my mother's room. It was hard to fathom that she was no longer where she usually was. I understood and accepted that she was gone. There was no doubt, no denial. I'm an engineer by training. I accept logic and reason and facts. They drive the universe and the decisions we make every day. I knew she was gone. It was just that when my mind would drift to something else, I would, for just a few seconds, simply forget that she was gone and wasn't in her bed behind that door. Now, even the bed was gone.

I still wasn't up to opening the envelope she'd left. Instead, I pulled out her list again and grabbed my iPad.

Financially, we were fine. I made good money at Facetech and banked most of it, as my expenses were very low. Mom wouldn't even let me contribute to the rent. She had never been particularly forthcoming with the state of her finances, beyond noting that she was not living beyond her means and that I'd be able to see it all clearly when she'd gone. In the bottom left-hand corner of the list, she'd written her banking log-in information. We banked at the same institution so I opened my online banking app and logged in as my mother.

I scanned the account summary page. She maintained only one chequing account and an RRSP account. I opened the first account and spent some time scrolling through the previous six months of activity. Mom was right. We weren't living beyond our means and it was pretty easy to follow. This was no financial labyrinth with shell companies and offshore accounts. Just a chequing account and an RRSP.

On the first day of each month a flat $5,000 deposit was made. It was not clear what it was as it showed up as a transfer from another account. This must have been what Mom had always called her "pension." It was the only monthly infusion of cash over the six months I scrolled through. I thought again about what François Meilleur had told me. It rang true now that I could see the account records. It would be highly unlikely for a monthly pension payment to be a straight-up $5,000 even. Pensions payments were usually derived from a complex algorithm based on years of service and your income from your highest-earning years. The monthly cheque would certainly have been a very strange number: $4,784.23 or $4,681.34. And even then, the number was rounded up to the nearest cent.

I had no idea how or why a flat $5,000 was arriving in Mom's account like clockwork every month. To be sure, I checked back several years and the mysterious monthly deposit was always there on the first of the month, as far back as I checked.

I looked more closely at the monthly disbursements from the account. Again, a predictable pattern emerged. On the second day of every month, $2,000 was transferred into Mom's RRSP. On the fourth of every month, $1,250 came out to pay the rent. On the eighth of every month, $794.23 was paid out to the PSW agency for our share of Malaya. I knew from doing the shopping that we spent about $400 each month on food and a couple hundred bucks on Internet and cellphone, which was the only other cost not included in our rent. And Mom was clearly banking some dough each month because her only chequing account had a balance of $12,459.55.

Mom's RRSP was managed by an apparently really nice and experienced financial advisor with the bank named Doug Evans. He kept track of how much Mom was allowed to contribute each year. She had urged me to get together with him, but since it meant meeting with a perfect stranger, I'd put it off. I clicked on the RRSP account. The balance was $356,871.26. Wow. I closed the banking app.

There was one call I felt I had to make, even though it wasn't on Mom's "To Do" list. I dialed.

"Dr. Weaver."

"Hi, Wendy, it's Alex MacAskill. I'm sorry for calling after hours."

"No problem, Alex, I was still doing some paperwork here. Is everything all right?" she asked.

"It happened last night and I didn't want you to read about it in the paper without telling you."

"Your mother?"

"Yes," I replied. "It's been a hectic day."

"And how are you feeling? Are you okay?"

"I swing between thinking I'm fine and reeling in shock that she's gone. There was so much to manage today, I haven't really had time to process what's actually happened."

"Sometimes it's the need to manage all the logistics that a loved one's death entails that keeps us functioning until we're actually able to deal with the reality of their loss," she said. "There's therapeutic benefit in having to write the obituary, deal with the funeral home, and handle all the other little details."

"Right. Even so, I think I'm okay. I mean we knew it was going to happen. She's been planning it for months. And everything unfolded today just as she'd envisaged. It's a very strange feeling, but I think I'm okay."

"Don't forget about your needs in all of this. I'm here, you know."

"Thanks. On the positive side of the ledger, I haven't given Gabriel a thought all day."

We talked for a few minutes, then said goodnight.

I cleaned up the kitchen and ran the dishwasher. It was getting late by then. I didn't feel like watching TV, so with nothing left to distract me, I reached first for the shiny black purse. As far as I could recall, Mom hadn't used it for years. Inside I found three new and unused white envelopes, like the sealed one in front of me. There was also a ballpoint pen, presumably used to write my name on the front. That was it. As I closed the purse, my eye caught something amiss. I opened the purse again and noticed that the inner lining along one side had pulled away from the wall of the purse revealing a perfect and reasonably secure hiding place for something flat and small. You might say the secret space was kind of envelope-shaped. I looked closely and decided the purse lining had been compromised by something other than wear and tear.

I closed the purse and picked up the envelope with my name scrawled on the front. It was almost certainly the last word my mother ever wrote. I could tell there was something inside other than paper. There was some weight to it, and I could feel it sliding back and forth, changing the envelope's centre of gravity when I tilted it. Turned out, what I found inside would change my centre of gravity. But I didn't know it then. I took a deep breath, slipped my finger under one end of the flap, and carefully pushed against the seam. It had not been sealed very well and opened easily. Before I could look inside, something fell out onto my lap.

Contorted in that strange, unnatural position,
every part of my body flexed and curved, but one.
A human dowsing stick.

CHAPTER 3

A key. I fished it out of my crotch where it had fallen. It was a key. I had no idea what it opened, but it was an old-style, flat, dull, brass key. The number 126 was stamped into the soft metal. Bus station locker? Nope. Wooden treasure chest? I didn't think so. Houdini's handcuffs? Unlikely. While I had no real experience in this area, it struck me that it might just be the key to a safety deposit box. I put the key on the coffee table. I figured the envelope had nothing more to offer, but I looked inside just to be sure. It wasn't quite empty. There was something lodged in the corner. I reached inside, pinched it between my index finger and thumb, and drew it out.

It was a small colour photo of me as a newborn. I recognized myself in the shot immediately. To be more accurate, it was only part of a photograph. I assumed it was originally a 3-by-5 print. The piece I held in my hand was about 3 by 2½, cut vertically down what I assume was the centre line from top to bottom. The standard white border ran along the top, left, and bottom sides but stopped at the cut right-hand edge. I was holding the left half of a colour photograph. I had no idea where the other half was.

The shot must have been taken very soon after I was born. I was swaddled in a light blue standard-issue hospital blanket, and my face had that just-delivered, pink pinched look. What little hair I had appeared still damp from my journey. I was cradled in the right arm of a man wearing jeans and a white T-shirt, no belt. But the man's face was not visible. In fact, the photo's top border cut off his head just below the chin, as if on purpose, by design, while the photo's cut right edge sliced off the other half of his body. Yes, it was a photo of a headless half-man with a newborn nestled in his right arm. With me nestled in his right arm.

I turned the photo over. There was nothing on the back except for an inked "0" written in blue ballpoint just on the left edge. A zero? The letter "O"? An egg? The mouth from Edvard Munch's *The Scream*? Who knew? I turned it over again and looked at the baby once more. The only certainty was that it was a photo of me shortly after my birth. I'd seen many baby pictures of me. But I'd never seen this one.

I put the photo and the mystery key back into the envelope, closed the flap, and sat it beneath my wallet on my dresser for safekeeping. Then I went to bed and slept deep and long for the first time in a while. There were no dreams that night.

The next morning, I decided I could no longer put off calling the funeral director about the final burial arrangements. (I guess when using the word "burial," it goes without saying that the arrangements were "final.") I'd avoided phoning the funeral director yesterday. It wasn't calling her in particular that I was trying to avoid. I didn't really like calling anyone. (Though I guess I'd much rather call them than meet them face to face. I know. Weird. You can thank Gabriel.)

"Susan Granger."

"Hi, Ms. Granger, it's Alex MacAskill calling."

"Oh, Alex, yes. I'm so sorry for your loss. I hope you were satisfied with our team yesterday," she said.

Well, to be honest, I bailed out for most of their visit. But they seemed very nice. Hard to believe their job is to drive around and pick up bodies. A great conversation starter in a bar, I guess.

"Yes, they were very efficient and helpful. Thank you," I replied. "I just wanted to confirm that the burial is in fact set for tomorrow at ten." Mom and I had met with Ms. Granger about fourteen months earlier when there was no longer any doubt about how my mother's illness would end.

I heard her clicking a mouse in the background.

"Yes, we're on track for the short graveside service and burial Thursday morning, that's tomorrow, here at Beechwood, at ten."

"Good. Thanks. Do I need to do anything?"

"Not a thing. We already have the outfit your mother asked to be buried in. She is already resting in the casket she chose. Our minister will preside, and it will be a very short and traditional committal service that will end with the casket being lowered into the ground. As you're the only family, we'd ask that you stand next to the minister. The service will last less than fifteen minutes from start to finish, as we discussed when we met with your mother and you."

I'm still stuck on the idea that someone had to dress my mother in her burial outfit. How do you get used to doing that? How hard is it to do for the very first time?

"So I should just arrive at the cemetery at 9:30 or so?"

"Yes, that would be fine."

She gave me directions to the actual plot on the cemetery grounds, and we concluded our call. It was nice to get off the phone.

Ever practical, my mother had insisted on a quick burial. She abhorred the idea of cremation, and there was to be no church funeral service and definitely no reception with its mandatory egg salad sandwiches and lemon squares. I followed her instructions to the letter, despite my affection for lemon squares. I wanted to honour her and thank her by carrying out her wishes. My mother's parents, the only grandparents I'd ever known, had both died about ten years earlier, within four months of one another. My grandfather died first of a bad heart, then my grandmother of a broken heart, fifteen weeks later. They'd had no other children. So I was the only one left. The end of the MacAskill line.

I referred to Mom's list, steeled myself for another call, and dialed.

"Royal Bank Rideau," the woman's voice said.

"Yes, it's Alex MacAskill calling. I'd like to speak to the manager, Shelagh Dunn I think it is, please."

"One moment, please."

"Shelagh Dunn."

"Hi. It's Alex MacAskill. My mother has an account with you, or had an account, and I also bank with you."

"Oh, Mr. MacAskill, I'm so sorry to hear about your mother."

What are you, psychic? Is the bank so all-seeing and all-powerful that you instantly knew when a customer died?

"Um, how did you know that she had, you know, passed away?" I asked.

"I read the obituary in the *Citizen* this morning. Lee MacAskill is not that common a name, and I'd dealt with your mother on more than one occasion over the years."

Wow. You are good.

"Of course. I'd forgotten it ran this morning," I replied. "I'm just wondering how we deal with my mother's account, now that she's, um, gone."

I heard her fingers flying over her keyboard.

"Well, it's really quite straightforward. You see, her account is jointly held. Both of your names are attached to it. With her passing, you become the sole account holder."

Wait, it was my account too? We had joint custody of the bank account? Why didn't she tell me?

"You're saying her account has also been in my name all along?"

"No, it shows here that she added you to the account about four years ago. You would have had to sign a signature card to make that change."

I had a memory shard of signing a couple of small cards from the bank that Mom had brought home one day. She'd said that the bank needed a next-of-kin signature for their records. I thought nothing of it at the time.

"I see."

"Yes, it happened the same time she arranged her safety deposit box."

Good segue, Shelagh. I was just coming to the box.

"Is it number 126?" I asked, knowing the answer.

"Yes, that's it."

"I have the key here. How do I go about getting access to the box?"

"You can just come down any time and we'll open it up, provided you have the key and some photo ID."

Kind of reminds me of drinking in my university years when I always had to present my driver's licence before they'd serve me. I'm told I look younger than I am.

"Oh, I didn't think I could just have access to her safety deposit box so easily," I said.

"Well, it's your box, too," she replied. "It was secured jointly, in both of your names. So you are now the sole owner of safety deposit box number 126."

Well, seems Mom was quite the little organizer. But why not tell me about it?

"I see. When I come in later today, could I also close out my mother's Visa account and cancel her card? I have my own Visa."

"Of course."

"I'd also like to talk about my mother's account to try to understand what's coming in and what's going out."

Like where this $5,000 is coming from every month that's been putting a roof over our heads and food on our table for all these years.

"No problem."

"Thank you. I'll be in shortly."

"That would be fine. And I'm sorry about your mother."

I decided to walk to the bank. It wasn't a short trip on foot, but I really needed the time and the air. I'd left Malaya back at the apartment. She'd arrived around 9:30, just as I was finishing up my call with Shelagh at the bank, and was now embarking on a complete cleanse of the entire apartment, including waxing the floors, dusting, and cleaning out the kitchen drawers. I hadn't realized that people still waxed floors. And dusting? Anyway, I tried to talk her out of it, but I didn't try for long. She was determined. It seemed to be how she was working through her grief. I had yet to figure out how to work through mine, other than shedding some tears at night and trying to stay busy.

It was a lovely day. Weather-wise, I mean. Just about room temperature with a light breeze. I pulled my Ottawa Senators ball cap down low, kept my eyes fixed on the ground, and walked. I didn't look at anyone else on the street. I seldom did, just to minimize the likelihood of being recognized. That hadn't happened for quite a while, years in fact. I guess I look a bit different now, the longer hair and all. Still, I don't like to take chances.

It took about twenty minutes at a brisk pace to bring me to the Royal Bank of Canada branch on Rideau almost at Nicholas Street. It was just past opening time, Wednesday morning, so the branch wasn't exactly brimming with customers. Just the way I liked it.

Shelagh Dunn was very nice. We sat in her office for about ten minutes. It didn't take long to transact what business we had. I showed her the death certificate and she scanned it with her fancy desktop device, then handed it back to me. In about thirty seconds, Shelagh had removed the name Lee MacAskill from the joint account that I now held all on my own. I literally watched Mom's name disappear from the computer monitor, leaving "Alex MacAskill" still standing at the top of the account summary screen. You die. You disappear. I'm not sure what I was expecting, but seeing her erased with the click of a mouse made her death seem all the more real.

"Can I ask about the $5,000 deposit that comes into the account on the first of each month?" I asked.

"Of course," she replied. "What can I help you with?"

"Well, my mother always referred to a pension she had, but I've since discovered that her employer has never had a pension plan, and certainly not one that would pay my mother a flat $5k every month. So I'd like to know where it comes from and why we receive it."

Not that I'm not grateful. Don't get me wrong. But it's a bit odd, don't you think?

"Let me have a look," she said, her fingers tinkling the keyboard.

When she reached the screen she wanted, she turned the monitor so I could see it and pointed to a line on the screen.

"Ah, there we go. You can see here that the monthly deposit is not via cheque, but through an international wire transfer from the FirstCaribbean Bank in Grand Cayman. FirstCarib is actually owned by the Canadian Imperial Bank of Commerce."

No shit! Grand Cayman? I guess that's better than a bank owned by some syndicate in Chechnya, or a paramilitary faction in Yemen, or maybe a community social club in Sicily.

"Just so I understand this correctly, each month, my mother's account, I guess I mean my account now, receives $5,000 from a Canadian-owned bank in the Cayman Islands?"

"Exactly," she replied.

"Is it always a flat $5,000?" I asked.

"For as long as I've been here," she replied.

This sounds like something straight out of a Robert Ludlum novel. The hair on the back of my neck just . . . well, it just did whatever neck hair does when something freaks you out.

"But who is sending it? Where is it actually coming from?" I asked.

And please don't tell me Grand Cayman is a haven for organized crime, or that this is a common international money-laundering scheme, or that drug money is the most likely explanation.

"All we know is that the money comes from the account of a numbered company, duly registered in Grand Cayman. And that's all we're permitted to know. That's all they legally need to disclose under international banking regulations."

What kind of world are we living in when you can receive money but have no idea who it's from, what it's for, or worse, when they're coming to get it back? Again with the Ludlum thing, or maybe LeCarré? Weird.

"I see," I replied. "My online banking app only goes back a few years. Can you tell me when these monthly deposits started?"

Shelagh Dunn swung the screen back in front of her, though I could still see it on an angle. She moused around a bit and banged in a few keystrokes. Then she stopped and scrolled up to the top of a large table filled with words and numbers in a very small font. She leaned in close.

"Okay, here we are. The first cheque arrived in the account January 1, 1991. Back then it was only $3,500 each month. Same bank, same numbered company as today."

That was a week after I was born. Seems a little young to be earning a salary.

Her fingers kept moving.

"It went to $4,000 a month in January 1999. Then to $4,500 a month in January 2007, and finally to the current level of $5,000 a month in January 2013."

A mysterious monthly payment, periodically adjusted for inflation. Sure doesn't seem like a pension benefit to me. Do you think my mother was an assassin? A drug lord? A spy? Kidding, but curious. Well, sort of kidding.

"Do we have any way of knowing if the monthly payments will continue now that my mother is, well, gone?" I asked.

"No, I'm sorry, we just don't know. I guess we'll find out at the first of the month."

"But couldn't I track down the numbered company and call them?"

Even though I really don't like calling people, particularly if they might be from the criminal classes.

"You can try, but it's usually a numbered company for a reason, particularly when headquartered in the Caribbean," she said. "There's really not much you can do. From our perspective at the bank, it's a perfectly legal and legitimate transaction."

Right. Spoken like John Gotti's lawyer.

"Thank you for the information," I replied.

We then closed my mother's Visa account. She was fully up to date on her payments, as I knew she would be. Finally, we excised Mom's name from the safety deposit box records, leaving me as the sole holder.

"Would now be a good time for me to check my safety deposit box?"

"Of course, as long as you have the key and one piece of photo ID."

I held up the key for her to see and then handed over my driver's licence. After she'd checked the key number and handed back my ID, she stood up and led me down to the back of the bank. As she walked, she jangled a set of keys she'd taken from her bottom drawer. Bankers and jailers were born to jangle keys. We stepped through what looked like a vault door – probably because it was a vault door – into a brightly lit, well, vault, with a low ceiling. Claustrophobes might have felt a bit antsy. All four walls of the vault were floor-to-ceiling grids of numbered rectangular doors, each with two keyholes. She stopped in front of number 126, chose a key from the jumble in her hand, and inserted it. She nodded to me and I inserted mine in the other keyhole. I felt like a soldier in a missile silo about to launch a nuclear strike. We both turned our keys and the door swung open, revealing a flat black box. She pulled the box out of its steel cubby and put it on the table in the centre of the room.

"I'll give you some privacy. Just call me when you're done and we'll lock it up again."

"Thank you for your help," I replied, as she left me alone in the vault.

I felt very strange at that moment. I sat down in one of the two chairs. My heart rate rose as I tried to figure out how to open the box. I finally saw that the top of it was really a hinged flap that simply swung up to reveal the inside of the box. I lifted the lid a few inches and then lowered it again before seeing what might be inside. I looked at my hands for a moment and breathed. I had no idea what I was expecting to find inside. Stacks of cash? A kilo of cocaine? Classified recipes from the

Cordon Bleu Institute? I took a few more deep breaths and folded back the flat lid.

No cash. No blow. No recipes. Just another white envelope, again, with my name written on it. The smooth, neat, and clean script was, again, unmistakably in my mother's hand, but before she was laid low by the relentless march of her vindictive, breath-taking disease. This did nothing to calm my pounding pulse. I stared at the envelope for a time without picking it up. I don't know for how long. I scanned the vault to confirm I was still alone, and then I picked up the envelope. No key inside this time. Nothing was moving inside. But it was thick, and it was sealed. As before, I used my finger to open it. My fingers were trembling as I drew out the folded paper.

I knew what it was immediately, instantly. I unfolded the document and smoothed it out on the table. My mother had affixed a single wooden Lucky Strike match to the top right corner of the front page with a piece of clear tape. It was the program from the 2005 Christmas pageant we'd put on at high school. I knew why it was there. I knew why the match was attached. I set it aside and reached again for the envelope. There was one more item inside. I pulled it out.

It was another photo, but a complete, uncut one this time, its white border completely circumnavigating the image. The left-hand portion of the photo looked very familiar. I was quite sure it was the half-photo I'd found in the envelope Mom had left for me under her pillow. There I was again, as a newborn, held in the right arm of a mysterious man in a white T-shirt and blue jeans. But what I couldn't yet fully process was what the other half of the photo revealed. My newborn self also appeared to be ensconced in the crook of the man's left arm, too. He was holding two of me. There were two interchangeable, absolutely identical babies.

With my mind nearly shutting down and refusing to assimilate what I was seeing, I thrust my hand into my pocket and yanked out my wallet. I pulled the folded envelope from the slot usually occupied only by fives, tens, and twenties. I removed the half-photo I'd discovered the day before and lined it up underneath the whole photo from the safety deposit box. I studied them both. Eventually I concluded that, yes, they were two copies of the same photograph. Everything from the left-hand portion of the whole photo perfectly matched the half-photo I'd brought with me.

I turned over the new photo and found my mother's handwriting. There was "2/3" in the top left corner, and "*December 24, 1990*" across the middle. That's when my memory nudged me. It shouldn't have taken so long, but I was not myself in that moment. I turned over the half-photo I'd brought with me and lined it up underneath the flipped whole photo. On my half-photo, the unexplained "0" was suddenly explained. It was in the same position as the "0" in "1990" on the back of the whole photo. (Have I lost you yet? Are you still with me?)

I turned over the new photo again and stared at it. The man, still with no face, but his torso finally whole, held me in his right arm, but also in his left. I was baffled. Was it trick photography of some kind? A double exposure? Photoshop? Hallucinations? I then noticed what looked like a tattoo on the man's left arm just above the elbow. The angle of the shot and the placement of the baby (me?) obscured it, but you could clearly see he had one.

Without being a rocket scientist or a brain surgeon, even I was able to conclude from my careful examination of the two photos that they were copies of the same shot. The notation on the back of the new one, "2/3," in the top left corner, suggested that there were, in fact, three copies of the same photo, and I was in possession of precisely one and a half of them. I was quite proud of my deductive reasoning. But I was probably doing all of this thinking and deliberating as a way to postpone considering the most pressing question. What the hell was I looking at?

I brought the complete version of the photograph closer and stared first at me in the man's left arm, and then at me in the man's right arm. I did that for a couple of minutes, scanning back and forth, without interruption. Then I sat back, closed my eyes, and tried very hard not to pass out. I consciously breathed slowly and deeply, my eyes still closed, but my pulse at wind-sprint rates. When I felt a little calmer, I opened my eyes to the photograph again. It was now obvious, unmistakable, and utterly clear to me, as it would have been to any fair-minded observer. I said it out loud before I ever said it in my head. I think I was trying to make it real.

"I am a twin. I have an identical twin brother."

The photo made it undeniable that we were identical and not fraternal. The two faces in the shot were literally one and the same. I looked for even the most minute facial differences in the two babies, and came up empty. I was – we were – one day old when the photo was taken. I assumed my mother snapped it, and that we were held in the arms of the father I never knew.

It dawned on me that this must have been what Mom had wanted to talk to me about the night before she died. Anger surged. I'm twenty-four years old and I find out after my mother dies that she gave birth to two sons on December 23, 1990. What's up with that? I was a twin. Who is he? Where is he? Is he even alive? Where are the other photos? Why didn't you tell me? How could you not tell me?

I tried and tried, but I couldn't think of a reason for her to keep this from me. I was mad. I was steaming. I think my anger was the only thing that kept me from blubbering. The swirling emotions of the moment and my mother's death fused in the vault of safety deposit boxes. I was a little messed up for a few minutes, but pulled myself together and wiped my eyes dry on my sleeve. What made all of this worse was there were no answers, and no easy path to finding them. I sat for another ten minutes staring at the photograph, trying to come to any other conclusion than the obvious one I'd already drawn. But I couldn't. No one could. The incontrovertible evidence was right in front of my eyes.

Shelagh Dunn stuck her head in.

"How are we doing in here?"

Well, my life's just gotten a whole lot freakier on account of discovering I have an identical twin brother. But thanks for asking. How are you?

"Just fine, thank you," I replied, coughing to cover any residual stress in my voice.

"We have a couple of customers here who need something from their box."

"Oh. Sorry. I'm finished in here."

I put both photos and the pageant program in the envelope and slipped it into the back pocket of my jeans. I closed up the now empty black steel box and slid it into the recess in the wall where it belonged. I closed the door and turned my key to lock it. Shelagh looked in, saw that I was ready, and entered to lock her side of Box 126.

I thanked her and left. I walked back but kept on going right past our apartment. I just didn't feel like going home yet. I carried on to Strathcona Park on the bank of the Rideau River. I really don't remember the walk. My mind was either empty or overflowing, I'm not sure which. I sat down on a bench along the water and didn't move for five hours. When I stood up from the bench, I was exhausted, but I had a new purpose and a new plan.

I was just about back at the apartment when my cellphone rang. I didn't recognize the number on the screen.

"Hello," I said.

"Hi, is that Alex?" a man's voice asked.

"Speaking."

"Alex, it's Doug Evans. I'm your mother's investment advisor at RBC."

I'm not sure you know this, Doug, but my mother really liked you. She said you were smart and kind – one of her favourite combinations. By the way, I just learned that I'm an identical twin. Don't you think no one should find that out at the age of twenty-four?

"Oh, hello," I answered.

"I just wanted to say I'm so sorry to hear the news about her. I really enjoyed working with her."

"Thank you."

"As well, I wanted to let you know, in case you didn't already know, that your mother instructed me to designate her entire Registered Retirement Savings Plan to flow to you. We made the arrangements with her lawyer several months ago. I've prepared the necessary paperwork and now just need your signature to complete the transfer."

"I see," I replied.

We talked for a few more minutes. More accurately, he talked and I added a few words here and there when required. We decided he would email me the documents and I would transfer my self-directed RRSP – which wasn't very big and held only a few mutual funds – over to him to manage along with what had been my mother's portfolio and was apparently now mine. I was comfortable with the plan. My mother really liked Doug. He seemed like a good guy.

"Doug, do you happen to know anything about the $2,000 Mom sent you every month? Do you know where the money comes from?"

"Nope, other than she said it was part of her monthly income. That's all I knew. But she never missed a monthly transfer. Are you intending to keep up the monthly contribution? It's a good idea if you can and still have the room in your RRSP," he said.

Well, if the mystery money keeps flowing in, we'll carry on with the $2k per month.

"I hope so. I'll know more in a couple of weeks," I replied.

"Sounds good," he said. "While I have you on the line, your mother was quite a conservative investor, meaning the annual growth pretty well matched the market, but it was secure. Does that approach work for you?"

I'm not the high-risk/high-reward type. Safe and secure. Slow and steady wins the race. Put my money on the tortoise, every time.

"Conservative works for me. Thanks."

Malaya was already gone when I made it home at 4:00 p.m. There was a note on the kitchen table confirming she'd be waiting outside her apartment building the next morning for me to pick her up for the burial, and that there was a shepherd's pie in the freezer.

I sat down at my laptop and Googled my way to a couple of different websites. I clicked through a few links to find what I was looking for and printed out a couple of pages from different sites.

Then I jumped in the car and drove to Facetech. I made it there by 4:30. Just in time. Before I lost my nerve, I went directly to Simone's office and stood outside her door. She was looking at something on her computer. I guessed YouTube, but it might have been Facebook. After a minute or two, I cleared my throat. She finally looked up. I somehow felt a little different. It might have been the new purpose and plan.

"Alex, I'm glad you're back. We've got so much to get done," Simone said.

I'm not back, you heartless tyrant. My mother died yesterday. Yes, yesterday, as in less than thirty-three hours ago. Which makes me wonder if there's even one tiny shred of decency lurking somewhere beneath your scales?

I came into her office and stood before her.

"I just came in to let you know that I'll be using my full three days of paid bereavement leave and my full ten days of unpaid bereavement leave."

"Three days? Ten days? Bereavement leave? What are you, nuts? I'm quite sure Facetech has no such policy. Anyway, I really need you on the Gold beta. That's got to be your priority. Besides, it'll help take your mind off of your father."

You have the sensitivity of a charging rhino and the empathy of a rattlesnake, but are less pleasant to be around than either.

"It's not a company policy, it's actually set out in federal and provincial legislation," I explained. "The company has no choice in the matter."

"Never heard of it," she replied.

You're kidding. What a surprise. You don't even know exactly what we do here, I hardly expect you to know employment standards legislation. Oh yeah, and you're a jerk, too.

I slid one of the pages I'd printed at home along her desk so that it was right in front of her.

"That just explains the relevant provisions of federal and provincial legislation. Under the Ontario Employment Standards Act, I'm entitled to ten days of unpaid leave. I'll start that the day after tomorrow. And under the federal Canada Labour Code, I'm entitled to three days of paid bereavement leave. I'll use them for yesterday, today, and tomorrow. The burial is tomorrow."

She was reading the printouts.

"I assume the ten days includes weekends," she said.

And I assume you're mentally deranged and obviously can't read.

"No, as it says right there, the legislation calls for ten *business* days."

"But according to this, I need to see proof of death before the leave can be granted," she said, looking smug.

How about I bring my mother's body in to the office for your inspection? Would that suffice?

I slid a copy of the death certificate over to her before she finished her sentence.

"Christ!" she snapped. "We have work to do here! Is this really necessary?"

Are you really necessary? I mean, really. What do you do other than yell and scream and kick your feet? Exactly how do you contribute to this company anyway, I mean other than destroying morale and starting a mass staff exodus you have no way of staunching?

"Sorry. It is necessary. Necessary and normal. Besides, the beta is on track. My work on it is pretty well done. Abby can take it from here."

"I have a call coming in now," she said, checking her watch and waving her hand in dismissal.

Would you like me to explain how the phone works again, like I did last week, so you can actually take the call?

"Okay. Just one more thing, I still have four weeks of vacation banked and I may need to use some or all of it, too."

She snapped her eyes to mine just as her phone rang. She looked at her watch again, and then at her phone. She reached for it, but hesitated. I pointed to the flashing button, and then gave her my best button-pushing gesture. She picked up the receiver, pushed the button.

"Ashe."

Yes, you are. A big one.

I left her office and walked over to my cubicle.

Abby heard me coming a mile away.

"Hey, Alex. What are you doing here? Are you okay?"

Well, other than my mother dying and Simone being such a twisted diva, I'm okay.

"Yes, I just came in to see Simone about my leave," I replied.

"You could have just called her. You didn't have to come all the way in when you've got more important stuff on your plate."

Maybe I wasn't just coming in to see Simone. I'm not sure, but maybe. Who knows?

"I guess. But there's a good chance she wouldn't have been able to answer her own phone. She has trouble with that."

She smiled, moved around to my side of the cubicle, and perched on my desk as I sat down.

"So how are you holding up? I've been thinking about you," she said, resting her hand on my shoulder in a kind of sisterly way. "The obit was really nice. I wish I'd met her."

I kind of wish you'd met her too. She would have liked you, and liked your, I don't know, your spirit, your gumption. She would have said, "I like your sass."

"Thanks. I'm okay. Lots to do to keep me busy," I said.

I paused, and thought, what the hell?

"Oh yeah, and I just discovered I have an identical twin brother I never knew about."

Her mouth opened but nothing came out for a second or two.

"Shut the front door!" she eventually said. I wasn't exactly sure what that meant. "Are you friggin' kiddin' me? You just learned you have an identical twin brother? That's a whole lot of insane."

I know. Completely and utterly wack.

"Yes, I know. It is."

"Well, come on. Out with it. What's the story?"

"Well, I found . . ."

"Hey. I'm over here," she said, waving. "Eye contact, remember?"

I know where you are, but you're kind of invading my personal space, so it makes me a bit edgy. If I turn my chair to face you, it brings my legs almost into contact with yours. I'm not good at leg contact.

I turned my head to look at her.

"Sorry. I found a baby photo in my mother's safety deposit box. And, well, I can show you."

I first pulled out my half-photo to show her.

"Here I am just one day after I was born. We have lots of baby pictures at home. I'd just never seen this one."

"Pretty cute for day one," she said. "Yeah, so?"

C-section baby. I'm told we tend to be cuter just after birth.

"Yeah, well, here's the same photo but including the other half."

I handed her the complete shot. I watched her eyes widen.

"Holy shit!" she said. "There're two of you. Totally the same! Farkin' doppelgangers."

Well, yeah, that's how identical twins work.

"Right," I said.

"So where is he? Who is he?"

I have no idea. Who knows if he's even alive? Even if I find him, maybe he won't want to see me. Maybe he knows about me and always has, but doesn't want to pursue it. Maybe he's dead. Maybe he's an asshole. Maybe he's nice. Maybe he's just like me in every way.

"I don't know."

"But you're going to try to find him, right? You gotta go find him!" she said. "It would be an epic fecking adventure."

Exactly. Why do you think I just subjected myself to time with Simple Simone? I have a purpose and a plan.

"I know," I replied.

PART TWO

My descent started, stopped, started, and stopped.
I could sense, but not see, the people below me.

CHAPTER 4

I could actually smell the fresh, damp earth underneath the swatch of fake green grass next to the open grave. The casket was resting on a kind of steel framework set up around the perimeter of the rectangular hole in the ground. It was really a lovely day. The sun was bright and warm in a clear sky. Malaya was standing near me. I'd picked her up earlier. She was a mess, crying quietly in the passenger seat beside me as I drove to Beechwood Cemetery. I was fine, at least then. I may have been fine because Malaya wasn't. It felt like I had to hold it together, particularly when she wasn't able to.

I looked up and scanned the crowd. And by crowd, I mean the four other guests arrayed around the grave. François Meilleur and three women from the Cordon Bleu restaurant were there. He'd asked me if they could attend and of course I agreed. The minister, who was right out of central casting, was in full liturgical regalia of dark flowing robes with a colourful sash around his neck, hanging down in front – and yes, I'm fully aware that it's probably not called a "sash." While he had a full head of bushy, grey hair, he took no special measures to tame it. The swirling breeze made his silver cranial corona even wilder.

We were just getting ready to start when I saw Abby making her way from the paved path over to the gravesite. I barely recognized her. She was wearing some kind of floral print summer dressy thingy. I'd only ever seen her in pants at the office. Her hair was tied back in a way I'd never seen in the admittedly short time we'd worked together. Her red-rimmed eyes suggested either a general emotional vulnerability at funerals, or an early morning fattie. I wasn't sure which.

She gave me a sad and empathetic look as she approached. Then she wrapped me in a brief but tight hug. I wasn't expecting that.

"Sorry about the waterworks," she said, pointing to her own eyes as she broke our embrace. "I suffer from a general emotional vulnerability at funerals."

Who are you?

"Right," I replied, remembering to make eye contact. "You didn't need to come. But thanks."

She squeezed my hand, let go, and stood next to Malaya. I felt oddly uplifted that Abby had come. I heard her introducing herself to Malaya as the minister of chaotic coiffures began the service. I know it's strange to say, but I wasn't really listening to what he was saying. My mind was elsewhere. I was trying to remember if I'd ever really, truly, felt whole, in my life. I didn't think I had, but I wasn't certain. How do you know what being whole really . . . really feels like? Up until then, I'd assumed it was my absent father that explained the nearly constant sense that something or someone was missing in my life. Perhaps it wasn't just my father. I'd read somewhere that twins actually start bonding in utero. So perhaps there was another explanation, beyond my father's absence, for somehow feeling bereft for most of my young life.

Just then, I thought I'd heard my own name. I came back into the moment, into the present, into the cemetery, and looked at the minister. On instinct, I nodded to him and hoped it was the appropriate response to whatever his invocation had been. He returned his attention to my mother's casket and carried on with the words of a psalm he'd committed to memory from reciting it at so many funerals.

With my head bowed respectfully, still I let my eyes wander a bit. The four from the Cordon Bleu restaurant were clearly moved by the proceedings. I couldn't tell if the minister's words were affecting them or if they were just burdened with the loss of my mother. It made me feel good that even in her very small circle, she had friends who mourned her passing. I lifted my eyes slightly beyond our humble gathering. A few hundred yards away, partly obscured by a large silver maple, a shiny black Mercedes was parked. The windows were tinted. The angle of the road gave me a partial view of the front of the car. Nothing was visible through the windshield, but I could just make out what looked like a front red licence plate. I hadn't remembered seeing the Merc there when we'd arrived.

"Alex?"

Yes? What? I'm right here. What did I miss?

I looked up and the minister and the rest of those assembled were staring at me.

"I think we're ready if you are," the minister said.

Oh, I'm ready all right. Um, ready for what?

He nodded towards the casket, his eyebrows bouncing.

"Oh, yes," I replied, stepping forward and pushing the button on the side of the steel framework, as I'd been shown earlier. The hum of an electric motor started and my mother's casket descended into the grave at an appropriately funereal pace.

It was all over a few minutes later. The minister performed his final words of committal, thanked everyone for coming, shook my hand, and walked back to the Beechwood Cemetery car that would return him to the office. Each of my mother's colleagues approached me again with words of condolence. I tried to look each one of them in the eyes. They also invited me to eat at their restaurant, Mom's restaurant, whenever I liked. I thanked them for coming and they made their way to their cars parked close by the grave.

In Abby's presence, Malaya was very quiet.

"I can drive you to the office after I drop Malaya at her apartment," I said to Abby.

"That would be great, if you're up to it. I bussed it here. I told the dumb-Ashe I had a dentist appointment this morning. She was not happy. And she'll know something's up when I show up in this get-up," she said, her hand grandly sweeping across her floral-printed self. "No one at the office has ever seen my bare legs, you know."

Or, with your hair tied back, so much of your face. You look nice. And it was really great of you to come when there's so much going on at work.

"Right," I said, smiling.

"It was a really lovely service, Alex."

I nodded.

Abby got into the front seat and Malaya sat in the back. I decided to sit in the driver's seat from which I've always found it much easier to control the car. We drove slowly through the green tranquility of the cemetery, back onto Beechwood Avenue, and then right on to Hemlock Road. I thought I'd be able to see Mom's grave from the road as we drove by. It's quite easy to drive and look to your right for your mother's fresh gravesite, but it's actually quite hard to drive *safely* and look to your right for your mother's fresh gravesite.

"Whoa!" Abby said, her hand braced on the dashboard. "That side of the line is for oncoming traffic. I recommend we stay on this side of the line."

Yeah, well, it's hard to stay in the lane when you're looking in the other direction. But I thought I saw something.

I steered us back into our lane and slowed down a bit.

"Right. Sorry. I was looking for my mother. You know, her grave," I explained.

I took another quick look to my right and saw the shiny black Mercedes now parked next to Mom's still open grave. A man in a dark suit with his back to me stood over the grave.

A honk brought me back.

"Yep! There's that pesky line again!" Abby said.

I could feel Malaya's hand gripping the back of my seat near my right shoulder.

"Sorry, again."

By this time, the trees obscured any view of my mother's grave. I tried the rear-view mirror but could only see the driver behind me raising his middle finger for my edification.

I had a strange feeling. I turned left at the first side street, I think it was Thornwood, hung a U-turn, and headed back the other way on Hemlock. By the time we reached the spot where I could see Mom's gravesite again, the man and the Mercedes were gone. Of course they were. If this were a movie, they'd be gone, so why not in real life? Shit.

"What's wrong? What did you see?" Abby asked. "Are you all right?"

I flipped another U-turn, right there on Hemlock, and resumed the drive to Malaya's apartment.

"Sorry. I just thought I saw someone at the grave who wasn't there at the service. But he's gone now. Sorry."

Malaya said she'd be at our place . . . my place, later this afternoon to resume the pristine apartment cleaning festival she'd started the day before. I tried to tell her it was unnecessary but clearly did not convince her. I gave Malaya a hug that she held for quite some time. I waited until she wiped her eyes again and headed inside her apartment building.

"She seems really cool," Abby said, when I slid back behind the wheel.

She's been a godsend for the last couple of years. I'm pretty sure my mother lived longer because of Malaya.

"She is."

"So what about your brother? Any progress?"

Are you kidding? I just learned about him twenty-four hours ago. And there was this little matter of my mother's burial to attend to, so I'm nowhere on my brother yet. But I'm on it now.

"No. But I'm starting just after I drop you off."

"Okay, but you must keep me up to speed. I can help. You may know that I'm good with computers and the interwebs and such," she said.

Yes, you are. I've seen your work. You're funny, too.

I smiled.

"I know. I will."

When I pulled up in front of the Facetech office building, she turned to face me and put one hand on my shoulder. I looked at her hand and then at her.

"Sorry, people say I touch too much. I can't help it. I'm a tactile person. I touch people. It's what I do," she said.

Touch away. I seem to find myself liking it. Not sure what that means.

"It's fine. Um . . . it's kind of nice."

"Are you okay? You know, I could turn my routine dentist's appointment into a full-on emergency root canal," she offered. "It could happen, you know."

"I'm okay. Thanks for coming."

It really meant a lot to me that you were there.

"It really meant a lot to me that you were there," I finally said, being sure to lift my eyes to hers when I spoke.

She smiled, patted my shoulder, and stepped out of the car. I stayed in the car, and exhaled.

I watched her walk into the building. At the door, she turned and waved before disappearing inside. I'm pretty sure she'd taken it upon herself to fix me, but even so, it felt good. Scoring the trifecta, a car horn honked in my direction for the third time in the last twenty minutes or so. I waved an apology to the driver behind me and started for home.

I wasn't sure entering my apartment would ever feel the same again without my mother in it. I'd had plenty of time to prepare for the inevitable, yet it was still surprising to arrive home and be alone. You can intellectualize the situation as much as you want – and I did quite a bit of that, thank you very much – but it still hadn't fully prepared me for the reality of her sudden absence. But in one sense, through her loss, I had gained a twin brother. It was time to find him, if I could.

I didn't really know how or where to start the search. I called the Ottawa Civic Hospital where I'd, or rather, we'd, been born nearly twenty-five years ago. It took a while to get anywhere. I finally reached someone in hospital records. It was a very simple question.

"My name is Alex MacAskill. I was born on December 23, 1990 at the Civic. My mother's name is, was, Lee MacAskill. This may sound odd, but I'd like to know if my mother gave birth to identical twin boys that day."

"Don't you already know?" the woman asked.

If I knew the answer, why would I be asking? I have other things I could be doing, like flossing, or baking a cake, or building an ant farm. Lots of things.

"No. You see, I've just discovered that I may have an identical twin and I'm trying to confirm it," I explained.

I heard her working a keyboard for a few minutes, before silence prevailed.

"I'm sorry, I'm not able to disclose that information except to the patient. Protection of patient privacy is a very big deal here."

The patient would be my mother, and I'm pretty sure she already knows the answer to my question.

"You mean, you can only disclose it to my mother?"

"If the patient, Lee MacAskill, is your mother, then yes."

Past tense. Was my mother.

"She died, Tuesday morning."

"Oh, I'm so sorry to hear that."

"So as her only next of kin, can you now tell me instead?"

"I'm sorry, but I can't," she replied. "The privacy laws are clear on this. But you can appeal this decision to the hospital ombudsman, if you wish. But I can tell you she'll not bend the rules on something like this. There's not much wiggle room here."

We had a brief discussion about wiggle room but I was getting antsy on the phone so I thanked her and hung up.

I then searched online for late December 1990 birth announcements in the *Ottawa Citizen*. Just having submitted Mom's obituary the day or so before, it was a little strange to be now searching birth announcements. The *Citizen* gets you coming and going, literally cradle to grave. It took a little mouse manipulation, but I eventually found my own birth announcement. It was just for one baby boy.

> *Lee MacAskill is proud to announce the arrival of her son, Alex MacAskill, 8 lbs, 6 ozs, born the night of December 23rd, 1990. Heartfelt thanks to Dr. Millar and the nursing staff at the Civic.*

Short and sweet. There were no other likely brotherly candidates among the birth announcements for that entire week. So I went online and tried to track down a certain obstetrician named Dr. Millar. It didn't take long to find him. The search engine spit back several pages of "Ottawa, Ob-gyn, Millar" hits. The first entry was his obituary from 2013. So far, my search was going exceedingly well. I might have had better luck finding my bro by staking out crowded intersections and scanning pedestrians' faces.

I checked my email and found one new message from Laura Park. Knowing what it was, I clicked it open anyway.

TO: Alex MacAskill
FROM: Laura Park
RE: You know

Hi Alex,
Sorry, but I'm trying to balance perseverance and pestering. Not sure if I'm succeeding. Please, I want to write about your story. I know it was a long time ago, but I also know how others have been affected by similar experiences. I think you might benefit. It might even help you put it behind you. I know from interviewing others who knew you then and were there that night that it had a profound effect on you. This might help. Could we talk, please?

Laura

I deleted her email. It was not the first time, and would probably not be the last.

Malaya arrived in the early afternoon. We tagged for old time's sake when she came in the door. She saw that I was busy working on my computer at the kitchen table, so she made the bathroom the goal of her cleaning mission. I didn't see her again for two hours. Pungent chemical scents wafted through the apartment. They effectively cleared out my sinuses while Malaya cleaned the bathroom. At about 3:30, my MacBook Pro and I moved to the living room couch so that Malaya could bring her frenzied cleaning road show to the kitchen. Not only did she sterilize the cupboards and counters, but she also broke out the oven cleaner and deployed antibacterial wipes against every square millimetre of refrigerator real estate, inside and out. It's a wonder neither of us passed out from the fumes. Actually, I may have passed out briefly at one point.

We had dinner together at the table at 5:30. For both of us, it had been our first real meal of the day. Chicken pot pie. We needed it. Both of us.

"My supervisor called me yesterday," Malaya said between mouthfuls. "With Mrs. MacAskill . . . you know, gone, I've been assigned to a new patient. I must start there on Monday. It's a little closer to where I live, but it's not the same."

"I know. She called and left a message here saying the same thing," I replied. "And that's just fine, Malaya. I'll be fine. You've done wonderful work here, and I'm grateful – so was my mother – but it's time. Maybe your new patient will be friendly and interesting."

She nodded. Then she squeezed her eyes shut and brought her napkin up to her face.

"It's okay, Malaya," I said in a spasm of originality. "It's okay."

"I don't usually feel so bad when a patient dies. There have been five other patients I've worked with who have died, and I was a little sad, but I was okay. Your mother was different."

"Yes, she was."

Malaya gave me a hug when she left and we even tagged one more time out in the corridor to close the circle. She was a little weepy as she disappeared into the elevator, and I may have been a bit, too.

Back to work. I thought about calling Melany Franken for advice on my search but ultimately decided against it, largely because it was well past quitting time when it occurred to me. I was about to pump the surname "MacAskill" into Google and start wading through the thousands of pages of entries, when I kicked myself. Obviously, my twin brother would not have my surname, if he were even alive. All I really had to go on was that he was born on December 23, 1990, in Ottawa.

Given its mass popularity, I tried Facebook next. I used the online community's help functions, with some assistance from Google, and learned that I could actually search Facebook by birthdate. So I plugged in December 23, 1990, and started to scan the results. It was a little like sipping from a water cannon. I tried to refine my search parameters to make it easier – like limiting it to males, born in Canada, who looked just like Ottawa's very own

Alex MacAskill – but there were serious limitations on the search function. Even excluding all those born on December 23 in a year other than 1990 seemed impossible. I gave up after marvelling at how many people in the world began their lives two days before Christmas as I had. Of course, it only found people who had included their birthdate in their Facebook profiles, and lots didn't. To make matters worse, I was also out of luck if no profile photo had been uploaded. Obviously, I needed to see the person to know.

It was a little like scouring the world for exactly the right haystack – and let me remind you, there are millions of gigantic haystacks from which to choose – and only then beginning the search for the teeny tiny needle hidden somewhere inside. And even if I somehow found that teeny tiny needle, it might very well draw blood. In short, winning the lottery three times in a row offered much better odds.

At 10:30, I realized I was ravenous, again. You wouldn't think scrolling through thousands of Facebook profiles until you were bug-eyed could lead to hunger, but there you are. I ordered a pizza, which seemed easier than reheating the leftover chicken pot pie. After all, the phone was in reach, but the fridge and microwave were a good four strides away.

I ate in front of the TV. *SportsCentre* brought me up to date on all the scores and highlights from the night in Major League Baseball. The playoffs were just around the corner and my Blue Jays were in the hunt. But I couldn't focus on baseball. I guess when your mother dies, and you've discovered after nearly a quarter-century on the planet that you have an identical twin brother, it doesn't just bring perspective, it inflicts perspective. Baseball, even the Jays reaching the postseason, didn't seem to matter so much any more.

I turned off the television, shoved the two remaining pieces of pizza into the fridge, and returned to the world of Facebook. It was really all I had to work with. At 2:45 a.m., I pushed back from my kitchen table and shuffled into the bathroom, overcome with the futility of it all. There must be a better way. I turned on the light. Every surface in the bathroom shone so much it hurt my eyes. It was as if I'd stumbled onto a TV set in mid-take. I could even see myself, in considerable detail, reflected in the lustrous floor. It would have to last for a while. Malaya's magic would not be returning to these parts any time soon.

I splashed some water on my face to sweep out the cobwebs and looked at my reflection in the mirror. My long hair hanging well below my ears, I looked like I was pining for the 1970s. I'd often tried to grow a beard. Nothing alters your appearance like a beard, so I really threw myself into the effort. But I simply couldn't do it. I could get a nice set of mini-muttonchops going, but there was a spot along my jawline on both sides that steadfastly refused to sprout hair of any kind or colour, to connect my sideburns with my chin spinach. So no beard.

I stared at myself for a long time. I was just lowering my eyes when the answer hit me like a runaway train. I am an idiot! I shoved a hairbrush and my MacBook Pro into my backpack, grabbed my car keys, and bolted out the door. Why had I not thought of it sooner? Why? I literally slapped the side of my own head while in the elevator. It hurt more than I'd intended, but I guess I deserved it.

It was strange driving through Ottawa in the middle of the night. The nation's capital is pretty quiet in the evening, let alone in the wee hours of the morning. I was nearly alone on the roads. I made it to my office in seventeen minutes flat, including waiting for a particularly long red light. In the elevator, the little news monitor mounted near the ceiling told me it was 3:06 a.m. I should have been dead tired. I had been dead tired not that long ago. Now I was wide awake. Too-much-caffeine-awake. Fallen-through-thin-ice-awake.

When the elevator opened, I walked right past the Facetech doors and into the men's room. The lighting inside was quite good, though the surfaces weren't nearly as polished and bright as in my own post-Malaya bathroom. I stood face-on to the mirror and raked my hair until there was some semblance of order. Then I grabbed my iPhone, opened the camera app, and took several shots of me in the mirror. For some, I held the camera below my face shooting up, for others I elevated it and shot downwards, always leaving my face unobstructed. Then I took my brush and parted my hair in the middle. I took more photos. Then I parted my hair on the opposite side from my traditional look and took more shots. I went through the same routine again – you know, left part, centre part, right part – but this time, I brushed my hair back behind my ears to at least simulate a shorter cut. More photos. I even wet my hair and slicked it straight back and flat against my head. It looked ridiculous, but I wanted to cover all my bases. Click, click with the camera. Finally, I turned slightly and took a bunch of off-centre, angled shots. I probably snapped a couple of dozen photos.

My security card let me in through the office back door that opened into the staff kitchen. It was very dark inside. I used the flashlight app on my iPhone to make it to my cubicle. I slipped my laptop into the docking station on my desk and my very large Apple monitor burst bright to life giving me all the light I needed. I unlocked my drawer and pulled out my Samsung Portable SSD T3 hard drive and plugged it in to my MacBook Pro. The three terabyte hard drive held the still-not-quite-yet-beta version of Facetech Gold, our latest and greatest facial recognition software. It was still too secret to run from our servers, hence the portable hard drive in my locked drawer.

Traditional facial recognition software is designed to identify similarities and differences across various facial features. Our faces have certain markers, or landmarks, that are distinguishable. Software is used to compare faces, measure certain point-to-point distances, put it all together, and declare whether the "base face" is the same as or different from test faces. Some of these defined measurements are the distance between the eyes, the width of the nose, the length of the jawline, and the depth of the eye sockets.

Some software also assesses the shape of the cheekbones. These distinguishing features are often called nodal points. Most experts agree that there are about eighty nodal points in each human face. Too much information? I don't think so. Bear with me. In an ideal world, the systems work best when the photos are taken head on, with good lighting, and very little facial expression. Current facial recognition software just isn't that effective. There are too many variables and too many limitations.

Not to sound like an infomercial, but at Facetech, we've refined the software to the point where we can examine about 120 nodal points with more precise measurements of other features never before included in similar software. We've also figured out how to accommodate varying lighting levels and face angles. Our estimates suggest that when it's ready for prime time, Facetech Gold will deliver a 40 per cent improvement in results. So it's a big deal in our world.

I moved all my bathroom mirror portraits from my iPhone to my laptop. Then I opened our software and spent several minutes uploading the photos to the Facetech Gold platform. I started by designating the first shot as my "base face." I was anxious as my cursor hovered over the big green Start button. I hesitated, just to let the significance of the moment hang in the air around me. What appeared on the screen in the next few moments could change everything. I clicked and a cartoonish face spun on the screen as our new software did its thing. In short, it was pawing through all the photos of faces on the Internet, comparing them to the base face I'd uploaded, and then spewing out the photos of those that matched and their respective URLs where they were found. It took a few minutes to do all of this. I know that doesn't seem like much time to accomplish such an extraordinary feat, but our goal was to turn minutes to seconds. And we were nearly there.

The whirling face vanished and the results screen appeared. I think I stopped breathing at this point, but even without respiration, my eyes and hands still worked. I looked at the photos and web addresses arrayed on the screen. I was an engineer. I did things methodically and logically, even when searching for my twin brother. I started at the top and worked my way down the list. A header line indicated that there were thirteen photos that "matched" the base face, or in this case, my face. I soon discovered that there weren't thirteen different photos. The first photo had come up ten times. It was a shot of me taken at the Facetech booth at the Consumer Electronics Show in Las Vegas a year earlier. I didn't even know the photo existed, but I remembered well the few days I had to suffer in our booth on the vendors' trade show floor. I hated every minute of it. So many people. And I had to speak to them like it was something I didn't mind doing. I was miserable. I wore a Facetech ball cap the entire time. The photo shows me being miserable, my bright red Facetech golf shirt and ubiquitous CES Vendor lanyard around my neck. But that aside, the software worked. It found me.

And there were two hits on a photo taken at a Facetech retreat at Chateau Montebello a couple of months ago. It was a group shot of a team bonding exercise everyone else had enjoyed and I had endured. There was Abby standing next to me, beaming. I looked like I'd just eaten a rotting prawn. Obviously, four of my colleagues in the shot had posted the photo to their Facebook walls. I had not. I had no Facebook account in my own name and no plans to start one. But several years ago I had opened a phantom account under an alias that allowed me to browse and search. I'd never posted anything.

Finally, there was a single positive result on a photo in someone's Flickr account taken at an Ottawa Senators hockey game. This one really showed the power of Facetech Gold. It was a selfie of a family of three ardent Senator fans taken by the father. There I was, two rows back and just barely in the shot, turned away from the family and watching the play on the ice. Even so, it came up as a match.

I was a little disappointed the software hadn't yielded more and different photos. But it was my first pass. I spent the next two hours selecting different base face shots from my bathroom selfie shoot and poring over the results. The same three photos of me kept emerging, along with two other shots, both taken at Facetech events. I was starting to feel discouraged. While the software was working well, it was only serving up photos of me. I skipped the remaining "long hair" base face shots and selected the first of my simulated short hair photos, with the part in my hair on the left side. The cartoon face set about its spinning. As expected it took about two minutes for the results.

The same photos once again filled the screen. Since I'd seen them all before, I scrolled to the bottom, where a single new photo slid into view. It was a shot of me standing and speaking at a lectern. My hands in the photo suggested I was in the midst of making a rather compelling point. The sign on the front of the lectern read "IAPP-UK Conference – London 2014." I thought back to that day in London when I'd given that keynote, feeling and looking calm, cool, collected, and confident. Then it struck me. I'd never ever been to London, and I hadn't been calm, cool, collected, and confident since late 2005.

When the spotlights found me, I could feel their warmth.
I was no longer cold, but something much worse.

CHAPTER 5

I was giddy. I was light-headed. My pulse was pounding. My stomach felt like someone else's. I couldn't tear my eyes away from him. It was strange and surreal to be looking at yourself knowing that it wasn't really you. I gathered myself and read the caption.

> *Innovatengage founder Matt Paterson addresses the 2014 conference of the International Association for Public Participation U.K., in London.*

Matt Paterson. Matthew Paterson. A good solid name. Looking at him was looking at me. There was really no longer any doubt. Certainty settled in my gut, belief in my heart, and conviction in my head. This was not just some guy who looked a little bit like me. This was not a fluke of birth in a foreign country an ocean away, where two parents produced a son who happened to resemble me in some respects. No. No way. It was clear. Utterly obvious to anyone with passable vision. We were once one egg. We split. We were born. Then we were split a second time . . . for nearly twenty-five years.

I had found Matt Paterson. I had found my identical twin brother.

While I stared at his photo, my mind raced. My thoughts swirled. I didn't attempt to rein in the chaos. I couldn't have if I'd tried. A split-second cerebral sampling from that frenzied moment yielded:

- Holy shit, I found him.
- Who is Matt Paterson?
- What does he do?
- Where is he from?
- I found him.
- What is Innovatengage?
- I want to show Abby.
- The miracle of a high-speed Internet connection and software I helped develop allowed me to locate a perfect stranger, and my twin brother, on a different continent, in under two hours. Unbe-fucking-lievable.
- What's his story?
- Mom, it's okay. Don't worry. Don't fret. I found him. It's okay.

- But why didn't you tell me?
- Short hair on us looks better, much better, but . . .
- Is he married?
- I wonder if anyone ever connects him to Gabriel?
- Does he have children?
- There's no wedding ring on his finger.
- I like his jacket but I don't think I could pull off that shirt.
- I feel different, now.
- I found him.
- I found him.
- I feel different.

Overwhelmed, I looked away from the screen for a moment and concentrated on breathing. I held my own hands. I rocked for a minute. I'd read somewhere that rocking is soothing to our species, in a primal sense. Then I looked back at the image I'd somehow found, my needle in the Internet's haystack. He was still there. Matt Paterson was still at the lectern, seemingly in full rhetorical flight. We almost looked noble, even heroic. In that instant, the need to see him move and hear him speak overpowered everything else. I flipped over to YouTube and typed "Matt Paterson, Innovatengage" into the life-giving search bar.

In an instant, there were several hits. The first one was from that same IAPP-UK conference. I stopped myself from hitting the Play button and hauled my earbuds from the side pocket of my backpack. The speakers on my MacBook Pro were pretty good, but I wanted the best audio fidelity I could get to hear him for the first time. I plugged in the buds and pushed them where they belonged. Then I hit the white triangle.

We were speaking with an English accent. He was speaking with an English accent. But it was my voice. Initially, I wasn't focused on what he was saying. I was listening to the lilt, the pitch, the timbre of his voice. Except for the accent, it was my lilt, my pitch, my timbre. After a few minutes, I started concentrating on his words and his performance. Even without speaking notes, he had an easy and confident speaking style. He cracked jokes on the fly that made his large audience laugh. In short order, it was clear he was funny, humble, self-deprecating, but very smart, confident, and fully engaged in the moment. For a time I narrowed my focus to three specific sentences early on in his remarks. At the 5:42 mark he said:

> In this era, earning the social licence to build massive infrastructure projects is not just an option, not just recommended, not just preferred, it's absolutely essential. Public engagement, scaled digitally, to secure social licence, has become the new corporate imperative. Ignore it at your financial and reputational peril.

I opened a notebook and wrote down these three sentences. I listened to them over and over, following the words I'd written, until I knew them by heart. I closed my notebook. Then I recited the lines, mimicking Matt's cadence and inflection. I worked at it for several minutes, repeating the lines, tweaking words, perfecting the accent. I don't know why I did this. Then, after listening to him one more time, I used an MP3 recording app on my iPhone to perform the sentences in my voice, in our voice, but with Matt's English accent. I'm good with accents. You already know I used to be an actor. It was a big part of my pre-Gabriel high school life. I loved the excitement of performing. I loved slipping into a different character, particularly if a foreign accent was involved. I loved the warmth of the stage lights, at least until I didn't.

I wasn't happy with my first few recordings, so I erased them. I played Matt again. Then I recorded those three sentences one more time. Got it. With a second set of earbuds I'd pulled from my desk drawer, I put Matt's YouTube clip in my right ear, and my iPhone recording in my left. It took me a minute or so to sync up the two tracks. When played perfectly together, it sounded like a single stereo recording from Matt's U.K. keynote. You honestly could not tell there were two different voices, largely because there was really only one voice. Our voice. Twins. Identical twins. I had found him.

It was now 6:45. Morning light was spilling through the office windows, though the sun would have to be much higher in the sky before it reached my cubicle. I spent the next half hour or so watching Matt Paterson in every YouTube clip I could find. Some were media interviews in which he spoke about his company or played the role of subject matter expert about digital public engagement, stakeholder consultation, and the concept of social licence. He was unfailingly articulate, polite, and informed. Occasionally, his obvious sense of humour crept in. I liked him. Even if he weren't my identical twin brother, I would have liked him. He came across as a nice guy who'd been well brought up. I stopped to wonder who had brought him up.

I easily found the Innovatengage website. Before reading about the company, I clicked on the Leadership Team menu item. Matt's name headed the list of four.

> ***Matt Paterson, Founder***
>
> *mattpaterson@innovatengage.co.uk*
>
> *Matthew Paterson started* Innovatengage *in 2013 following a short stint as a political staffer for the Secretary of State for Business, Innovation, and Skills. Before that, he earned a Masters in Social Science of the Internet from Oxford where he examined the concept of "social licence," and the Internet's potential to scale public and stakeholder engagement, an emerging staple of modern government and business. The award-winning* Innovatengage *platform Matt Paterson conceived is changing the way organizations engage with their audiences. He is a sought-after speaker, and lives in London.*

I read his short bio through twice. He'd gone to Oxford. He'd worked in British politics. He'd started a company when he was twenty-three and built an online engagement platform. He had an email address. I had his email address. I could just fire off an email right that second if I wanted to. I could have connected with him right then. Hell, I could have picked up the phone and called him right then. At that hour, he might have just been munching on a sandwich at his desk. This thought elevated my heart rate. I leaned back from my computer. I had only one chance to make that first connection. And I'd never get it back if I botched it. It was tempting, but I needed to think.

By then, people were drifting in to the office. Some nodded my way, or waved, though many just ignored me as they passed through to their cubicles. They weren't jerks. In fact they were really very nice, almost to a person. They'd all, at one time or another, tried to engage me, tried to involve me in the day-to-day office social dynamic. You know what I mean. "How was your weekend?" "Can you believe what Simone said in the status meeting yesterday?" "I think Susan and Brent might be seeing each other." "Is that a new top?" Okay, no one has ever asked me about a "new top." But the other stuff, yes. They'd all tried. But I just couldn't ever seem to give them enough back to keep myself in the play. I just couldn't.

I smelled Simone breeze in shortly after 8:30, which was early for her. She wore the same powerful, trachea-constricting fragrance every single day. Always the same scent. Always. Actually, neither scent nor fragrance was anywhere close to the right word. But "stench" just sounded too harsh to my ears, though my nose was on board. While I waited until she settled herself in her glass-walled office, I read a little more about Innovatengage on the website. It was referred to as a "start-up" in the "About the company" section. There were two principal lines of business. First, Innovatengage developed, and was constantly innovating, an online engagement platform that allowed organizations to move their costly public and stakeholder consultation programs on to the Internet where so many more people could participate. Instead of attending an inconveniently timed and located public information session in some sterile hotel function room or community centre, interested individuals could visit the engagement site online, review the same materials, ask questions, respond to surveys, watch a video about the project, offer feedback on any aspect of the project, upload an audio comment or question, and almost anything else you could conceive.

Instead of always seeing the same fifteen well-known stakeholders attending the town hall meeting and providing utterly predictable feedback, the Innovatengage platform allowed thousands of people to go online and participate in a meaningful exchange. Through this innovation, Matt's company could scale the old-school, bricks-and-mortar regional road-show stakeholder consultation program, making it far more effective and efficient, and far less costly. And many more people had the opportunity to participate. Win-win. Very cool, I thought, and with an almost limitless market potential in what Matt described in one of the YouTube videos, this emerging age of social licence.

Second, the consulting side of the business provided customized advice and counsel to clients on how to develop and execute successful public digital engagement programs using the Innovatengage platform. If I understood it correctly, you didn't need to buy the advice and counsel if you didn't want or need it. Clients could just pay Matt's team to put their own branding on the Innovatengage platform, and then the client could take it from there, on their own. Interesting.

I glanced over to Simone's office. There she was, ensconced behind her desk. Let's get this over with, I thought. I got to my feet and forced myself to walk over to her office door. I just stood there, knowing that I'd entered her peripheral vision. I waited a bit, and eventually she looked up. I managed a slight smile. Her face did not say, "Hey, Alex, it's great to see you. How are you holding up?" No, her expression was more along the lines of "You, again. What do you want this time?" I'm quite good at reading her facial expressions.

"It's you, again," she said. Then she sighed in a very big way – big, as in hyperventilating big. "I've got a bad feeling about this. What do you want this time? My nine o'clock is going to call any second."

What do I want this time? Well, how about what I've always wanted? But alas no, you keep showing up every morning.

"Um, there's been a major development related to my mother's death that means, well, I just have to take care of a few things," I replied. "Sorry."

"What exactly do you mean? What's happened?"

I found out about three hours ago that I have an identical twin brother in England who doesn't even know I exist, and I have to find him. That's what's happened.

"I can't really say, but I must travel out of town for a few weeks, and then . . ."

"Stop!" Like one of the Supremes, she raised high her stop sign hand. "Wait! Just wait! For a moment there I thought you said you were going out of town for a couple of weeks. Surely I misheard. I did misunderstand you, didn't I?"

Your ears are working fine. It's your brain and people skills that are constantly misfiring.

"Yes. Technically, you misheard me. I said a *few* weeks, not a *couple* of weeks."

"Don't you fuck with me, Alex," she snapped – and I mean she snapped in every sense of the word. "Do not – I repeat – Do. Not. Fuck with me! I am right out here on the ledge!"

Yeah, well, why don't you put us all out of our misery and just step off?

The eyes and ears of every other person in the vicinity were trained on Simone's office as her voice reverberated throughout the floor. Even Abby in our remote cubicle popped up from behind our partition like a startled meerkat with a pained look on her face.

"Sorry. I have no choice," I said, looking at the floor. "I'll use the rest of my bereavement leave and then I'll start on the four weeks' vacation I still have. Sorry."

"Alex!" she shouted.

I physically recoiled from the impact of her vocal waves striking my chest.

WHAT!

"Yes?" I replied in almost a whisper.

"The Gold beta is mission-fucking-critical to this company and it's all on my head. Are you reading me? I'm sorry your father died, but the Gold beta must be rolled out on time, or none of us here are going to have a job."

You want mission-fucking-critical? At this precise moment, finding a twin brother I never knew I had is my idea of mission-fucking-critical.

She stopped to breathe some more before continuing.

"So I don't care if you need an emergency heart transplant or if the steel plate in your skull needs rustproofing, taking time off right now is JUST NOT HAPPENING!" she shrieked.

Oh it's happening. It's happening.

I had nearly retreated out of her office, but realized that I needed to move back in. The thought of Matthew Paterson in London somehow made it a little easier to step back into the furnace.

Let's try it again and I'll speak slower.

"Again, my role in Gold is essentially over. The code is written. It works. The platform works. We've done all the QA we can . . ."

Her face instantly morphed from rage to rage-perplexed. It was a subtle change, but I got it.

"Sorry, Quality Assurance. We've done all the Quality Assurance we can at this stage. As I've explained, it's now over to the UX team – sorry – User Experience team and Design to make it look pretty. My part is done. Over. Finished. It's off my desk. Abby can handle any minor coding variances that UX and Design might need."

She actually looked frightened. Well, frightened and apoplectic.

"No. No. No . . ."

Thankfully, the phone on her desk rang. Her nine o'clock call, right on time. She froze and stared at her phone.

"Um. I'll just speak to HR on my way out. See you when I get back. I'll stay in touch with Abby," I said as calmly as I could.

She remained transfixed by the phone, by then on its third ring. On ring five, I pointed to the flashing button.

"I know. I know!" she yelled, reaching for the phone.

I spoke to Carleen, our HR director, on my way back to my desk. She was very curious about what had just gone down in Simone's office. I explained. I was just as cryptic about the true reason for my unplanned hiatus from the office, but she was completely reasonable and sympathetic about it all. She also apologized for Simone's psychotic behaviour, though she used a milder term. I think it was "somewhat unusual behaviour." I thanked her.

Abby waited one nanosecond after I sat down at my desk before using her feet to propel her swivel chair to my side of the partition.

"What the fork was that all about?"

Fork?

I remembered to make eye contact.

"Nothing. Just Simone being, you know, Simone," I replied.

"Yeah, but she sounded deeper in bat shit there than she usually does."

Yep, and that means a whole lot of bat shit. Full immersion.

"Well, I just told her I'm going away for a few weeks, you know, to deal with some family stuff. And she wasn't very happy about it."

"But Gold is off your plate now. You've done your time on it. It's good to go," she said.

"That's what I told her, but still she's . . ."

"I know, a whacked-out wing nut with several bolts loose, with a whole lot of venom looking for a home," she interjected.

"Right," I agreed, and then made sure I was making eye contact. "Um, Abby, it meant a lot to me that you were there yesterday. Thank you. I mean it."

She smiled and put her hand on my arm.

"It's okay. That's what you do for friends," she replied. "I know you'd be there for me."

I hadn't actually realized that we were friends. But I'm starting to get it now.

"But more importantly right now, what's your plan? In fact, why the firk are you even here, anyway? You're supposed to be tracking down your twin bro. Come on. Get on it! The next time I see you, I want to see two of you."

Funny you ask. It seems I just found him.

"Well, I just found him – my twin brother, I mean," I said. "I found him."

I hadn't planned on telling her. It just kind of happened in the moment. I couldn't seem to stop myself.

"Wait, you found him already?" she asked, her eyes assuming a cartoonish diameter.

"I did."

"Shut the frank up!" she said in a voice better suited for saving ships from shoals.

I jumped in my chair and, after landing, looked around furtively.

"Sorry. Shut the frank up!" she whispered. "What are you talking about?"

I leaned in closer to her.

"I found him."

"Where is he? Ottawa? Toronto? Canada?"

"London, England," I replied.

"England? But how did you find him?"

I just pointed to the mock-up for the new Beta Gold branding pinned to my bulletin board. It took a few beats.

"No fracking way! You didn't!"

I certainly fracking did.

"I did."

"And it really worked? Show me. Show me!"

I turned my MacBook Pro towards her and flipped back over to the Gold beta platform. My first simulated short-hair bathroom photo filled the screen.

"Hmmm, I like the brushed-back shorter look. You should cut it that way," she said.

No way. Gabriel and I prefer longer hair. But thanks anyway.

I just shook my head.

"And you got a hit on this shot?" she asked, still looking at my photo.

I just nodded.

"Yeah, well, don't keep me in suspense," she urged. "Let's see him. Come on! I'm dying here."

She was rubbing her hands together and had an almost gleeful look on her face. To heighten the impact of the moment, rather than showing her the listing of photo matches, which included lots of shots of the real me, I turned the computer so that only I could see the screen. I flipped back to YouTube and cued up Matt Paterson's London keynote address. Then I handed Abby one earbud while I inserted the other in my own ear. This worked fine because we were so close together. I turned the screen towards her and started the video.

It was interesting to watch her face when Matt appeared and started talking. It freaked her out a bit. She pushed her chair back and away from the screen, yanking the earbuds from both our ears.

"No way! No way! This is not happening," she said.

Then she rolled back in close, took both earbuds for herself, and concentrated on Matt.

"You're messing with me. This is you, right? This is you before you became, you know, who you are now, right?"

What do you mean before I became who I am now? Are we that different?

"No. I've never been to London. I don't do a lot of conference keynotes, as you might imagine."

She knew I was speaking the truth. She knew.

"Other than the accent, you sound identical. You look identical, except he's got way better hair. You could look like that," she said. "It's just so surreal looking at this. Oh, did you see what he just did with his right hand? Back it up. Stop. Go. Okay, right there. Did you see what he did?"

Matt had just said something and emphasized it with a hand gesture that looked like he could have been cradling a small bird, but he wasn't.

"You do that! You do that when you're making a point," she said.

"I don't think I've ever done that," I replied.

"Trust me. You make that move. That's your move. It's the same move," she insisted. "This is flarkin' freakin' me out."

I returned one earbud to my right ear, then I moved the cursor to the 5:42 mark of the YouTube video.

"Listen," I said.

I played my twin brother's three sentences for Abby, and then played them again. After the second time, I hit pause and said, in my own voice, but in Matt's accent:

"In this era, earning the social licence to build massive infrastructure projects is not just an option, not just recommended, not just preferred, it's absolutely essential. Public engagement, scaled digitally, to secure social licence, has become the new corporate imperative. Ignore it at your financial and reputational peril."

Then she stared at me for quite a long time, apparently stunned.

She signalled with her right hand. I understood and performed the lines a second time.

If you don't close your mouth soon, barn swallows just may nest in there.

"I'm out of frickin' words! That was amazing. You are amazing. Great accent. You and he are one and the same," she said. "Okay, after that, I'm done. I'm all in."

We watched a few more videos and then I showed her the Innovatengage website with Matt's photo and bio. She studied the photo intently, for quite a long time. Then she put her hand on my knee, shaking her head, still looking at Matt on the screen.

"You never knew? Never knew anything about him? Nothing?"

You think I'd spend half the night with Gold searching if I knew about him?

"I had no idea. None."

Then she turned in her chair so we were face-on to one another. She took hold of my hands in hers. I looked down at our coupled hands. The cuff of her shirt had ridden up her wrist a bit, revealing on the inside of her right forearm a tattoo of what looked like a fountain pen. It was small but intricately detailed, and quite beautiful.

"Look at me," she instructed.

I looked at her.

"You really must find him," she said. "I'm an only child. All I ever wanted was a sister. I still want one. You must go right now, and find him. Do you copy?"

What do you think I'm going to do? I'm not an idiot. Well, not often. Of course I'm going to find him. What else is there to do?

"I know. Yes, I copy. I'm going. That's what I was just explaining to Simonesaurus Rex in her office."

"Wait, you told her about, you know, Matt?" she asked, looking a little hurt.

Are you deranged? Of course not! In her current state, her head might have exploded.

"No. No. I just told her it's an important family matter related to my mother's death."

Abby nodded in relief, still holding my hands.

"You have to find him. I mean it."

"I know. I will," I replied.

"And you have to keep me in the loop every step of the way," she said. "Wait, maybe I can come with. I have some vacay coming to me."

No way. I just found out we're friends. Let me get used to that idea first.

"I'm afraid you have to stay here in case UX or Design modifies anything on Gold that means changing some code or writing some new lines. You being here is the only way I can go," I replied, tilting my head towards Simone's office.

"Okay, but you let me know where you are, and what's going on. I've got a stake in this now that you've told me. I'm in this thing, right?"

"Right. I'll keep you updated, often, I promise," I said.

We sat there in silence still holding hands for a few seconds. It was kind of weird, but it was also kind of nice.

"So, I was thinking of emailing Matt or calling him, you know, just as a first step. Maybe Skyping him?"

She looked up in thought. I've noticed that's what Abby does when she thinks. She looks up. Eventually, she looked back down at me and shook her head.

"No. Don't," she said. "Think about it. It's weird. Someone calls and says 'I think I might be your identical twin brother.' Or worse, puts it in an email. It's a nonstop express ticket to a restraining order. Even Skype isn't quite right. You're too far away. He won't believe you until he's looking at you in the flesh, up close, until you're standing right in front of him. You kind of need that element of surprise for him to believe it. So no calls, no emails, no letters, no texts, no Skype. You have to go to him, physically, in person. Methinks that's the only way."

My thoughts exactly. Besides, I hate calling strangers on the phone, even if we were womb-mates for nine months, twenty-five years ago. On the other hand, I don't exactly like meeting new people in person, either. But if he's looking at me right in front of him, I think I'll be okay.

"Okay. That's it then."

She released my hands. I was kind of sad when she did.

I loaded my laptop into my backpack. On a whim, I slipped the Facetech Gold portable hard drive into my pack as well, breaking a boatload of company internal security rules. Then I nodded at Abby and left.

As I drove home, I found myself steering the car towards Dr. Weaver's office. Made sense. I needed to fill her in and let her know I'd be gone for a bit. It was just past 10:00 a.m. by that time. I knew Dr. Weaver didn't start seeing patients until 10:30, so I took a chance.

Her waiting room was open and empty when I arrived. She'd heard the door and came out of her office.

"Alex? I don't have you down for this morning," she said. "Again, I'm so sorry about your mother. Is everything okay?"

"I'm okay, but I do have some rather shocking news, and since you're kind of in charge of my mental stability, I thought you should know about it."

She waved me into her office.

"We've got a bit of time before my first patient."

It took me only fifteen minutes to lay it all out for her. Having explained the story to Abby, I was more efficient when telling Wendy Weaver. I trotted out the safety deposit box photo. I showed her the facial recognition software on my computer. Then I played her Matt's keynote YouTube video and mimicked the three lines as I had with Abby. Wendy didn't need any more convincing.

"Truly extraordinary. There can really be no doubt. I don't know what to say. I'm flabbergasted," she said. "I know now is not the time to talk about this, but you're so good with accents. I really think we should revisit the theatre therapy idea we've been discussing."

"Yes, we can do that later. But I have a higher priority right now."

"You mean, meeting Matt Paterson?"

"Yep."

"Don't you think you should take some time to think this all through, to consider all the options, and only after that make a decision about next steps? I can barely get my head wrapped around what you've just told me. It must be even more shocking for you. Why not take your time, be cautious, and not rush into any decisions?"

"I know that sounds sensible, and it probably *is* sensible, but I think my course is clear. Yes, I know this only happened about four hours ago, but I actually feel quite calm now, and I think I know what I have to do."

"Alex, I don't want to rain on your parade or trample your enthusiasm, but sometimes these reunions don't play out as expected," she cautioned.

"What do you mean?" I asked. "Are you saying I shouldn't pursue it, pursue him?"

"No, no, of course not. I'm just suggesting you contain your expectations. It'll be a shock to your brother if he doesn't already know."

"What do you mean 'if he doesn't already know'? How could he know about me and not try to find me? Come to think of it, if he's like almost everyone else in the world, he's probably already seen me in my big moment. He just didn't know who I was."

"Well, let's just think it through a bit. There are a few possibilities," Dr. Weaver explained. "Maybe he knows, tried to find you, failed, and gave up looking. Or maybe he knows but is scared, or just doesn't want the cataclysmic upheaval in his life."

"No, I don't think so. That really doesn't sound likely to me. I'm pretty sure he has no idea he has an identical twin living in Ottawa, Ontario, Canada."

"You may well be right. Okay, you're probably right. But just prepare yourself for the full range of reactions you might get when and if you meet Matt Paterson."

We talked for another ten minutes until we heard the waiting room door open. It was time to go.

When I got home, I spent the rest of the day making arrangements. It really is amazing what you can accomplish on the Internet. I had two calls that afternoon from Abby pining for updates. I told her everything that had happened since leaving the office. It didn't take long. I found it easier to talk with her over the phone, but I kind of missed her habit of touching me on my arm or hand or knee when we talked. I didn't read much into her tactile approach. I'd seen her do the same thing with other colleagues at the office, and even with Malaya when we'd dropped her off after the interment ceremony. Still, it was nice. She said Simone had been locked in her office most of the day dealing with something that may or may not have been related to the Gold beta launch.

Speaking of the Gold beta, I plugged in the portable hard drive again and opened the program. Another idea had just hit me. The software had already worked once for me that day, maybe it would work a second time on a different target. I started by going to YouTube and typing a single word in the search bar. I clicked on the first video that came up. I knew it well – painfully well. I moved the time cursor along to the 11:38 mark and then froze the frame. Using a few keystrokes and my mouse, I put a virtual border around the pixelated face of a young woman in a red dress, seated in a crowd. My computer made the familiar camera-clicking sound to signal I'd just taken a screen shot from the video. It was not a good photo. Quite blurry, actually. But it was the best I could get. The video was shot long before the days of high-definition home video cameras. Besides, the young woman was not really in focus to begin with. After all, she was not the star of the video. She was just part of the background. Nevertheless, I thought it was worth trying.

I loaded the photo into Facetech Gold as my "base face" and hit the big green Start button. As it had many times already that day, my heart started beating faster in anticipation of the results. In less than ten seconds, the "Base Face Failure" error message flashed on the screen. Shit. The shot I'd lifted from the video was just too blurry for the software to work. The nodal point measurements simply could not be made. I tried again with the same result. Oh well, one missing-person search at a time.

An hour later, I was all set. I was nervous, perhaps even terrified, yet knew I was doing the right thing for the right reasons. I hadn't felt this confident about anything for quite some time. I went to bed around midnight, but just lay there for a while watching more videos of Matt on my iPad. I couldn't really stop. I woke up at 3:09 a.m. in the grip of a vivid dream. Simone Ashe had been choking me, her hands working my neck at full throttle. Awake in a sweat, I found my iPad resting on my neck and pressing up against my throat. I pushed it aside to permit normal respiration, and in that instant was struck by a terrible thought. I leapt out of bed and searched our apartment – my apartment – from stem to stern.

It had taken me about an hour and three-quarters to find my twin brother. But I found him. It took me two hours and seven minutes to find my passport. But I found it. Then I slept.

I heard them all gasp below in unison, and then felt the currents and eddies of their simultaneous exhalations wash over me.

CHAPTER 6

I landed at Heathrow Monday morning. It was drizzling. Though I'd never ventured across the ocean, my mental image of England always featured grey skies and rain. It was no longer just a mental image. I was nervous at passport control though I need not have been, because I passed through without incident. When the officer asked the purpose of my visit, I kept it short and sweet but one hundred per cent true. "Visiting family" was all I said. She welcomed me and waved me on.

I didn't sleep much on the flight. The man seated next to me made sure of that. He slept the whole way but snored to beat the band. And I don't use "beat the band" as just a metaphor. I tried listening to a Rolling Stones concert available on one of the in-flight audio channels, but the snoring juggernaut next to me drowned out Mick and the boys – and that was quite an achievement. I tried reading a book but that didn't work. I tried watching a movie. No dice. So I reclined my seat, closed my eyes, and just thought about the preceding several days. It had been less than a week since my mother had died. Man, how the world could change in such a short time.

I was convinced my mother had been about to tell me about Matt. If she had not been so fatigued that last night, she would have told me. I was sure of it. How else could you explain the envelope in my name and the key inside? But why had she not told me earlier in my life, say, when I was ten, or fourteen, or seventeen, or twenty? Perhaps she was ashamed about giving up Matt as a newborn, if that's what happened. Perhaps with each passing year, the thought of explaining it all to me – that I had an identical twin brother – became too heavy, the burden too great. The accumulation of time? The accumulation of guilt? Of shame? Who knew? But she'd given me all the pieces. Now I just had to put my family back together again.

It may not come as a shock that London Bridge Hotel is located near the south end of the famous bridge that spans the Thames in the heart of London. (I was able to confirm that contrary to popular belief, London Bridge is actually not falling down.) I arrived around 10:00 a.m. An attractive young woman checked me in, smiling the entire time. I was lucky my room was ready, given that it was not even lunchtime. We'd just about finished the paperwork when I remembered.

"Could you tell me how to get to the London Bridge Tube station?" I asked. "I assume it's closest."

"Yes. It's very close, about a two-minute walk. Jeremy, our concierge on the front door, can show you the most direct route when you're ready to go."

"Thank you."

"My pleasure, Mr. MacAskill," she replied, handing me my key card and Wi-Fi log-in instructions. "And our full buffet breakfast is served each morning in the Londinium restaurant, from seven to ten."

I don't think I can stay for the full three hours, but thanks.

"Thanks."

I wasn't too concerned about the cost of the four-star accommodation. While London hotels are notoriously expensive, I was fine, financially, and this trip was worth it. Besides, this location meant only a short public transit trip to my final destination.

My flight had left Toronto's Pearson airport at 8:30 Sunday night. I'd spent the weekend repacking my suitcase, removing and adding items each time. I was restless. I wanted to go while I still had my nerve. But I couldn't find a seat on a Saturday flight. I'd slept in until about ten Sunday morning and felt alert and excited as soon as my eyes opened. I'd packed a final time late on Saturday night, so I was ready to go with several hours to spare. To kill the time until my flight to Toronto, where I'd connect through to Heathrow, I jumped back on my computer, determined to learn more about my identical twin brother. I'd already exhausted the first few pages of Google search results on Friday, so I ventured deeper. I was glad I did.

After wading through a raft of Matthew Patersons online who weren't my identical twin brother, I finally found a hit on *my* Matt Paterson that wasn't related to Innovatengage. It was a 2011 article in the *Guardian*. I then quickly found several more media stories about the same thing. In late 2009, Matt's parents, Eva and George, had been killed by a drunk driver in a collision on the M25. Matt would have been in university then for his undergraduate degree, before he'd gone to Oxford. How terrible. I felt a strong pang of pain and sympathy for him as I read the articles. I sat back in my chair for a moment and thought about how I'd feel if Mom had been taken in the same fashion.

The stories were not so much about the collision itself, though there were a few news photos of the aftermath at the crime scene, but about the eventual court case. The impaired driver had been charged, tried, and convicted of what British law calls "causing death by careless driving while unfit through alcohol/over prescribed limit."

What was interesting about the story was that even though the driver was immediately charged, the whole thing was dropped when some key evidence went missing. That must have been crushing for Matt at the time. Curiously, about eighteen months later, the charge was reinstated. This time they proceeded to court and won. A few media stories noted that Matt was an only child and had attended each day of the trial. There was one photo in the *Daily Mail* of my twin brother leaving the courts after the driver was convicted and sentenced to four years in prison. So Matt had no family left . . . except me.

After I'd unpacked and put my clothes in the dresser and closet, I took a shower. Then I coiffed my hair with the blow dryer provided. Despite my long hair, I seldom used a hair dryer. But it was right there. When in Rome, etc. Then I clipped my nails. After that, I got dressed, turned on the TV, and proceeded not to watch it for a time. I used the shoe-shine kit in the bathroom to do a number on my loafers. A first for me. There was also a sewing kit in the bathroom, but my clothes were in pretty good shape. I checked out the mini-bar in the room, but took nothing. Finally, I lay back on the bed and stared at the ceiling for about fifteen minutes. It was then about 11:20 a.m.

When I could think of nothing else to do – and believe me, I tried – I took a few deep breaths and headed out the door. I got to the elevator, pushed the down button, and then spun around and returned to my room. I sat on the bed and hyperventilated for a few minutes.

I couldn't just show up at Innovatengage. I didn't even know if Matt was in the country, let alone at his office. And even if he were there, what would he say? What would he do? Would he even agree to see me? Would he believe my story or think I was just some freaked-out plastic surgery–loving stalker? And I couldn't avoid meeting at least some of his work colleagues. I loathed meeting strangers, particularly when I feared one or two of them might recognize me for something other than looking strikingly like their boss. This idea didn't seem quite so perfect any more. Now that I was just a short Tube trip away from pay dirt, it seemed there were suddenly a whole lot of cons and only one pro. On the other hand, the one pro was quite compelling. I might just find my long-lost identical twin brother.

I pulled out my cellphone and thought about sending Abby a text, until I realized it was only 5:15 a.m. in Ottawa. But just thinking about Abby and her enthusiasm for my mission made me feel a little better. I rose and left the room a second time.

I walked southeast to the London Bridge Tube station. After figuring out how to pay my way onto a train, I travelled three Tube stops north to the Old Street station. I was headed for what is called East London Tech City, the third-largest tech start-up cluster in the world, after San Francisco and New York. In fact, there were plenty of rumours at our office that Facetech would soon open a London office in the same part of town. Sitting on the train, I reviewed my carefully conceived, detailed, step-by-step plan and attendant contingencies. Here goes. I would hang around Matt's office building until I spied him. Then I'd just walk up and stand in front of him. Yep. That was it. That was the plan. That's what I had. And yes, I'm quite aware that it's not really what an observer of sound mind would ever call a plan. It was more of a loose notion than a plan. More of a hazy inclination. All right, it made ad hoc seem anally retentive. I know. But I'd come this far. I'd figure it out.

It was 11:50 when I walked out of the Old Street Tube station and west along Old Street. As was my habit, I pulled the Ottawa Senators ball cap down low on my head. It held my long hair in place, partly obscuring my face. I did not want to be recognized. It was a short walk to the Innovatengage office, housed in a reasonably good-looking building known as Classic House. I recognized it from having studied it on Google Street View the day before. It was, more or less, on the southwest corner of Old Street and a strange little road called Martha's Buildings. No, I'm not making this up. There really was a street called Martha's Buildings. I know. Just the kind of confusing nomenclature to make navigating a gigantic metropolis so much easier for a London virgin like me. But I'd made it. And I'd found it necessary to speak to only a couple of strangers thus far.

There was a pub on the first floor of Classic House called the William Blake. I'm not making that up either. I know there's this romantic notion that London has a pub on every corner. Well, from my observations since arriving earlier that morning, pubs aren't quite that ubiquitous, but conveniently, there really was one in Matt's building. I'd checked it out before my flight and learned it enjoyed a solid online reputation. I slipped in and snagged a two-person booth in the front window with an unobstructed view of the main entrance to Classic House. It was quite a nice little pub – dark hardwood floors, comfortable seating, old fox-hunting prints on the walls, and a long bar with multiple taps presumably offering multiple draught beers. The lighting was dim enough for atmosphere and just bright enough to prevent collisions. I liked the place.

Innovatengage was five floors directly above me, but I figured every employee, Matt too, had to enter through the front doors directly in my line of sight out the window. I felt good about my prime position. Think of it as a stakeout, but without the unmarked police car, dysfunctional partners, bad coffee, and doughnuts.

Despite common courtesy, I kept my cap on my cranium while seated in the pub. I kept my head lowered but my eyes raised to the passing pedestrians outside.

"What'll you have, luv?" said the older woman who materialized next to my table, startling me. "Oh sorry, luv, I didn't mean to sneak up on you. Usually customers come up to the bar to order."

You didn't surprise me. That strange high-pitched noise in my throat was to signal that I'm ready to order a drink.

"Oh, right. Just a pint of Guinness, please," I replied. "Thank you."

"Coming up, luv."

Then she did a very understated double take and turned back to look more closely at my face. She scrunched up her nose a bit as if trying to place me. I looked back down at the table and tried to avoid further eye contact. Gabriel? Probably. Or maybe hanging out in a pub likely frequented by my identical twin brother was not one of my better ideas if I wanted to avoid attention.

She was dressed neatly, but casually, in green corduroy pants, a cream-coloured turtleneck, and a green vest of some kind. She moved and spoke with the weary authority of an owner. Never once in my life had Guinness crossed my lips. I'm really not much of a beer drinker. But, you know, the Rome thing, again.

I watched as she pulled the Guinness herself behind the bar – I think "pulled" is the correct term, isn't it? Then, when I just stayed in my seat, she walked it back to me, placing it on a cardboard Guinness coaster in front of me.

"Will you be joining us for lunch? Everything is up on the blackboard there," she said, pointing.

All of a sudden I was quite hungry. I hadn't noticed it until she reminded me about the midday meal and our daily need to ingest nourishment. I scanned the blackboard.

"Yes, thank you. Shepherd's pie, please."

"A very wise and popular choice," she said.

Yeah well, I really have no idea what a ploughman's lunch is or Welsh rarebit, so shepherd's pie was an easy call. I have at least some faint notion of what it is.

"I'm glad," I said.

"American?"

How should I know? You're serving it.

"I don't think so. I just assumed shepherd's pie originated over here."

"No, no, luv. I meant, are you American?"

Nice. Here I thought we were getting along so well and then you insult, defame, and malign me. I'm Canadian. There's a big difference. Huge, in fact.

"Canadian."

"Oops. So sorry, luv. No offence meant. But you somehow look familiar."

Then she turned and disappeared into the kitchen just behind the bar.

I tried my Guinness. To my palate, unburdened as it was by much draught beer–swilling experience, Guinness felt like a milkshake in my mouth. I wished it had tasted like a milkshake or had actually been a milkshake. Still, I sipped it slowly, as I had no idea how long I'd be sitting there. I devoured the shepherd's pie when it arrived. It was really quite good, but it also didn't hurt that I was hungry enough to eat a horse between two mattresses. I think the ground meat, peas, and mashed potatoes helped settle the Guinness sloshing around in my gut.

With the lunch crowd starting to arrive, I broadened my surveillance zone from the main entrance of Classic House to include the interior of the William Blake itself. Over the course of the next few hours, people streamed in and out of the front doors of the building and the pub. Twice I recognized faces I'd seen on the Innovatengage website as Matt's colleagues. They knew him. They worked with him. They saw him every day. I know I'd probably already seen many of the company's employees, but they only posted photos of the leadership team on the website. One of them, the chief technical officer, entered the building around 12:30. I kept my head down as I watched her approach. She was smiling. I decided she looked like a good person. Then she was in through the doors and gone, presumably to the elevator, or rather the lift. The chief marketing officer then appeared quite suddenly at the bar and ordered a sandwich, not "to go," as we would say in Canada, but "to take away." When he turned around towards me as he waited, I buried my head in my shepherd's pie and didn't look up until he was gone, his wrapped-up ham and cheese in hand. All he would have known was that an Ottawa Senators hockey fan with a fierce focus on his food was in the pub, provided he knew what the logo on my hat signified.

And that was it for the rest of the day. No Matt. He never showed up. I stayed and watched faces all afternoon and into the early evening. Nothing. After the CTO and CMO left the building around 6:30 and the flow of weary workers dwindled to a trickle, I thought it was safe to call. I pulled out my iPhone and dialed. I wasn't worried about my name showing up in the caller ID window. Alex MacAskill was a name that would mean nothing to anyone over here. I made my way through the company directory and selected Matt Paterson. It rang three times.

"Hi, it's Matt Paterson and you've reached my voice mail on Monday, September 22. I'm out of town today on business but if you leave me a message, I'll return your call Tuesday morning. Cheers."

Cheers. How English. I hung up without leaving a message, and then called three more times just to hear his voice. I somehow sensed there was something gentle, even kind, in his tone. It's hard to explain, and perhaps I wasn't particularly objective about it. But I liked his voice. Not just that it was *my* voice with a lovely English lilt. It went deeper than that. Knowing that he wasn't upstairs but that he'd be there the next morning, I got up and left the pub. Then I immediately turned around and returned to pay for my Guinness and English culinary staple. I had a lot on my mind that night.

I hadn't realized how exhausted I'd been from the transatlantic crossing and attendant time change until my head hit the pillow. I managed to text Abby about the day's events but shortly thereafter I was down deep for the night. No tossing, no turning, no dreaming. Just a full-on, deep sleep. So deep that I had no idea where I was when I awoke, though I figured it out eventually. My iPhone had logged in several texts from Abby demanding elucidation, elaboration, and clarification on my paltry summary from the night before. I spent a few minutes responding to her, expanding on my fruitless first day in London.

By 7:30 a.m., I was back on Old Street. I had no idea if Matt was an early riser, but I wanted to cover off that possibility. Of course, the William Blake didn't open until ten, but there was a little boulevard park-like green space with tall trees and benches that circled the trunks of some of the larger trees where I could sit. It was directly across the street from the entrance to Classic

House and the Innovatengage office. I settled in the lee of a large tree but on an angle that allowed me to monitor the entrance of the building. I didn't think there was underground parking in the building so I figured he'd be coming from the Old Street Tube station along with the rest of the commuting crowd. Given the proliferation of start-ups in the area, it seemed a fairly young and confident crowd striding by, making their way to their offices. I'd bought a carton of orange juice at a little stand in the Tube station. I pulled it from my jacket pocket, rammed home the little pointy straw it came with, and drank. It was lukewarm and almost tasted like orange juice. Almost.

It was 7:51 a.m. I saw him from a distance. I knew it was Matt long before I could see his face. It was how he walked. It was how I walked. It was how we walked. I stood up but slid further behind the tree. I watched as my own facial features came into focus as he sauntered along the sidewalk towards Classic House on the other side of the street. So here we go. I took two deep breaths and sat down on the bench again, my back to the tree, my back to my brother. I peeked over my shoulder as Matt Paterson disappeared into the building. Was I really going to just dash across the street and leap in front of him? No, I don't think so. But I'd found him.

He hadn't seen me. I was certain of that. Clearly, no innate, brother-to-brother, telepathic proximity alarms had been triggered in his head. He hadn't so much as looked my way. But it was my identical twin brother. No one could look quite so much like me and not be. There was no doubt in my mind. Oh sure, we may have doppelgangers out there roaming the earth. But they just sort of look like you from a certain angle. Vicki Lawrence and Carol Burnett. Or maybe Will Ferrell and Chad Smith, the drummer for the Red Hot Chili Peppers. But when you saw them together, you quickly realized they really just resembled one another. If my hair were short and I stood next to Matt Paterson, no one would say we "resembled" one another. We "were" one another.

I sat on that bench in a kind of trance, eyes on my feet, thinking about what to do next, for the next two hours and more. It was the sound of bells in the distance that seemed to break the spell. A church was chiming 10:00 a.m. I surveyed my surroundings. A few stragglers were still entering the building, but in general, the coast was clear. I stood up, strode across the street with purpose, and slipped back into the William Blake. They were still vacuuming – "hoovering" was what they told me – but I stepped over the cord and claimed my window booth for the second day in a row. I passed on the Guinness shake and ordered an orange juice, hoping it might taste a little more like OJ than what I'd purchased in the Tube station earlier. The same older woman who called everyone "luv" delivered my juice a minute or two later. Much better.

From my jacket pocket, I pulled the envelope Mom had left for me and extracted the half-photo of me cradled in the right arm of the person I assumed to be my father. I stared at it for a few moments. I snuck a glance at my watch: 10:23. I pulled off my cap and raked my hair with my right hand, a habit that came with longer locks. That's when I heard my voice order a latté to take away. My eyes had been focused on the front entrance of Classic House through the window. In an instant I realized there must be a second entrance to the pub from inside the lobby of the building.

I looked up when I heard my, his, our, voice, just as Matt Paterson turned from the bar and looked in my general direction. I froze, my right hand still stuck in mid-hair-rake, pinning my soft and manageable tresses behind my ear. Our eyes locked briefly as he swept the room with his gaze. He turned back to the bar, stopped, then slowly swivelled his head to meet my eyes once more. His eyes widened. His eyes narrowed. He turned his body now to face me. He took a small step towards me and stopped, his head slightly tilted like a Labrador's when you call his name.

Just relax, Matt. Don't flip out on me, now. I know it's a shock. It was to me, too, and I was sitting alone in a bank vault. But just try to hold it together and all will be made clear. This is no time to lose it.

"Matthew," I said quietly.

It was the only word I could utter. I released my hair, letting it fall long again. I slowly slid out of the booth and stood to face him. I gestured with my left hand for him to sit down. I said nothing after uttering his name. My heart was making so much noise in my chest I thought surely he could hear it. We kept staring at each other, saying nothing, just a few feet and a quarter-century between us. He broke eye contact briefly to look me up and down. He looked quite swish, at least to my somewhat underdeveloped fashion sense. He was wearing tight, narrow-legged blue pants, a rather funky brown leather belt, cool low-cut red running shoes that looked more for fashion than fitness, and a tight, white button-down shirt. I forgot what I was wearing and looked myself up and down when he did. Jeans, sort of brownish desert boot–like shoes, and my favourite blue-plaid flannel shirt from the Northern Trapper spring line. No belt. I'd forgotten my belt.

Clothes aside, I could see that he could see that we were obviously made in the very same mould. Height, weight, build, face, skin, hair colour, hands, all the same. All that separated us was the length of my hair. Okay, he probably wouldn't have been caught dead in my blue-plaid flannel shirt, but it would have fit him perfectly.

Come on, Matt. Stay with me, bro. And I do mean bro. Have a seat and we'll talk. We'll talk for a very long time. Just make it to a sitting position, please.

"Matthew," I said again. "Please." I waved my hand again for him to sit across from me. Looking at him, I felt at least a bit of my omnipresent shyness drain away. This was my brother. He was family. My only family.

He raised his hands, closed his eyes, and shook his head as if trying to banish this apparition. But I was still before him when he took his hands away from his face and his eyes opened again.

"Who are you?" he asked.

Isn't it obvious? Can't you tell just by looking at me?

I said nothing but again pointed to the empty seat opposite mine. He looked at it and then at the table. His eyes and mouth opened wide when he saw the half-photo of me. He stared at it for a moment, his brow and forehead compressed in what appeared to be incredulity. If Matt had seen his own face in that moment, I think he might have described it as "gobsmacked."

"Where did you get this?" he demanded as he reached for it. "How did you get this?"

Easy, Matt. Stay calm. You'll get all the answers I can provide. That's why I'm here. That's why I came to find you. That's why I drank a whole Guinness yesterday. I can't believe I found you.

I still had no words lined up in my mouth. Matt grabbed the photo and studied it. Soon a whole new level of puzzlement creased his face. He tilted his head again, I assume, processing. He stared at that half-photo for a long time trying to figure it out. Then, slowly, almost as if he dared not, he turned the photo over, examining the back. He cycled through so many different facial contortions I gave up trying to interpret them. That's when all the colour suddenly drained from his face, and he sank into the seat. I dropped back into mine, facing him.

That's it, Matt. Good. You made it. You're here. We're here. Finally.

"Matt, your latté's here, luv," the woman said from the bar before disappearing into the kitchen.

Sit tight, Matt. I'll get it. Don't move! Do. Not. Move.

"I'll get it," I said.

I jumped out and fetched his latté. I placed it on the table and resumed my seat as he carefully placed my half-photo, baby face up, on the table between us. Then he hauled his wallet from his front right pocket, stuck his fingers in a little slit inside, and pulled out a battered, curved, and creased half-photo of his own.

Holy shit! Where did you get that?

"Holy shit!" I said. "Where did you get that?"

Matt ignored me and slid his up against mine. What had been half was now whole. Two arms now. Two babies.

I can't believe it. Where did you get that? Who gave that to you? Was it my mother? Our mother?

"Who gave that to you?" I asked again, more urgently than before.

Matt held his hand up to silence me. I complied. He then turned his long-suffering half of the photo over. There, in blue ballpoint ink, in my . . . in our mother's hand, it said:

1/3 December 24, 199

He flipped over my half-photo and pushed the overturned halves together. With them reunited for the first time in nearly twenty-five years, the script on one half lined up perfectly with the script on the other half to yield:

1/3 December 24, 1990

He still hadn't touched his latté. I pointed to the envelope still lying on the table between us. He picked it up, opened it, and withdrew the full photo. He placed it beside the recently reconnected bisected photo to confirm it was in fact the same shot. He stared at it for a long time.

"I'd always wondered why it was only half a photo. Now I know," he said, still studying the full shot.

Yep. Now we both know why. That, bro, I guess is what they call "the big reveal."

He turned the photo over and just nodded when he read in our mother's hand:

2/3 December 24, 1990

He took a very deep breath, almost as if it might be his last, placed the photo back on the table, and stared at my face for what seemed like a long time. It was probably under a minute, but for someone like me who's tried to avoid careful scrutiny of his face, it felt like a very long time. But I forced myself to keep my eyes fixed on his.

"Would you mind pushing your hair back again?" he asked in the same tone he might have used to ask for the salt shaker.

I'll do it, as long as you don't ask me why, against all societal trends, I choose to have such long hair while still hating heavy metal. Please don't ask.

I lifted both hands this time, pushed my hair back behind my ears, and held it there in place. He just stared.

"Eerie and uncanny," he said, shaking his head. "Thank you."

No problem. But remember our deal.

I released my hair. He looked down again at the baby photos, then quickly back up to me.

"I don't even know your name."

"It's Alex," I replied. "Alex MacAskill. I was born in . . ."

"I know. In Ottawa," he interjected. "It stands to reason."

So you know where you were born. I wondered if you would.

I nodded.

"So, Alexander," he said.

Nope. Not Alexander.

"No. Just Alex."

"Right then. Well, Alex MacAskill, I'm Matthew Paterson," he said, offering his right hand. "Where the hell have you been all my life?"

Okay. Good. So you're on board. The doubts have dissipated. We can move past wondering if it's true and on to how and why it happened.

I gripped his hand to shake it. But he held on to it beyond the customary duration. He shook his head.

"This somehow does not do the occasion justice," Matt said, standing up while still holding my hand in his.

He pulled me up and out of the booth, and into what I guess you would call a brotherly embrace, the first I'd ever experienced.

Whoa, Matt. Easy. I'm not a real hugger, but . . .

I generally didn't do very much hugging, so this should have felt strange to me. But somehow it didn't. In that moment, it was both natural and almost overwhelming. We stood there, arms around one another, for a moment or two, or three. It took a Herculean effort for me not to burst into tears. We both had watery eyes when we eventually pulled apart and resumed our seats. My chronic reticence left me in silence. So I just looked at him. It felt like I was smiling continuously, but I seemed to have lost the ability to know for sure.

"I don't know what to say. I don't know what to do," he said. "I have a million questions orbiting but I don't know where to start."

Don't worry about it! There is no guidebook for this situation. We just have to navigate it on our own. But we're here together. That's what's important. I've sort of gotten used to the idea in the last few days. But I know what you're feeling right now. I know.

"I don't know what to do or where to start either," I replied. "But I've had some time to get used to this idea, so you should start. Ask whatever you want. Ask in whatever order the questions come to you. I don't have anywhere to be right now."

"Shit!" he said and reached for his phone and punched in a number. "Just give me one second."

I'm sitting right across from you. I'm not going anywhere. Take all the time you need.

I remembered only then that also in the envelope still resting on the table was my high school Christmas pageant program from

2005 with the wooden Lucky Strike Mom had taped to it. I did not want to get into that with Matt right then. It wasn't time. Maybe it would never be time. So while he focused on his cellphone, I slid the envelope over to me and off the table into my lap. I shoved it in my back pocket as he lifted the phone to his ear.

"Karen, it's Matt. Yes, I'm downstairs. Yes, I got my latté, thank you. But I've just realized I've got something to do today outside of the office. I'd forgotten completely about it. Can you bump the team meeting to tomorrow, same time, and let everyone know my day today is now rubbish and I probably won't be back until tomorrow? Thanks. Yes, but only if it's mega-urgent. Right. Cheers."

He ended the call and put his phone down on the table.

"Sorry. Where were we?" he asked. "I mean, other than just discovering that for my entire life, I've had an identical twin brother growing up in, I assume, Canada."

I nodded.

The floor is yours, Matt. We just have to start somewhere. So fire away.

"You were about to ask questions and I was about to attempt answers," I replied.

"Right. I'm almost too overwhelmed to fathom any of this, let alone ask sensible questions."

Who cares if they make sense? Just ask.

"They don't have to make sense. Not much about this makes much sense at all. Just ask," I said.

"Right, then. Well, this is a weird place to start, but why do you wear your hair long? I mean, it looks fine. But I'm just curious."

Wait a second, Matt. We agreed you wouldn't go there. Remember? Anyway, it's a long story. Sometimes people recognize me for the wrong reasons and it's, well, it's fucking embarrassing.

"Um. It's kind of a long story. I've had my hair like this for the last decade or so. Not really sure why. Maybe I'm trying not to resemble, um, somebody."

"Who are you trying *not* to resemble? Me?"

No, not you, me. I don't want to look like me. Well, when you think about it, that's the same thing. But it's not because of you. It's because of me.

"No, not you. Not at all. I'm trying not to, um, well, look like me."

"But we look the same?"

"Yes, but this isn't about you. It's all about me. I can't explain now. I just can't. It's too soon," I explained.

"Fair enough," Matt said. "Right then, when did you learn about, well, about me? When did you know you had a twin brother?"

"It was last Tuesday night when I first laid eyes on the half-photo, and Wednesday morning when I first saw the whole photo."

"Obviously there's a third photo. Do you know who has it?"

I think our father has it, whoever he is.

"No idea," I answered. "Unless it's with the headless guy in the photo."

"Right. And just who do we both think the guy in the photo is?"

You know and I know.

"If I had to guess, I'd say it's probably our father. Who else would be holding us the day after our birth?"

"Right. That's what I've always thought," Matt replied. "Wait! Do you know who he is? Have you met him?"

"No and no," I replied. "We know absolutely nothing about him. Not even a first name."

"So how did you come to have the photos?"

"My mother," I replied. "*Our* mother."

It was as if it hit him only in that instant. He executed what kind of looked like a very mild, understated version of the classic Warner Brothers cartoon character double-take shiver, but without the over-the-top sound effects.

"Our mother. My mother!" he said, looking past me somewhere for a moment before coming back. "My mother. Is she here in London with you?"

Pass. Any other questions? Any different questions?

Shit.

Above me, I could hear them laughing.
No, not really laughing so much as snickering.

CHAPTER 7

I liked him enormously. I guessed I loved him, in that familial sense, almost instantly. Perhaps it was something like when a mother bonded with her newborn. That afternoon in the William Blake pub, I bonded with my identical twin brother, more than two decades late. I knew. I could feel it because in a very short time, call it a few hours, I was almost "inside-out" with Matt, as Dr. Weaver would have put it. I felt like I could say out loud to him what I really wanted to say rather than what usually came out of my mouth. And bear in mind, we were both still reeling from the shock, he more than I. Still, he was warm and funny and thoughtful, and completely accepting of the unlikely news I had broken to him. The finally reunited half-photos and our identical appearance – my long hair notwithstanding – left the truth beyond doubt. Shock? Yes. Doubt? No. Not a shred.

"But how did you find me?" he asked as if just then recognizing how miraculous it all was. "The world is big. There are more than seven billion people on the planet. How did you find me from a single photograph?"

"Well, you could say I followed our face," I replied.

He furrowed his brow and turned his head just a bit.

"Okay, I need more than that."

"If we'd been fraternal twins, I may never have found you. But we are identical. That saved us," I said. "Maybe fate pushed me into my current job, but I helped write the most advanced facial recognition software available. I work at Facetech."

I paused and watched as understanding dawned.

"Right. Facetech. So you searched for your own face and I popped up," he said.

"Exactly."

"Brilliant. Very clever," he said.

Well, the software really kicks ass.

"Thanks," I replied. "But perhaps not as clever as you might think. The idea didn't occur to me until after I'd spent far too many hours scouring Facebook for photos of guys born on our birth date."

It took me about an hour to encapsulate the narrative of my life thus far. Matt asked me to go first. I think it was helping him process what had just happened. I described what had always seemed to me to be my idyllic childhood. Just Mom and me. A happy mother and a happy kid. When I got to my high school years, I talked about my love of acting and of Cyndy Stirling. I did not mention Gabriel or his role in my eventual breakup with Cyndy. I hadn't decided whether I ever would. I did say I experienced what I described as "a bit of a setback" in high school, but because of when, and how, I said it, Matt likely assumed it was all about the dissolution of my high school romance. And that was fine with me.

I took him through my university years, my software engineering degree, and Mom's diagnosis. He'd never heard of idiopathic pulmonary fibrosis. Neither had our mother, and neither had I before that doctor's appointment when everything changed. This seemed like an appropriate time to break the bad news. Like the nervous driver who makes three right turns to avoid making one left turn, I usually went to extreme lengths to avoid emotionally charged conversations. But I knew I owed Matt more. My identical twin brother deserved more.

So I told him of our mother's recent passing. This hit him harder than I expected it would. But we moved past it reasonably quickly. In fact, he seemed to understand that we wouldn't have been together that afternoon in the William Blake had she not died. In a way, bringing us together had been her parting gift to both of us.

The owner sauntered over to see if we wanted any lunch, given the hour. We did, and ordered. She then spent the next several seconds staring from Matt to me, and back again. It was the first of countless future occasions when people stared, questioned their grasp on reality, and perhaps briefly believed in the possibility of cloning.

"Um, Maggie, I believe that's your jaw on the floor there, just next to your left foot," Matt said, pointing. She closed her mouth. "Maggie, this is Alex MacAskill, my twin brother. He's visiting from Canada."

"How wonderful! I didn't know you had an identical twin," she said as we shook hands.

"Funny you should say that," Matt said, looking at me. "Anyway, we're just catching up after not seeing each other for a while."

"Lovely to meet you, Alex," Maggie said before heading back to the kitchen to place our lunch orders.

I don't remember what we ordered. I don't really remember eating whatever it was we'd ordered. I just remember looking at, and listening to, my brother. I noticed after a while that I simply could not take my eyes off him. It was also clear that he was keeping his gaze completely focused on me. I guess that's not surprising. We were studying one another's faces and seeing our own. We were isolated in our own little private fraternal universe. Not to get too weird about it all, but it was like we were back in the womb, just the two of us. Okay, I admit, that does sound a little weird. But we were making up for a quarter-century of lost time. It was surreal, and strangely calming.

"Okay. Your turn," I said after Maggie had cleared our lunch dishes.

"Right," he replied. "Well, you've probably pieced some of it together already, but I was adopted in Ottawa about two weeks after I was born, after we were born, by the nicest, kindest couple I've ever known."

Names?

"Names?"

"Right. George and Eva Paterson. Dad was an electrical engineer, born over here, in Chester, just a bit southwest of Manchester. He grew a bit restless early in his career at British Telecom, so he took a job with Northern Telecom in Ottawa. He thought of it as an adventure. You know, visit the colonies and all. This was in 1985, if I remember correctly."

Carry on.

I nodded.

"He met my mother, my adoptive mother, Eva, on the job, in the company cafeteria. She worked in the marketing department trying to translate the technology George was helping to develop into pithy and understandable language for the sales team to use. Apparently, it only took a couple of meetings before she asked him out. He said yes, and that was that. Eighteen months later they were married in Ottawa and honeymooned in England, visiting Dad's family."

He paused.

Well, don't stop there. You're just getting started.

"Okay, then what?" I pressed.

"Well, they tried to have children, but it seemed they couldn't. I never found out why. They didn't talk much about that period," he said. "So I think it was early in 1989 when they pursued adoption."

"And in December of 1990, we arrived," I added.

"Exactly. Apparently I was a ward of the province for a couple of weeks before I was adopted in early 1991."

"But how did you get back here?" I asked.

"My father, George, got a great offer from British Telecom to return to England. BT was going through lots of tumultuous changes, having been privatized, and were desperately trying to stay on top of cellular technology, so they staffed up on engineers. In early '92, we came to London. I was barely one year old. So I have no memories of Ottawa. None.

"After that, I had what I would describe as a typical English upbringing. My mother loved London. She didn't work outside of the home while I was growing up, and she didn't really need to. My father was doing very well at BT.

"So I was a good student, played football, cricket, and rugby, like every other schoolboy, and I pined for a brother."

His eyes widened when he said this.

"Yes. I did want a brother, didn't I?" he said, almost talking to himself. "I always thought it was strange – actually, it felt strange – not to have a brother. I just thought I wanted a live-in mate, but maybe it was more than that."

I nodded.

Don't stop now.

"And then . . ." I prodded.

"Right. And then I went to Oxford for my undergrad in what they call philosophy, politics, and economics . . ."

Whoa. Hang on.

"Wait. How did you get to Oxford? Isn't it tough to get into?" I asked.

"Well, I aced the admissions test and the written submission for my chosen field of study. I guess they also liked my personal statement that was part of the application. Then I seemed to score well in the interview. I also had good references and strong marks. They called me in January 2009 to tell me I was in for that fall term. And I snagged a scholarship, too. I loved it there. I was in Balliol. That was my college."

And then the accident happened, right? 2009?

"I'm really sorry about your adoptive parents. I read that they, um, lost their lives in a car accident," I said. "It would have been pretty soon after you landed at Oxford. That must have been very hard."

"Actually, I never ever think of it as an 'accident.' The guy was smashed when he drove into my parents on the M25. He made it home alive, eventually. My parents never did. I was gutted. It was hell on earth."

It took all my resolve to reach out and put my hand on his as it rested on the table. I didn't really do things like that, and hadn't for a very long time. But it felt like the right thing to do.

I'm so sorry. That must have been horrible.

"I'm so sorry. That must have been horrible," I said. I kind of patted his hand with mine and then withdrew it. "I read about the court case online. The story popped up when I Googled your name."

"It was very difficult and it all happened just when I was finishing off my first term at uni. It knocked me for six and I almost lost my spot at Oxford. But then I pulled it together. My parents were so proud that I was at Oxford, it felt as if I owed it to them to make it through. So I just shut it all out and tried to focus on my studies."

Yeah, but the bastard got off.

"I read that the driver got off, at least the first time around," I said.

"Yes. I was in my third year of undergrad then. That was not fun. The police kind of botched the investigation and 'misplaced' the actual breathalyzer test results, so the charges had to be dropped long before it ever got to court. I admit I briefly entertained the thought of some good old-fashioned vigilante justice, but my parents would have been horrified. So I just buried it deep and carried on."

"How do you 'misplace' breathalyzer results?" I asked.

"We never got to the bottom of it, but my lawyer heard rumours that the drunk driver had friends on the force. But he got his in the end. It's over now. I'm over it, now."

I don't know how you ever get over something like that. That must have been rough.

"That must have been rough. I'm so sorry you had to go through that," I said. "So it eventually went to court?"

"Yes, it did. It was very odd. About eighteen months after the charges were dropped, the breathalyzer test results miraculously reappeared. The case was reopened and off to court we went. In a way I'm glad it happened that way. I was in much better shape a year and a half later."

"I read that you went to court every day."

"I did. It was hard. But there was no option. I felt I owed it to my parents to be there. I also gave a victim impact statement from the stand during the sentencing hearing. That was not pleasant, either."

"Geez."

"Yeah, well, you've had your burdens," he replied. "I can't imagine what it must have been like to care for your mother, for our mother, in those last few months."

Okay, enough of the depressing talk.

"Anyway, so you finished your undergrad and then promptly did a master's, too, right?"

"Yes. I just kept going. I didn't yet feel ready for the real world. I managed to stay in residence at Balliol for my entire Oxford tenure. I was very lucky, although living in Hollywell Manor, built five hundred years ago, had its own special charms."

"Okay. So you graduated. Then what?"

"Thanks to some political contacts I made during my graduate project, I landed a short contract job straightaway on the political staff of Sir Vince Cable, the Secretary of State for Business, Innovation, and Skills. He was very interested in my work on how the Internet might scale the cultivation of social licence for major industrial projects. I'm really more of a Labour guy, but this policy area was right up my street."

I chose that moment to deliver my best Matt Paterson impression, accent and all, reciting those three sentences I'd picked up from one of his YouTube appearances.

"In this era, earning the social licence to build massive infrastructure projects is not just an option, not just recommended, not just preferred, it's absolutely essential. Public engagement, scaled digitally, to secure social licence, has become the new corporate imperative. Ignore it at your financial and reputational peril."

His mouth and eyes opened wide at the same time.

"How did you . . . I think I've said those words. Those are my words. That was my voice," he sputtered.

"Actually, it's our voice," I replied. "Anyway, it's no real mystery. You gave a keynote at a conference and it's on YouTube. I just memorized a few lines and mimicked your accent."

"Bloody brilliant. The actor. It was like listening to myself. It was an out-of-body experience," he said, shaking his head. "And by the way, we're in England now. I don't have an accent. You do."

"Right." I laughed.

I hadn't noticed how crowded the pub had become. I looked at my watch. It was 6:10 p.m. We'd been sitting there engrossed in our reunion for pretty well the entire day. I was shocked at how quickly time had passed. The booth we occupied was quite private. Unless you were standing right at our table, you really couldn't see much of us.

"Hey, I see a few of my colleagues over at the bar," Matt said after scanning the room. "Let me introduce you."

Matt started to stand up. I put my hand on his arm.

No. Not now. Please. I can barely handle meeting you. I'm really not up for meeting strangers.

"Um, Matt, can we leave that for another time?" I asked. "This has been a lot to absorb. I'm a little overwhelmed. Not sure I'm up for meeting new people now."

He sat back down, nodding.

"Sure. No worries," he replied. "We've got lots of time."

"Thanks."

We ordered dinner and more drinks. As with our lunch, I barely remember what we ate or drank – though I can confirm the beverages were alcoholic. But I recall every word we exchanged, every story, every revelation.

At one point I looked up and saw Matt staring at my hands.

"I hold my hands in exactly the same way," Matt said, shaking his head.

"What?"

"Your hands. The way you just interlocked your fingers. I do that, too."

I looked at my hands, fingers laced. Wow. I moved my hands to my lap.

"Anyway, it seems you didn't stay in politics too long," I said.

"No. It really wasn't for me, I guess. But I learned a lot, particularly about how governments go about consulting with stakeholders and average citizens. Sometimes they're genuinely interested in hearing outside views and sometimes they're not. But one thing is certain. Setting up an evening information session in a local church basement to explain plans to locate a few dozen wind turbines around the town just isn't very helpful if you're really trying to connect with the people affected. The same people show up every time and the masses stay at home. I had an idea of how we could do a much better job of it. So I left and started Innovatengage."

"That was brave. How did you know what to do?" I asked.

"I didn't. I made lots of mistakes, but luckily, most of them were relatively minor. I managed to get the big decisions right, at least most of the time."

"But how did you start?"

"Well, I'm not much of a techie, so I knew I needed a coder who could take this idea I had and actually build the engagement platform. So I used some of my inheritance to hire a software engineer. She's still with me as the company's chief technology officer. Hiring Isabella was one of the best decisions I've ever made. She not only took my ideas and created the online platform and interface, but she actually made it better than I'd envisaged."

Well, what did you expect? That's what software engineers do. We build amazing things. We're an extraordinary breed. Surely you've noticed that.

"Well, that's what software engineers do. We build stuff," I replied.

We sat in our two-seater booth in that pub, in our own little world, until closing time – 11:00 p.m. There was no sense of the passage of time that afternoon and evening. We were both startled when our nightshift waiter – Maggie had left hours earlier – let us know they were closing in ten minutes. I knew a lot more about Matt by then. He knew a fair bit about me, too, but not everything. At my suggestion, the waiter used my iPhone to take a photo of Matt and me, his arm draped over my shoulder. I emailed it to Matt. It seemed we should have some formal record of our historic reunification. It was a great shot, with both of us beaming. It almost looked as if we'd just found each other again after a twenty-five-year separation.

We left the William Blake and walked back towards the Tube station.

"So where are you staying?" he asked.

"At the London Bridge Hotel."

"You're joking," he said, smiling. "Why did you pick that hotel and that area?"

"Well, it seemed central and was only a short subway ride, sorry, Tube ride to your office. Why? It seems like a perfectly good hotel."

"Yes, it's a fine hotel," he replied. "I live just a short distance away. I bought in the area for the same reasons you looked for a hotel here. Uncanny. Thinking on the same wavelength. As if we're related or something. And by the way, you're no longer staying at the hotel. You're staying with me."

"I'm fine staying at the hotel. I don't want to impose."

He stopped walking. So like a good twin brother, I stopped walking.

"Impose? Alex, it's impossible for one twin brother to impose on the other, particularly when we're catching up on so much. That's a family rule. We're not having a debate about this. You're staying with me."

We started walking again and were almost at the Old Street Tube station.

"Besides, I just recently lost my roommate so I've got lots of room, right now," Matt said.

"Roommate?"

"I guess we haven't covered my relationships yet. But I just broke up with my girlfriend. She moved out a month ago. We'd been together about a year."

"Shit, I'm sorry," I said. "What happened?"

"Well, it was time, I guess," he replied. "Or at least she thought so. Without descending into cliché, there just didn't seem to be enough room in my life for a fledgling company and a serious relationship. They both needed my attention and I just couldn't balance the two. I suppose I decided what was more important. I feel bad about it, but also a little relieved. What about you?"

Oh, well, you know, I'm in great shape on the romantic front. Couldn't be better. I haven't been in a serious relationship since high school. You remember the Cyndy I mentioned earlier. You heard me right, brother. That's nearly ten – count 'em – ten years ago. Oh, but there is this woman at work who kind of scares the crap out of me while at the same time making my stomach feel a little queasy when she's around me. So, yeah, things couldn't be better.

"Hello? Alex?"

"Sorry. Let's just say it's been a little while since I was in a serious relationship," I admitted. "But there's a slim chance something might be happening with someone at work."

"Wow. This twin thing is powerful. We look alike and sound alike. We both work in the online world. We both lace our fingers in the same way. We both lost our parents. And the topper, we both have the same luck with women."

Right. We're exactly the same. You broke up with your girlfriend a month ago. I broke up with mine a decade ago. Yep, that's pretty much the same story. Twins-ho!

"Right."

At Matt's insistence, I checked out of the London Bridge Hotel. We piled into a cab out front. Matt said we could easily have walked to his condo, but we'd both had a few drinks and my suitcase was heavy. The cabbie turned onto a strange little street known simply as Wild's Rents and pulled up to what I thought looked like an old warehouse. I was quite pleased with this observation because, as it turned out, it was in fact an old warehouse refurbished as high-end condo units. And I mean high-end. Matt's was amazing.

He heard my sharp inhalation when he opened the door and fingered the touch pad on the wall to bring up the lights.

Holy shit! Killer condo.

"Wow! Killer condo," I said.

"I like it," Matt replied. "Let me show you around. It won't take long."

Well, it'll take longer than a tour of my apartment.

I slipped off my shoes and pushed my wheelie suitcase out of the way.

"So this is the gigantic open space that sometimes makes me feel as if I live in a gymnasium," he started with a sweep of his hand.

I was going to say the deck of an aircraft carrier, but gymnasium works.

It was a sprawling open-concept configuration, and the words that flitted into my mind as he led me in were "expansive" and "expensive." There were exposed wooden ceiling beams above and gleaming hardwood floors below. The massive central space was wide open and contained a living room, dining area, library/workspace, and kitchen. The large windows along one wall made the room seem even larger than it was, even at night.

The furniture was perfect for the space. Clearly, care had been taken designing the interior. There was a white and fluffy couch and matching chair. A funky glass and wood coffee table sat on a white rug. Cool end tables on either side of the couch each supported ultra-modern halogen lamps. The kitchen was all stainless steel from the counters and appliances to the light fixtures and barstools. It looked like the kitchen you might expect to see on the *Millennium Falcon* – or any similarly appointed intergalactic cruiser – only larger.

Contrasting with this, but strangely not appearing to conflict with it at all, was the more traditionally styled dining area with a large polished dark wood table with matching claw-foot chairs. A companion buffet sat opposite the table against the wall, above which was a large abstract painting. In fact, the grey walls held several large pieces of art that looked to my untrained eye to be very valuable.

I loved the library/workspace in the corner, defined on the floor by a very traditional and ornate Persian rug. The desk was old but on it rested a MacBook Pro sitting in a docking station and a large Apple monitor. Antique bookcases provided some privacy and partially hid a very comfortable-looking brown leather chaise longue for reading or for pretending to be telling Sigmund Freud about your dreams.

I couldn't imagine living there. Our entire Ottawa apartment would have fit in about a third of the footprint of this one central room.

Matt took my elbow and guided me through the three large bedrooms, each with its own sparkly bathroom. Again, wow.

"You can bunk in here," Matt said, flicking on the light in bedroom number three. "I'm just down the hall if you need anything."

I just nodded in a bit of a daze and fetched my suitcase.

Matt walked to the kitchen and opened the fridge.

"Beer?" he asked.

I really shouldn't. We've been drinking all afternoon.

"Um, sure. Thanks."

He grabbed two and walked to the sliding glass doors at the far end of the room. I'd completely missed them on the tour. He slid open the door and led me out on to a large wooden deck, populated with wooden furniture, including a table and umbrella combo and six really comfy-looking chairs. We sat down. A nice wooden privacy fence did its job, providing the illusion that perhaps we weren't in central London after all.

"The view is no great shakes from here, but you can actually see stars on those few days when we don't have cloud cover," Matt explained.

Innovatengage must be raking in the dough to pay for this castle. Congrats!

"You have an amazing condo, Matthew. It's beautiful," I said. "Your company must be doing very well."

"The company is coming along, but it's still a start-up," Matt replied. "I bought this place with money from my parents' estate. My father did very well at BT. And there's really no more secure and lucrative an investment than London luxury real estate. And I decided I might as well enjoy it as it appreciates."

"Makes sense."

"Well, maybe not entirely," Matt continued. "I bought this place before I started the company. I would have scaled down my living arrangements had I known I was going to have to fund a start-up. We're now heading towards a second tranche of VC financing to get us up to the next growth plateau. It would have been helpful if this particular investment were a little more liquid. But we're doing fine."

"Would you mind if I had a look at the back end of your platform some time?" I asked.

"Anyone coming into this conversation late might think that was a very personal question," Matt replied. "But since you're my long-lost identical twin brother . . ."

"And a software engineer," I reminded him.

"Right. And as a software engineer, you're welcome to check out my back end. In fact, I'd like your thoughts on it. I think we can get a little lost in our own weeds sometimes. A third-party view makes sense."

"Great."

He looked at me for a few minutes in the dimness of the light spilling through the sliding glass door.

"I still can't believe this has happened. How is one supposed to feel? I've completely lost my bearings. But I know it's all true. Logic demands it. You really can't question the evidence. It's unassailable."

I nodded.

"You'll need some time to process it all," I said. "I've had a few days now for it to sink in, and that's really helped."

He shook his head again.

"Listen to your voice!" he said. "It's my voice."

I smiled in agreement.

I know. Isn't it fucking awesome! Isn't it great?

"I know. Isn't it awesome? Isn't it great?"

"It's bloody mind-blowing," Matt replied. "That's what it is. Mind-blowing."

He stood up and moved over to the fence to look out on the city. I joined him there.

We leaned on the fence, looked out at the city, drank our beer, and talked for another half-hour or so. I oscillated between scanning the cityscape and looking at my twin brother, just to confirm yet again that this was really happening.

I know it might sound a little creepy that we couldn't keep our eyes off each other. But it didn't feel that way. Now that we'd both accepted that we had found one another, and that we were unquestionably, undeniably, unimpeachably formed from the same single zygote, there was a warmth and a connection that felt almost overwhelming. In hindsight, I realized it was almost certainly love – a familial love – that had arrived at breakneck speed. It was not the brotherly love that builds slowly over the years as twins grow up together, sharing a womb, sharing a room, sharing adventures, joys and disappointments, and sharing so much idle time. This was not the typical slow-build. No. This was more like a detonation. And it felt like it.

"Don't move!" Matt said.

"What? Why? Is there a scorpion on my shoulder?" I asked. "A spider?"

"Don't move," he repeated. I stood stock-still. "Now look at how you're standing."

Matt watched as I froze but lowered my eyes to take in my own physical set-up. I was standing sideways to the fence, leaning on the top rail, my outside leg supporting all my weight while my inside leg was bent and crossed over, resting easily on the deck. My inside forearm lay flat along the fence rail, a bottle of Heineken in my hand. My outside arm was at my side, slightly bent at the elbow – which is where my arm usually bends – my hand resting in my pants pocket.

"Yeah? So?"

"Now look at me," he instructed. "Bizarre and brilliant!"

I realized that Matt, facing me, was fixed in precisely the same pose, right down to the way his fingers wrapped around his Heineken on the top rail of the fence.

"Did you just copy the way I was . . ."

"Of course not. That would hardly make this so interesting," he interrupted. "I just looked down and noticed that we were both standing in exactly the same position. And this is how I always stand here. It's my restful, contemplative pose. Apparently it's yours, too."

"Yes, but this is also my 'I really can't believe this is happening' pose," I replied.

Matt laughed, using my laugh.

We stood in silence for a minute or two.

"So what really happened with your high school sweetheart?" he asked. "You were a little cryptic about it, earlier."

You don't want to know and I'm not yet ready to tell you.

"Oh, you know early romances. It was very intense for quite a while. Then something happened, and it was never quite the same after that," I said, instantly regretting being quite so explicit.

"It's the 'then something happened' part that's intriguing. Did you get her pregnant?"

"No. Hardly. We were fifteen at the time. We'd, you know, talked about sex – we talked about everything – but weren't quite there yet. No it was, um, something else."

I realized through all of this I'd been shuffling my feet and looking down like a six-year-old being scolded for breaking a neighbour's window. The vibe had changed.

"Hey. Are you all right?" Matt asked.

No, not really. I'll tell you about Gabriel sometime, but just not now. Not today. Not yet.

"Yeah. I'm fine. Just a little overwhelmed by everything, I guess."

"Understandably. But listen, Alex, you're my twin brother, my identical twin brother," Matt started. "It's obviously completely up to you what and when you choose to share with me, but just know that what we have, by virtue of our shared birth, no one else in the world has. No one. So whenever you're ready, I'm here."

He looked briefly out over the city before turning back to me and continuing.

"You know, I would love to have had a brother to talk to growing up. We've both grown up without any siblings. We've both missed out on so much – on each other. I'm thrilled this has happened and at the same time, I'm a little angry that neither of us knew about the other until now. What would we be like today if we'd grown up together? Where would we be? Who would we be? We could have really helped one another out."

"Yeah, well, now we can," I croaked, hoping the lump in my throat wasn't as big and obvious and visible as it felt. "Better late than never."

"Better late than never," he repeated. "Even though we've never ever met before today, the fact that our mannerisms are so eerily similar is either very weird or it's not weird in the least. I'm now thinking it's the latter."

"It's really not weird at all. We have the same DNA," I said. "It would be very weird if we *weren't* so much alike."

"DNA. Right," Matt said. "Hang on, I just had a thought. We both know what the results would show, but let's take one of those consumer DNA tests anyway, just to etch it all in stone. It would be a fitting way to commemorate our reunion. Fifty years from now we can pull it out and show our grandchildren."

"I like it," I said. "I'm in."

Ten minutes later I was horizontal in the dark of the bedroom. I was so tired I wasn't. My last act of the night was texting Abby the photo of Matt and me from the William Blake.

"I found him" was all I wrote to accompany the shot.

It was early evening in Ottawa, so I was not surprised when she immediately responded.

"OMFG!!! So happy for you. Details! All of them. Now! Abby xo"

I just stayed still, not that I could move much.
I knew any movement would make it worse.

CHAPTER 8

"I was just making sure this all hadn't been a dream," Matt said. "Sorry if I woke you."

He was standing in the bedroom doorway, fully dressed. Morning sunlight streamed in around him from the wall of windows behind, making him look either deified or radioactive.

"You didn't," I replied. "Even with the time change, I've been awake for a while. It's hard to sleep when your mind is still grappling with something this big."

He nodded.

"Coffee is ready when you are."

He swung the door closed. I just lay there for a few minutes in a kind of reverie. Beyond the satiny comforter gathered around me, a feeling of serenity, calm, and I guess happiness enveloped me. I could have sworn I'd felt satisfied, happy, content, many times before in my life, but never at this level, never on this scale. And it actually felt rooted deep inside me, anchored there, secure, rather than just draped over me, perhaps to be pulled away at any second. It was a different feeling, more vivid and vital, with a kind of permanence I'd never experienced before. A blend of the physical and the emotional. I suddenly felt like me for the very first time. I lingered a little longer, savouring the sensation. After a few minutes, when it failed to dissipate or diminish in any way, I got up. The digital clock on the nightstand said 6:55.

I took a very quick shower, shaved, and pulled on clothes I might have worn to work that day had I been back in Ottawa. I figured Matt might drag me to his office so I wanted at least to look the part. The prospect of being the target of intense scrutiny from a small army of hipster techie strangers made my pulse pound. But I knew it was unavoidable. And it was worth it to spend more time with Matt. I was still at the stage where I didn't really want to be too far away from him. We'd covered a lot of ground the day before, but still we'd barely scratched the surface of our separate lives.

"I don't even know how my twin brother takes his coffee," Matt said when I emerged from the bedroom and made the long walk to the kitchen. "How weird is that?"

"Lots of milk, no sugar," I replied. "This place looks even bigger and better in daylight."

It was bright and sunny in the great interior space. It was like being outside while inside.

"The light certainly helps me wake up in the mornings, though blundering around temporarily blinded does have its hazards."

He poured and doctored my coffee, then handed the mug to me.

"Thanks."

"So, Alex, odd as this might seem when we have twenty-five years to catch up on, I don't think I can avoid my office a second day in a row. We have a lot going on, what with heading into another round of financing while juggling several client engagements. I hope you don't mind."

"Matthew, there's no rush now. We've got lots of time," I replied. "I'm not heading back for at least a couple of weeks. Maybe I should just hang out here for the day."

"No bloody way. Just because I have to work doesn't mean we have to be separated. You're coming to the office," he said. "I do have some pull with the company, you know. And I have just declared it 'bring your long-lost twin brother to work day,' for the foreseeable future."

All those people? All those strangers, staring at me, pointing at me, talking to me? Excruciating in the extreme. No, I don't think so.

"Okay," I replied, trying to hide the physical manifestations of "sucking it up."

I'd already tried to say it several times that morning, but it wasn't until we were walking along Old Street, just a few minutes from Innovatengage, that I finally found my voice.

"Um, you know, Matt, about this morning, I'm not really what you would call a people person. I'm not good with new people. It freaks me out a little. It's the curse of the introvert."

Matt turned to make eye contact as we walked towards the Classic House entrance.

"I know, Alex. I know," he said. "Don't worry. You'll be fine."

You know? What do you mean, you know? No you don't. You have no idea. You have not begun to have an idea. Gabriel, meet Matthew. Matthew, Gabriel. No, you really don't know.

"You know? Um, you probably don't," I said. "I'm fine with you. I'm assuming because you're my own flesh and blood. But I'm shy, in a very big way, in a 'shy on steroids' way, in a 'Is that guy mute?' way. I get really nervous around new people. Sometimes paralyzed. So maybe we don't have to meet all forty-eight of your employees at a big all-staff meeting. It's hard enough for me to get through my own company's weekly staff meeting. I don't think I can handle being an agenda item on yours. So can we just take it slow?"

Matt stopped and took hold of my arm.

"Alex, it's okay. I know. Trust me. I know. I have eyes. I like to think I'm a quick study. I spent all day with you yesterday. Maggie, the other waiter, the cabbie, the woman on the Tube, the hotel guy, the old man on the platform who asked if we were twins. I know. We'll take it slow."

It's that obvious? I thought I was rockin' it yesterday. I forced myself way out of my comfort zone. I actually nodded to the Tube woman, and I said "Thanks" to the hotel guy. For me, that's bordering on loquacious.

"It's that obvious?"

"Don't worry about it. I've got it covered. No staff meeting. No boardroom lunchtime meet and greet. I wouldn't do that," Matt said.

Wow, thanks, bro.

"Thanks, Matt. I mean it. Thanks."

"It's nothing," Matt replied as we resumed our walk. "But it is a little perplexing, isn't it? I mean, we have the same genes and I'm often accused of being an extreme people person, a turbo-charged extrovert. I love meeting new people. I like reading the room and working out how to connect with different personalities. Odd that we're so different in that respect."

"Yeah, well I'm quite sure my issue is not based in our DNA. It's more of a learned behaviour," I explained. "I'm comfortable with people I know and trust. It just takes me some time to come out of what may seem to be a thick, sometimes impenetrable shell."

"I know. You're covered."

When the elevator door opened directly into the very hip and open Innovatengage office, my heart rate spiked so high I figured I could cross tachycardia off my bucket list. Large tables were populated by lots of computers and young men and women. Tight jeans, plaid shirts, and hoodies ruled. Nearly all the guys had closely cropped hair, while half of them also sported bushy hipster beards. There seemed to be just as many women as men.

People were bustling about. Two women were playing a Foosball game. Two guys were yukking it up in a very cool-looking kitchen off to the side. A young woman sitting close to the front looked up and saw us, grabbed a file from her station, and headed our way. Great. She was wearing a high-wattage smile.

"Good morning, Matthew. And it's great to meet you, Alex. I'm Karen. And just so you know, Matthew would have crashed and burned long ago without me."

What? What did you say? How did you know my name?

"Oh. Um. Nice to meet you, Karen," I stammered.

"I wish it weren't true. What she said about me, I mean," Matt said. "But she's right about that crash and burn thing."

She handed him the file folder, gave me a wink, and sauntered back to her place at the table. I looked at Matt. He just nodded and started walking towards the glass-walled office at the far end of the big open space. It made me think only briefly about the Ashe-can's office at Facetech.

To reach Matt's office, we had to navigate the long walk through the maze of work tables and the more than forty staff who worked at Innovatengage. I followed Matt, keeping my eyes on his feet and trying to paper over my anxiety with nonchalance. Not sure it was really working.

It started when we reached the first set of tables and continued for our entire journey.

"Morning, Matthew, Alex."

"Welcome, Alex."

"Hey, Matt. Hi, Alex."

"We're all good on the Shell engagement, Matthew. It's up and running. Hey, Alex."

"G'day, gents."

"Nice to have you here, Alex."

And that was just a sampling. A wave of gratitude for Matt's kindness washed over me. I don't know how he'd done it. I'd been with him the whole time. Yet somehow, he'd prepared his entire staff for the arrival of his freakishly shy identical twin brother. And they got it. No big deal. No freak-outs. No staring. Just "Hi, how are you, great to meet you, welcome."

I spent the trip smiling and nodding at everyone who greeted me – and a lot of people greeted me. Everybody greeted me. It was not unlike arriving at my own office at Facetech, only warmer and without the promise of mayhem and meltdowns from Simone. Matt replied to everyone, waved to a few on the other side of the room, and spoke briefly to the woman who'd updated him on the Shell engagement. But he kept us both moving towards his office. When we finally made it, he slid open the glass door and closed it behind us.

I exhaled.

"Now that wasn't so bad, was it?" he asked, turning to me.

Thank you. I don't know how or when you did it, but that was a potential throw-up moment for me and you made it go away.

"Thank you. You told them. You prepared them. I don't know how you did it or when you did it, but they all knew who I was."

"Alex, look at us. They would have known who you were without me telling them," he said. "But I did email the team late last night just to take the edge off our little surprise. We've got too much going on here at the moment for all of them to be as distracted as I am."

"Thanks for that. Very thoughtful," I said. "Seriously, I dread those situations and you made it, well, you made it so much easier. Thank you. I wasn't even queasy by the end of the walk."

"Forget it. It's nothing," he replied.

Well, it's not nothing to me.

While we were safely ensconced behind the glass wall of Matt's office, he took a few minutes to describe how the floor was set up. He pointed to various clumps of tables and staff as he talked.

"Over there in the corner is the platform development team. Great coders, all. They're working on the next iteration of the platform, adding new functionality, and ensuring it's secure and well protected. Right next to them is the platform maintenance team. They keep the current generation of the platform in fighting trim. They also serve as the Help Desk for our clients who have white-labelled our platform and are using it on their own."

He pointed to another cluster.

"In that corner, the UX team work with our designers to make enhancements to the interface. While we want the look and feel to stay the same for our clients, we also need to be constantly making improvements and adding new functions.

"On the other side over there, the team that's dressed slightly more upscale handles marketing and new biz development. They're a little less geeky but still know the platform and what it can do, cold. They're really strong at selling. I help them land the business and then turn it over to the team of engagement consultants who sit over there," he said, pointing.

"The engagement consultants work with the client to determine how best to set up the online engagement to deliver on their goals. Finally, the smaller team over there handles engagement communications. Their job is to promote each engagement so that the intended audiences actually know about them and can participate. We've learned that if you build it, they won't necessarily come. So it's all about driving traffic."

What about you?

"What about you? What do you do?"

"Good question. Sometimes I wonder," Matt replied. "I'd say I'm the digital public engagement subject matter expert. I try to make sure our platform at least accommodates, and often actually defines, best practices. So it's not just about the technology, it's about advancing our understanding of the field, as lofty as that sounds. I also work on what's next, what's around the corner."

"You seem to have brought together all the pieces of the puzzle," I said.

"We hope so. The trick is to make sure all these people don't live in their own silos and that they commit to working together, fully integrated. That's the key."

"Which is why you put them all together in one giant room?"

"Precisely. Plus, open space is cheaper to build than office walls."

I pulled my MacBook Pro from my backpack, turned it on, and slid it onto his desk.

"Do you have time to show me the platform?" I asked.

"Of course."

He swung my computer around so he could see the screen and logged me into Innovatengage Wi-Fi. Then he typed in the URL.

"I'm going to set you up with administrator log-in credentials so you can explore what we've built," Matt said. "Your user name will be 'AlexMacAskill' and I'll set your password as 'Twins1990.'"

"Nice," I replied.

"There, you're in," he said, rotating my laptop back to me. "You're obviously looking at a standalone version, not the actual working site. But this will show you how it all works and get you into the code, too, if you want to see it."

Oh, I want to see it.

"But first, let me show you the actual site in action."

He opened a new window and took us to the site of the British Pipeline Agency. The BPA was seeking public input on various aspects of a new section of pipeline near the Hertfordshire Oil Storage Terminal. The home page featured four cards examining route, construction, impact on the environment, and impact on endangered species. Each card featured an image, a headline, a few introductory sentences, and a Participate Now button. By clicking through, you could read as much or as little as you liked about each subject, watch a video, examine more images and infographics, and then complete a survey. You could also examine three different options for the cosmetic design of the pipeline and then use what Matt called a Likert scale to record your level of approval or disapproval, as the case may be. You could also see what others had said.

"Do you have to register before you can participate?" I asked.

"It's up to the client, but it really helps to require some level of registration so we capture a bit of demographic info and at least an email address. The platform yields more insights when we know who's participating."

"Makes sense," I said.

"So the comms team promoted this engagement nationally, but really focused on the Hemel Hempstead area, where the storage facility is located, and the towns closest to the route of the proposed pipeline. We used media relations, advertising, an email campaign, and social media to build awareness of the engagement."

"Impressive," I said.

"The last time BPA engaged the public, they ran a series of regional public meetings that cost them about £100,000. In total, 234 people attended."

"Not very many," I said.

"Right," he agreed. "So far, nearly 4,500 people have viewed the site online and filled out the survey."

"Wow."

"Of course, we can track each interaction and then, with the help of census data and other available demographic data, and whatever registration information we gain, we can slice the numbers any way we want, by geography, income, gender, education level, political orientation, etc. It gives our client real insight and helps them design and build the pipeline based on the views of those directly affected."

Right, but if the people can't stop the pipeline from being built, do they really care about voting on what colour it's painted?

"Right, but there's still going to be a pipeline built, whether people want it or not. Right?"

"Well, in this instance, yes," he agreed. "Sometimes the engagement platform is used to seek meaningful and influential input from stakeholders and the public. Other times, it's used simply to inform target audiences or help the client more effectively sell what they're going to do anyway. It's up to the client. But the system works best when the client is truly looking for input and not just putting a check mark in the public consultation box."

He showed me several other quite fascinating engagements they were working on. Then he opened the administrator's dashboard on the standalone version so I could begin to explore how the platform was actually built. Now we were in my world.

"Have a look through the code if you like," Matt suggested. "I have to sit down with the new bus dev team on a pitch we're doing tomorrow. But just let me know if you need anything. Oh, and you and I have a lunch date at a local consumer DNA lab. No needles, just saliva."

"You've been busy," I observed.

"I don't sleep very well," Matt explained. "But until then, feel free to root around in our platform code. I'd really like your thoughts on it."

"I'm on it."

"Should I have Isabella come in and walk you through the back end?" Matt asked.

Nope. No thanks.

"I think it's better if I just find my way through it, and if I have questions, then we can talk to Isabella."

"Whatever you like."

He closed the door behind him when he left. I looked up and noticed that several of the Innovatengage team were looking my way. They tried not to be too overt about it, but it didn't take advanced powers of observation to see they were struck by the presence of a second, quieter, long-haired Matt.

Despite the prying eyes on the other side the glass, I dove into the Innovatengage proprietary platform program code and started to relax. There's a comfort in being in familiar surroundings. For me, being immersed in code is like going home.

Not bad. Actually, it was quite good. I saw how they made it all work. It was sensibly done. I immediately saw some improvements that could yield efficiency benefits and opened up a Word document to record my suggested revisions. By throwing in some shortcuts and tightening up the code here and there, I was able to get it to run somewhat faster. Sometimes the gains would accrue to the end user. Other changes would make it easier and faster for

Innovatengage or their clients to upload content. I worked on it for an hour or so. Matt slipped in and out, and occasionally, someone came in to meet with Matt while I perched in the far corner of his office, my MacBook Pro in my lap. I kept my yap shut when others were in Matt's office – standard operating procedure – and my cranium in the code.

Matt spent quite a bit of time on the phone to various people. As far as I could tell, he'd spoken to his lawyer three or four times and to at least three venture capitalists. He was in pitch mode, and man, was he good. So cool, so articulate, so witty, so thoughtful as he answered and asked questions. It was an impressive display. I simply couldn't imagine doing what he was doing. I'd have been a complete wreck, yet there he was, his feet up on the desk, his eyes closed some of the time as he concentrated, reeling off thoughtful opinions, detailed tech talk, and amusing but relevant anecdotes, as casually as small talk with me. I was beginning to understand how and why he was so successful at such an early age.

When he hung up the phone and seemed not about to dial some other angel investor, I brought my computer over to the desk and turned it towards him.

"This is very well designed. The platform is solid and uses all the latest tricks and techniques. I'm impressed," I said.

"I'm relieved to hear you say that, given that software is not my forte."

"I found some minor efficiencies that should give you a bit more speed when navigating the site or when uploading content. And

I have some other thoughts on some additional functionality that would allow you to host fully interactive, real-time discussions right on the site without too much more work or complexity. But it's tight and tidy."

Matt smiled and shook his head.

"I can't believe we're sort of working on this together," he said. "Yesterday morning, it was just another day. Today, I have an identical twin brother pointing out enhancements to the Innovatengage platform. That's almost too much to fathom."

"If I think too hard about it, I get completely freaked out," I said. "So to hold it together, I try to focus on smaller, practical, everyday things, like breakfast, the pound-to-Canadian-dollar exchange rate, and code."

"We'd better go," Matt said, looking at his watch.

We made the long walk back to the elevator.

"See ya, Matt."

"Bye, Alex."

"Have a good lunch, Alex. Make sure Matthew pays."

"Ciao, Alex and Matt."

We weren't going to eat. At least not right away. Ten stops on the Tube later, and a two-block walk brought us to GeneCorp Labs. If you signed some forms, flashed some identification, answered a brief questionnaire, paid £150, and surrendered a cheek swab, you, too, could find out if Bob's your uncle. Or in our case, if Matthew Paterson and I were in fact identical twin brothers, born of one mother and one egg. Neither of us had any doubt, but it would be nice to have it locked down and an official piece of paper.

"Do you really think it's worth the money to verify what anyone with eyes can see is obvious?" Sandy, the lab technician, asked as she readied what looked like large Q-Tips.

I said nothing but looked at Matt.

"I see you're not on the GeneCorp sales team," Matt said. "You make a good point, but let's do it anyway."

She swabbed both our inner cheeks and stowed the swabs in clear ziplock bags.

"If you give me your mobile number, I'll text you when we have the results. The RapidHIT process should only take about ninety minutes."

What used to take weeks, sometimes months, could now be done in ninety minutes. The swab is inserted in a RapidHIT machine the size of a small photocopier, and an hour and a half later, out pops a DNA profile.

Matt and I found a small café down the street from the lab. I ordered minestrone soup while my brother chowed down on a club sandwich.

"So are we going to talk about it?" Matt asked. "This 'learned behaviour,' as you put it?"

No, we are not going to talk about it. How did we get back on to this? Is there something remotely unclear about my request for more time?

"Talk about what?" I replied.

"Come on, Alex. I may be able to help. If you can't talk about it with me, who can you discuss it with, Wendy Weaver?"

What the fuck! How do you know Wendy Weaver?

I did my level best to disguise my shock when that name crossed his lips, but still, my knife, fork, and spoon wound up on the floor in a cacophonic clatter. I slowly picked them up, breathed deeply, and then said in sort of a high-pitched yelp:

"What the . . . How do you know Wendy Weaver?"

"Whoa!" he said. "I don't know Wendy Weaver. Never met her. Never laid eyes on her. Never heard of her. But when you were in the shower this morning, your mobile rang. I didn't answer it, but the name Dr. Wendy Weaver flashed on the screen. Is she a psychiatrist?"

No!

"No, of course not. Psychiatrist? Ha!" I said.

"Okay, then who is she?"

"Um, well, she's a psychologist I see now and then, um, twice a week."

"Do you talk to her about the learned shyness thing?"

"Well, yeah. We've talked about it a bit . . . a lot," I conceded.

"Did you talk to your mother about it?"

"Of course. She was always there for me. I'm not sure I would have made it without her."

"Alex. Our mother can't be there for you now. But maybe I can be – you know, your identical twin brother. I sense this thing, this event – whatever it was – changed you somehow. I mean we're alike, identical, in so many ways. But we're not really the same at all in other ways."

I said nothing and kept my eyes glued to the tabletop.

"Look, I want to help. I'm concerned. Your psychiatrist . . ."

"Psychologist," I interjected.

"Right. Sorry," he said. "Your psychologist knows about it. Our mother knew about it. Why not talk to me about it? Can't you expand that audience from two to three?"

Audience of three? Ha! If only.

"That's just it, Matt. The audience isn't two, it's more than 827,000,000 and growing every day."

He looked perplexed.

"Matthew, you're right. You are my twin brother. I will tell you all about it, probably more than you ever wanted to know," I said. "But I just can't right now. Not today. It's not time yet. I'm not ready yet. Okay?"

"Of course," he replied. "So something did happen."

Oh yeah. Gabriel happened.

"Oh yeah. Something happened all right."

Matt's phone pinged. He looked at his screen and then turned it so I could see the text.

"Results are ready."

I wasn't that hungry any more anyway, though I'd eaten most of my soup. We paid and hoofed it back to the lab.

"Congratulations, you're related," Sandy said with a smile, as she handed us the results sheet.

I pressed in shoulder to shoulder with Matt so we could both read the results. It didn't take long. Our DNA showed a perfect match on all markers. Identical twins. No doubt. No uncertainty. No question. Identical twins.

Matt turned and gave me another hug. I still wasn't used to hugs.

Five minutes later we were back on the Tube heading for Old Street station. There weren't too many others on the train at that time.

At one point, we stopped in the tunnel between stations and just sat there for a few minutes.

"So, Matt, um, has anyone ever come up to you thinking they recognized you from somewhere?"

Matt thought about it for a few seconds.

"Not that I can recall," he replied. "Why?"

Sorry, I'm not quite ready to share, yet. Soon.

"Just curious, you know, with us being identical twins, and all."

After the workday ended at about 6:20 and most of the staff had left, Matt and I ended up in the same pub in the same booth where we'd met the day before.

"Let's hoist a glass to DNA technology," Matt said, clinking his glass of Guinness with my bottle of Heineken.

"To DNA testing and identical twins!" I said.

Two beers and no food later, Matt put Guinness number three on the table between us and put both his hands on my arms.

"Okay, you have to do me a favour," he said. "It was so amazing the first time, you must do it again."

"Happy to. But first, you must tell me what it is I must do again so I can do it again," I replied.

"Could you please impersonate me again? That was shocking to witness. That was bleedin' brilliant."

I took a moment to get into character and reload the lines from my brainpan. And then . . .

"In this era, earning the social licence to build massive infrastructure projects is not just an option, not just recommended, not just preferred, it's absolutely essential. Public engagement, scaled digitally, to secure social licence, has become the new corporate imperative. Ignore it at your financial and reputational peril."

Matt's mouth sagged open as he shook his head.

"Unbelievable. Impeccable. The voice, the mannerisms, the inflection, the tone, the pacing. Everything," he said. "How do you do that?"

"Well, I'm an actor. I worked very hard at acting in high school. I loved it. Modesty aside, I think I'm still sort of good at it."

"Can you do some more accents? That's the most impressive part of your performance."

"Can I do more accents? Does Donald Trump use hair product?"

Then, in quick succession, I repeated Matt's same three sentences in the voices of Sheldon from *The Big Bang Theory*,

Barack Obama, Sean Connery from his James Bond period, and finally, Mike Myers as Fat Bastard in the Austin Powers films. I had dozens of voices I'd been practising for years. I'd added many more since becoming a Netflix member and watching all the old TV series and movies I'd never seen before.

Matt was nearly on the floor in hysterics.

"Brilliant! Bloody brilliant!" he wheezed. "I think your talents are wasted in software engineering."

"Thanks. I think."

His breathing had almost returned to normal. I took another long draw from my Heineken, parched from my little one-man show.

"But you don't strike me as someone who would naturally gravitate to acting. You know, being on stage in front of lots of people, mostly strangers."

You just can't stay away from it. But it totally makes sense.

"Think about it, Matt. When I'm acting, it's not just that I'm inhabiting someone else's character, it's that I'm no longer inhabiting my own. I'm somebody else. I'm no longer shy. I'm no longer nervous. I'm no longer worried about being found out, of being called out or put down. In a way, I'm liberated from myself when I'm in someone else's shoes, wearing their clothes, speaking in their voice, shouldering their problems. It's like a heavy weight is lifted. I don't expect you to understand. Not yet. You don't know enough, yet. But you will eventually."

"Well, that was rather deep," Matt replied. "I won't push you. I'll give you all the time you need. But I'm ready when you are."

"Thanks, Matthew."

He looked past me for a moment as he took a long swallow of his beer.

"You know," he said, "if we'd grown up side by side, we'd have dealt with this together long before now. It would be behind you, now, behind us."

"I know."

I spent the next morning sitting with Matt and Isabella Prochillo working our way through the Innovatengage software. I doubt I could have done it without Matt there. He seemed to sense this and helped a great deal as I tried very hard not to sound like I was being critical of Isabella's work. In reality, she'd done an amazing job on the code and I found several different ways of telling her that, particularly when I was about to suggest an improvement. But I need not have worried. She was a true professional and seemed excited at the enhancements I proposed. She even gave me a hug just before she left to brief her team so they could implement most of my changes and incorporate them into the next software update, which was imminent.

"Now that wasn't so bad, was it?" Matt asked after she'd departed.

"She was great," I replied. "Smart and nice – a rare and wonderful combination in software engineers."

"All right. With that out of the way," Matt said, "it's time you and I turned to our next pressing challenge."

"Can't we just bask a little longer in the afterglow of our triumphant reconnection?"

"No, we can't," he replied solemnly. "Our story isn't complete until our family is complete. It's time to track down our father."

Oh sure. No problem. Why don't we crack cold fusion and cure cancer while we're at it? And then after lunch, we'll move on to the crisis in the Middle East.

"Oh sure. No problem. Do you think we'll be gone overnight?" I replied.

He didn't even acknowledge my gift for sarcasm. Rather he ignored my comment, sat down at his desk, and lifted the lid on his laptop.

"Matt, finding you was actually kind of easy after I discovered the photo," I said. "But that photo won't help us find our father. So where do we start?"

"Let's start at the very beginning," he replied in a kind of rhythmic voice.

Please tell me you're not about to sing a song from The Sound of Music.

"Please tell me you're not about to sing a song from *The Sound of Music*."

"I was thinking about it, but perhaps another time," he said. "Instead, why don't we review what we already know about our mystery father?"

I got up from the couch at the other end of his office and moved to a chair in front of his desk. I leaned forward, my elbows on the desk.

"Okay. I'm with you."

"We know our father was in Ottawa at least for a period of time around the date of our conception and then of our birth, assuming the photo is of our father," Matt said.

"Right," I agreed. "We also know our father clearly went to some lengths, with Mom's complicity, to keep his identity a secret. They didn't want us to know about him. And they apparently didn't want us to know about each other, either. That's going to make it hard. And that's about all we know."

Matt's fingers were working his touchpad and keyboard.

"We actually do know something else. And we know it from the very photo you just dismissed," Matt said.

He swivelled his computer so I could see the screen. He'd obviously scanned the photograph I'd found in Mom's safety deposit box. Propelling his chair around to my side of the desk, he used the touchpad to enlarge the photo. Then he repositioned part of the enlarged shot to centre stage. Filling the screen was our father's left arm cradling Matt's diapered baby ass.

"You see? We do know something else," Matt said, pointing. "We know our father had a tattoo."

"Yeah, right," I said. "That really narrows it down. I'm sure we'll bump into him on the street any day now."

PART THREE

After their collective gasp, it took what seemed like a long time before anyone said anything. It wasn't as long as it seemed.

CHAPTER 9

The enlarged photo was a little blurry but still revealed more details of the tattoo than you could see in the original.

"Right, then," Matt said, as we both stared at the left arm of the man we assumed was our father. "What do you see?"

"I see two parallel diagonal lines that disappear at the top beneath some red shape with curvy borders, and at the bottom they go under your baby butt resting on his forearm. Two more diagonal lines cross the first two towards the bottom, but I can see even less of them."

"What else?"

"And I see a small black circle, or maybe a black ball, below the crossed diagonal lines," I continued. "And finally, I see two complete letters and part of a third. We've got an uppercase 'K,' a lower case 'a,' and what looks like it might be an upper-case 'H,' though it's smaller than the capital 'K.' Weird."

"Perhaps it's a capital 'A' with the top cut off from our view," Matt offered.

"Maybe. So the options are 'KaA' or 'KaH,'" I said, spelling out the two word fragments. "Neither makes much sense."

It felt like I was too close to the image, that it was too big to take in clearly. So I stood up, stepped back from the screen a couple of paces, and turned to view it again.

"Hmmm. I'm not sure it's a black circle," I said. "I've just discerned a slight change in the shade of black along the lower portion that makes it look more like a disk than a circle or ball."

Matt nodded. "I see it now."

I was getting a little bug-eyed from staring at the image with such intensity. I looked away and surveyed the office scene playing out on the other side of the glass. There was a lot going on. Two different groups were meeting in different corners of the office. A Foosball tournament seemed to be in full swing. And the sales and new bus dev team was projecting a PowerPoint deck onto a blank wall, presumably in anticipation of an upcoming pitch. Still, something was nudging at my consciousness – a memory, perhaps. Something.

Matt was silent.

I turned back to the screen and finally saw it. I don't know why I hadn't seen it before, but now that I had, it was almost unmistakable.

Holy shit, I'm an idiot, a blind idiot.

"It's a puck," I said, moving closer. "It's a *puck*. So those aren't just two sets of parallel lines crossing at the bottom, those are two hockey sticks. And now that I see it, if I'm right, that red thing at the top could be part of a flag, probably Canadian by the colour."

"I don't see it." Matt sighed.

"If it were a soccer ball, or a cricket ball, you'd see it. National context is everything, here," I explained. "And remember, we're only seeing half of the tattoo. You're rather unhelpfully sitting on the other half. But if we were seeing it all, I suspect we'd see two hockey sticks angling down and crossing just above the puck in the middle. I once received a similarly configured hockey crest for losing a peewee tournament."

"'Peewee tournament'?" Matt said. "I'm not sure I even want to know what that entails. It sounds like some kind of team toilet-training ritual."

"Stay with me, Matt, we're almost there," I said. "I don't really know what else is going on in the image – those letters are really baffling – but now that I've made the hockey connection, that really does look like crossed sticks and a puck to me."

"I wouldn't have seen that in a million years," Matt said.

"I should have seen it long before now. Hockey was my game, at least until I gave it up when I was fifteen."

"So you're certain it's something to do with hockey?"

"Not completely certain. But it's somewhere to start," I replied. "Besides, we're talking Canada here, so hockey is always a good bet."

"I guess it's a start, but I think we could use some help," Matt said.

I watched as he saved the enlarged image as a jpeg and opened up a new email message. He hit "To:" and selected "Entire Organization." In the Subject line, he simply wrote "Help?" Then he wrote this message:

Hi gang,

Alex and I are trying to solve a mystery. We think this somewhat blurry photo of part of a tattoo on the inside of a man's left arm might be related to ice hockey – at least that's what my Canadian brother Alex sees. The red shape might be a flag (Canadian?), but again, we're not sure. And we have absolutely no idea what the letters (either 'KaA' or 'KaH'?) mean. Any ideas?

Thanks,

Matt

He hit Send.

When we got home that night we snagged a couple of beers and took them out on the deck.

"Feel like an Indian tonight?" Matt asked.

What?

"Well, um, no, I think I feel like my usual Canadian self," I replied. "I'm not sure what it means to 'feel like an Indian.'"

"No. It's a Britishism that simply means do you want to order Indian take-away for dinner," he explained. "You know, to eat."

"Ah. Got it," I said. "Then, yes, I guess I do feel like an Indian, though I'm not crazy about that line."

Matt was already dialing his iPhone. He placed the order and then checked his email. He discovered he'd already received five responses to his company-wide electronic plea for tattoo help.

The first four were inconsequential and offered no new insights. Matt thought they were well-intentioned staff who simply wanted to register that they had received, reviewed, and thought about his email, even if they couldn't really shed any new light on the tattoo. But the fifth email, from Oksana Lysenko, a Ukrainian immigrant – I remembered her accent – and one of the coders I'd met on my first day in the office, was different. It was quite different.

Hi Matt,

I agree with Alex. I think this is a hockey tattoo. The partial word makes no sense in English, but in Russian, it's quite a different story. I think the whole word in Cyrillic might be Канада. In English, the word is "Canada." I suspect the red shape at the top is probably part of either the Canadian or old Soviet flag, not sure which. If it's the Soviet flag, it dates the tattoo to before the breakup of the Soviet Union, so pre-1991. I wish I could tell you more about it. But I play hockey Tuesday nights and my coach is Russian. He actually works with the IHUK national women's team. He's quiet, but nice. Do you want me to see if he will talk to you?

Oks

Two days later, Matt and I were sitting at a snack bar table at the Lee Valley Ice Centre in northeast London. I could barely sit still and Matt was as fidgety as I was. Pavel Dubov was not tall, but he was very well built. I put him at about fifty-five years old. He'd just finished running a practice on the ice when he arrived at our table, as Oksana had arranged. We shook hands and then sat down.

"Okay, so I am here," Pavel said, in his pronounced Russian accent. "What is this about hockey tattoo?"

As we'd agreed, Matt took the lead.

"Thanks for agreeing to meet with us," Matt opened. "We're trying to learn anything we can about a tattoo that may or may not be Russian in origin, and we think it may have something to do with hockey."

Pavel nodded as Matt pulled up the enlarged image on his iPad and slid it over to him. He picked up the iPad, pushed his glasses up on his forehead, and examined the photo closely. At one point he extended his arms to move the image further away from his aging eyes. Finally, he started nodding and the first faint trace of a smile took hold of the corners of his mouth.

"I have not seen one of these for great many years."

"So you recognize it?" I piped up, my excitement overtaking my reticence.

"I think, yes."

"What can you tell us?" Matt asked.

"Well, I cannot be sure, but I think is a tattoo made before first great series against Team Canada in 1972," he said. "I remember reading something about it years ago."

"The Canada–Russia series, the Summit Series?" I exclaimed.

"Yes, but we called it the Canada–USSR series."

"Paul Henderson scored the winning goal, right?" I asked. "It's a famous moment in Canadian history. I learned about it in school."

Pavel winced at the name.

"Always with Paul Henderson," Pavel said. "Thank you for reminding me. It was huge failure, big defeat for us. It took us years to recover."

I clammed up again.

"So we can assume that whoever took the trouble to have this tattoo inked on his arm was a true fan?" asked Matt.

Pavel's still not fully formed smile made a return appearance.

"Actually, you can say even more than that. As I remember, this tattoo was created only for players on national team. No one else could have one."

"So you think the man in this photo was a player on the Russian national ice hockey team?" Matt asked.

"The Soviet team," Pavel said. "Possibly he could have been one of the coaches or trainers, but this I don't know for sure."

"Is there anything else you can tell us about the tattoo?" Matt asked.

"I think no. This was just before my time. I was just boy in 1972. But Dimitri Dumanovsky, guy I know, could tell you lots more."

"Who is Dimitri?" Matt asked.

"For my rubles, he is best hockey historian of Soviet era," Pavel said. "If anyone can tell you about this tattoo and who is wearing it, it will be DD."

I couldn't believe we might be closing in on our father. I could barely contain myself. But I did. Matt, however, wasn't plagued by the same constraints.

"Brilliant, Pavel! That's amazing!" Matt shouted. "Where can we find Dimitri Dumanoskovitch, Dumanovskolav, Duman-whatshisname?"

"Dumanovsky. Dimitri Dumanovsky," Pavel replied. "Where can you find him? Well, I think you can still find him where he's always been. Moscow."

Less than a week later, we were sitting in the departure lounge at Heathrow when another of her emails arrived.

TO: Alex MacAskill
FROM: Laura Park
RE: Please . . .

Hi Alex,
As you can see, I don't give up easily. I truly believe that talking about that day could be therapeutic, even cathartic, for you, and maybe for me, too. Don't you think it's time? It's been nearly ten years, almost an entire decade. Your

perspective on the event is now informed by all those years of living, and growing, and reflecting. Don't let this imprison you any longer. I implore you to speak with me about it. I promise you the piece I write will treat you and your experience that day with the reverence and respect it deserves. Please, I'll come to you anywhere, anytime.

Laura

I didn't respond, but neither did I delete it this time. I was too tired and excited to deal with it just then. It had been a very hectic several days since our meeting with Pavel Dubov. To be fair, making arrangements to fly to Moscow wasn't nearly as onerous as I'd expected. There was some red tape involved, no pun intended, but not much. We had to obtain a visa from the Russian Embassy on Kensington Church Street in London. The embassy was employing a fancy new high-tech fingerprint scanning procedure that actually helped speed up the process of securing a visa. With neither of us checking boxes for international fugitive, underworld kingpin, violent warlord, escaped money-launderer, or petty criminal, Matt and I seemed to pass their little digital fingerprint test.

We'd already agreed that we wouldn't specify on our visa applications that we were heading to Moscow in search of our long-lost father. We feared that might complicate matters. So we just claimed we were visiting Moscow on vacation. With passports and visas in hand, we boarded our flight without any issues. Matt did the talking. I opened my yap only when required to. That's how I liked it.

Our Lufthansa flight left on time, landed in Frankfurt ten minutes ahead of schedule, and then took off again on time. We didn't leave the plane until we landed at Domodedovo Airport about four minutes late. I'd never been to Moscow. Then again, I'd never been to London or Frankfurt either.

We picked up our bags and passed through customs without incident, I mean other than dealing with my usual anxieties. When the passport control officer stared at me for quite some time, I was sure he recognized me. I kept waiting for him to pop the question, but it never came. He eventually stamped my passport and waved me through. I joined Matt in the main concourse and we then caught a cab for the trip to our hotel. Domodedovo Airport is about forty kilometres south of Moscow. It took quite a while for the cab to get us to the Courtyard Marriott Moscow Paveletskaya. Neither Matt nor I were in a position to know whether the taxi driver had chosen the most direct, efficient, and inexpensive route. The hotel was really quite nice, and very Western. Were it not for the signage featuring Cyrillic alongside English, we could have been in Montreal or Cleveland. Even with the favourable exchange rate, we still opted to share a room with two queen beds. By the time we'd settled into our room on the fifth floor, it was nearly 6:00 p.m., local time, three hours ahead of London.

"This isn't so bad," Matt said. "I'm not exactly sure what I was expecting, but this is just so . . . so Western."

"I know. I thought it might be a little less colourful, a little dingier, drab, grey, overcast, drizzling, with a lot of small, old dented cars, with people bundled up in utterly nondescript earth-tone clothes, lined up at grocery stores, looking forlorn, and two men in ill-fitting suits following us without really caring that we knew."

"I was actually just talking about the hotel, not the social history of the Soviet Union," Matt said. "Have you read lots of Cold War–era spy thrillers?"

Dozens and dozens.

"Well, maybe a few."

"It's been nearly fifteen years since the breakup of the Eastern Bloc," Matt said. "Time to let go of your Evil Empire image. Russia is a different country now, in many ways."

"I suppose," I conceded. "But even though they swapped communism for capitalism, I think they've hung on to the corruption and are still about as democratic as your garden-variety banana republic."

"I dare say you're right about that. As you might imagine, we haven't exactly targeted Russia in our next big new business development offensive," Matt said. "But we're here and we really should at least try to play the tourist in the hours we have until our meeting tomorrow. Who knows how much time we'll have afterwards?"

You mean go out in a strange new city filled with strange new people? I don't think so.

"I was thinking of maybe staying here, having dinner in the restaurant and getting to bed early for our big day tomorrow," I said.

"Come on, Alex, it's really only mid-afternoon for us. Indulge me."

When we got down to the lobby, an empty cab was idling in front.

"That's our man," Matt said, heading straight out to the taxi.

The driver rolled down his window and then rolled his "r" when he said, "Paterson?"

"Yes, Paterson," Matt replied, without rolling his "r," and climbed in.

I followed. There didn't seem to be any other option.

Matt wouldn't tell me where we were going. He just kept telling me to be patient and that I'd enjoy myself. While our hotel was more on the outskirts of Moscow proper, our taxi was clearly headed downtown. It was warm and the sun was still quite high in the sky. Moscow looked not unlike many major metropolitan cities. A mix of high-rise and low-rise buildings, busy streets, highways around the periphery, and lots of people, some striding down the avenues with purpose, many others milling about seemingly without any place to go. About forty minutes later, the cab pulled up next to an old but beautiful building, fronted by a row of pillars.

The cab driver uttered his second word of our little road trip.

"Bolshoi."

Matt had already arranged for us to see *Giselle* at the famed Bolshoi Theatre. Two tickets were waiting for us at the box office. I hadn't been to too many ballets. Okay, I'd never been to a ballet, probably because it had never occurred to me to go to a ballet. It should have occurred to me. I loved it. It was truly beautiful and told a story just as effectively and powerfully as any movie or novel. And the theatre was stunning. It wasn't massive, but was so beautifully designed it took my breath away. With about 350 seats on the floor, there were six, yes, six different balconies rising around the inside perimeter of the theatre. Wonderful architecture from 1776 – thank you, Wikipedia. The music, the dancing, the emotion of the story, the theatre itself, all made me feel, well, alive.

I looked up often to marvel at the gold, ornately appointed ceiling. I pushed Gabriel from my thoughts as I let my eyes flit over, but not dwell on, the lighting bays high above the audience. It was all quite magical.

At the intermission, I turned to Matt.

"You were right. This was a much better idea than staying in the hotel room for the night."

"Alex, a prostate examination is a much better idea than spending your first night in Moscow in a hotel room."

"Well, thanks for making it happen and for dragging me along."

"No worries, mate."

With Pavel Dubov's help, we'd arranged to meet Dimitri Dumanovsky at ten the next morning, though we weren't very specific about our interest. From our one telephone conversation, it was clear that despite a heavy accent, Dimitri's English was quite good. I guess that made sense. It would be difficult to become a recognized hockey historian, even in Russia, without at least a passing understanding of English, or perhaps French. It would be like being a bull-fighting expert and not knowing Spanish, or a chess authority without knowing Russian. After all, Canada is hockey's birthplace and founding world power.

The VTB Ice Palace is just a short walk from the Avtozavodskaya Metro station slightly southeast of downtown Moscow, and conveniently located only one Metro stop south of our hotel. Now you know why we'd chosen the Courtyard Marriott.

With directions from Vaclav, the hotel concierge, Matt and I easily found the Paveletskaya Metro station and boarded an only moderately crowded southbound train. We stood near the door, holding onto the grab bars conveniently provided.

"Same routine when we get there?" I asked.

"Absolutely, Alex. That works well for me," he replied. "I'll take the lead."

"Thanks."

The VTB Ice Palace – and I could never find out what VTB stands for – houses the Russian Hockey Museum and the Russian Hockey Hall of Glory. A young player with a hockey bag and stick waiting just inside the entrance directed us to Dimitri's office on the upper mezzanine of the complex. A team was practising on the ice three floors below. His door was open, revealing an office you might expect belonged to a hockey historian. Posters, photographs, plaques, sticks, and pucks were mounted on almost every square inch of wall space. Old wooden filing cabinets and a few newer, industrial grey steel filing cabinets were arrayed around the perimeter of the room. Some drawers were open and overflowing with paper. I suspect they were open because they could not be closed. His desk was large and, beyond an older-looking desktop computer and monitor, completely covered with file folders, paper, and abandoned take-out food containers.

Dimitri, dressed casually, sat with his back to the door in an old wooden wheeled desk chair, focused on his outdated CRT computer display. The pale yellow linoleum floor beneath his feet no longer shone, if it ever had. I walked behind Matt as he approached the open door. I was sure he'd heard us approach. I'd even manufactured a cough as we closed in on his office in the hopes that he'd turn around. But no. We stopped outside his door. Matt knocked on the doorjamb.

"*Da*," the man said, still with his back to us.

"Dimitri Dumanovsky?"

"*Da*," he repeated.

"Matthew Paterson and Alex MacAskill," Matt said. "We're here from London to meet you. We talked on the phone."

"*Da*. I remember," he said, finally turning. His chair protested the swivel with a noise that sounded like the grinding gears of an ancient tractor.

"Come in, come in," he said, clearing debris from two guest chairs we hadn't even noticed.

"I am Dimitri," he said, facing us and extending his hand.

"I'm Matt, and this is my brother, Alex."

Dimitri clearly read too much into the word "handshake." It felt like he might have been trying to dislocate my shoulder.

"Sit down. Sit down," he said, pointing to the chairs now free of hockey detritus but not dust.

We sat down.

"Sorry about mess," Dimitri said. "Not much people visit me here."

"No problem. Thanks for meeting with us."

"So why you come great distance from London, where hockey is not good, to talk to me about hockey? Pavel did not tell me much. You did not say much on the phone. So what can I do?"

Matt pulled his iPad from his backpack, displayed the enlarged photo of the partially obscured tattoo, and passed it to Dimitri.

"We're trying to learn about this tattoo," Matt said. "Pavel Dubov thought you could help us."

"Pavel is a smart man. But why you want to know about this? Two young brothers, 'tweens' I think, from London, where hockey is not good. Why?"

"Alex is actually from Canada and is a very good hockey player," Matt said, pointing to me.

I kind of smiled but didn't know what else to do.

"Okay, but still why you want to know about tattoo?"

Matt looked at me with his eyebrows elevated. I just seemed to know what he was asking. I nodded once.

"Well, Dimitri, you're right, Alex and I are twin brothers. Just a few days ago, we met each other for the first time since we were born. Alex didn't know about me and I didn't know about him."

Matt then took the iPad from Dimitri and brought up the un-enlarged version of the photo showing two newborn babies in the arms of a man in jeans and a white T-shirt, and handed it back to him. Pavel looked from the photo to the two of us, and then back to the photo again.

"Dimitri, we're here to see you because we think the man in the photograph is the father we've never known. We're trying to find him."

He looked back to us again.

"You don't know who is your father? You never met your father?"

We shook our heads in unison.

"Not since that photograph was taken nearly twenty-five years ago," Matt replied.

Dimitri looked at the floor and sighed.

"My father passes away just four months ago. He was ninety-four. I am seventy-one," Dimitri said with a far-off look in his eye. "I knew my father for seventy-one years, for the whole of my life. Long time. Now he's gone."

"I'm so sorry for your loss, Dimitri. We didn't know. We're both sorry," Matt said, reaching out his hand but not quite touching his shoulder. "We only knew our father for a few minutes when that photo was taken. That's all. Will you help us?"

Dimitri lifted his moist eyes to ours again. "*Da*."

Dimitri Dumanovsky stood, walked past the steel filing cabinets, and stopped in front of one of the wooden filing cabinets. He pulled out the balky middle drawer, waded through some files, then closed the drawer. He knelt on the floor to open the burgeoning bottom drawer. He thumbed through several files, searching. He was talking to himself, or perhaps to the filing gods.

"*Da!*" he exclaimed, withdrawing a file folder and hauling himself back to his feet. He cleared even more historical hockey flotsam from a small round table by simply tipping it over and dumping whatever had been on it onto the floor in one corner of the office. He dragged the table over and positioned it in front of where Matt and I were seated. Then he plopped down in his wheeled wooden chair and rolled himself over to join us. He dropped the thick file on the table. Written on the tab in black ink was "СССР-Канада 1972."

He flipped open the file and started riffling through it as if he knew exactly what he was looking for. Though they were somewhat obscured by his flying fingers, I saw game sheets and team line-ups fly by, and some photographs, and newspaper clippings, some in English but most in Russian.

"Eureka!" Dimitri shouted, holding up a single sheet of paper.

Apparently "eureka" is the same in Russian and English. He placed the paper on the table and turned it so we could see it.

"Eureka, indeed!" Matt said.

The paper showed a full-colour hand-drawn detailed sketch of the elusive and exclusive tattoo. It was exactly as Oksana, and my memories of a long-lost peewee hockey crest, had suggested.

Two hockey sticks crossed diagonally with a puck placed in the middle, just below where the sticks crossed. The straight blade of each stick was fully clothed in black tape. Above the puck it said: Канада-СССР. The year 1972 was centred just under and between the two billowing national flags representing Canada and the Union of Soviet Socialist Republics. This was, without a doubt, the design tattooed on the inner left forearm of the man in our mysterious bilateral baby photo.

"That's it!" Matt said after examining the sketch and comparing it to our enlarged photo. "No doubt about it."

Matt looked at me. I nodded in vigorous agreement.

"Yes, that is it, certainly," Dimitri agreed. "There were two sizes. One small and one large. The man in the photo has the large tattoo. If he choosing smaller one, big baby would cover it all. We would never see it. We would never know."

"This is brilliant, Dimitri. Thank you," Matt said. "Now, Pavel said only players on the Soviet National Team could have this tattoo. Is that correct?"

"Almost correct," Dimitri replied. "In point of fact . . . Is that how you say it? In point of fact?"

"Yes!" Matt and I replied, perfectly synchronized.

"Good. In point of fact, not just players was permitted to have tattoo installed, if I could say it that way. Also coaches, trainers, and equipment staff could wear it, too."

I'd already done some research on the Soviet team. I mustered my resolve, took a deep breath, and looked across the table at Dimitri.

"So that means we've narrowed it down to the thirty-four candidates," I said quietly. "That's the twenty-nine starting and reserve players, along with the one coach, one assistant coach, one team doctor, one trainer, and one equipment manager, for a total of thirty-four possibilities. Are we missing anyone? Is that right?"

"*Nyet*. You are not right for two reasons," Dimitri declared. "Number one, the Soviet coach, Vsevolod Bobrov, was scared of needles – everybody knew – and he never even thought he would be having tattoo. And number two, the team decided they would only have the tattoo on their . . . how do you say this . . . dominating hand? Domination hand?"

"Dominant hand," Matt and I said together.

"Stupid me," Dimitri said, shaking his head. "*Da*, dominant hand."

He then turned back to the full iPad photo.

"You see? Your father, and I hope he is your father, has tattoo on his left arm. He was what Americans call a 'lefty.'"

He smiled and seemed pleased by his use of slang.

"I thought all Russians were 'lefties,' by definition," Matt said, chuckling.

"I do not understand what you are meaning," Dimitri replied.

"Sorry," Matt said. "Never mind. I was kidding."

"Okee-dokee," Dimitri said, smiling. "I like this phrase, okee-dokee. Is fun to say."

He returned to the thick file folder in front of him and again flipped through the pages until he stopped and withdrew a document.

"These are physical characteristics of each player. I think it will tell us what dominant hand each player has."

He flipped through the pages, jotting down names on a small notepad he withdrew from the pocket of his pants. When he turned the final page of the stack, there were only five players' names on his list.

"What about the non-players?" I asked. "How do we find out if they were left-handed?"

"You," Dimitri said pointing to me. "Alex, yes?"

I nodded.

"Come with me."

Dimitri grabbed a stack of old VHS tapes from a shelf near the door and walked into the corridor. I followed. Down the hall, he turned into a much smaller office with a TV and VCR sitting on a trolley. A lone empty chair sat in front of the screen.

"These are tapes of series in '72," Dimitri started. "We already know Bobrov has no tattoo. So you must look at tapes and watch assistant coach, he's young one, and trainer, one with moustache who opens one bench door, and equipment manager who opens other bench door. See if they do anything that says what hand is strong one."

"Okay. I can do that. What about the team doctor?" I asked.

"*Da*. Try tape for Game Six," Dimitri suggested. "That is when your Bobby Clarke, no sportsman, slashed the ankle of our best player, Valeri Kharlamov. His ankle was broked. Team doctor came to ice then. Watch him."

We spent the rest of the morning working through our fatherly candidates. While Matt and Dimitri tracked down the five left-handed players on the list, I worked on the non-players. I thought it would be a difficult and tedious process, but it was neither.

I started with the Game Six tape. The play-by-play was in Russian. I found the audio distracting so I turned the volume down so it was just loud enough for me to hear names. I eliminated both coaches within the first ten minutes of the broadcast. Even though Dimitri had already taken Bobrov out of the play, the head coach compared notes with his assistant coach, Boris Kulagin, during a break in the action. Both coaches were holding notebooks in their left hands and pens in their right. Good enough for me to declare them both righties.

Partway through the first period, Aleksandr Gusev broke his stick and headed for the bench. I watched as the equipment manager quickly fetched him a new one. He used his right hand to grab the stick from the rack behind the bench, and then again to hand it to Gusev, who was skating by. Definitive? No, I don't think so. But confirmation came a few minutes later in the game when the TV cameras again focused on the Soviet bench during a stoppage in play. The equipment manager picked up a water bottle and tossed it to one of the players about halfway down the bench. The bottle flew from his right hand. Now it was definitive. You don't throw with your weaker hand. That was three of the five already accounted for. Just the trainer and team doctor left.

Right before the end of the first period in Game Six, with the score still deadlocked at 0–0, Yuri Lyapkin, a defenceman, had his bell rung when Peter Mahovlich plowed him into the boards. The Soviet trainer was quickly escorted onto the ice, using his right hand to hold onto the arm of the linesman. Not conclusive evidence of another righty, but it was a start. Then when the trainer knelt down beside Lyapkin, he used his right hand to unsnap the player's helmet, even though his left hand was much closer. Good enough for me. Another check mark in the right-handed column.

By this time it was almost noon and I was dying to know what progress Dimitri and Matt were making with the players. But I had just one more candidate to rule in or out, as the case may be.

I used the fast-forward button to move quickly to about the midpoint of the second period when Bobby Clarke's famous two-hander felled Valeri Kharlamov. I watched for any sign of Vladimir Krupin, the Soviet team doctor, but he never stepped onto the ice. Kharlamov limped, under his own power, to the dressing room, where apparently no cameras recorded Dr. Krupin's examination.

Rather than watching more tapes, I decided to bring Google onto my team. Dimitri had already logged me into the Wi-Fi network, so I simply plugged the doctor's name into the search bar and hit Return. There were plenty of entries in Cyrillic that meant nothing to me. But there was one English article on the *Hockey News* website from 2012, commemorating the fortieth anniversary of what, in Canada, we called the Summit Series. The article recounted in bone-crushing detail the Bobby Clarke slash and its aftermath. The piece included an interview with Dr. Krupin from 1987 wherein he claimed Kharlamov's ankle was indeed broken and that he'd immobilized it and given him a local anaesthetic so he could continue playing. Kharlamov had returned to the ice later in the second period. Well, that was all very interesting, but what really mattered to me were these two closing sentences:

> *It was the only interview Dr. Vladimir Krupin ever gave about the infamous Clarke slash. He died in a Moscow hospital in 1989 after a heart attack at the age of 72.*

I was done. I'd confirmed that none of the non-players associated with the 1972 Soviet National Hockey Team was left-handed. None of them was our father. That meant that he must have been a player. It made me wish I'd not given up hockey. Another decision Gabriel and I made together that I'd like to take back.

When I returned to Dimitri Dumanovsky's office, Matt and our resident Russian hockey historian looked at me in anticipation.

"Progress. I've conclusively determined that four of the five non-players were right-handed," I announced. "I couldn't figure out which hand the team doctor favoured but it really doesn't matter. He died a year before we were conceived."

"Blast," Matt said. "We've made progress too, but haven't found him yet. We've already eliminated four of our left-handed players."

"Just give me the topline," I asked Matt, while Dimitri buried his head in another file cabinet.

"Okay, in summary, two of the left-handed players actually died before January 1990, one from cancer and the other in a car accident. So they were eliminated from our little investigation, in the truest and most permanent sense of the word," Matt explained. "Three lefties remained. We moved next to Anatoli Firsov. He was a left forward on the 1972 team."

Dimitri rolled his eyes.

"Actually, we call them left wingers," I corrected.

"Right then, he was a left winger, but he was not a starting player. He saw very little action in the series. But he went on to be first a player, and then a player coach for the Soviet Red Army team in the old Soviet League, retiring in early 1992, as the Eastern Bloc broke apart. Still, he was a possibility. So we tried to confirm his whereabouts around March 23, 1990, when you and I were likely conceived."

"Right. I'm with you. And?"

"Well, the Soviet hockey season was still on in March. So Dimitri pulled the game sheets for the Soviet Red Army team for all the games in the early months of 1990," Matt said, holding up the stack of game sheets. "Firsov played for the team in all nine games in March. He scored twice, as Dimitri put it, 'had two assists, and was assessed four penalties' across those nine games. With never more than four days between games, it is highly unlikely, indeed almost impossible, that in the middle of this stretch of games he could have suddenly flown to Ottawa, met our mother, and grown close enough to her to, well, to be an equal partner in our conception, and then jet back to Russia in time for the next game. It just doesn't make sense. So we've ruled out Anatoli Firsov."

"Shit," I said. "I can't really argue with that. Okay, three down, two to go. Who's next?"

"Leonid Veselov, another lesser-known player who only took a few shifts in the tournament," Matt said. Dimitri looked up and shook his head at the name. "Over to you, Dimitri. Why don't you tell Alex why Leonid Veselov is not our father?"

"Sorry, Alexei, but our friend Leonid is also not him."

He turned to his computer and pulled up a newspaper article and photo. He pointed to a youngish-looking man in the back of a police car.

"Leonid Veselov?" I asked.

"Bongo," replied Dimitri.

"I think you mean bingo."

"Stupid," he said. "Bingo. It is Leonid leaving court to start four-year prison sentence for nasty bar fight. I think it was about somebody's girlfriend and lots of vodka."

"But then," Matt interjected, "his four-year sentence was extended to eight years when he was implicated in a prison riot. But in good news, he was scoring champion for the prison floor hockey team."

"When was he locked up?" I asked, though I already knew the answer.

"June 1985 to July 1993," Dimitri reported.

"Four down, one to go," I sighed. "Who's the lucky final prospect?"

"Yuri Golov is his name," said Matt. "And we've saved the best for last."

"Well, by the process of elimination, Yuri must be our man," I said.

"Based on what we've found so far, you might be right," Matt said.

Dimitri frowned and waved to cede the floor to Matt.

"Right then. We've checked his hockey records, and Yuri Golov was very young when he was on the team in 1972. He was a nineteen-year-old army officer and did not play much in the series. Like our earlier candidate, Anatoli, Yuri also played in the old Soviet League afterwards. The most recent reference Dimitri can find had him playing for Dynamo Moscow early in 1990.

There's nothing in the Russian media after that. It's as if he disappeared."

"Okay, then what?" I pushed. "Don't keep me hanging here."

Matt then turned his laptop around to show me another newspaper clipping on the screen, this one in English.

"Then I found this courtesy of several online search engines. It's a 1991 *Toronto Star* article about the University of Toronto's Varsity hockey assistant coach, Yuri Golov. It also says he was working with Hockey Canada to help get Team Canada ready for the Lillehammer Olympics. This must be our father."

The photos Matt had found online showed a very Slavic-looking man – high cheekbones and a strong jawline – with no obvious physical similarities to us.

"We couldn't find any record of him in Canada before 1991, but that doesn't mean he wasn't there. Besides, he is our only option."

"I have just found little bit more on Russian Internet," Dimitri said. "It seems still Yuri Golov is alive."

He called up an article in a Yaroslavl newspaper from June 2011 about a new industrial bakery that had recently opened. There was a photo in the story showing ten bakers gathered around one of the large new ovens. Yuri Golov was identified in the photo, third from the left. Dimitri used the Zoom function to make the photo larger.

"Hello, Yuri Golov," Matt said when it was obvious we'd made a positive ID. "So, Yuri Golov, former member of the Soviet

National Hockey Team, and potential father of identical twin sons, is now living in Yaroslavl and working as a baker?"

"Correct," Dimitri replied. "And I just found a Y. Golov in online telephone directory for Yaroslavl."

"Where is Yaroslavl?" I asked.

"About 250 kilometres north and east of Moscow where Volga and Kotorosl rivers meet. There is some history there, but is not great town. But they do have new bakery," Dimitri said.

We agreed that Dimitri should call but would not tell Yuri Golov about us. He suggested he just ask Yuri if he could come to Yaroslavl to see him about some old hockey records he was trying to assemble and maybe ask him a few questions about his time in the old Soviet League.

"Could we go tomorrow?" Matt asked.

Dimitri checked his old-school paper desk calendar for the next day.

"I am hockey historian. Most days are clear."

He called, and the phone rang and rang and rang. Dimitri frowned but kept the phone to his ear. Finally, just as he started to hang up, we all heard someone pick up on the other end.

"Yuri?" Dimitri said in a heavier accent.

He then spoke to someone for about six minutes and hung up.

"It was Yuri, our Yuri," Dimitri said. "He sounded hanged over. But he said yes to see me tomorrow, but not until twelve. I told him I had two friends who might be with me. He said okay. You have got me now curious. I guess we are going to Yaroslavl."

Someone shouted, "Kill the spotlights!"
But they stayed very much alive.

CHAPTER 10

We met Dimitri on the platform of the Moscow Yaroslavskaya station at 7:15 for the 7:35 departure. We'd taken the Metro from our hotel that morning, like so many other commuters.

"You have my ticket?" he asked.

"Right here," I said, handing it over.

"We should get on now or seats will be gone."

We managed to find three seats together. Dimitri took the single seat facing backwards so Matt and I could behold the breathtaking scenery as it flew past our window. Kidding. The only aspect of the trip that was breathtaking was the foul odour emanating from the young, rough-looking man sitting directly across from me. Our knees touched on occasion. Dimitri, sitting next to him, seemed unaffected by the stench.

I tried to sleep for some of the four-hour run, but that was not going to happen. Both Matt and I had been awake most of the night in anticipation of meeting our father. I'd Googled part of the night away trying to find out more about Yuri Golov. Given my limited ability to read Cyrillic – and by limited, I mean non-existent – I was left with very few English entries. I found a brief reference to him as a volunteer coach with the local Yaroslavl hockey team. Matt had spent the night doing the same thing.

I sent a long update email to Abby, who'd been texting me every twenty minutes or so. Despite my inability to keep her textually satisfied, I'd been thinking about her quite a bit. Not on purpose. She was just there.

"I read that Yuri Golov is still involved in ice hockey in Yaroslavl," Matt said.

You can just say "hockey," not "ice hockey."

"Yes," Dimitri replied. "He is helping to rebuilding city's KHL team, the Lokomotiv, after the tragedy."

"What tragedy?" Matt asked.

"Four years ago, whole Lokomotiv team was killed on their way to their first game of season. The plane crashed," Dimitri explained. "It happened just when they take off. Then poof! Whole team gone."

"That was in Yaroslavl? I remember that," Matt said, turning to me.

"It was big news in Canada," I said. "Very sad."

"The team now is back, but it takes time to be good," Dimitri said. "And they are not as strong as before."

The malodorous man next to me seemed to be growing more pungent with every passing kilometre. I'm quite proficient at holding my breath, but not breathing for four hours is slightly beyond my capabilities. For reasons other than brotherly bonding, I leaned towards Matt, sitting beside me.

Beyond near-asphyxia, the four-hour trip passed uneventfully in what felt like eight hours. We took a taxi from the Yaroslavl Glavny train station. It was a short drive to the nondescript, low-rise apartment house – I actually can't describe how nondescript it was. I almost nodded off when looking at the building for the very first time. It must have been designed and built during a nationwide architects' strike. The only aesthetic flourish was a piece of blue-painted plywood covering a broken window in the front door.

There was no security system and no way to buzz up to a tenant. We just walked directly up the stairs to the second floor, and down a dank, dirty, and dimly lit corridor that smelled, to me, very much like a dank, dirty, and dimly lit corridor. But compared to my neighbour on the train, it was quite pleasing to the nose.

Dimitri stopped in front of a door with a number 6 stencilled on it. He looked at us. My heart was attempting to break free from its moorings, it was beating so fast. Matt looked a little calmer but still excited.

"If I am you, don't expect too much," Dimitri said.

Then he knocked on the door. Nothing. Again he knocked. Nothing. And a third time knocking, or pounding more like it.

Still, not a sound from within. So that's it then. We'd come all this way, and now this. I shrugged my shoulders, giving up, but Dimitri shook his head and went at the door again like he was working the speed bag in a gym.

"Yuri!" he shouted through the door. "Yuri Golov!"

He shouted other words but none I recognized.

After a few more seconds of silence, we heard it. The guttural groan that escaped beneath the door wasn't so much a sound as a surrender. We waited. We heard him banging around within, though I had no idea what he was doing. Inside, the loud crashing and banging noises made me wonder if one of those automated self-propelled vacuum cleaners was running at high speed but programmed to navigate a completely different apartment. Eventually, we heard him struggling with the door lock, as if he might be unfamiliar with it. Then the door opened. Standing there barefoot, in a grey hoody and jeans, was the towering presence of Yuri Golov. Looking closely, I knew we had the right guy, but he was barely recognizable from the photos we'd spent the night studying. He hadn't shaved in a long time. There was a reasonably fresh cut above his right eye. His hair was longer than in any of the photos we'd found online, and to call his mop unruly would be an understatement of monstrous proportions. He stood before us, swaying gently, fists clenched at his sides. He looked even older than his sixty-three years. I had the distinct impression that he was not happy to have been roused at the ungodly hour of 12:15 p.m.

"Yuri, we spoke yesterday," Dimitri said. "I'm Dimitri Dumanovsky."

"Why English?" Yuri asked.

"Sorry, my friends speak only English and they wanted to meet you."

"I told you come at noon," Yuri said.

"Yes, Yuri, you did," Dimitri replied. "Sorry we're a few minutes late."

"Late? It's after noon now?" he asked.

"Yes, Yuri. It's 12:15."

He stood there for a few more seconds until he noticed my wristwatch and pointed to it.

I held up my arm so he could see the watch face and confirm the time.

"Sorry," he replied. "It feels like very early in morning. Come in."

He led us inside and closed the door behind us.

We stepped carefully and clustered near the kitchen counter where there was just enough floor space to accommodate the three of us. It was what we in the West would call a bachelor apartment. It was also what we in the West would call messy beyond all comprehension. One large room, a pull-out couch, a galley kitchen, and a small bathroom in the far corner near the sole window. The chaos in the apartment suggested either a recent bomb blast or perhaps a Force 12 hurricane. A strange smell, like freshly baked alcohol-infused bread, lingered. There was life's debris everywhere. In one corner of the kitchen floor, there were several empty clear bottles with a green label featuring a bear. I'd already learned this was the cheapest, rotgut, local vodka of choice, Dobry Medved, or Gentle Bear. I noticed a half dozen more empties scattered near the couch and a few on the windowsill. Then something else caught my eye near the bathroom door. It was a shallow box filled with more vodka empties. Oh yes, I also noticed there were some vodka empties, yes, Gentle Bear, spilling out from under the couch and crowding our feet. The apartment was a veritable Gentle Bear sanctuary where the protected species was allowed to multiply and flourish.

"Okay. You are here. I am here," Yuri said, looking at Dimitri. "What do you want to know?"

Dimitri shook his head and pointed to us, or rather to Matt.

"All right then, Yuri, I'm Matthew Paterson from London, and this is my twin brother – we're identical twins – Alex MacAskill, from Canada, more specifically, from Ottawa, where we were born."

There was absolutely no flash of recognition or concern or resentment or anything when the words "identical twins" and "Ottawa" sounded in the same sentence. I watched him closely to see the ruble drop behind his eyes, but it never did. He seemed utterly unfazed.

"Okay, so why are you twins here in Yaroslavl?" he asked. "I still don't see why. Explain to me."

Yuri's command of English was quite good. There was an accent, yes, but he was easily understood.

"We just have a few questions to help us solve a bit of a mystery," Matt said. "We're looking for a member of the 1972 Soviet National Hockey Team who was also in Ottawa in 1990. We know you lived in Canada for a while when you coached at the University of Toronto. When exactly did you arrive in Canada and how long did you stay?"

Yuri looked at the ceiling and winced with cerebral effort.

"Okay, let's go fast so you can leave and I can lie down again," Yuri said. "I arrived in Toronto in early November 1990, and I stayed until sometime in 1992. Okay?"

"We think you may have arrived in Canada early in 1990, and that you were in Ottawa in February or early March," Matt persisted.

"*Nyet*," Yuri said. "*Nyet, nyet, nyet*."

He shook his head and turned to engage Dimitri in a heated conversation in Russian. We could only watch. Then Yuri fished through a drawer in a beaten-up desk under the window. It took him a few minutes to find what he was looking for. When he did, he handed Matt what looked like a certificate of some kind on card stock, and then pointed to a line at the bottom.

"I'm sorry, I can't read this," Matt said. "It's in Russian."

Dimitri took it from Matt and scanned it, nodding his head.

"I'm sorry, but Yuri is right. He was in Moscow in February for six-month alcohol rehabilitation program that finished July 1990. That is the date on this certificate."

"You weren't in Ottawa in March 1990? You didn't meet a young woman?" Matt asked Yuri.

"No. I was not allowed to leave facility. And I've never been to Ottawa. Just Montreal, Winnipeg, Toronto, Vancouver, and Hamilton."

You must have been in Ottawa. You're the only player left. You're our only option.

"It makes no sense," I said, unable to stop myself. "Do you have a tattoo on your left arm?"

"*Da*."

I pulled the photo from my backpack and held it out to him.

This is you, isn't it? It has to be you!

"Isn't this a photograph of you?" I asked.

He took the photo, stared at it, and furrowed his brow. He did not give off the air of someone who was looking at himself. He shook his head.

"No," he said. "Is not me."

Bullshit! It has to be you. Who else is it then?

He handed me the photo and then pulled his hoody over his head, revealing a white T-shirt underneath. So there he was, in jeans and a white T-shirt, just like our father in the photo. He then turned to show us his tattoo. It all crashed down around us then. Yuri pointed to his tattoo and then to the tattoo in the photo.

"You see, tattoo is same, but mine is on outside of arm not on inside, like in photo," he said. "Some players have on outside, some on inside. I want people to see it so I have tattoo on outside of arm. Story over. Visit over."

Matt looked at me. He looked as gutted as I felt. At one and the same time, I was crushed that Yuri Golov was not our father and happy that Yuri Golov was not our father. I think Matt felt the same way at the same time.

"Why did you stop with hockey?" Dimitri asked. "You were good. Big and powerful. Good hard shot. But also a thinker on ice, too."

Yuri looked like he might cry. He stared at his feet for a few seconds before responding.

"I stop for the same reason I was fired in Toronto," he said. He nudged an empty vodka bottle with his bare foot. "Fucking Gentle Bear. Fuck Gentle Bear."

By 2:30 we were back on the train for the return trip to Moscow. Dimitri seemed more discouraged and dejected than we were. We'd asked Yuri who he thought the man in the photo might be. He wracked his brain and came up with a few names, every one of which we'd already researched and rejected. And that was it. I don't remember much about that train run. I just turned my face to the window, closed my eyes, and tried very hard not to think about it all. This technique didn't really work very well. The Yaroslavl baker was not our father.

"Are you so sure about the dates?" Dimitri asked as the train eased back into Moscow Yaroslavskaya station at 6:40 p.m.

"It's one of the few things we actually are certain about," Matt replied. "We were born December 23, 1990, we were only a week premature, so we had to have been conceived mid-March 1990. Those are the facts. We can't control them. We can't change them."

We thanked Dimitri for his efforts and offered to take him out to dinner. He seemed a little reluctant to say goodbye, but eventually declined our invitation. I gave him my cell number in case he needed to reach us. We shook hands, then he walked to his car in the parking lot nearby, and Matt and I headed for the Metro.

We both felt terrible, miserable, cheated. We'd come all this way, gotten so close, only to hit a brick wall, or perhaps an iron curtain. I'd never really experienced such excitement followed so quickly by such disappointment. It wasn't just emotional. There was a physical side to it, as well, that's hard for me to describe. But it can't be good for you.

We made it back to the hotel shortly after seven and realized we were both famished. We didn't even go to our room, we headed straight for the hotel restaurant. When the waiter approached, I ordered a steak, medium rare.

"Is that how you always order it?" Matt asked, ignoring the waiter for a moment.

"Yep."

"Me, too. No surprise, I guess." He turned to the waiter. "Sorry, the same for me, please."

We were finishing our crème brûlée when my iPhone vibrated with a text. I figured it was Abby looking for another update. Beyond the long email I'd sent the previous night, I'd kept her informed and texted photos on our train ride north, but I hadn't yet broken the news about our failed mission to Yaroslavl. As it turned out, it wasn't a text from Abby, it was from a number I didn't recognize with what I thought was a Russian country code.

"Where you are now?" it read.

"Who is this, please?" I replied.

"DD"

"Matt, it's Dimitri," I said before turning back to my iPhone.

"Where you are?" he texted again.

"Restaurant at the Courtyard Marriott Pavel. Hotel," I texted back.

"Meet me in hotel bar in 20 mins," his next text read.

"Okay. Why?"

"Just meet me there in 20."

"K"

We charged our meal to our room and then moved to the bar. We took a booth along one wall. It was a very quiet night. In fact, save for a few young couples on the other side of the room, we were pretty much on our own. The music was Western rock and roll and it was quite loud. We ordered beer, Heineken for me and a Stella Artois for Matt. Fifteen minutes after we'd taken our seats in the bar, Dimitri arrived. He acknowledged us with a glance, quickly scanned the room, and then walked straight to the counter to speak to the bartender. The guy nodded and moved to the sound system control panel at the far end of the bar. He turned the music up even louder. Then Dimitri joined us. He turned down Matt's offer of a drink. He looked anxious, nervous.

He opened his mouth and I presume some words came tumbling out but they were lost in the raucous music.

"Pardon?" Matt and I both said.

Dimitri tried again, but again, whatever sound emerged from his gaping mouth was lost to the pounding backbeat.

I have no idea what you just said. In fact, I'm not sure any sound came out of your mouth.

"Sorry?" Matt said, pointing to his ears and leaning in close to Dimitri.

"*I won't be staying long enough to drink!*" Dimitri shouted.

"Is everything all right?" Matt asked.

Dimitri shook his head but whatever he said was again overpowered by the music.

Still can't hear you!

Matt waved at the bartender, who miraculously noticed. Matt pointed to his ears again and used hand gestures to persuade the guy to turn down the music. He did.

Dimitri looked annoyed and leaned in closer.

"For what I have to tell you, is safer for music to be loud," he said.

Right. We'll both be safer but with permanent bilateral hearing deficits.

"Dimitri, yelling at one another so we can hear is not going to work very well either," Matt said.

"Okay, but lean in," Dimitri replied.

We leaned in, so that anyone observing us would instantly know we were sharing deeply privileged and sensitive information. We looked like we were planning a hit or, at the very least, a multi-million-ruble drug deal.

"Okay, what's happened?" Matt asked.

"Shhh! Not so loud," Dimitri scolded.

"Sorry. What's happened?" Matt whispered.

"Something didn't feel right," Dimitri started. "It didn't hit me until I was just looking at my 1972 national team list on computer again. I saw there was only twenty-nine players listed. But I know there was thirty. And it all came back to my memory. I finally figure out problem, and then I wished I didn't figure out problem."

Dimitri shook his head and looked around the room as if ensuring we weren't being watched. I almost looked under our table but didn't think Dimitri would appreciate my sense of humour.

"Okay. Here it is. Here's news. There was a second backup goalie on the national team who made trip to Canada in '72, but never played a game and never even got dressed. I completely forget about him, maybe on purpose. I remembered there was thirty players, not twenty-nine," he said, looking up and shaking his head.

Then he leaned in even closer and used his curled index

finger to beckon us into a tighter huddle. So we moved in closer. Dimitri took one final look around the restaurant before turning back to us.

"Alexei Bugayev," he said. "Alexei Bugayev."

Who is he?

Matt and I looked at each other, then back at Dimitri. We both shrugged and shook our heads at the same time. Uncanny.

Dimitri pulled out his phone, called up a photo, and turned it so we could see it. It was an action shot of a goalie in his crease wearing the now familiar red jersey with CCCP across his chest.

"Is this Alexei whatever-his-name-is?" Matt asked.

"Yes, but look more closely," Dimitri instructed.

Matt squinted at the photo, studying it.

"Well, the bloke looks very sweaty, but that's all I see," Matt said. "What am I supposed to be looking at? I'm not following."

"You don't play hockey, do you?" Dimitri asked.

"Well, not beyond one painful week of field hockey at school."

"Field hockey," Dimitri snarled, and angled the phone so I could examine the shot.

"He's a lefty," I said, immediately.

"You played hockey!" Dimitri replied. "Yes. He is lefty. And he was removed from the team's history. It is like Alexei Bugayev never played on the team."

"But why?" we both asked at precisely the same time and in the same tone.

"Well, and this is where my help will have to be over," he said, glancing around furtively, "Alexei Bugayev was not great goalie. He was not even good goalie. But he was very calm and very good with languages. His time with national team meant he travelled a lot at young age."

"Okay, but what does that mean?" Matt asked.

I thought I knew where we were headed, but I kept it to myself in the hopes I was wrong.

"It means Alexei Bugayev was scouted and recruited at young age and I don't mean by national team. His goalie skills were really not good enough for national team. So let's just say, he was not third-best goalie in Soviet Union. But still, there he was, on team, travelling to West."

He was a spy, right?

"Spy," I said. "Alexei Bugayev was a spy." Dimitri shushed me and looked around. Then he nodded, and looked very uncomfortable doing it.

We leaned in again.

"As I remembered Alexei, more and more of story came back to me. When Alexei was seventeen and playing at tournament in Finland, he was scouted by agent who worked in Russian Embassy in Helsinki. Within one year he was on national team. Everyone who knows hockey was shocked, but no one said nothing. They knew not to. Alexei was good with languages. He spoke Finnish, German, and English and French."

"How do you know this?" Matt asked.

"I was the one told to remove him from hockey records," Dimitri explained. "The first call came from someone who worked for Central Committee member. Then I got a visit from someone who didn't tell me his name, and I decided not to ask. It happened very long time ago. I almost forgot about it."

He stopped to survey the room again.

"I'm sorry, but this is all I can do. I don't know any more than I told you. And now I don't even know you. I cannot go any deeper. It's up to you now. And I would be careful. I will deny everything if this comes back to me."

"Can we at least have the photo?" I asked.

"I cannot email it. I'm sorry."

"Of course not, but you can Airdrop it to my iPhone and no one will even know," Matt said, pulling his phone out.

Matt gently took Dimitri's iPhone out of his hand and completed the transaction.

"So is Alexei Bugayev our father?" I asked as Dimitri started to slide out of the booth.

"He could be. He's only lefty we don't check."

"Before you go, how do you spell his name?" Matt asked, ready to type it into his phone.

"A-L-E-X-E-I, B-U-G-A-Y-E-V."

"And he worked for the KGB?" I said.

He shushed me again and leaned in very close to us both.

"We don't call it that any more. But Alexei Bugayev was very much KGB before world changed in '91. I don't know where he is now, what he does now, or even if he's alive now. And I don't want to know." He shook our hands a last time, stood, and walked out of the restaurant.

I think we were both a little shell-shocked by Dimitri's revelation. He'd only been with us in the bar for about fifteen minutes, but so much had changed so quickly. I realized in that moment that I'd never really believed Yuri Golov was our father. The idea just hadn't sat well with me. It never quite fit. It never quite felt right. There was no instant connection, no involuntary surge of recognition. When I looked at his photo or at him when we'd met, it had left me cold. Now, even though I was looking at Alexei Bugayev through the wire mesh of a goalie mask, I felt something. I can't explain it. But something was there – perhaps only wishful thinking – but it was there.

"What do you think?" Matt asked.

"It's less what I think and more what I feel," I replied. "I feel something when I look at him. And I can't even see his face."

"Me, too," he agreed. "Come on, we've got work to do."

We got up and headed briskly for the elevators in the lobby. I was reaching for the Up button when the bartender caught up with us. He didn't look pleased to see us.

"You did not pay," he said.

Five minutes later, when we were back in our room, we each pulled out our laptops and agreed on an approach. I started searching online for vintage hockey card dealers. We needed a good, preferably colour, photo of Alexei Bugayev where we could actually see his face. Matt's job was to take a broader approach and start Googling Alexei Bugayev.

It took me less than ten seconds to find my way onto what seemed to be the largest and most popular online trading card site on the Internet. At least, that's what they claimed on the home page. They offered trading cards across countless sports and from the worlds of music and entertainment. I simply typed "Alexei Bugayev" along with "1970s" and "Soviet National Hockey Team" into the search bar. I suddenly felt very hot. My stomach tightened as I hit Return.

In less than three seconds, I got four hits. Who knew that the Soviets also produced hockey cards just like the North American versions, with stats on the back and everything? Four small thumbnail images appeared. The first three were the same, showing the action shot of a Soviet goalie behind his wire mesh mask. In fact, it was the same photo Dimitri had shown us on his phone. But the fourth thumbnail showed the classic face-on, head and shoulders shot, of the player wearing his official team jersey. The card was dated 1972. I clicked on the thumbnail and a larger version of the card instantly appeared, crisp and in focus. Alexei Bugayev. I enlarged the full colour photo so it filled my screen. There he was, at age twenty-two, looking right at me.

I can't explain why I knew he was my father, our father. I couldn't point to his eyes, or his nose, his hairline or the shape of his chin. It was nothing in particular, but everything in general. I knew. In my head, in my heart, in my gut, I knew. I followed his left arm down to the bottom of the frame to his elbow. Of course, the sleeve of his red jersey covered it, but I knew lurking beneath was a tattoo of two flags, two crossed hockey sticks, and a puck. I just knew.

"Matthew," I said, quietly.

He looked over at me as I turned my screen towards him. His face changed when he focused on the photo. I could tell before he said it, he knew, too.

"Holy shite. You found him."

"We found him."

Matt came over and perched on the bed beside me. We both just stared at the photo for a while. Alexei Bugayev was quite good-looking, with wavy brown hair parted at the side. He wasn't smiling, but I wasn't sure Soviet hockey players were allowed to smile, except perhaps upon scoring. Some Russians have that distinctly Slavic look, like Yuri Golov, Leonid Brezhnev, Vladislav Tretiak, Anatoly Karpov. But Alexei Bugayev did not. I snagged a screen shot of the trading card photo and Air-dropped it to Matt's computer.

It was hard to stop looking at the photo on my screen, but we had much more to do. To avoid having to jump up and cross the floor whenever one of us discovered something, Matt grabbed his laptop and sat on the bed beside me, pillows between our backs and the headboard. It was kind of like John and Yoko's bed-in for peace in that Montreal hotel room all those years ago, except we weren't under the covers. That would have been weird.

I joined Matt in a straight-up Google search on "Alexei Bugayev" filtered for "relevance." There were dozens and dozens of hits on his name, far more than I thought a KGB operative would ever want. We coordinated our efforts as we followed online trails that sometimes suddenly turned cold and other times gave up important information. In about three hours of dedicated effort, we were able to assemble many, many disparate strands of information, from many, many disparate sources, and knit together a reasonably coherent and convincing story about Alexei Bugayev across the last thirty-five years or so. There were some newspaper articles, magazine pieces, blog posts, photos, book excerpts, and even some archival video footage courtesy of YouTube.

Rather than reliving the avalanche of information through which we sifted, let me package it up in a more orderly fashion.

In several articles we dug up, and in three book excerpts we found, Alexei Bugayev was identified as a KGB operative working in North America in the 1980s and early '90s, usually attached to the Soviet Embassy. From 1981 to 1987, he worked in the embassy in Washington, D.C., holding a variety of titles, including trade attaché and cultural exchange director.

Then the big moment arrived in the form of an article in the *Ottawa Citizen* from October 12, 1989. In the story was a quotation about Canada–Soviet trade relations from Alexei Bugayev from an interview he gave at a meeting of the Conference Board of Canada held at the Westin Hotel in Ottawa. He was referred to as an economic advisor at the Soviet Embassy in Ottawa. And it all made sense. I could see how it all happened. It fit together perfectly.

"We've got him," I said. "This cinches it."

I showed Matt the article.

"Well, it certainly looks as if we're on to something," Matt said. "But I really would like this to be airtight before we claim victory."

Oh, it's airtight right now.

"I think we're pretty close to airtight right now. You see, there's something you don't know yet," I said. "I know how Alexei Bugayev met our mother."

Matt stopped, closed the lid of his laptop, and gave me his full attention.

"Pray, enlighten me."

"We know from the *Citizen* piece that he was posted to the Soviet Embassy in Ottawa and worked there at least in 1989. What you don't know is that the Soviet Embassy, now known as the Russian Embassy, is located on Charlotte Street in Ottawa and that it's just around the corner from the Cordon Bleu school and the restaurant where Mom worked for most of her adult life."

"Go on," he said, nodding. "Don't stop now."

"If Alexei Bugayev were on crutches, or in a wheelchair, or decided to drag himself by his lips, it still wouldn't have taken him more than a few minutes to reach the restaurant where our mother worked every weekday. It's that close to the embassy,"

I said. "Matt, Mom often mentioned the Russian diplomats who would come in for lunch. She called them 'regulars.'"

"Okay, then you're right. We've got him. The circumstantial evidence is bulletproof," Matt said. "So, we've both lost the only parents we *ever* knew, and we've just found the one parent we *never* knew."

"Well, we now know who he is," I said. "But where is he?"

"Hang on," Matt said.

He opened the lid of his laptop and I watched as he filtered the Google search results, not by relevance, but by time, calling up just the results from the last year. Brilliant. The final piece fell into place.

A story in the *Guardian* from two months ago quoted Alexei Bugayev on the state of the Russian economy.

"Jesus, Mary, and Joseph," Matt whispered. "He's been hiding in plain sight."

Alexei Bugayev was identified in the article as the senior economist at the Russian Embassy . . . in London.

I stayed calm and stock-still – a deer caught in headlights that kept on shining.

CHAPTER 11

"Who is Gabriel?"

I would have flinched had I not just been waking up, with the dull, flat morning light slipping into the room around the window blinds. It took a moment to remember where I was – the sign, for me, of a deep sleep. Maybe I hadn't heard what I thought I'd heard.

"Alex? You awake?" Matt asked, standing at the bathroom door.

Well, I wasn't, but I am, now.

"Yeah," I croaked. "Are we late?"

"Not quite. I was just awake for some reason."

And you thought I should be, too.

"What time is it?" I asked.

"About 6:10."

Did you really just say 6:10?

"Did you really just say 6:10?"

"I did. Sorry if I woke you. I thought you were already conscious, given that you were talking a while ago," Matt said.

Talking?

"Well, I must have been channelling a voice from one of my insomniac past lives because I was definitely not awake."

"Really? So sorry then," he said. "So who exactly is Gabriel?"

WTF?

"Why would you ask me that?"

"You said his name out loud about four times in kind of an agitated state about twenty minutes ago," Matt replied.

Shit. Don't tell me that. Are you serious?

I'd been starting to feel better about Gabriel. I hadn't dreamt about it for a while. Or so I'd thought. But maybe I was still dreaming but just not remembering. Shit.

"You're kidding," I said. "I guess I must have been dreaming, but I don't remember anything about it. And I said 'Gabriel'? Weird."

"You distinctly said 'Gabriel,'" Matt confirmed. "You were mumbling so I couldn't make out much else. So again, Alex, who is Gabriel?"

Shit. Not "who" but "what."

I looked at the ceiling and said nothing for a time. Matt seemed to know not to fill the space. He waited.

"The question is not 'Who is Gabriel?' but 'What is Gabriel?'" I said.

Matt waited. But I was done, at least for the moment. He waited some more, but it was still not time.

"Right then. What is Gabriel?"

Not now. Not yet.

I turned away from him, onto my side, and said nothing.

"Okay," Matt said. "When you're ready."

Thanks, bro.

"Thanks."

"You know, for identical twins who have the same DNA, whose mannerisms are astonishingly similar for two people who were separated nearly twenty-five years ago, who seem to think the same way about things, who have gravitated towards the same interests, we certainly have our differences," Matt said.

Do we have to go over this tired ground again? Not now. Not yet.

"Matt, we've had this conversation."

"Yes, I know, but it was never resolved."

Not now. Not yet.

"I think it was sort of resolved," I replied. "Remember when I said not all differences are gene-related? Well, shit happens, and well, shit happened."

"Yes, but that's exactly what I mean. The 'shit,' as you so delicately put it, is the part we never resolved."

Not now. Not yet.

I lay there in silence for a minute or two more, and he let me.

"I know," I said.

"Right then," he said, again. "When you're ready."

"Thanks."

"You fell asleep last night and I didn't want to wake you up," Matt said. "But I changed our Lufthansa flights to this morning. We should get going, soon."

I was sitting in the departure lounge at Domodedovo Airport waiting to board our flight, while Matt was standing up, talking to his office on his cellphone. They had a big important meeting with a venture capitalist coming up and it was hard to get ready when Matthew was in Moscow. It was a good thing we were heading back to London.

I emailed Wendy Weaver to report on our progress and that I'd obviously been dreaming of Gabriel again, though I had no memory of it this time. It was my second email to her since leaving Ottawa. I let her know that I was essentially "inside-out" with Matt, which felt good, but that I hadn't yet introduced him to Gabriel. She'd strongly suggested in her response to my first email that I bring Matthew into the tent as soon as I felt I could. That was my plan, too. But not now. Not yet.

I had actually mustered the courage to FaceTime Abby. I left Matt to his phone call and found a relatively isolated corner of the lounge. I stuck in my earbuds, hit her number in the FaceTime sidebar on my iPad, but it just rang and rang. She didn't pick up. That's when I realized if it was 11:30 a.m. Moscow time, it was 3:30 a.m. in Ottawa. Oops. Sorry, Abby. So instead, I typed out a hasty update email about our failed trip to Yaroslavl and Dimitri's subsequent revelation about Alexei Bugayev. That was the first time it hit me. I finished my Abby email and hit Send. Then I returned to my seat next to Matt, who was finally off his call to the office. They were about to call our flight.

"Matthew, I think I may have been named after Alexei Bugayev," I said. "My birth certificate simply says Alex, not Alexander."

"Hmmm," he replied.

"They couldn't give me the formal name, Alexei, as that would be too strong a link to a KGB agent operating in Canada."

"And they couldn't bring themselves to go with Alexander, so they just shortened it to 'Alex,'" Matt said.

"Wild," I said. "I don't know why it didn't occur to me before now."

"So just to summarize what we now know, for the forty-seventh time since last night," Matt began. "Alexei Bugayev, a left-handed member of the 1972 Soviet National Hockey Team, who made the trip to Canada for the big series, joined the KGB in the midst of his less-than-distinguished hockey career, largely due to his gift for languages. When he finished playing hockey, he assumed official roles in Soviet embassies in Washington and Ottawa as a cover for doing whatever KGB agents do in foreign lands. Eventually he worked at the embassy in Ottawa in late 1989 – and we have the documentary evidence to prove that – and so he was probably still in Ottawa in early 1990 for the big moment of our conception. Finally, you could easily throw a cricket ball from his office to the very restaurant where our mother worked during the same period."

"Right. Adding to that, we've already eliminated every other possible left-handed Soviet hockey playing candidate," I replied. "Then, when we were born at the end of 1990, I was given the name Alex . . . just Alex."

"That is one big community of coincidences all lined up next to each other."

"Except they aren't coincidences, are they?" I asked.

"No, they certainly are not," concluded Matt.

I lifted my iPad and pulled up the 1972 hockey card photo of Alexei Bugayev. We just looked at it for a moment – the eyes, the nose, the chin, the hairline, the earlobes, the mouth. Perhaps we were seeing what we wanted to see. I concede that possibility. But, still, there was enough to satisfy the eye of at least the mild skeptic.

"First, you found me," Matt whispered, as he gently bounced a fist off my thigh. "Now, we've found him."

Three minutes later, we boarded our flight back to London.

I dozed off a few times during the flight and hoped I hadn't been talking in my sleep again. We landed and sailed through customs. Twenty-five minutes after we'd touched down, Matt and I were in a taxi. Courtesy of the three-hour time change, it was still mid-afternoon when the cab turned onto Wild's Rents and pulled up in front of Matt's condo.

"Please wait for us, we're just dropping off our bags and will be right back down," Matt said as we piled out of the car and grabbed our luggage. We dumped our bags just inside the door of Matt's unit and were back in the cab about two minutes later.

The Hollywood line, "Russian Embassy and step on it!" shimmered in my mind. But I left it there.

"Russian Embassy, in Kensington Palace Gardens, please," Matt said, and we were off again.

"Should we call or just show up?" I asked.

"On the off chance he's there, I'm not sure alerting him is wise, given the twenty-five-year effort he's made to stay out of our lives," Matt replied.

It was about 4:15 when the taxi parked in front of the old two-storey stone building. We'd been there to get our visas a couple of weeks before. I wondered if our father had been there at the same time.

One of the two young women seated behind glass at a reception station just inside smiled when we pushed through the doors and stood before her. Well, Matt stood before her, and I stood behind Matt. Strangely, there appeared to be no one else ahead of us seeking the services of the Russian Embassy. Our lucky day.

"Can I help you?" she said with just the slightest hint of a Russian accent.

"Yes, thank you," Matt said, stepping up and assuming his role. "We're here to see Alexei Bugayev, if we may."

"Do you have an appointment arranged with Mr. Bugayev?"

"Ah no. It's kind of a surprise, a rather big surprise," Matt replied. "We haven't seen him for a very long time and hoped to see him again, today."

"I see. Could you give me your names, please?"

Matt looked at me. We didn't really have any choice. Providing false names to the Russian Embassy didn't seem like a particularly good idea.

"I'm Matthew Paterson and this is Alex MacAskill," Matt said.

"Citizenship?" she asked.

"British for me, and Canadian for him," Matt replied.

She looked puzzled.

"Are you two not related?"

No, I've never seen this man before in my life.

"Um, distantly," Matt said with a smile.

"If you two could please sit down over there," she said, pointing to a couch against the wall of the foyer. "I will determine if Mr. Bugayev is available to see you."

She opened a door at the back of the reception station and walked out into the hallway. She slipped the wrong way through the X-ray scanner staffed by two large Russian security guards direct from central casting, and escorted us to the couch. She stood there until we both sat down.

"I do not know how long this will take, so, please, be comfortable here," she said before heading back through the scanner and disappearing up the staircase.

I was too keyed up to sit, so as soon as she was out of sight, I stood up and paced around the open foyer.

Five minutes later, the phone on the security guards' desk rang. The bigger of the two uniformed guards – and they were both big – answered the phone. He had that classic heavy Brezhnev mono-brow, and appeared rather well suited to his profession. Soon after lifting the receiver to his ear, his eyes met mine. I know that because I was watching him closely. I just had a faint sense that the call was about us. He spoke for a moment longer and then hung up the phone. He stood and walked over to me. His English was not as refined as the receptionist's.

"You must please to sit down," he scolded, waving his hand towards the couch where Matt sat. "This area is secure area. Please to sit down."

Well, when you put it that way, so friendly and all.

I said nothing, but quickly made my way back to the couch. Matt and I sat there not saying anything, just waiting. About half an hour later, the phone at the security station rang again. The same big guard answered, and right on cue, lifted his eyes to Matt and me on the couch. He spoke in Russian for a moment and then hung up. He leaned over to his only slightly less gargantuan colleague and whispered to him, covering his mouth with his hand, presumably to prevent us from lip-reading – a wise precautionary measure given how often I resort to lip-reading Russian. I really didn't think this was a positive development but Matt didn't seem troubled at all. When I looked at him, he offered nothing more than a smile and a nod.

The two guards stood and approached us. Matt and I stood up.

"Finally, I guess we're in," Matt said as we turned to face the advancing guards.

"Wishful thinking, but I don't think so," I replied.

Brezhnev mono-brow gripped my arm and his colleague gripped Matt's.

"Hey!" Matt said.

"Sorry, but you must to leave now immediately," he said, guiding Matt towards the door.

I was similarly led, but I held my tongue, which is my standard approach in most public situations, anyway.

"Wait. What's going on? What have we done?" Matt asked in the strained tone of someone being manhandled by a gigantic Russian security guard.

"We do not know, but do not do it again," the guard said. "If you apply for visa again, it will not to be approved."

By this time, they had muscled us both out the front door of the embassy, released us, and pointed for us to leave the property. They watched from the steps as Matt and I, affecting the appearance of a normal departure, walked down the stone path to the street. We walked quickly, trying not to run.

"What the hell was that?" Matt said when we'd moved around the corner and out of sight of our two new Russian friends.

"Did you notice that the couch was directly in front of the security camera hanging from the ceiling?" I asked.

"No, but every embassy in the world has security cameras."

"Yes, but in our case, I think it means that our father knows who we are, and doesn't want to see us, wants nothing to do with us."

"Or he just didn't recognize us," Matt countered. "I mean, he hasn't seen us since our Kodak moment with him twenty-five years ago."

"I think he knows who we are."

Thirty minutes later we were back in the condo, crushed and confused.

"Well, it's not the end. It's just another setback," Matt said. "We've had a few since this started."

I don't know why I did it, but I pulled out my laptop and ran another search on the name Alexei Bugayev. I filtered for new results in the last twenty-four hours, just in case there was something new. As luck would have it when all seemed lost, there was one new entry we'd never seen. I saw it had been found by a Google search bot about forty-five minutes earlier. I clicked on it.

It was a landing page promoting a conference hosted by the Confederation of British Industry at the Savoy Hotel in London. A bright red banner at the top of the page pulsed to draw viewers' attention.

> Please Note This Conference Programme Change:
>
> Due to unavoidable travel plans, tomorrow's conference luncheon talk by the Russian ambassador, entitled "Future Trends in Russian–U.K. Trade," will now be delivered by Alexei Bugayev, senior economist at the Russian Embassy. Tickets are still available.

"Okay, we have another chance." I turned the computer so Matt could see the screen.

"It's tomorrow at the Savoy," Matt said. "We're going."

And it was done. Matt reserved two tickets online, this time using a false name and the company credit card. So we had another chance. We spent the evening trying not to be discouraged. We had a few beers and ordered in food. That night I told Matt I felt like an Italian. But he seemed puzzled by the expression. Apparently, the line only works when you're hankering for Indian food.

Matt had to spend some time on Innovatengage work. The presentation to the venture capitalist was important and needed his focus. He spent a good part of the evening on the phone with colleagues who were still at the office.

"If you have to go to the office, don't worry about me," I said. "I can wallow just as easily here on my own."

"Thanks, but I just don't feel like going in right now. They've got it under control."

So we wallowed together until we both turned in early. I didn't sleep much and I doubt Matt did either.

The room at the Savoy held four hundred people for lunch and they all seemed to be streaming in at the same time. Most wore standard-issue conference lanyards to identify themselves. Those without, like Matt and me, were obviously just attending the luncheon. Behind the lectern at the front, a Russian flag stood alongside the Union Jack. We arrived early and snagged two seats at a table at the front and just to the right of the lectern. Maybe this was provocative on our part, but we wanted to leave nothing to chance. We wanted to see him up close, and more importantly, we wanted him to see us so we could easily gauge his reaction.

We reserved our seats by tipping our two chairs up to lean them forward against the table. This seemed to be the standard method others in the room had adopted. We then retreated to a crowded back corner of the room in an attempt to keep a low profile. Eventually the room settled and everyone took their seats. We waited until a well-dressed man approached the front and stepped up on the riser. Lunch would be served after the speech so that Alexei Bugayev, our father, would not have to contend with the clatter of cutlery during his remarks.

"Wait. Not yet," Matt said, touching my elbow as we held our ground at the back.

"Good afternoon, ladies and gentlemen," the man at the lectern said. "Welcome to the fourteenth annual conference of the Confederation of British Industry. I'm your luncheon host, David Ward, managing director of the CBI. Beyond the informative sessions you've already attended this morning and those you will attend this afternoon and over the course of the next two days, I'm very pleased that we've managed to secure interesting and diverse luncheon speakers as well. Today, speaking on the important topic 'Trends in Russian–U.K. trade,' we were to be hearing from the Russian ambassador himself. Regrettably, his return to London from Moscow has been unavoidably delayed. But, in his stead, we are fortunate to have with us the senior economist at the Russian Embassy, Mr. Alexei Bugayev. He is a long-serving diplomat who has previously held economic positions in Washington, Ottawa, Geneva, and Paris, before being posted to London five years ago. Ladies and gentlemen, please join me in welcoming Mr. Alexei Bugayev."

"Now," Matt whispered.

We picked our way through the tables as quickly as we could and arrived at our seats just as our father arrived at the podium from the other side of the room. He placed a file folder of speaking notes on the lectern and looked out at the crowd. He was smiling. Then the movement down to his left as Matt and I belatedly took our seats seemed to catch his eye. He turned his head only slightly and looked directly at us. Then he flinched, as if he were being electrocuted. I don't mean by lightning or the electric chair, but perhaps by a half-dead car battery. It may not have been obvious to the rest of the audience, but the impact of our proximal presence was certainly clear to Matt and me. His reaction unequivocally solved yesterday's mystery of whether he actually knew who we were. But how he could have recognized us so readily after such a long separation was just one of a raft of new questions.

"He knows us!" Matt whispered.

Either that, or he recoiled because we're shockingly ugly, repulsive, and grotesque.

"I know," I whispered back.

I thought he was quite a handsome man who had aged well. I noted with some satisfaction that he still had a full and flowing head of longish hair that was neatly parted and styled. As if out of respect for his host country, he wore a subtle tweed suit, complete with vest, white shirt, and a quiet patterned tie. The facial similarities both Matt and I perceived in the old hockey card photo were still discernible at his current age of sixty-four. The KGB notwithstanding, to me, he looked gentle and kind.

Alexei Bugayev quickly recovered his composure. As is standard luncheon speech protocol, most in the crowd had been clapping and had not even noticed him falter in the instant. He studiously avoided further eye contact with the front table to his left, keeping his eyes trained on the middle of the room well behind us. Head down, he took a moment to gather himself and arrange his papers, as the audience applause died away. Then he donned rimless glasses, took a deep breath, and lifted his eyes.

"Ladies and gentlemen, I thank you for your warm welcome. I bring greetings from the ambassador along with his deep regret that he cannot be with you today. I can tell you, he was very much looking forward to this event, but alas, in the world of international diplomacy, ambassadors are not always in control of their time. I, too, regret that he is not here, as it means that I am."

He paused to let a chuckle run through the assembled.

"Not that I am ungrateful for this opportunity, but luncheon speeches are not generally part of my repertoire, and our ambassador is very good at the microphone. So please bear with me and I will do my best."

I loved the sound of his voice. His command of English vocabulary and syntax was perfect, with just a slight, almost charming, Slavic lilt. Despite our presence, he spoke with intelligence, humour, confidence, and even something that approached charisma leavened with modesty. He seemed to be addressing the middle and back of the room. He never once let his eyes linger on any of the front tables, let alone ours.

A very odd sensation descended on me. Later, Matt admitted to feeling the same thing. We both knew, without reservation, that we were in the presence of our father. It wasn't rooted in logic and reason, but was something far more visceral, primal, and personal. I felt calm and – I don't know how else to put it – complete. It was strange, new, and comforting at the same time.

I really didn't listen to what he said, but to how he said it. I wasn't focused on content but on his presence, his tone, style, and mannerisms, the way he moved his hands, the way he held his head, even the way he turned the pages of his notes, and held the edge of the lectern. I studied him, utterly secure in who he was to me.

He spoke for about thirty minutes, though even without really taking in exactly what he was saying, it passed quickly for me. Then all too soon, it was winding down.

"I realize that I am the single obstacle remaining to serving what I know will be a lovely lunch here at the famed Savoy. On behalf of the ambassador, I reiterate my gratitude for this opportunity to be with you to discuss the very bright future of trade between our two nations. I regret that I cannot stay for lunch. I am rushing off now to another important engagement but wish you well and hope that our paths will cross again. Thank you."

The audience applauded enthusiastically as our father snatched his folder of speaking notes, stepped quickly off the risers, and very nearly trotted to the nearest exit. It was the door to the kitchen, but he strode through it as if he knew exactly where he was going. A few seconds later, two other well-dressed men, clearly caught off guard by our father's unorthodox and hasty escape, headed through the door, too.

"Come on," Matt said, leaping to his feet and rushing towards the same kitchen door.

I was one step behind. A few people behind me expressed mild consternation that we were plowing through the crowd quite so aggressively.

"Sorry," I heard Matt say to no one in particular. "Pardon me."

I said nothing but kept moving.

The kitchen staff weren't quite prepared for yet two more luncheon guests to come barrelling through their work space, but one of them kindly pointed a wooden spoon down a small aisle to the left. I assumed it was sign language for "they went that way."

"Thanks," Matt said as he hustled down the corridor.

I followed just behind. The aisle took a ninety-degree turn to the right. When we came around the corner, we just caught a glimpse of our father ducking out an emergency exit. Behind him, his two colleagues, who now looked less like luncheon guests and more like Mafia muscle, stood and faced us, blocking the exit.

"Back this way," I said to Matt. "We passed another door."

"Right."

We dashed back the other way but were in the grips of the two men before we could even get near the other fire door.

It was obvious from their strength and the skilled way they immobilized us while still propelling us, that we were in no position to escape or overpower them. They guided us right back out into the still crowded luncheon ballroom. I almost tripped a server carrying a large oval tray precariously bearing ten plates of chicken. She managed to stay upright, though her tray did not. Despite the cushy carpet, it made a very impressive noise when it hit the floor. Our assailants were smiling and nodding to people as they "escorted" us through the room and out into the lobby of the Savoy. I wish there was more we could have done but we were completely helpless in their hands. In hindsight, we could have screamed or shouted, but neither Matt nor I wanted to draw any more attention to ourselves than we already had.

We wound up out on the sidewalk, still held by Russian embassy "officials."

"Do not bother Mr. Bugayev, again," one said. "Is this clear?"

"But . . . um . . . we know him. He knows us," Matt said. "We just want to talk to him."

"He does not want to talk to you. Do not try to contact him again. That is a last warning. Mr. Bugayev has no wish to see you yesterday at the embassy, today, or tomorrow. He is very busy and has no time for this. If you persist even more, we will speak to the authorities."

I wasn't sure who these "authorities" were, but I wasn't about to ask him.

They then waved down a taxi that pulled up beside us. They shoved us into the cab, slammed the door, and banged on the roof. The driver seemed to know what that meant and eased back into traffic.

"Where to, gents?"

"I suppose we're headed to Wild's Rents and Decima, near the Tower Bridge, please," Matt said.

"I don't know what to say. I don't know what to think," Matt said as we reclined on his couch, quite tuckered out from our little luncheon encounter with our father.

"He knows who we are. That much is certain," I replied. "I can't imagine not wanting to see my own twin sons after being apart for twenty-five years. His reaction makes no sense."

"I don't think we're in possession of the full story. I mean, how did he recognize us? His reaction to seeing us strongly suggests he's seen us before, maybe more than once. Something else is going on here."

"Maybe, but he's certainly made it clear he doesn't want anything to do with us. And that little kick in the gut feels just awesome, really quite lovely."

"Hang on," said Matt. "Let's not jump to any conclusions, just yet, though I know it looks a little bleak right now. I think we really do have to get him alone, somehow."

"Well, we could stake out the Russian Embassy and then tail him to his home," I suggested. "You know, try to reach him when he's not officially on Russian territory flanked by burly Bratislav and muscle-head Mikhail."

"It might be a little difficult to shadow him without being discovered given that we have no idea what we're doing and he seems quite able to recognize us," Matt said.

"Ah, but I'm an actor, remember? If I take the time to prepare, I think I could walk right up to him and he wouldn't know I'm his own flesh and blood. That's what actors do."

"I dare say," Matt conceded. "I just didn't think we'd have to wear a false nose and glasses to get close to our own father."

We ordered in Chinese food. By the time it arrived, it was after 8:00 p.m. We were both starving as our premature exit from the Savoy meant we'd missed our lunch. We ate pretty much in silence sitting at either end of the couch. I felt a little better after gorging on sweet and sour chicken, but we were both still depressed. Dramatic emotional swings take their toll. There was the ride up to euphoria when we beat the odds and found our father, thanks to a twenty-five-year-old photo of a partial tattoo. Then the unexpected plummet to despair when he rejected us, twice.

I took half an hour after dinner to craft an email update to Wendy Weaver. Then I texted a slightly more detailed version of the day's developments to Abby. In true Abby fashion, she replied expressing her deep sympathies for Matt and me, and then calling our father an asshole.

"Listen, whenever I'm depressed, I watch *Chariots of Fire*, my favourite film of all time," Matt said, grabbing the DVD from the bookcase.

"No shit!" I replied. "I love that film."

"Of course you do," Matt said. "You would."

"I'm serious. Ben Cross is amazing in it. Such brooding intensity."

"Would you like to see it now?" Matt asked.

"Well, it's a little late to start it, but what the hell?"

"It's never too late for *Chariots*."

He grabbed two beers from the fridge, joined me back on the couch, and hit Play.

It really was a great movie. Matt and I took turns reciting lines we'd both committed to memory. Matt took on the Eric Liddell role, while I handled Harold Abrahams. Eventually, it seemed we both nodded off. It was after midnight when I woke up. The DVD was playing some of the bonus features, and Matt was sound asleep at the far end of the couch. Something had wakened me, but I didn't know what. Then I heard it again, a very soft knock on the front door. I nudged Matt.

"What?" Matt said, as he sat up. He looked at the TV. "What did I miss?"

"What you just missed was a knock on the door."

Just then a third, slightly louder knock sounded. With a quizzical look on his face, Matt hoisted himself from the couch and headed to the front hall. I was not far behind. He swung open the door. There, alone, stood Alexei Bugayev.

PART FOUR

Above me, there was silence. They were gone.

CHAPTER 12

Alexei snatched a final glance down the corridor behind him, stepped inside quickly, and closed the door. He stood there facing us, his hands trembling, his eyes glistening.

"My boys. My sons," he said. "I'm so sorry for all of this, for everything."

He turned to Matt and embraced him.

"Matthew."

Matt seemed in shock, but eventually reciprocated. They rocked a little bit. I heard our father sniffle once before he let go of Matt and turned to me.

"Alexei," he whispered, as he locked me in a bear hug. I was ready and hugged back.

"I prayed this moment might come someday, somehow," he said. "But I couldn't see what could possibly bring about this moment. But you figured it out. You somehow cracked the code."

We let go of one another and stepped back. Our father was wearing jeans and a short-sleeved dark blue patterned shirt, untucked.

We just stood there, three points of a triangle, looking at each other.

My customary reticence vanished in the moment. I don't know why, or maybe I do. But it was gone. I hadn't uttered a single word to the man standing before me yet I felt completely "inside-out" with him.

"So it's true," I said. "It's all true. We did figure it out. You really are our father."

He smiled through tears and nodded.

"How did you do it? How did you find me?" he asked.

I don't know how Matt and I choreographed what happened next. We exchanged no signals, no knowing glances. We each just played our part on instinct. At the same moment, we both raised our right arms, extended our index fingers, and pointed to his left forearm, perfectly synchronized. Our father looked puzzled until Matt then grasped our father's left wrist and turned it to reveal the tattoo. We'd only ever seen part of it. But now we examined the entire tattoo.

He still looked puzzled. I walked over to the kitchen table, pulled the one and a half photos from the envelope, and returned to the rest of my family. (I like how that sounds.) I handed the whole photo to our father and pointed to the obscured tattoo, while Matt fished his half photo from his wallet to line up with my half. Alexei Bugayev was shaking his head, his eyes moving from the complete photo in his hand to the bisected photo in mine. He handed the photograph to Matt and then reached for his own wallet. I knew what was coming. So did Matt. We looked at each other and smiled.

Our father opened his wallet and reached into a slot in almost precisely the same way I'd watched Matt do the same thing a week earlier. He withdrew a photo folded in half. We knew. We were both still smiling and nodding. Father opened the photo and held it next to the other photos Matt and I held. We took the photos over to the coffee table and laid them edge to edge, finally reunited after nearly a quarter of a century. I couldn't help myself. I reached over and flipped our father's photo, as certain about what I'd find as I was about anything. And there it was.

3/3 *December 24, 1990*

"But the tattoo is not enough to explain it. You cannot even see it in the photo," Alexei Bugayev said. "I still don't understand how you found me, or how you found each other."

Matt looked at me.

"If we tell you the story, will you then tell us your side, why you left, how you could do that, where you've been, and why you were so eager to avoid seeing us?" I asked.

He winced and nodded.

"Yes, of course, of course," he replied. "You are both owed so much more than the story, but it is at least where I will start. It is not a simple story, but you deserve to hear it. Now that you have brought us together, now that you know the truth, this long and painful masquerade can finally end."

I spent about twenty minutes recounting my search for Matt. From my mother's passing to finding the photo in the safety deposit box, from using the software I'd helped bring to market to flying to London and facing Matthew for the very first time. I spared no details. Then I turned to Matthew and he took over. He spent the next half hour describing in considerable detail how we'd enlarged the tattoo, figured out the hockey sticks and puck, and the Cyrillic spelling of Canada. He talked about our meeting with Pavel Dubov in London and with Dimitri Dubanovsky in Moscow. He relayed the story of our ill-fated trip to Yaroslavl to meet Yuri Golov. Matt spent some time on our final encounter with Dimitri when we first heard the name Alexei Bugayev. He skimmed over the last couple of days and our visits to the Russian Embassy and the Savoy. After all, our father was well aware of those events.

"I'm so impressed with your ingenuity and dedication," our father said. "I was convinced you'd never find me. And that when the time was right, I would find you."

"Okay, I can't wait any longer," I said. "Please, tell us what we need to know."

"I've waited a long time for this moment," he said. "I've thought a lot about what I'd say if I ever got the opportunity. So let me start with three truths that I want you to keep in mind as I tell you this tale. These are very important.

"First of all, I loved your mother very much and never stopped loving her, not when she was ill and not after she died. It sounds cliché, but she was my one and only true love. Until I met her, I'd always rejected that romantic notion. But I have never loved anyone more, and will never love anyone more. I cannot imagine being with someone else. Second, I know you think I completely deserted you, abandoned you. But I didn't, at least not entirely. You couldn't see me, but I was there. Finally, number three. Your mother loved you both so much, whatever decision was made twenty-five years ago. You have suffered for it, she suffered for it, and I have suffered for it, but I have always tried to do the right thing for both of you and your mother. Okay, will you try to remember these things when I am speaking?"

Matt and I nodded, as if on cue.

"Okay, now the story I never ever thought I'd be telling my two sons, my twin boys."

He made us sit down on the couch and he stood up in front of us, to present his case. My heart was pounding.

"This story starts long before your mother and I met. I was first approached by the KGB when I was still a teenager, playing hockey. I had no brothers and sisters. That made it easier for them. Also, for some reason, I was good with languages. I did several radio interviews for my team at a big tournament in Finland. I knew a little of three different languages back then, I mean other than Russian, Czech, and Ukrainian, which I already knew. I learned by listening to a short-wave radio in my bedroom. I found a few books too that helped. Language skills are very important to the KGB. A man talked to me in Helsinki, and then again at other tournaments in Grenoble and Oslo. And that is how it all started. I wasn't a member of the KGB then. I was just in the recruitment process that usually takes many years. At the time, I did not even know it was the KGB.

"At eighteen, I joined the army and went to university in Moscow to study languages and economics. Most soldiers do not get to go to university, but my superior officers permitted it and I was readily accepted. I know now that my path was carefully planned by the KGB. I was encouraged to continue to play hockey, though my interest in it was fading. And to be honest, I was not that good. I was a goalie, but you already know that. But playing for the national team meant international travel. And playing for the national team is a good cover for a covert officer of the KGB.

"I earned my degree in the spring of 1972. After we lost the famous Canada–USSR series that summer, my hockey career officially ended and I started working for the KGB in foreign capitals, always at our embassy.

"Now you may think that I was involved in lots of undercover work, spying, assassinations, and espionage. But I was no James Bond. I was an economist who could speak six different languages. I was no spy in the Hollywood sense of the word. I spent my days gathering and analyzing important economic and industrial data about the country I was stationed in and neighbouring nations. My work was much more focused on making the Russian economy stronger. But I admit, others I knew were real spies. All major countries were doing it. I felt I was serving my country. I still serve my country.

"In the summer of 1987, we had a bit of diplomatic trouble with the U.S. government that was never made public. Anyway, as part of a negotiated agreement, I, and several colleagues at the Soviet Embassy in Washington, were recalled to Moscow. I spent only a month back in Russia before I was posted to the Soviet Embassy in Ottawa. I loved Canada. The Ottawa climate is very much like Moscow, except it's colder in the winter than it is at home. And that is very cold. But I could watch the second-best hockey in the world."

He looked at me when he said it. I just raised my eyebrows and tilted my head.

"Okay, maybe hockey is played the best in Canada. Anyway, I liked my job in the embassy. I was promoted to economic advisor and learned a lot from economists in the federal government and at Carleton University. But most importantly to us, I met Lee MacAskill. The embassy is just around the corner from a cooking school, the Cordon Bleu school. They have a restaurant there called Signatures. We would go to lunch there often. It was not expensive and it was very good quality. Also, the first time I went, this wonderful, kind, beautiful woman showed me to my table. I didn't ask her name that first day, but I knew I would come back.

"The next week I learned her name. The week after that I ate alone at Signatures every day. On Friday, I asked her out. She said no. The next week I again ate alone at Signatures every day and asked her out on Friday. This time, she said yes. And we fell in love. I was already in love before she said yes, but she fell, too, in time. We were inseparable. And just so you know, we had to be so very, very careful. I was still technically part of the KGB. Having a brief affair, not to mention a full relationship, with a Canadian woman represented the classic and powerful security risk. I was breaking every rule in the KGB handbook unless the relationship was cultivated as part of an assignment. And it was not. This was no 'honey trap,' as we used to call it. This was just love. Pure, simple, wonderful, love. So we had to be extremely cautious. I would have been sent back to Moscow on a leaky fishing boat and then on to Siberia if our relationship had ever been discovered. So it was a love that could never be acknowledged."

"That must have been very difficult and dangerous," Matt said.

"Both. But it was worth it. Then you were born on December 23, 1990, a day I'll never forget. Such beautiful baby boys."

He stopped and looked at the ceiling for a moment. It seemed almost as if he were gathering himself, preparing himself, steeling himself. Then he lowered his eyes to ours again.

"I blame myself for what happened though your mother carried almost overpowering guilt with her always," he said slowly.

"Two days after you were born, I had to leave the country suddenly on an unexpected assignment in . . . well, in another part of the world – I cannot say where. It was supposed to take only three days, but it didn't go as planned and it was twenty-eight terrible days until I could get back to Ottawa. When I was gone, your mother descended into what was recorded in her hospital chart as severe postpartum depression, what is called postnatal depression in the U.K. Feeding the two of you was very difficult and painful. She was not herself and went down deep into what she told me later felt like a dark emotional and psychological hole. She said she couldn't think straight, and was so tired all the time she could barely move. And worst of all, she said she had grave, overwhelming doubts about being able to care for you."

He stopped talking and stared at the floor for a time before lifting his head to look back at us.

"A social worker and a nun from the hospital chaplain's office were involved. They spent a lot of time with Lee. As far as they knew she was a single mother on her own in a very difficult position, marked by clinical depression, severe postnatal depression. I don't know how much they influenced her, but seven days after you were born, and five days after I had to leave Ottawa, she signed the papers to put you both up for adoption."

"Both of us?" Matt and I said in unison.

"Yes. But your mother seemed to emerge from her depressed state about a week later. She said it was like a fog lifting. She fought to get you both back. But by that time, Matt, you had already been adopted. For some reason, your adoptive parents were never told you had a twin."

He paused to let it all sink in a little. Then he started again.

"I knew none of this until I returned two weeks later. By that time, Alex, you were back with your mother, but Matt, you were already with your new family and beyond our reach. Lee cried almost all the time. I tried to fix matters, but there was nothing that could be done. I'm so sorry."

"Wouldn't the authorities have needed your permission as well to put us up for adoption?" I asked.

"Normally, yes. But no father was registered for your births. Your mother refused to expose me. In the eyes of the hospital and adoption officials, she was a single mother with full authority. So you can see why I blame myself. We both carried this secret – this shame – that you now both know."

I remember Mom crying a lot in my childhood. Whenever I would ask her why she was sad, she'd always say they were tears of joy that I was her son. The crying jags decreased over the years, but never fully stopped.

I realized Alexei was still talking.

"I was with her as often as I could in that first year, but there were strange things going on in Moscow and across the Soviet Union. Two days after you turned one, the Soviet Union collapsed. By that time, Matthew was already in London with his new parents, who were both wonderful people. But in early January, I was sent back to Moscow."

"I would have thought the collapse of the Soviet Union would have finally freed you up to stay in Canada without any fears," I said.

"That is an understandable view, but it was not true. It was far from true. It was a very dangerous time to be in the KGB. I cannot tell you much about it, but I was doing my best and doing what I thought was best for the two of you and your mother. In the nineties, when the KGB became the Russian SVR, or Foreign Intelligence Service, I was posted to the Russian embassies in Paris, Geneva, and then here in London. My days of espionage for the Soviet Union, not that I ever really had many, were over. My interest in economics gave me the ability to move past my KGB history and climb through the diplomatic service. I suspect I'll never be an ambassador, but I'm happy as a senior economist."

Then it dawned on me. The Cayman Islands.

"Just to go back a bit, you've been sending my mother $5,000 every month, right? You've been supporting her, supporting us, all this time," I said.

"From the very beginning and still now," he replied. "It is nothing, and far less than I wish I could have done as your father."

"How did you get the money?" I asked.

"I saved it. I've always earned reasonable money at my embassy posts. It was and is my responsibility. And I have only modest and simple needs."

I just nodded.

"I have watched you both grow up and have tried to look out for you," he said.

"How have you looked out for us?" Matt asked. "We've only just met."

"Again, that is a reasonable and understandable view. But it is not the complete story."

"And how did you even find me and my new parents?"

"Matthew, I was a KGB officer. Let's just say there was not much information, confidential or not, I could not obtain," he explained. "I was so deeply sorry when that drunk killed your parents. That was such a tragedy. I have watched vodka do terrible things to Russia. Drinking and driving is a plague in my country. When that murderous driver escaped justice, I, and some former KGB operatives who owed me favours, managed to persuade a particular police officer to 'rediscover' the evidence that he had unlawfully suppressed. When the charges were reinstated and the trial called, it was because of that new evidence."

"That was you?" Matt asked, sitting up. "You made that happen?"

"I wish I could have done more. You were alone. I felt helpless," Alexei said. "And when you bought this wonderful apartment, did you ever wonder why that higher competing offer was mysteriously withdrawn at the last moment so you could get this place?"

"My agent just said something about another unit in a different building coming available so he pulled out of this one," Matt said.

"That is true to a point. Let's leave it that I 'encouraged' the other bidder to see the wisdom of buying the unit he ended up buying."

Matt cast his eyes around his beautiful condo.

"Thank, you, um, Father, if I can call you that. I had no idea."

"How could you know? It was not for you to know."

Our father then came over to my end of the couch and perched on the arm. He put his hand on my arm.

"Alex, my namesake, I am so sorry about Gabriel. I did all I could. We managed to get many sites to pull it down in the beginning, but it became too big. We couldn't keep up. And now it is impossible. I'm also deeply sorry things did not work out with Cyndy, all because of Gabriel. The whole affair was monstrous and horrific. But it was a long time ago now. It is over, long over."

I looked over at Matt. He was leaning forward, focused on Alexei and me. I looked back at our father, who still had his hand resting on my arm. I was still processing what he'd just said. Eventually, I regained my faculties and turned my eyes to the floor.

"It's not over for me," I said, almost in a whisper. "The stats grow every day. New people know about Gabriel every day. Yes, it was ten years ago, but it's not over for me."

"Okay, okay. Yes, you are correct. But when was the last time someone recognized you from Gabriel?"

I thought for a moment.

"It was 2009," I replied.

"Yes. Six years," Father said.

"Right, so what I'm doing seems to be working," I insisted.

"Or it's over and the world has forgotten," he said. "Even if you are right, at what cost? At the cost of . . ." Our father paused. "At the cost of . . . you?"

"So we're back to Gabriel. When can I get in on the family secret?" Matt asked.

"You have not told him?" our father asked.

"Not yet," I admitted. "Soon."

"Your brother should know about Gabriel. He can help."

I nodded.

"I still cannot believe I am here," our father said, standing up from the arm of the couch. "But it is late and I should really go. I will not keep you longer, but here is something of great importance that you must accept. Even now, all these years later, it still cannot yet be publicly known that you are my sons. Even though I have not really been in the field for many years, the perceived security threat of this secret remains and could be used against me and even against you. This is why I had to avoid you at the embassy and at the Savoy. It is also why I took such strong measures to ensure my visit here tonight was undetected. I am no longer a spy, but until I'm no longer at the embassy, until I retire next year, we must keep this among us alone. I'm sorry it must be this way, but it is important. Do you understand?"

Matt and I nodded.

"If it were known, I would be recalled to Moscow immediately."

"When can we see each other again?" Matt asked. "There's still so much to talk about."

"It will depend on several factors, but now that we are together, there is no chance of us not meeting often. It will just take some planning. I will contact you. Perhaps I will bring food and we can cook a late dinner together some night . . . a family dinner." He choked up a bit on that final phrase and raised his hand to his mouth.

As he was about to open the door to leave, an image flashed into my mind.

"Wait, you were at the cemetery that day in Ottawa, weren't you?" I asked, though it was no longer really a question.

He looked at me. His face softened.

"Not until after the burial. I had to wait until everyone had left, to pay my respects."

"I saw you, standing by the grave, afterwards, as we drove by. If only I'd known who you were."

He teared up again.

"I visited your mother shortly before she died while you were at work and the wonderful Malaya was shopping. There's never been anyone else for me, and there never will be," he said before turning to Matthew. "I'm so sorry you never knew her. You would have liked her. You would have loved her."

He hugged us both and slipped out the door.

"Do you believe the man who just left is our father?" Matt asked.

"There's no doubt left in my mind."

"Nor in mine," Matt concurred. "Alex?"

"I know, Matt. I promise. Tomorrow morning. First thing. I promise."

I held it all together until I closed my bedroom door. In the dark, in my bed, I cried for my mother. It wasn't my idea. I hadn't scheduled it. The grief came rushing out of me in waves and shudders. It was almost what I thought convulsions might feel like. I buried my face in my pillow to dampen the sound, but still Matt may have heard. But he left me. I cried for what Mom carried with her for so long. I cried for the enforced separation from the man she clearly loved. I cried for my father's guilt. I cried for Matt never knowing Mom. I cried because she was gone. I don't really know how long it went on. But I was utterly drained when it passed. I could hardly lift my head. But I actually felt better, calmer, grounded, ready. That surprised me. Maybe it shouldn't have.

When Matt walked into the kitchen at 6:45 the next morning, I was already there waiting for him at the table. I got up to pour him a cup of coffee and drop the bread in the toaster. I also lowered two eggs into the already boiling water. He kept his peace and sat down to start on his coffee, a medication he seemed to need that morning after our very late night. I'd slept straight through until about five and then had tossed and turned and thought about what I was about to do, the story I was about to share. I spent time mapping out how I would tell Matt my tale. I'd only ever told one other person this story. Of course my mother already knew. She'd been in the auditorium when it had all gone down. But it took me nearly two months of therapy sessions before I could bring myself to tell Wendy Weaver. Now it was Matt's turn.

Five minutes later, I'd extracted the eggs, popped and buttered the toast, and set the plate in front of Matt so he'd have something to do while I was prattling on for the foreseeable future. I stayed on my feet. I wanted to be able to move around while regaling him with my sad little tale.

"Brilliant," he said. "Thanks."

"So, do you have an hour right now so we can get this over with?" I asked. "I don't want to start if you have to leave in the middle."

"Alex, for Gabriel, the time is yours. I need to get to the office at some point this morning to get ready for the big pitch, but the floor is yours, now. I know this is important to you, so it's important to me. Plus, our father already seems to know all about it, so I'm feeling a little left out."

"You won't be for long," I replied. I took a deep breath. "Okay, I'm going to tell you more about Gabriel than you probably want to know. It derailed me in high school and is still getting in my way today. Even telling you, my own brother, is hard. I've only ever told one other person and I remember how hard that was. So just let me talk. Don't interrupt. Just let me get through it all, and then you can ask all your questions. Okay?"

"Of course. I promise," Matt replied. "But just to help me with context, is this why there are two Alexes?"

"What do you mean?"

"Well, you know, with me, when we're by ourselves, you're open, funny, articulate, thoughtful, etc. But when others are around, particularly strangers, 'open Alex' morphs into 'closed Alex.' You lower your head and your eyes, you take two steps back, and you clam up. When you have no choice but to speak, you respond in one-word answers, never say anything more than the bare minimum, and you never make eye contact. Voila, the two Alexes."

"Oh, those two Alexes," I replied. "Then yes, the second Alex, taciturn, anxious, timid, and shy, is brought to you by the good folks at Gabriel."

"Right then. Let's hear it."

"It was 2005. I was almost fifteen and in grade ten. I was having fun. I was doing well in school. I had at least some friends. I loved the Drama Society and auditioned for all sorts of roles, landing some great ones. I really loved acting. I wasn't different, ugly, geeky, fat, bald, skinny, or effeminate. I didn't dress weirdly. I didn't have bad breath. I didn't have severe acne. I didn't have a speech impediment. I wasn't a teachers' pet. In other words, I exhibited none of the traditional markers that might attract bullies. Except perhaps for being in the Drama Society. On the other hand, there were lots of other guys who were into acting but who did not earn the attention of jackasses and jerks.

"Anyway, for some inexplicable reason, two assholes, one a big burly loud jock and the other a smaller sycophantic follower, latched on to me and wouldn't let go. It was as if they'd chosen me because I wasn't their usual fare. Perhaps they'd wanted to change things up that year. Who knows?

"I recognize what I just described sounds like the set-up for a young adult novel, but stay with me."

Matt just nodded.

"I auditioned for and won the role of the angel Gabriel in the big Christmas pageant, a major production staged every year. The production values and staging techniques in the show were to be bigger, better, and more sophisticated than ever. And I was excited about it. I was pumped.

"For my big scene, when I appear to Mary to tell her about the surprise son she's going to bear, I was to be lowered on a cable from the ceiling lighting bay in the school auditorium in my spectacular gold sparkly costume complete with real feathered wings, to give my speech hanging some seventy feet above Mary and the audience."

Matt jumped to his feet.

"Good God, Alex, you're . . ."

"Stop, Matt!" I said, raising my hands. "You promised. Let me finish, and then you can jump to your feet. Sit."

He held his hands up in surrender and lowered himself back to his chair.

"So when the stagehand lowers me into position, three spotlights are unleashed and there I am, seemingly hovering in mid-air, as angels do. I deliver my lines. Mary understandably quakes. Then the spots are doused and the stagehand cranks me back up into the ceiling lighting bay. He pulls me up through the hatch in the floor of the little room, and then I'd wait there until the second half of the show. Then I'd do it all again, this time imparting angelic wisdom to some poor, innocent, ill-informed shepherds, who were watching their flocks by night. I confess, I was nervous at the first few rehearsals, dangling so high off the ground. But I got used to it, and eventually it was very cool to be hanging in mid-air.

"On show night, I arrived early, as I always did, and grabbed a Coke in the cafeteria. I was sitting with a few other members of the cast talking about the show, when Jackson and Cam, my friendly neighbourhood bullies, sauntered in. Jackson sat down on one side of me, and Cam on the other. My cast mates made a hasty retreat. Jackson grabbed my Coke and took a swig while Cam put me in a gentle headlock. With my head pressed against Cam's rib cage, I tried to reason with them." I recalled the scene as if it were yesterday.

> "Come on guys, can we please do this some other time, I've got a show to do and I really can't be late," I said, trying not to antagonize them unduly.
>
> "Sure," Jackson said, sliding the Coke back along the table to me. "That sounds reasonable. Let him go, Cam-man, he's got a show. Have some respect."

Matt was nodding his head. I suspect he was moving ahead in the story without me.

"Anyway, then they both just stood up and walked out of the cafeteria," I continued. "So as you can imagine, I was quite surprised and relieved by their withdrawal. It wasn't really in character for them to back off so easily and quickly. But I thought nothing of it. After tangling with Jackson and Cam, I downed the rest of my Coke. But it didn't taste quite so refreshing. In fact, it quite literally left a bad taste in my mouth. But I had no time to worry about that, so I grabbed my costume and sat through the director's last-minute instructions and pre-show inspirational talk. Twenty minutes or so later, I headed up the backstage staircase to the ceiling lighting bay where I would change into my costume.

"Now here's where it gets embarrassing to talk about, though not nearly as humiliating as it was to endure that day. But, even though I was excited to be in this production, my excitement had never quite manifested itself as it did right then as I climbed the backstage stairs."

"I know, Alex. I know. I've seen the video," Matt said. "You were, um, somewhat aroused, physically."

"Right. Delicately put, and absolutely true," I replied. "And, of course, you know. You and millions of others."

"God, I'm sorry," Matt said.

"Anyway, I knew from personal experience that it was not unusual for fifteen-year-old boys to, as you say, be aroused, at almost any time, day or night. I remember that well at that age. But this was different. This was more intense, severe, almost painful in its, um, rigidity, if I'm making myself clear."

Matt nodded.

"I didn't think much of it at the time, but I do remember being thankful I had long flowing gold lamé robes to cloak my, um, excitement. Anyway, when I reached my perch in the ceiling bay, the stagehand who was supposed to help me into my harness and make sure my wings were configured properly was nowhere to be seen. Again, I thought little of it and simply started changing into my gym shorts, which I wore beneath my costume. I heard footsteps on the catwalk outside but it wasn't the stagehand who showed up, it was Jackson and Cam. They each carried a video camera, which I thought was a little odd. Just to cut to the chase, as I suspect you've figured out the outcome already, they stripped me naked, buckled me into the harness to which my wings were already attached, duct-taped my wrists behind my back, then folded my legs up behind me and duct-taped my ankles to my wrists. If you can picture it, my body was fully arched with my wrists and ankles secured behind my back. In my arched position, you can imagine what part of my naked body was soon going to be most prominent in the eyes of the audience below.

"My extreme condition was not lost on Jackson. I remember his every word."

> "Fuckin' brilliant. That stuff worked. It really fuckin' worked," Jackson said, pointing to my crotch. Cam seemed shocked, even mortified, by what he saw. But not Jackson. "Wow, MacAskill, you seem really, *really excited* to be in this show. Your excitement is totally and completely *hard* . . . to miss," Jackson said.

"Finally, they very securely duct-taped my mouth closed. The only sound I could make would have you looking for pigeons in the area. I'd struggled a bit, but Jackson was a huge, mean defensive lineman, and probably could have pulled off the stunt even without Cam's extra hands. I was horrified and humiliated, but also resigned, if that makes any sense at all.

"The auditorium lights dimmed and I heard the familiar soundtrack to the show's opening number booming from below. I'm quite uncomfortable in the full arch position, but can do absolutely nothing about it. Cam is following the script for the show. This was the kind of well-planned operation I'd seen watching old reruns of *The A-Team*."

> "Okay, it's coming up. I guess you can open the hatch," Cam said.
>
> "Roger that," Jackson said, as he pushed open the floor hatch right next to me. "Let's get him up so we can get him down."
>
> "Right," Cam said as he grabbed the winch control and hit the Up button.

"I felt myself lifted up so I was arched face down, horizontal to the ground. They positioned me over the opening. All I could see below was darkness. I could feel a draft wafting up through the hatch."

> "I see my little blue pill is still doing its thing to your thing. Now remember, MacAskill, if you're still like that in six hours, call a doctor. Okay, down the hatch you go," Jackson said, as I shook my head vigorously, making more pigeon sounds. "Don't fight it, MacAskill, this is going to be epic."

"Then, just before Cam hit the Down button, Jackson tapped his index finger hard on my forehead."

> "I know even you're not dumb enough to say anything about this to anyone," he sneered.

"Then Cam lowered me down through the hatch while Jackson made sure my wings made it through the opening. And then I was alone, in the darkness, being lowered to my position, seventy feet above the audience. I stopped at one point, before I should have, and for an instant, I wondered if they'd come to their senses and the prank was over, that maybe they'd just winch me back up before the spots flared. But no. An instant later, my slow descent continued. I stopped again after what felt like the usual time span. I visualized the little piece of red tape on the steel cable that marked the perfect hanging length. Having rehearsed this show so often, the music told me exactly where we were in the script. At the appointed moment, I look down and towards the back of the auditorium. Right on cue, a spotlight found Mary walking down the centre aisle. Then she stopped, as did her light. I could sense rather than see the audience below me.

"I remember preparing myself for that moment, for what was about to happen. I decided to stay stock-still. I thought thrashing around would just make it worse. Three, two, one, and the three large spots from three different angles pierced the darkened auditorium and pierced me. I could feel the heat. And there I was, alone, illuminated, every part of my body flexed and curved, save one. A human dowsing stick. You could say I put the arch in ARCHangel, as it was soon to be known by pretty well the entire world.

"A few seconds elapsed while the eyes of the audience grew accustomed to the bright light but they never grew accustomed to what it illuminated. I heard a collective gasp from below and snickering from above. It took a little time for the audience to comprehend exactly what they were looking at. When I say 'a little time,' I really mean about four beats. Then all hell broke loose."

Even though he'd already figured it out, Matt was mesmerized by the story. Both his hands kind of cupped his forehead in an expression of what I thought looked like horror and sympathy. He just kept his eyes on mine. He was about to say something, but my raised hand silenced him.

"People shouted, 'Kill the lights! Kill the lights!' but it took another sixty-eight seconds for two of the three spots to shut down. I was counting. By that time, Jackson and Cam had fled through a skylight in the lighting bay to the school roof. Their last act was locking the door of the lighting bay from the inside, where one could find the controls for the largest of the three spotlights, still focused perfectly on my winged, arched, medically aroused, and naked body.

"I hung there in the spotlight for the next twenty minutes until the janitor finally forced the door of the ceiling lighting bay. You would have thought the audience might have been asked to leave the auditorium. But they weren't. Finally, the third spot was extinguished, throwing me into welcome darkness, at least for a few seconds until some bright bulb brought up the house lights. I remember thinking, please winch me back up. Please crank me up. Nope. Less than a minute later, the janitor only seemed to find the Down button. I was being lowered directly into the outstretched waiting hands of far too many parents eager to help in my rescue.

"When I was still about thirty feet off the ground, I locked eyes with those of a young woman about my age who was wearing a bright red dress. I didn't recognize her. She never took her eyes off mine. There was a look of pure unadulterated empathy on her face as she covered her mouth with one hand. She looked outraged that I was enduring this personal and all too public humiliation. I'd never experienced such a personal connection with anyone before or since, and just through deep and penetrating eye contact. In the years since, I've searched for her but have always come up empty. I'm still searching.

"Eventually, I felt many outstretched hands supporting me and one large coat covering me as I finally made it to the auditorium floor. They unharnessed me, cut the duct tape, releasing my appendages – I mean the ones that were previously trussed up like a Christmas turkey. I distinctly remember someone saying, 'It's all right, son, it's over now.' The only thought running through my mind was 'It's not over. It's only just started.'

"Exactly ninety-three minutes later, the full nine-minute video of my naked descent, crisp and clear, perfectly edited, lit, and shot, appeared on what was then a small, brand-new fledgling online platform called YouTube. At least four cameras were used to create the video, which meant that Jackson and Cam had accomplices in the audience. The video was shared and reposted across the Internet hundreds of thousands of times over the years, usually with a blurry patch censoring my 'excitement' at being exposed in quite so dramatic a fashion. But the blurry patch never quite did its job and there were plenty of versions of the video without the modesty blur. So it's true. I was, and still am, the star of the very first viral video, the gift that keeps on giving year after year."

I looked at Matt, who appeared to be in the throes of early onset PTSD.

"Okay, you can now finish the sentence you started in the early stages of my story," I said.

"ARCHangel. Holy shite, you are ARCHangel. I can't believe it," he said, shaking his head in apparent disbelief. "My own twin brother, ARCHangel!"

"Yes. I know. Believe me, I know."

Matt grabbed his iPad from the table and Googled "Top ten viral videos of all time." Every listing on the first page of Google results had ARCHangel at number one. It was not just the first viral video in the earliest days of YouTube, it was the video with the most all-time views, and we're talking in the hundreds of millions.

"So what happened, I mean to you, afterwards?" Matt asked.

"My life changed in that YouTube instant. Everyone, and I mean, everyone, knew who I was. I grew my hair long as fast as I could grow it. I changed schools on four separate occasions, but each time, it was only a matter of days before my true ARCHangel identity spread through each new school faster than virulent mononucleosis."

"Wasn't there an investigation?" he asked.

"The school did what it could, but when I remained silent and refused to cooperate, their hands were tied," I explained.

"So what did you do?"

"I stopped going and finished high school by correspondence. I never left our apartment. I withdrew, physically, emotionally, socially, and psychologically. Within four weeks of what my mom and I came to call 'Gabriel,' I broke up with Cyndy Stirling even though she was loving and supportive and would have stood by me through it all. But I just couldn't handle it. I kept right on growing my hair and started wearing big ball caps so I didn't look quite so much like the poor sap in the video. I looked more like a Metallica roadie. I just went to ground. I kept my eyes and head down through my software engineering degree. I barely said a word to classmates or professors, and I took every possible online course I could find. Then I somehow landed the job at Facetech – how I survived the interview I'll never know – and

I've been toiling in a cubicle farm ever since, still with my head down and my mouth closed."

"But it's been nearly ten years, a whole decade," Matt said.

"For you, it's a long time ago," I tried to explain. "For me, it's always right there. Always."

"But I know the real Alex MacAskill. I've met him and seen him in action. He's in there somewhere," Matt said, leaning across the table and tapping my temple. "We just have to bring him out."

"We have a term for that," I explained. "My therapist calls it 'going inside-out.' You know, taking the inside-my-head voice and letting it loose on the outside world."

"Right, inside-out," he said. "By the way, what were the names of those two assholes who visited this tragedy on my twin brother?"

"Why?"

"I just want to know their names in case I ever bump into one of them, with my car."

"Jackson Trent and Cam Forster."

"Do you know where they are now?" Matt asked.

"I think Cam actually went to law school, but I could be wrong. And I heard Jackson worked for a long time as a groundskeeper at the Royal Ottawa Golf Club. But that was quite a while ago. I have no idea where they are now. Frankly, I don't care."

"I wonder if they have any idea what they've done," Matt said.

Then he stood up, came around the table, and gave me a hug. He pulled back a bit so he could look me in the eye at close range while his hands still gripped my upper arms.

"What a horrific ordeal. Thank you for telling me. I know that wasn't easy. I cannot imagine what it's been like for you all these years – and if anyone can imagine it, I should be able to," he said. "So I think I'm starting to get it now. I think I can at least begin to understand."

You're about to drop a "but" on me, aren't you?

"But let me just make two observations," Matt continued.

Careful.

"Firstly, you are obviously a very strong person. That's even clearer to me, now. From personal experience, I've come to believe that resilience is something we really only discover when confronting adversity. You, my brother, are blessed with a shitload of resilience. And secondly, last time I checked, 2005 was ten long years ago. You told our father it's been six years since someone even recognized you as ARCHangel. And remember, in the ten years since the video was posted, I cannot recall a single soul ever asking me about Gabriel, ever, and I do cut quite a striking resemblance to the star in that video. Not once has it happened. So it makes me wonder if you might be too close to the situation to examine it dispassionately. And that maybe you're still fighting a battle that actually ended quite a few years ago. At least it's food for thought."

I know. I know. I'm trying.

"I know" was all I could muster.

"Those two bastards probably have no idea what they've done," Matt said.

Two spotlights finally doused, then the third. Good.
House lights up. Not good.

CHAPTER 13

With no familial mysteries left to solve, Matt could finally focus on getting ready for his big pitch to a high-flying American venture capitalist. And I figured I'd better help him as much as I could. After all, I felt responsible for pulling him off his top business priority that week. On the other hand, I did think Matt's reasons for ignoring his day job were quite compelling. As in, "Gee, I'm sorry I've been away from the office a bit lately, but I've just reunited not only with the identical twin brother I never knew I had, but also with my birth father who I haven't seen since I was one day old. But I'm back now. Any messages?"

Neither of us mentioned our father, though his silent presence shared our minds alongside the more pressing task ahead. I wondered when we'd see him again. We had so much lost time to recover.

"This is not your standard, run-of-the-mill VC pitch," Matt said as he swivelled a full 360 degrees in his desk chair.

We were alone in his office as he rotated. CTO Isabella Prochillo, and Matt's CFO, whose name I can never seem to remember, Michael something-or-other, had just left after working with us for an hour and a half on the presentation.

"You keep saying that," I replied. "Even though I have no idea what a standard VC pitch looks like, why is this one so different?"

"Stephanie Mosel is, well, she's . . . mercurial. She's famous for backing winners. She's made an astonishing amount of money on some amazing outlier start-ups. But she's . . . er . . . different. She doesn't just immerse herself in the spreadsheets. She's a bigger thinker than that. Unlike most investors, she judges opportunities on a broader range of factors, some of them not particularly business-focused. You never really know what's going to catch her eye and push a deal past the finish line."

"So you've met her before?" I asked.

"No. Never. She doesn't hang out with the other angel/VC crowd on the playground. And she doesn't mingle much at the big meet-ups and conferences. You don't reach out to her. She finds you."

"How did you land an audience with her?" I asked.

"As I said, she found us. She called, said she'd been watching us for quite a while and heard we were ready for a new investment round. So she invited me to present to her."

"Who else is going?" I asked. "Isabella and Michael what's-his-name?"

"No. Remember, she's mercurial. We've got only one opportunity. She lays down the rules for the pitch, and we follow them, or it's a very short meeting," Matt explained. "I'll be the only one presenting and she'll be the only one listening. No slides. No support. No sound and light show. Just spoken words. That's how she does it. One on one. Principal to principal, with a platform demo only at the end."

"Why set it up that way?"

"I don't know for certain, but I suspect she's not just assessing the big idea, the market potential, and the business plan. She's also judging the entrepreneur – as a person, I mean. What and how I choose to present is a reflection of how I think and what I believe is important. She's judging me, and my brain. She wants to kick *my* tires, not just the company's."

"That actually sounds quite sensible," I replied. "Except for the part where she never gets to meet the talented people you've gathered around you to take this idea from paper to practice. That, too, is an important part of your leadership, isn't it?"

"Mercurial. It's her call."

"So let's hear the pitch again," I suggested. "The more often you practise it, the better you'll be able to deliver it without it sounding so rehearsed. That was my preferred acting method. Practise it so many times that it seems spontaneous, as paradoxical as that sounds."

"Right."

Matt rolled his chair back up to his desk to refer to his notes.

"Try it standing, and without your notes," I suggested. "I think you'll be much more impressive that way, and you can sustain eye contact for the whole show."

"Well, I don't want her to think she's being stalked."

"She won't. I imagine she's used to being the centre of attention," I replied.

I went and stood next to Matt's chair. I waited until he stood. Then I sat down.

"Okay, I'm Stephanie."

"I'm not sure I can do the whole thing off the cuff," Matt said.

"That's the point. It's not off the cuff. You've carefully planned the pitch. It has a logical, even at times, dramatic, flow. Now you want to deliver it like it's emerging fully formed, on the spot, from your steel-trap mind," I said. "Hey, that didn't sound half-bad."

"Of course, when I stumble, it's a very short trip from steel trap to claptrap," he said. "Is this the approach you use in the boardroom?"

"What are you, nuts?" I replied. "I don't do boardrooms. I don't do presentations. I do cubicles. I write code. Good code, great code, beautiful, elegant code. But I don't present. I'm talking to you right now from my earlier life as a once-avid actor interested in the art of the compelling performance – and by compelling performance, I am not referring to my most famous moment in theatre. That was quite unrehearsed."

"Well, I suppose it's worth a shot," Matt said.

He scanned his notes a final time and then handed them to me for safekeeping. He walked in front of his desk and turned to face me.

"Thanks so much, Stephanie, for giving me some of your valuable time. I know that time is money, and I hope in thirty minutes you'll agree it was time and money well spent," he opened. "In short, we have found a way to scale the all-important process of public and stakeholder engagement so that it reaches a much larger audience, yields more meaningful insights, and often breaks down the adversarial dynamic inherent in the search for social licence."

Nice opening, bro.

And away he went.

Matt, his team, and I had worked hard on what was supposed to be a thirty-minute pitch. There were three major sections. He opened with a story about arrogant executives of a Canadian oil company who clearly didn't understand the concept of social licence. They mistook regulatory approval granted on a pipeline project as a green light to put shovels in the ground. The spontaneous, immediate, and well-organized backlash from residents, environmentalists, naturalists, First Nations groups, climate change activists, and scientists stopped the company in its tracks, despite their having all the necessary government approvals to proceed. The pipeline has still not been built.

Matt didn't miss a beat as he told the story. It was obviously not the first time he'd recounted this tale. It took about six minutes for this opening piece.

The second section was all about how organizations, institutions, companies, and governments had typically engaged their stakeholders to earn social licence. He covered the waterfront from open houses to public meetings, stakeholder outreach to direct mail, telephone surveys to print advertising, you name it. He then inventoried the problems with these outdated techniques. Chief among them, of course, was the inability to reach, and sustain engagement with, average citizens in numbers large enough to be meaningful. It was easy to connect with passionate stakeholders, but what you heard from them was predictable. But what about the masses? You can't truly earn social licence without them.

He flagged a few times, stumbled over his words, but always found his feet. I could see him making mental notes as he navigated this section of the presentation. It took Matt about nine minutes.

Finally, he went in for the kill with the passionate and potent story of how his Innovatengage digital solution helped earn social licence for a major mass transit system expansion in Manchester. It seemed to me that Matt was at his most compelling when talking about the potential of his digital platform to alter the public consultation landscape, to give private- and public-sector organizations a powerful new way to engage, educate, track, and learn from the audiences most important to them. I was quite moved by the strong feelings he brought to his words. It was clearly not his first rodeo.

Matt used up the remaining fifteen minutes with this final portion, but it seemed only about ten. It was a strong close.

I stayed with Matt for a good chunk of what remained in the day, practising and offering advice from the acting side of my experience. My software engineering expertise was not a factor in our preparations. In particular, I think I was able to help almost at the micro, line-by-line, level. I suggested strategic pauses to enhance the impact of certain pay-off phrases. We worked on his energy, inflection, gesturing, pacing, body language, movement, and eye contact. We practised key lines over and over until they were all right there, perfectly cued up in his brain. Occasionally, when he didn't quite understand a point I was trying to make, I would step in and demonstrate, doing my best impression of Matt, accent and all. By this stage, I felt utterly calm and relaxed with him.

We punched up several lines and practised various delivery styles until we found the most persuasive yet authentic approach. We spent quite a bit of time on tempo. Matt was a good student. While he had never acted, even in school productions, I suspected he would have had great success on the stage. By the end of the afternoon, I knew his lines as well as he did.

We returned to the condo, ate pizza on the deck, and then, just to lock it in, we practised some more. He was really nailing it by late in the evening. He'd never before prepared in this way for any kind of a pitch. But by the time we went to bed, I knew he saw the value in it and felt confident. As he said goodnight, he looked drained to me, and I noticed his voice growing hoarse. No surprise.

By then, we were both exhausted. I Googled Stephanie Mosel and read a bit about her. I don't even remember falling asleep, but I do remember being roused from my coma in the morning – at least I assumed it was the morning. I rolled onto my back and looked into my own eyes. Two beats later I realized Matt was hovering over me. His eyes were wide and he was waving his hands around a bit. He kept pointing to his mouth and throat. It was nice of him not to make any noise. I wasn't yet ready for noise. It was then I noticed he was wrapped in a blanket, shivering even while beads of sweat glistened on his forehead.

"Matt?" I said, still emerging from deep sleep. "Is that you?"

He offered a facial expression that clearly communicated something sarcastic, like "No, it's Margaret Thatcher. Who do you think it is?"

"What's wrong?" I asked.

He then leaned down to my ear, which was a little weird. He whispered so quietly, I almost missed it.

"Voice. Gone. Completely."

The air pushed from his lungs when he whispered was easier to discern than his words.

He stood up, still shivering. I was awake then. He had dark circles beneath his eyes. His hair was spiky with perspiration. He looked terrible, miserable. He looked sick. Perhaps he was sick.

I know. Yes, you're right, I am a quick study. Always have been.

"Are you all right? What's wrong?"

He leaned down again to my ear where I assume more words were issued, but I could understand none of them.

"Sorry?" I replied. "Can you say it again, maybe out loud this time?"

He was midway through a very dramatic eye roll when he turned on his heel and disappeared from my room. I heard him rooting about in the kitchen. Drawers were opened and shut. About thirty seconds later he returned, a small notepad and pen in his hand. He wavered a bit as he approached my bed, even staggered. I moved over in time for him to collapse on the edge of my bed. He was still shivering. For the first time, I noticed him sniffling and snorting – though those two verbs hardly do his performance justice – and running his index finger back and forth beneath his nostrils. I handed him a Kleenex from the box on my nightstand. He nodded and blew his nose. A beach towel might have handled the onslaught, but one Kleenex did not. I handed him the box. He nodded again.

When he seemed to have his nasal effluvia under control, he piled his overly taxed Kleenexes in a mound on the bed beside him, picked up his pad and pen, and started writing. He dashed off a few lines before thrusting the pad in front of me.

> *Woke up at 2:30. Headache, sore throat, congestion, hot flashes then chills, no voice,* NO VOICE! NONE, *feel like shite, am in deep shite*

"What, you can't make a sound? Total laryngitis?"

Matt opened his mouth and tried to say something. His lips were moving. He pushed air across his vocal cords but all I heard was a slight whoosh.

"Don't force it," I suggested, knowing less than nothing about laryngitis. "Try a very gentle whisper."

I leaned in close to him.

"I'm fucked," Matt said so softly I almost missed it. The hard *k* sound helped.

He was holding his iPhone and looking at it periodically. Sweat was pouring down his face. He shucked off the blanket and sat there in a pair of boxer shorts. It was surreal. His body was a precise copy of mine. For some reason, I thought of Dolly the cloned sheep. Matt was shaking his head. He picked up the pad and pen again and started writing.

S Mosel is going to phone to confirm. Soon.

"Can't you just email her and tell her what's happening?"

Matt shook his head with such violence chiropractors in the area surely felt a disturbance in the Force.

He opened his mouth and I leaned in again.

"No, no, no. It's her protocol. I must take the call or we're done," he whispered with my ear nearly pressed up against his lips. I know. I'm sure it looked odd. But even then, I barely understood him.

"When is the call?" I asked.

Matt shook his head, shivered once, and turned his phone towards me. It said 7:59.

"She's not calling at eight, is she?" I asked. "She can't be calling at eight."

Matt nodded, looked at his phone again, then using the fingers of his right hand, started counting down, five, four, three, two, one.

The digital display clicked over to 8:00 and I held my breath. Nothing. A few seconds passed. Nothing. I began to breathe again when his phone rang with a very loud Led Zeppelin ring tone. I almost knocked the lamp off the nightstand.

Matt was moving the index finger of his left hand toward the green button showing on the incoming call screen.

"You can't answer it!" I shouted. "You'll sound like a wheezing Hannibal Lecter, only more evil. You'll botch the deal."

By then we were on the second ring. He shook his head again and kept his finger poised over the button.

"You can't take it. I could barely understand you when my ear was practically inside your mouth."

I don't know what made me do it. I really don't. Perhaps love for my newfound brother? More likely a complete and precipitous suspension of rational thought.

I grabbed the phone from his hand. He made no move to take it back. The third ring had just finished and we were headed for the fourth. I closed my eyes, took two deep breaths, returned to the moment, and hit the green button.

"Matt Paterson," I said in my best Matt Paterson voice.

"Good morning, Matt. It's Stephanie Mosel, but you already knew that, didn't you?"

"Well, I know your protocol, so yes, I was expecting your call and I'm certainly glad you made it," I said.

"Well, I could be calling with bad news," she said.

"True, but I can't help but think you have others to make those calls for you," I replied.

I glanced at Matt and then looked away fast. His face was white and registering primal, sasquatch-sighting shock.

"Gold star for you, Mr. Paterson," she said. "We're a go for our meeting tomorrow. Four p.m. I have to be at Heathrow by six to catch a plane."

"And by plane, you really mean your own Gulfstream G280," I said.

"That's two gold stars, Mr. Paterson. I like an entrepreneur who does his homework," she replied with a little laugh. "We're wheels up at 6:45 so we'll have at least forty-five minutes together before I'll have to dash, so make them count."

"We'll be ready. Or rather, I'll be ready," I replied. "I'm hoping by 6:45 you won't just be wheels up, but cheque book out, as well."

"Ha! You can leave that part to me. See you tomorrow at the Four Seasons, Park Lane. You'll be met in the lobby and brought up to my suite."

"Thank you, Stephanie. I'll be there in the lobby on time. I'll be the one in the red sombrero."

"Ha! No need for the hat, though it would be an amusing sight. We know what you look like," she replied.

"Right then. And thanks again for the meeting," I said. "I know time is money, so whatever time we have together, I'll make sure it's time and money well spent."

"Until tomorrow, then," she said. "Goodbye."

"Goodbye."

I hit the red button to end the call and then collapsed on the bed. I heard Matt furiously scribbling on his pad. When I opened my eyes, he was holding his words in front of my face.

> *Bloody brilliant! How did you do that? I was listening to . . . myself!*

He then bent down and whispered something I couldn't hear or understand, though I did catch another hard *k* sound.

"Sorry?"

He leaned in even closer to my ear, like Mike Tyson on Evander Holyfield close, and whispered. "Fucking brilliant!" was all he said.

I just lay there, eyes closed, hyperventilating.

Matt tapped my leg. When I opened my eyes again, he pointed to the "How did you do that?" phrase on his pad. He then embellished his query by lifting up his shoulders and hands and shaking his head in disbelief, the perfect physical manifestation of "How did you do that?"

"Matt, that's what actors do. We act. We assume someone else's character. We impersonate people. I just impersonated you, a role for which I seem to be quite well-suited."

Matt then scrawled the word "SHY!" and turned the pad so I could see and pointed at my chest.

"Yes, I know. But that's a whole different thing," I tried to explain. "I'm shy. But you are not. So when I'm playing the role of Matt Paterson, I am not shy. I'm you. That's what it means to act."

He opened his mouth again, but I couldn't hear him. All I got was one syllable. I think it was a hard "k" sound, but I wasn't sure.

"Pardon?"

Matt leaned down to my ear yet again and whispered, "Fucking brilliant. You nailed it, er, you nailed me."

Matt, who really did look terrible, spent the day at the condo going over and over his pitch, but only in his mind. He didn't utter one word all day to save his voice for the big meeting the next day. I got a little deeper into my acting by performing those important lines in the pitch that I thought he could punch a little more. It was kind of nice always having the floor and never being interrupted. But Matt, I think impressed with my thespian prowess, listened intently and nodded as he heard my subtle key line delivery suggestions – a pause here, heightened eye contact there, lowering the volume and slowing the pacing for the big finish. My silent captive audience and I worked every line in the entire presentation for most of the day.

Calls from CTO Isabella and CFO Michael came in now and then as they monitored Matt's progress. I was convinced that by uttering not a word for the entire day, he'd be able to speak by nightfall. At least that's what Wikipedia's Laryngitis entry promised, the last word on the condition. We waited until about nine that evening to assess his progress. I stood before him as he opened his mouth.

Not a sound was heard beyond the faint rushing of air from his mouth.

"Did you just try to say something, or were you just practising opening your mouth for when you do try to say something?" I asked.

Matt looked crushed, which effectively answered my question. He tried for a few minutes and managed to croak out a few lines that sounded slightly less melodic than Linda Blair's possessed voice in *The Exorcist*.

"Wait," I said, holding up my hand. "That's enough. You'll make it worse. Well, it would be hard for it to be worse, but you won't improve it any by talking."

Matt flopped back on his bed, where he'd spent most of the day. He was not happy.

"Kit."

"Sorry?"

Matt motioned for me to lean down, so I did.

"We're fucked," he whispered, his breath tickling my ear.

"Not yet we're not. Can we not just postpone the meeting for a week?"

He shook his head and tried to speak.

"I know, I know," I cut in. "She's mercurial and has a protocol."

He nodded.

"Well, we've got nineteen hours till the meeting. I can't believe you won't have improved enough to make yourself understood by tomorrow afternoon."

I was wrong.

By eight the next morning, he reported his temperature as 103 degrees. He alternately huddled under his covers shivering and stood on his deck in next-to-nothing, sweating profusely. He felt and looked miserable. By noon he was worse and had still not produced a sound that even remotely resembled his voice, or any human's voice.

"You have to cancel," I said. "You can't do the meeting. Not today."

Matt shook his head for quite a long while. By this time, he was using an app on his iPad that turned his texting into a woman's monotone voice with an English accent. He typed for a few seconds and hit the Play button.

"No way. We cannot cancel," the woman's flat voice recited. "She makes the rules. We blow off this meeting and we blow off the investment. It's over."

"I know, I know," I replied.

Matt nodded. Then his expression changed. He looked up at the ceiling for a moment. He appeared to be deep in thought.

Uh-oh. No. And then he started nodding again and smiling and mouthing what I thought was the word "yes" though he produced no sound of his own. He typed and hit Play.

"I have an idea," his iPad proclaimed.

Shit. It was my own fault. I'd brought this on myself.

"No, you do not have an idea! You have no ideas! Do not go there," I jumped in. "Do not even think about making a plan to consider perhaps contemplating going there. Do not."

More typing. Play button.

"It's our one shot. It's the only way."

And we were off. The debate raged. I was somewhat put off arguing with an iPad that sounded vaguely like a supremely bored Helen Mirren. At a few heated points in our discussion, I found myself directing my counter-arguments towards the iPad. It was strange.

An hour later I was weakening and wavering. Two hours later I was actually considering it. Three hours later I was wearing Matt's clothes and a friend of his was cutting my hair, staring from Matt's head to mine and back again, her scissors flying.

Matt was right. In light of Stephanie Mosel's well-earned reputation, it was the only way to salvage at least a shot at securing her critical investment. I was well beyond nervous and anxious. I was scared, but if I wouldn't do this for Matt, my own twin brother, then who would I do it for? In the end, deep down, very deep down, I think it's possible I wanted to do it as much as I felt obligated to do it.

By noon, Matt's voice still showed no signs of returning any time soon. We made the final call and then spent the next two hours undertaking final preparations. That meant that Matt struggled to stay awake as his fever really took hold. He couldn't help himself. He'd be in the middle of explaining something to me and then he'd have to lay his head down and drift off to sleep for a few minutes. He'd wanted to bring Isabella and Michael over to help me prepare, but I demurred. I was much more comfortable alone with Matt.

When he was on his back and out of the play, I read several documents and articles he'd gathered for me that articulated his vision for the company and his ideas on social licence and digital public engagement. Then he'd rouse himself and we'd work through the pitch a few more times. Finally, we spent the last hour before I had to leave working on the questions he expected Stephanie Mosel to pose. With about thirty-five minutes until Isabella was to pick me up to drive me to the Four Seasons, I stood and presented to Matt one last time. Throughout my performance, he was smiling and nodding, and pumping his fist. I didn't think Stephanie would be responding the same way.

When Isabella buzzed up from the lobby, Matt stood and made a last-ditch attempt to use his voice. Nothing but air. I picked up my laptop for the platform demo as well as the aptly named leave-behind document I was supposed to, you know, leave behind with Stephanie. I was ready. Terrified but ready. Petrified but ready. Paralyzed but ready.

Matt hauled himself out of bed and put his hand on my shoulder as we walked to his front door. Then he faced me and gripped my upper arms in his hands. He opened his mouth, then closed it again. Finally, he just mouthed "Thank you." Then he hugged me and patted my back. I'm not sure if he noticed I was shaking.

The Four Seasons Park Lane was the most luxurious hotel I'd ever seen. Being in a completely different world seemed to help me shed my own persona and slip into Matt's. It was acting. I was an actor. It was time to act. When Isabella pulled up at the front entrance in her tiny Ford Fiesta, I left my nervous nauseated self in the front seat and stepped into the beautiful lobby as Matthew Paterson, confident, poised, articulate, and thoughtful entrepreneur. At least, that's what I kept telling myself. It was 3:55.

"Mr. Paterson," the well-dressed young American man said as he approached.

"Yes. You're Robert, aren't you?" I said, or rather, Matthew said.

"I am," he replied, looking surprised. "How did you know that?"

"Your photo is on the website."

"Right! Well, good to meet you. We can go right up, Stephanie is ready."

The word "suite" hardly did justice to the palatial luxury of the rooms mercurial investor Stephanie Mosel occupied on the top floor of the Four Seasons Park Lane. I'd never seen anything like it, though Matthew possibly had. So I kept my awe to myself.

"Matthew Paterson, I recognize you from all the YouTube videos I've been watching," she said. "I'm Stephanie Mosel."

She looked older than in her online photos. She was dressed in a simple but elegant blue suit, and her blondish hair looked as if it had been carefully coiffed moments earlier. For all I knew, it had been. I hadn't seen his departure, but Robert had disappeared.

I shook her hand and beamed, as Matthew would have.

"Stephanie, so nice to meet you in person, finally," I said. "And yes, I am Matt, and I'm currently reviewing in my mind all the YouTube videos you may have suffered through."

She laughed.

"Don't worry. If I'd seen anything amiss, you wouldn't be here now."

"Right. Of course," I replied.

"Sit down, please," she said, indicating one of two plush couches in front of the large but inactive fireplace.

I sank into the couch facing her and put my laptop and our leave-behind document on the glass-topped coffee table between us. I noticed with some interest, even surprise, that I was calm in my new body and breathing normally.

"Okay, then. I'm here to listen," Stephanie said. "We've got about forty-five minutes before I must dash, so let's make the most of the time we have. The floor is yours, Mr. Paterson."

I made the split-second decision not to stand to present. Given the couch-facing-couch configuration of the room, I thought it would have looked too contrived and artificial to stand and present across the coffee table. But I sat up, leaned forward, and made solid and sustained eye contact. Abby would have been proud of me.

"Thank you. I'm so grateful for this time," I began. "The roots and future of Innovatengage lie in a commodity that is now as critical to the global industrial economy as oil prices, wage levels, and interest rates. Securing social licence has become central to doing business on this continent and on yours. To drop directly to the bottom line, we have found a way to scale the all-important process of public and stakeholder engagement so that it reaches a much larger audience, yields more meaningful insights, and often breaks down the adversarial dynamic inherent in the search for social licence. Our online platform helps public- and private-sector organizations get on with building the major projects that will yield continued economic growth and higher investment returns. That is why I'm here, and, I imagine, it's why you invited me."

I stayed on track. I clung to the script like a shipwrecked sailor to an overturned lifeboat. I made it through all three sections of the pitch without stumbling. I seemed to remember all the nuances I'd suggested to Matt when he'd been rehearsing. I focused not just on the lines, but on my vocal inflection, tone, pacing, and volume as well. I knew how long my presentation was, so I didn't feel the need to rush. I often gestured with my hands, the way Matt did, animating my sentences. Again like Matt, but very much unlike me, I smiled through much of my monologue, but not so much that it was psycho-creepy. I held eye contact with Stephanie throughout, except when forecasting what the future might hold for Innovatengage and how the search for social licence might evolve in the coming years. Only then did I allow myself to look past her to some far-off point in the distance. Well, I thought it was a nice touch.

Because she'd given me the floor and had not interrupted, my presentation felt more like traditional theatre. I knew my character and my lines, so I inhabited the former and delivered the latter with complete focus. But when I finished and she started asking questions, it suddenly morphed into an improvisation exercise, though we'd worked hard on anticipating her concerns and queries. I felt my heart rate rise though I'm quite certain she didn't notice. My pulse quickened not so much out of anxiety, but more from excitement. I liked improv.

She'd ask me a question. I'd recognize it as one for which we'd prepared, or at least a version of one of them. I'd nod thoughtfully, look briefly upwards, apparently deep in cerebral machinations, and then I'd deliver an articulate response Matt and I had carefully crafted hours earlier. At one point, Robert materialized in the room, nodded at Stephanie, and then disappeared again.

"I know the answer to this question, but I want to hear your version," she said. "Why has social licence suddenly become such a big deal? Used to be when you got regulatory approval, you could bring in the backhoes and bulldozers and get going. What's happened?"

I paused, though I didn't need to.

"The idea is to minimize the investment required to build projects. Our experience is that the cost of managing and eventually overcoming well-organized opposition, dealing with work interruptions as activists handcuff themselves to equipment, pipelines, old growth trees, etc., is higher, much higher, than taking the time up front to understand and, to the extent possible, involve, accommodate, and assuage public, community, and stakeholder concerns. Give them a say in *how* you do what regulatory authorities have already said you *can* do. Beyond saving money, and often time, in the long run, it has the added benefit of being the right thing to do," I said.

I paused again before continuing.

"The term social licence may be new, but what it represents has been sought by builders for as long as we've been building railroads, power stations, and sewage treatment plants. We just have a more effective means now of securing it than we've ever had before."

"Understood. And that may be true right now, but what about five or ten years from now?"

"Well, Stephanie, given the climate change imperative, volatile oil prices, the move to solar, wind, and other power-generating options, I simply cannot foresee a time when cultivating social licence will not be a growth industry, year after year. And a premium is paid to those who are first in the market. We're ready to be first in with a much bigger footprint than we have now."

Not bad. We knew that one was coming. But of course, it's difficult to anticipate every question.

"Okay. I admit it. I'm very impressed. I like what I've seen from the research our due diligence already turned up. I like what I've heard from you today and I think your take on social licence is bang on," Stephanie said. "As you know, it's not uncommon for a group of angels or a VC to demand a thirty-five or even forty per cent stake to fund a start-up. If I proceed, I have no intention of demanding such a high level of share ownership in Innovatengage for my money. Why do you think I feel that way?"

Uh-oh. Hadn't planned for that one. Think. Think. I offered just the first faint traces of a smile as my mind raced. I turned back to her.

"You do not want such a high stake because you rightly fear that it would irrevocably change the character and culture of Innovatengage and how it actually feels to work there. And you don't want to tamper with a dynamic that has worked very well thus far."

She said nothing, but nodded through narrowed eyes and a growing grin.

Robert appeared again, this time looking a little more anxious. He pointed to his watch, though that gesture was completely unnecessary.

"We're done, Robert. Calm yourself," she said.

"I was hoping to show you a platform demo," I said.

"No need. I've been through the platform many times on the many engagements currently underway," she replied. "But I do have one final question before I must, quite literally, fly. When you and I spoke two days ago, I told you I'd be back in London next week and we'd have more time for this initial meeting then. But you proposed staying with a shorter, likely more rushed encounter today. Why?"

WTF? I hope I didn't look as bowled over as I felt. Reaching. Reaching.

"It's really quite simple. You're a very busy person with many balls in the air. Seven days is a very long time. Much can happen in a week. To me, the certainty of a short meeting today was preferable to the mere likelihood of a longer meeting next week. Besides, if today went well, I figured we might be meeting again next week anyway."

"Smart," she replied. "Why don't you ride with me to Heathrow and then my driver will get you back home afterwards?"

On the drive to the airport, we did not talk at all about Innovatengage, social licence, or whether she'd invest. She asked me a series of quite personal questions. I hadn't really expected that, but I figured being open and forthcoming was the right play. Plus, I was feeling a strong connection with her, and I think that made it easier to venture into the personal realm.

She already knew about the car crash that had claimed Matt's parents. But she was quite surprised when I told her about the recent reunion of two long-lost identical twin brothers. I figured there was no harm, and perhaps some benefit, to bringing her into that exclusive circle. She was blown away. I was blown away as I listened to myself recount an abbreviated version of the story. It really was quite extraordinary.

"Well, I'd really like to meet your brother some time," she said as we neared the private planes access gate at Heathrow.

"We can make that happen," I replied. "Alex is a little quieter than I but he's a brilliant coder, absolutely brilliant."

"Most coders I know are quiet," Stephanie replied. "And you really do look alike?"

"I'd say so, yes."

The car pulled right up to the sleek Gulfstream.

"Customs staff are already on board waiting for you," Robert said as he got out of the front seat.

"I enjoyed our meeting, Matthew," she said, offering her hand. "Thank you."

I shook her hand.

"I appreciate your time. I know it's precious," I said as I handed her our leave-behind document. "A little transatlantic reading. Strat plan, financials, and growth projections."

She took the package, got out of the car, and headed to the plane. Robert scurried just behind her.

Forty-five minutes later, the black Mercedes pulled up in front of Matt's building. I could barely contain myself. I was exhilarated. I was on fire. I was ready for my close-up, Mr. DeMille. Still in character, I thanked the driver and climbed out, affecting nonchalance as I entered the building. I stepped off the elevator and walked down the corridor to Matt's apartment. I was about to bust down the front door when I heard Matt inside talking on the phone. Yes, talking. It was muffled and I couldn't hear what he was saying, but it was clearly his voice. I walked in. He looked up with eyes wide and immediately coughed into the phone.

"Alex is back, I have to go," Matt said into the phone in a raspy, breathy voice. "I'll give you a full report as soon as I have it." He hung up, rushed over to me, and grabbed my upper arms.

"Well?" he croaked.

What the hell? Your voice is back.

"Your voice is back," I said.

He winced and rubbed his throat.

"Well, I wouldn't say it's back. Isabella could hardly understand me on the phone. But it's clearly making a valiant attempt," Matt whispered. "It just happened about forty minutes ago, out of the blue. Fever and voice."

I just looked at him.

"Come on, tell me what happened!" he said, pulling me into the living room. He lay back down on the couch and pulled the comforter from his bed on top of him.

I sat in the chair and gave him a full report. It took me about half an hour to tell the story. I tried to remember every detail.

"And she asked you to drive to Heathrow with her?"

I nodded.

"That is a very good sign. Brilliant! Just brilliant!"

His voice was nowhere near normal, but he could make himself understood. He sounded a little like Darth Vader after a three-day debate with the Rebels.

Matt was over the moon. He kept asking questions and then clapping his hands at the responses I'd given. The phone rang. On instinct, I reached for it as I had for the last couple of days while Matt had been mute.

"Hello," I said.

"Hello, is that Matt?" I froze when I heard the unmistakable but somewhat distant voice of Stephanie Mosel.

"Um, no, this is his brother, Alex," I managed. "Um, let me get Matt for you."

I pulled the phone away from my ear, closed my eyes, and breathed for a few seconds.

I looked at Matt. He shook his head then pointed at me. I lifted the phone back to my ear.

"Matt Paterson," I said.

PART FIVE

Below me, I locked onto the eyes of a girl about my age in a red dress. There were tears in her eyes as she stared up at me, her hand over her mouth.

CHAPTER 14

"It's Stephanie Mosel calling from somewhere over the Atlantic," she said.

"Hello, Stephanie. You sound like you're in the next room," I said. "Thanks again for seeing me this afternoon."

"I'm glad we could meet," she said. "I liked what I saw and heard. You've clearly thought through this next phase of your growth and identified the client sectors that will fuel it. Very comprehensive. The numbers in your plan look reasonable and realistic, though I do want you to stretch. My team in San Francisco is already digging in to your financials just to make sure nothing comes up strange. We may have some more questions for you in the coming days. But I really just wanted to let you know that you should be feeling good right about now, because I'm feeling good."

"Then I'm definitely feeling good," I replied.

"And you were wise to have stuck with today's meeting time even if it was a bit rushed," she said. "As it turns out, my schedule just changed for next week. Seems I won't even be in London. I'll be in New York. Do you think you might be able to come over to Manhattan next week? I'll be there until Wednesday. I'd like to move this along quickly so you can get ramped up on your growth plans."

"New York? Early next week?" I said, eyeing Matt. He nodded so vigorously it was a miracle he didn't pass out. "That sounds great to us, to me."

"Excellent," she replied. "We'll be in touch with the details. When you're here, we can decide on the investment and what our mutual obligations are."

"That sounds wonderful. Looking forward to seeing you next week," I replied. "I may have my brother in tow, if that's okay."

"If that's okay? I'd love to meet your other half, genetically speaking."

We closed out the conversation a few seconds later. I was actually eager to hang up so we could start celebrating. It sounded like the deal was as good as done. Matt, who seemed to be making a rapid recovery, had been bouncing up and down in front of me as I finished the call.

"Unbelievable!" he said after I ended the call. "You've got a real future playing me. So we're going to New York. That sounds like a positive development."

"I should really head back soon anyway, so I'll tag along to New York on my way back to Ottawa," I replied.

"Can't you stay a little longer? We've only just met and we've spent exactly no time with our father. We've got some catching up to do."

"I know, but I have a job and a cranky boss who wants me back in the cubicle farm yesterday so it's easier for my colleagues and me to continue saving her bacon," I explained. "But I'll be back and I hope you'll visit Ottawa some time, your ancestral home."

"It just doesn't seem right to have been separated for twenty-five years, reunite for a week or so, and then separate again. Why don't you stay and work at Innovatengage? I have some pull with the founder."

"Thanks, but I already have a job, and Ottawa is home," I replied. "By the way, why did you tell me today's meeting was our one and only shot with Stephanie? She told me she offered you a longer meeting next week when she expected to be back in London."

He looked a little taken aback. He didn't quite blanch, but the question clearly caught him off-guard.

"Well, um, I thought a bird in the hand was better than a maybe meeting next week," he said, his voice still hoarse. "Turns out I was right."

The whole family had dinner together that night at Matt's condo. Our father arrived well after dark, bearing wine and what we learned was a classic Russian dessert, chocolate-covered prunes. Who knew? We'd made the dinner arrangements after Dad, if I can call him that, texted us both on what he described as a safe phone. I know this will sound strange, exaggerated, and idealized, but after the first hour, it was almost as if we'd been together all our lives. There was a natural chemistry among us, a bond that ran deeper than friendship. Some of the common physical mannerisms Matt and I had seen in one another, we now saw in our father. If either of us harboured any doubt when he arrived that Alexei Bugayev was indeed our biological father, it was banished within an hour. We talked late into the night and covered a lot of ground.

"You must have been ready to assassinate Bobby Clarke when he broke Kharlamov's ankle in '72," I said. "I watched the video. It looked like Clarke was swinging an axe."

"I was not dressed for that game, but was up in the commentary box watching," our father said. "We were outraged. But then again, we had our own tricks in the corners, too. Subtler, but no less effective. I can tell you, my KGB colleagues had some other ideas for Mr. Clarke, but they were never pursued."

He was warm, thoughtful, engaging, and full of stories.

"You know, the KGB really wanted me to have my tattoo removed," he said. "It makes no sense for an agent to have such a distinguishing mark that can so easily identify you. It is like a brand. But '72 was a special time for us all, even if I didn't play. So I somehow always managed to avoid having it removed. Lucky for me. Lucky for us."

At one point, when he was telling us about his time in Ottawa working at the Soviet Embassy and courting our mother, his eyes welled up and he fell silent for a moment to regain his composure.

We had three more late-night dinners together, the last of which was the night before Matt and I were to fly to New York. That dinner carried on to well past midnight. By the end, I was not only inside-out with Matt, but with our father as well. It was 1:30 in the morning when I said goodbye to him. We both knew we'd see each other again and often. We just weren't exactly sure where and when. Alexei hugged me for a long time, his hand cradling the back of my head, perhaps as he had done on December 24, 1990. Then he slipped out the door, along the corridor, and down the stairwell.

The next morning, Matt and I were at Heathrow awaiting our flight to LaGuardia. Abby sent me a cranky text asking about developments. I apologized and replied that she should check her email inbox in ten minutes. I then typed a longish email bringing her up to date on all that had happened, which included a short version of reuniting with our father without referencing the whole KGB thing. I also told her I was coming home in a few days.

Two minutes after I'd hit Send, she replied:

Alex,
It's friggin' amazing that you found your brother AND your father. I'm so happy for you. But I'm glad you're coming home. Some serious shit is going down around here and I think you need to be here for it. Don't bother asking what's happening. I have no idea, but something is definitely up. See you when you're back.

Abby xo

I emailed Simone to tell her I'd be back in the office three days hence. I was about to close down my computer as our flight was about to be called, but an email had just arrived in my inbox. It was yet another missive from Laura Park. I almost ignored it, but didn't.

Dear Alex,
In case it wasn't already obvious, I'm persistent. I'm serious about talking to you. This is more than just one of those "where are they now" features. I really want to showcase the impact viral videos can have on their victims. I've already spoken to Numa Numa boy, the backyard Light Sabre guy, the boy whose little brother Charlie nearly bit off his finger, and a bunch of others. But you're the first and arguably the most shocking viral video in the history of YouTube. We can do it without photos and without formally identifying you. But others might learn how profoundly their actions can affect

others. You'd be doing something in the public interest, something that might actually help other victims, or perhaps more importantly forestall some jerk's prank on another innocent person.

I'd read all this before but read it again because it was moderately less boring than waiting for boarding to start. Matt was on his phone to his office. But then I read her closing line.

You know, you weren't the only one affected that night in your high school auditorium. I was there when it happened, almost directly above me. I was transfixed, not by the whole scene, but really by the look on your face, in your eyes. I couldn't look away. It haunts me. It's why I'm writing this piece, to try to understand not just its impact on victims like you, but to try to figure out why it has such a hold on me. You wouldn't just be helping other victims; you'd be helping me, personally, I mean. Could we please meet?

Laura Park

I read her last few sentences several times. No. It couldn't be. Why hadn't she said this earlier? I hit Reply and typed:

What were you wearing that night? (And I don't mean that in a weird, creepy way.)

I bounced my heels up and down as I sat there waiting for her reply and for our boarding zone to be called. Just before I closed the lid on my laptop and rose to join the line, her reply arrived.

Bright red dress.

Holy shit. Why hadn't she told me this in her first email? I closed my laptop and stood beside Matt in line. Several people looked at the two of us and whispered to their companions. For the first time in a decade I didn't fear they'd recognized me from a certain viral video. Rather, I knew they were just observing that a set of identical twins was standing together in an airport lounge. I was learning that that was enough to turn heads and trigger double takes. At the gate, the airline employee stared at the photo in my passport and then at me.

"I just had a haircut."

She looked closely and waved me on to the flight. My hair was now even shorter than Matt's. We decided to trim even more in the hopes that Stephanie would accept the real Matt as the same person who'd met her the previous week at the Four Seasons Park Lane. A brush cut, right down to the wood, had been proposed, but I refused. Still, my hair was cut shorter than it had ever been, even in Gabriel's time. It might have been the haircut, but I felt different after the events of the previous week. By different, I mean better, happier, more comfortable, less anxious, closer to whole, more like myself, if that makes any sense. The flight was long but uneventful, though identical twins sitting together did stimulate some interest from the flight attendants.

We met in Stephanie's Manhattan office in the heart of Wall Street. She was not alone this time. Three of her staff sat alongside her at the boardroom table while Matt and I sat across from them. Matt handled his "reunion" with Stephanie very smoothly. He asked about her flight from Heathrow and thanked her again for having her driver take him back home from the airport. With my very short hair, she had no idea Matt's understudy had stepped in for the previous performance. That was a relief. Plus, there was no longer a need for me to fake an English accent.

It became clear soon after the meeting started that Stephanie was going to invest. The discussion focused on the terms of the deal, not on the possibility of a deal. In keeping with my standard operating procedure, I said very little in the meeting and let Matt carry most of the load. However, late in the proceedings, one of Stephanie's colleagues asked a technical question about the software that supported the Innovatengage platform. Matt could easily have answered, but turned to me for a response. I started off a bit haltingly, but found my way and soon got into the moment. After all, software was my safe harbour.

Ninety minutes after the meeting started, Matt and Stephanie signed a binding term sheet for her investment and commensurate ownership stake in the company. Lawyers representing both entities would hammer out the actual legal agreement in the coming week or so. But the deal was essentially done.

"Thank you for this vote of confidence," Matt said. "I was kind of expecting that you'd want more shares."

"That's what you said last time we met," Stephanie replied. "Too many good companies have been ruined by VCs that get too deeply entangled in operations. I need you to remain the creative and cultural leader of Innovatengage. That's how I protect my investment. So unless or until you're heading off the rails, it's your show."

The next morning, Matt knocked on my hotel room door. We'd booked into the Algonquin. It was an old and noble Manhattan hotel, but the rooms were very small.

"Okay, our work here is done," he started. "But will you indulge me and join me on a bit of a mission? I'd rather not say much about it, but it makes no sense if you don't come with me."

"I have to be back in my cubicle in two days," I reminded him.

"No worries. It won't take that long," he said as he handed me two boarding passes stapled together.

"What would you have done if I'd refused?" I asked, looking at the boarding passes.

"I was pretty sure you wouldn't."

Three hours later we boarded an Air Canada flight to Toronto, then connected to an Ottawa flight. It seemed we were going home.

Four and a half hours after leaving LaGuardia, a Blueline taxi dropped us off at the Chateau Laurier. It felt very strange to be back in Ottawa. I felt different from when I left a few weeks earlier. So much had happened. So much had changed.

"You do know that I have a perfectly serviceable apartment in the Glebe, right?" I said.

"What's a Glebe?" he asked.

"A neighbourhood just south of the downtown core. It's about a six-dollar cab ride from here."

"But this is easier. Besides, we're celebrating," Matt explained.

We checked into two different rooms and met in the lobby twenty minutes later.

"Now what?" I asked.

"Patience. We have three stops to make. It's all arranged," Matt said.

He checked his iPhone map app and led me out the revolving doors of the Chateau Laurier. We walked for ten minutes to a downtown office building known as World Exchange Plaza. We walked directly to the elevators and boarded one. Matt hit the button for the twentieth floor. Laurendeau-Rousseau was one of Canada's largest law firms and occupied Suite 2000.

Matt approached the young man who sat at the reception desk.

"Hello. We have a meeting in the Trudeau Room," Matt said.

"Mr. Paterson?"

"Yes, that's right."

"Just down the corridor, second door on your right."

Matt and I walked down the hall and into a small conference room. A large oil painting of what looked like Georgian Bay hung on the wall. A plate of cookies and a carafe of coffee waited on a side table.

I was about to say something, but Matt raised his hand to stop me. We could both hear the soft footfalls of someone approaching along the corridor. We heard them stop just outside the open door, and pause for a moment. Then through the door came the unmistakable figure of Cam Forster. Even though ten years had passed, I'd have recognized him in a Ninja Turtle costume.

He closed the door and turned to face me. He looked upset, distraught. I looked at Matt. Using his index finger, he just gently pushed his chin up to shut his gaping mouth and then pointed at me. It seemed my yap was hanging open. I closed it.

"Alex, I wasn't sure you'd have come if I told you," Matt said. "This is important, for both of you."

Cam then took a few fledgling steps towards me. He looked stricken. On instinct, I braced myself for his traditional headlock, but it never came. Instead, he extended his hand. I shook it and he drew me into a hug. He wasn't exactly sobbing, but he was snuffling and held the embrace longer than seemed appropriate.

"Alex, I'm so sorry," he said. "I was a jerk, an asshole. I didn't know what I was doing. I'm so sorry."

He let go and we all just stood there.

"Sorry, I thought I'd be able to hold it together," Cam said, "but then I saw you, and, well . . ."

You get used to holding it together.

"It's okay, Cam," I said.

"No, it's not okay, Alex. I just slipped into Jackson's orbit. He seemed like a big shot and I kind of liked how it felt to be around him. But the ARCHangel thing just went way too far. Way too far. I was horrified as it was happening, but I was in too deep by then. Or at least that's how it felt."

I get that. Jackson was a big shot.

"Cam, you don't have to . . ."

"Yes, I do. I need to. I really do," Cam insisted. "I even made a lame attempt to stop the whole thing. Not that it worked. But I stopped your descent about fifteen feet earlier than I was supposed to. The lights would have missed you. But Jackson noticed. And he was not happy about it. He pushed me away and hit the button again until you were right in position, that stupid piece of red tape right where it was supposed to be. I'm so sorry I didn't do more. And you have to believe me, I had no idea about the Viagra. Jackson just told me to distract you in the cafeteria, so I did. That's when I put you in . . ."

You don't have to remind me. I know. I was there.

"I know, Cam. The headlock. I remember," I said. "But who shot the video?"

"We shot some of it from the lighting bay but we couldn't just stay there for the whole scene. We would have been caught. But what I didn't know was that Jackson had threatened three grade niners into shooting the scene from their seats. We met up afterwards, gathered up the memory cards, and then Jackson stitched the video together and uploaded it to YouTube. I'd never even heard of YouTube and had no idea that was his master plan."

Who knew he could edit video? Clearly a man of many diabolical talents.

"Well, he did a pretty good job on the video," I said. "It still drives a lot of traffic."

Cam winced.

"I know. I know. Look, Alex, I'm so sorry. When it went viral, I was a bit of a basket case for quite a while. I was paralyzed. I should have called you, but I just couldn't do it. Plus, I kept waiting for the principal or the police to show up at my door. But they never did, because you never squealed. And now I'm a lawyer because you kept our secret. Thank you."

Don't think I wasn't tempted. But the toothpaste was already out of the YouTube.

"It would have just made it worse. Even more people would have watched the video if I'd turned you both in," I replied.

"I've thought about it a lot over the last ten years, but still, I never called or wrote. I should have. I just couldn't. I'm sorry."

It was a long time ago.

"It's fine, Cam. It was a long time ago."

"Yeah, but now whenever I read another article about bullying and the consequences, I think of you and ARCHangel and my role in it, and I feel sick."

I wonder how Jackson feels?

"It's okay, now, Cam. I know Jackson was in charge."

"Cam, perhaps you should tell Alex what you told me on the phone, about your pro bono client," Matt suggested.

"Right. Well, as part of working through my ARCHangel guilt, I'm doing all the legal work for Kids Help Phone gratis. It's nothing compared to what I did to you," Cam said. "But I can't turn back the clock. I wish I could. But it makes me feel a little better to help them out."

Good for you.

"Good for you, Cam," I said.

"And meeting you today, something I've wanted yet dreaded for a very long time, an inexcusably long time, well, it lifts a little weight from my shoulders. I hope it does the same for you."

It's a little early to tell, but I think it might.

"I'm glad we've connected again. Thanks."

We talked for a few more minutes about what it was like finding Matthew after so many years. At one point, I saw Cam looking from Matt to me, and back again. It was then that I noticed that Matt and I were both standing in the identical position, feet shoulder-width apart, our arms hanging free in front of us, our hands held together by interlocked fingers, our thumbs crossed, too. Identical and a little eerie.

Cam apologized another forty-seven times before hugging me for too long again. Then he gathered himself and walked us back to the reception area.

When Matt and I emerged from the elevator on the ground floor, he put his hand on my shoulder. There had certainly been a lot of hugging and touching in my life since I'd found my twin brother. I realized I liked the sensation and what it meant.

"So? How do you feel?" he asked.

"Better, I think. A little lighter," I replied. "But how did you find him?"

"Come on. You gave me his name when you told me the story and Google did the rest. It's not hard to find a lawyer working in Ottawa when you have a name," Matt said. "Then I just called him up to make sure I had the right guy. It took a while to explain who I was and what my rather unusual connection was to you, but we pushed through. It was like he'd been waiting for my call, or maybe your call. He was ready."

"But you didn't have to keep it a secret from me," I said.

"Really? Think about it. If I'd suggested this, would you really have agreed? Would we have just met with Cameron Forster if I'd told you?"

I stopped walking and thought about it.

"Okay. Fair point," I conceded. "I probably would have pushed it off or just said no."

"But now that it's done, was it helpful?"

"Comfortable? No. Helpful? Maybe," I said. "Thanks for making it happen. You had other things on your plate this week. It was a thoughtful, um, brotherly thing to do."

"Don't thank me yet," he said, as he raised his hand to hail a taxi.

We settled in the back seat of the cab. He read the address off his iPhone for the driver.

"No, Matt," I said.

"Alex, yes, it's important. Please," Matt replied. "It's part of all this."

It was close to five when we arrived. Most had left the building. The football team still toiled on the field, running drills. Thankfully, no one seemed to be in the main office or the foyer. My high school had changed very little in ten years. I hadn't been inside since that night, since Gabriel, or what the rest of the world knew as ARCHangel.

"Are we expected? We're not meeting anyone, are we?" I asked.

"No and no," Matt replied. "You're just dropping something off."

I looked at him, puzzled.

"Baggage" was all he said.

He looked around the front foyer and pointed to the two sets of double doors on our left.

"In here?" he asked.

I nodded. He walked over and tried the doors. They were open. The lights weren't on, but the windows on one side gave more than enough illumination. It was smaller than I'd remembered. Filled with people, it had just seemed so much bigger. Alone in the auditorium, we walked down the centre aisle. Instinctively, I looked up to the ceiling and found the lighting bay. Then I let my eyes follow my descent to the altitude where I'd stopped and the spotlights found me. A calm settled over me then as it inexplicably had that night ten years earlier.

"Do you want to go up?" Matt asked, nodding his head towards the lighting bay.

I shook my head.

"Don't need to," I replied. "Everything seems smaller, now."

"Maybe it wasn't packed to the rafters that night as you remembered it," he said.

"No, no, it was definitely packed to the rafters. It just seems smaller without the people, and in daylight. Smaller in every way."

Matt kept a respectful distance and waited.

I moved to the third row from the front, fourth seat over, 3D, and sat down.

"This is where she sat."

"Red dress?" Matt asked.

I nodded.

"I couldn't take my eyes off her. She kept me calm and breathing all the way down."

We stayed only a few more minutes. I knew the cab was still idling in the turning circle out front.

"One more stop?" I asked, as we climbed into the back seat of the taxi.

Matt nodded.

"Are you okay? We can call it a day and forget the final act," Matt offered.

"No, let's finish it," I replied. "I think I feel better than I thought I would. So I might as well see it through since you've already organized the whole tour."

But the address he gave the driver was not the one I'd been expecting. It was a short trip. The cab pulled up in front of the main entrance of the Ottawa Hospital, and we got out. Inside the lobby, Matt seemed to know where he was going. We boarded an elevator. When the doors opened, the sign on the wall opposite said "Oncology." Matt turned right and started down the corridor, scanning the room numbers. Then he halted, turned around, and walked back the way we'd come to the hallway on the other side of the elevators. Matt soon stopped in front of a room with the door propped open. I looked inside and saw a small figure curled in the bed. Various tubes snaked from machines and IV stands into various entry ports in the patient. I did not recognize him. I looked at the patient's name and number posted outside the door and could not reconcile the name with the figure in the bed. His eyes were open, though he'd not yet noticed us.

Matt gently knocked on the door but stepped to the side so that only I was framed in the doorway. The man looked at me, squinted, blinked a few times, then grinned as he rolled over onto his back.

"Holy shit. As I live and barely fuckin' breathe, and I won't be for long, the ARCHangel is in the house!" Jackson Trent's voice was a much softer version of the one I remembered. "Hope you've still got your wood on!"

Then he was wracked by a coughing fit. I was shocked. I would never have recognized him. His coughing slowed and stopped. I walked up to his bedside.

"Um, hi Jackson," I stammered. "It's been a very long time."

"Not long enough, boner-boy. But now that you're here, I want to thank you for being such a pussy that night. It made the greatest prank I ever pulled a piece of cake," he said.

By this time, Matt had entered the room.

"This is my brother, Matthew."

Jackson barely looked at Matt, then came back to me.

"My best fuckin' stunt ever. You made me famous," Jackson said.

"Actually, I think it's the other way around," Matt said. "You made Alex famous, and not in a good way."

"Yeah, well, fuck you," he whispered. "ARCHangel was my greatest achievement. I still watch it a few times each week, just to keep the numbers up. It was fuckin' brilliant. I was fuckin' brilliant. And you walked right into it. We were going to do it anyway, but when we found you in the caf and you actually had a fuckin' Coke in your hand, it was like winning the lottery. It was meant to be."

There was a pause when all we could hear was the hum of the machines and Jackson's laboured breathing as he recovered from his own words.

"What's wrong with you?" I asked. "I mean, what are you sick with?"

"Lung cancer. Stage fuckin' four," he replied. "It showed up eight months ago after I thought I'd beaten melanoma. Too much fuckin' sun on the golf course. That's what started it all. Thought I was just allergic to the new fertilizer we were using on the course. But it was the big fuckin' C, again."

"I'm sorry," I said, still barely recognizing the slight figure hunched in the bed as Jackson Trent, Bully of the Year, 2005.

For the first time I saw the clear plastic tubing hooked behind each of his ears delivering oxygen through two prongs in his nostrils. I hadn't really noticed this earlier, I think because it was such a familiar sight.

"I'm sorry you're sick," I said softly. "And for what it's worth, I forgive you for, you know, for ARCHangel."

"Yeah, well, fuck forgiveness and fuck you," he said, lifting his head off the pillow and giving me a look of pure contempt. I finally recognized Jackson Trent in the hospital bed. "I don't want your goddamn forgiveness. You had it coming with your pansy-ass acting. You fuckin' asked for it. And it was a thing of beauty. It was perfect. Probably the only perfect thing I ever did. So fuck forgiveness."

I suddenly felt what I can only describe as closure enter the room and wrap itself around me. I had not expected it to be so palpable. But there it was.

I walked over to the bed and put my hand on Jackson Trent's arm, above his intravenous. I gently patted it, twice.

"See you, Jackson."

Then I turned and walked out of the room, with Matt two steps behind.

"Yeah, well, fuck you, ARCHangel. See you on the other side."

I stared at the girl below, her face a blend of sympathy and rage. But those eyes. Her eyes. New sounds above me, then vibrations.

CHAPTER 15

"It's an extraordinary story. I'm very happy for you and Matt," Wendy Weaver said. "And finding your father, too. It's amazing."

We were in her office the next morning. She'd made room for me on short notice. I was sitting where I always sat, but it felt different. Everything felt different.

"But before we get too far ahead, tell me more about your acting debut as your twin with that American investor," she asked. "Clearly you pulled it off, but how were you feeling when it was actually happening? What were your emotions? What were you thinking?"

"Funny you should ask. This never happens, but for some reason I had no worries about her recognizing me as Gabriel. Strangely, that fear wasn't even in my mind. Maybe that's my actor's arrogance kicking in," I said. "And I felt very calm and comfortable when I was finally in the room with her. Odd. I was terrified when we pulled up out front, but just fine when I stepped out of the car and the performance started."

"Why?" she asked. "Why do you think you felt that way?"

"You already know why, but you really want me to say it, right?"

"Am I really that transparent?" Wendy asked.

"Either that or we've both been doing this for far too long," I replied. "But to get to your point, the only conclusion I can draw is that I was not myself when I was in the meeting, therefore I was not anxious and over-wrought as I usually am with strangers. I was playing Matt. I was acting. Alex MacAskill wasn't in the room, so I was safe."

"Not to pound the point into the ground, but you were totally relaxed, confident, and calm, even on the inside, during the meeting?"

I nodded.

"That sounds nothing like the typical post-Gabriel you, but very much like Matt's natural state," she said. "Do you see where this is going, what this means?"

"That I'm an outstanding actor whose talents are being wasted as a coding cubicle creature?"

"Perhaps, but it also means that you are actually capable of being relaxed, calm, articulate, warm, witty, and friendly, in public settings. You proved it in that meeting. Furthermore, from what you've told me, it sounds like Matt and you have very similar personalities, dispositions, and attitudes, as one might expect when the two of you share the same DNA. Now stay with me here. So isn't it just possible that while you were acting as Matt, you were in fact portraying who you would truly be had Gabriel not intervened? That acting as Matt actually liberated you to go completely inside-out with a total stranger?"

"Let's not read too much into it," I said. "I really was acting as Matt. I wasn't just being Alex with an English accent. I was Matt."

"Do you really know that? Are you certain?" she asked. "Let me put it another way. Isn't it true that if you'd gone in there and performed as Matt in exactly the same way as you did, but without affecting an English accent, it would almost be like the real Alex MacAskill saying out loud what you usually keep inside your head? Can you not see that?"

I said nothing as I tried to follow her logic, not that it was too cerebrally taxing. I think I knew that what had happened in the last week, and even in the last day, was significant. But I was still circling it, reluctant to venture too close.

"Alex, listen, this is important. I think this is a big step forward, even if you haven't really picked up on it," she said. "Don't lose this momentum. Remember what it felt like to be in that meeting. Remember that you pulled it off, that your performance was convincing. And use that sensation, that memory and that knowledge."

Even though I thought she was probably investing too much in my meeting with Stephanie, I had come to trust her judgment over the years.

"By the way, what about the Gabriel dream?" she asked. "When was the last time you had it?"

"Hmmm, now that you mention it, not since our last night in Moscow," I replied. "That might be a record."

We spent the next twenty minutes until my time was up talking about the Gabriel Closure Tour that Matt had so kindly organized the day before. I already loved Matt. He was my identical twin brother. Love is somehow built in, even after such a long separation. But his insight and thoughtfulness in tracking down Cameron and Jackson and taking me back to my Gabriel ground zero left me with such a strong feeling of warmth and gratitude towards him. He had so much on his mind yet he still had room in his head and his heart to worry about me, to try to fix me, to help me move past my past. After visiting the skeletons in my closet the day before, I was keen to sustain the momentum and tie up one more loose end.

It was just coming up to 3:30 p.m. I waited in the bar just off the lobby of the Chateau Laurier, Ottawa's grand old hotel, opened in 1912. Preferred by power brokers of all ideological stripes for more than a century, the Chateau was the scene of many seismic events that had shaped Canada's political landscape. Framed black and white shots by the renowned photographer Yousuf Karsh hung in the bar. Hemingway, Einstein, and Churchill looked down from the walls, even Stephen Leacock.

As an exercise, I decided to follow Wendy Weaver's advice. As an actor, I planned to play the character of one Alex MacAskill, but in that fictitious world where Gabriel had never happened. It was acting, but if I performed the role well, I might be the only one who knew. Strangely, it was an idea that had never occurred to me.

She was right on time. Even without the red dress and a bird's-eye view, I recognized her immediately. When I saw her, my heart did something I can't really describe. It had been so long. She had no trouble recognizing me and picked her way through the tables to greet me, her hand extended.

"Laura Park," she said as we shook hands. "So glad to finally see you again in the flesh, after so many . . ."

Nice. It's going to be like that, is it?

She grimaced, then looked horrified.

"Shit! So sorry. I don't know why I said that. I meant nothing by it," she said, even though I was smiling by that time. "We're not starting that way. We are not."

She turned, walked four steps away from me, performed a rather theatrical turn, and approached me a second time.

"Hi, I'm Laura Park. Wonderful to see you after so many years."

Better. Your eyes haven't changed.

"Alex MacAskill. I'd recognize your eyes anywhere, and that's not a come-on line," I said, re-shaking her hand. "I really can't believe we're actually meeting."

We sat down and ordered drinks from the roving waiter.

"Just to get it out in the open right off the bat, I will never forget locking eyes with yours as I dangled above the audience," I said. "You couldn't possibly know this, but you really helped me that night. You really helped me survive that night."

"Really? You're kidding. Well, I'm glad I was helping, but I had no idea," she replied. "I was just so horrified for you. That another human being would do that to someone else was a harsh wake-up call for me about the real world. I just wanted to reach up and help you down, but I could only stare at you and not look away. Your eyes were pretty wild that night, unsurprisingly."

Yeah, well, I was caught a little off-guard, you know, being plied with drugs, stripped naked, and suspended high above the crowd. Cirque du Soleil it was not.

"Yes, well, I wasn't wearing my usual costume," I replied. "But you wore a bright red dress. And you never did look away. You sometimes had your hand in front of your mouth. But your face and your eyes said so much to me, meant so much to me in those moments. It really was like you were with me, on my side. I'll never forget that. I don't know what would have happened if you'd not been there below me. I've been looking for you ever since, to thank you, I mean."

"Well, you ignored almost all of my emails."

I wouldn't have if you'd mentioned the red dress right off the top.

"That's because until your last one, I had no idea who you were, that you were there that night, that you were the girl in the red dress," I explained. "If you'd mentioned that in your first email, we'd have met months ago."

She paused and looked down for a moment. Uh-oh.

"Um, this is a bit awkward," she started.

Here we go. I wondered how long it would be before you asked. You want to know what was so arousing about hanging high above the audience bound, gagged, and trussed like a pig on a spit.

"But there is one detail I'm still trying to understand, as a journalist, I mean," she said. "I don't know if it was the pressure or terror of the moment, or maybe it was . . ."

"Viagra," I interjected. "That's what it was. The little blue pill."

"Sorry?"

"The Coke I was drinking about an hour before the show was laced with it, obviously without my knowledge. It was all part of their master prank."

"Ah, okay, okay. Got it. That makes total sense, now," Laura said. "That's just cruel and inhuman."

Yet it seems to have been the highlight in Jackson Trent's soon-to-be-foreshortened life.

"Why were you there in the auditorium that night?" I asked. "I'd never seen you around the school, never seen you before or after. Where did you come from?"

"My cousin, Jessie Bain, was in grade nine at your school. I was visiting her for the weekend. Turned out she was a shepherd in the pageant, so I went to watch," she said. "And then when the spotlights found you and I realized what must have happened, my heart just broke for you."

I could see that in your eyes.

"I could see that in your eyes. I don't know how you managed to be so clear with your eyes alone, but I knew exactly what you were thinking. It was like the Vulcan mind meld. I just knew you were with me. It was like you were communicating with me. It helped keep me calm through the entire ordeal. But afterwards, I could never find you. And I tried. I wish I'd known you were Jessie's cousin. I knew her a little bit from the show."

"I had no idea you were looking for me. Anyway, that night really stayed with me. When I eventually pursued journalism, we were always told to dig underneath the story, to try to understand not just what happened, but what lay behind it, and what did it mean for the key players, over time."

You mean, "How did it change the key players, over time?"

"Hence your emails," I suggested.

"Right. I really want to write about the broader impact of viral videos on the lives of those victimized in them," she said. "I really think it's an important story. And now that video has taken over the web, the kind of prank that was pulled on you is happening more and more with horrendous consequences."

Oh, I'm well aware of the consequences. Okay, I'm ready, but no names, no photos, and no links to the video. Deal?

"Well, I think I'm finally ready to talk about it, but I do have some, I guess you'd call them conditions, before we can move forward," I said.

"I figured you might," she replied. "What do you have in mind?"

That nobody, who doesn't already know, learns that I, Alex MacAskill, was the unwilling engorged aerial exhibitionist known as ARCHangel.

"It's pretty straightforward, I think," I began. "My real name is not to be used in the story. The name of the high school is not to be mentioned. No reference is to be made to Ottawa or even Eastern Ontario. And, of course, no photos. Sorry if that seems restrictive."

But it's no more restrictive than what I've been living with for the last ten years.

"Done. No problem. I hadn't planned on using any of that information unless you were comfortable. I'm totally fine moving forward without it," she replied. "In fact, your identity is not the point at all."

"Where and when would the story run?"

"I'm a freelance writer, but the *Globe and Mail* weekend section has accepted the story idea. December marks the tenth anniversary of YouTube and the uploading of ARCHangel. They want to run the story on the second weekend in December as we head into the craziness of Christmas."

Merry Christmas to all, and to all a good night.

"Okay, so what do we do now?" I asked.

Laura pulled a small digital recorder out of her purse and placed it on the table between us.

Whoa!

"Well, if you're ready and have some time now, I would just

like to ask you a series of questions and that'll probably be it," she replied. "I may need to call you back as I write the story just to clarify a few points. Then someone from the *Globe* may call you to fact-check some points in the story, but they've already agreed to protect your anonymity."

"Okay," I said, eyeing the recorder. "But the audio files will never be released, right?"

I mean, tell me you're not working on the "ARCHangel Unveiled" podcast.

"You have my word on that."

I believe you. I believe those eyes.

"Thank you," I said. "And one more thing, could I read the story before it runs?"

"That is very unusual, but then again, this is not your average freelance piece," she said. "If you don't let anyone know that you saw it prepublication, I'll agree to send it to you, but it'll just be between us. Does that work?"

"That works for me."

"And just to be clear, the story is not just about you. I'm also highlighting several other V3s, I mean viral video victims."

Wait, you cooked up a name for people like me?

"You call them V3s?"

"Sorry, just to myself."

But I'm the star of the piece, right, even if I'd rather not be?

"But given the timing of the article, I figure my part of the story will be quite prominent in the piece, right?"

"Right. That is true. It's hard to avoid. You were the first and are still the biggest."

Isn't that just awesome. How gratifying.

"You do know that for ten years I've been trying to put all of this behind me, right?" I asked.

"Of course," she said. "But I really believe this article, and the very act of sharing your insights for it, may well be part of closing that door once and for all."

You are good.

"Okay, then," I said. "I'm in."

We spent the next hour and a half together. It was much less traumatic than I feared it would be. I suspect – no, I know – I wouldn't have been so calm had our encounter been three weeks earlier. Then again, I would never have agreed to see her three weeks earlier. She was thorough and direct, yet sensitive and understanding. Laura Park was not exactly the dispassionate journalist writing the story from a distance. In part, it was her story, too. I suppose in the spirit of exploring our common ground, she spent some time telling me how that night affected her. She claimed to still be carrying around some unresolved feelings about the human species courtesy of that Christmas pageant in December 2005. I knew what that felt like.

We parted just after 5:00. She promised to email me a draft in the next two weeks. After she'd gone, I sat there in the lobby bar and decided I felt better.

I pulled out my iPhone and dialed Malaya. I hadn't really kept up with her while I'd been gone, so she didn't even know I was back in Ottawa. She didn't pick up. Despite the hour, she was likely still at work in the home of her new patient.

I still had some time before Matt and I were heading into the Byward Market for dinner just a short walk to the east of Parliament Hill and the Chateau Laurier. I banged out an email while I waited.

Dad,

(Hope you don't mind if I call you that. I'm making up for lost time.)

I was thinking, you really don't need to keep sending $5k a month over to me. I have a well-paying job, and Mom's investments, largely thanks to your monthly stake, have left me in a very comfortable position. I'm fine. Instead, maybe you and Matt can figure out how you can invest in Innovatengage. That might be a win-win, particularly if they ever decide to go the IPO route.

Yesterday, Matt took me on a guided tour down memory lane, here in Ottawa. I think it's been very therapeutic. I'm pretty sure I'll be back in London for a Christmas visit. I'll keep you posted until then.

Alex

I watched the screen of my phone just in case Dad responded. After all, it was close to midnight in London and he'd likely be alone, perhaps with his "safe phone" near at hand. Sure enough, a few minutes later, his email appeared.

Son,

(I'm honoured you addressed me as "Dad.")

Matt has texted me already about what happened yesterday. Even if it is difficult, he is trying to help. So am I. You are his brother and my son, though neither Matt nor I have been able to do our part until now. As you say, I think we are trying to make up for lost time. Still it remains hard for me to be the father I now wish to be. But I am now intending to retire earlier than I had planned, maybe even before the end of the year. The thought of only seeing Matt and you at clandestine meetings after dark is hard to take. We will be free from all of this soon. In the meantime, perhaps I can find a reason to visit our embassy in Ottawa. All of a sudden, it seems quite urgent for Canada to strengthen its trading relationship with Mother Russia.

With a father's love,

Dad

I had a little moment sitting there all alone while the after-work crowd ambled into the bar. Then I ordered another drink.

"You already know our platform backwards and forwards. In fact, you've already made improvements to it that thoroughly impressed Isabella," Matt said, leaning towards me on his elbows.

We were sitting in an Italian restaurant called Vittoria Trattoria in the market. It had taken us only a few minutes to walk from the hotel. It was a beautiful, warm night, making it hard to imagine the subzero temperatures just around the corner.

"Matt, I have a good job, a great job, at Facetech. We're doing stuff right on the bleeding edge," I replied.

"Yes, but you could be doing that same level of advanced work at Innovatengage, and we could all be together, you know, the way most families are."

"Matt, Isabella is very good at what she does. I've seen her work up close," I countered. "You don't want her nose out of joint by having me there in a role that seems to replicate her job."

"No, you're misreading the situation and the role," he said. "This is Isabella's idea. She wants you to come. I've not pressured her on this at all. You would be coming in as R&D lead. Her role is to keep the current platform online and optimized. Your role would be to work with me to figure out what Innovatengage 2.0 will be. There's no overlap with Isabella at all."

"It's a very nice offer. But this is my home. I live here and I like my job. I even kind of miss my job, parts of it, anyway. I need to get back to it."

It went on like this for most of the dinner. We actually got a little drunk that night. And when I say "a little drunk" I really mean something else. The confluence of so many big emotional events in the last couple of weeks seemed to trigger a kind of catharsis in us both. Yes, that's the right word, I think. Catharsis. I don't mean we got hammered, threw alternating fits of hysterics and weeping as we celebrated, and then got thrown out at closing time. No. It wasn't like that at all. We were thrown out well before closing time. I'd share more details if they weren't so hazy, jumbled, and a little disquieting, in my memory. I do not remember how we got back to the Chateau Laurier. I suspect it involved seeing it from the sidewalk outside the restaurant and then stumbling towards it along a very meandering route till we somehow found the Wellington Street revolving doors to the lobby. On the floor of my mind lies a memory fragment of negotiating those revolving doors. I know it's not a happy memory, but that's all I can recall. What I do know is that despite each of us having rooms booked in the hotel, I woke up to find Matt crashed out on the couch in mine.

My first act in the morning, when I became capable of rational thought, was to secure late checkouts for us both. Matt was still sprawled on the couch, passed out or asleep, or more likely a little of both. I hauled the spare blanket from the shelf in the closet and covered him with it. Then I took a shower. I stood under the strong, full stream for just over an hour, though it felt like just a regular ten-minute shower. When I emerged, it was nearly 11:00 a.m. Matt was gone but had left a note in his barely decipherable hand.

> *Bro*
> *I'll call about a late checkout and then I'll be in my shower. Meet you in the lobby at 1:00.*
> *Bro*

Matt had a three o'clock flight booked to Toronto where he'd catch his London flight later that evening. We said very little to one another in the cab. I think it was a combination of our shared hangover and a dawning realization that having found each other after so many years, we were about to separate again, this time voluntarily. It didn't really feel right.

I waited with my bags while Matt checked in at the Air Canada counter. I would just catch a cab to my apartment from there. Matt joined me a few minutes later. At the Ottawa airport, security and the gates are downstairs. I walked him down the long flight of stairs but could really go no further. The line-up for security snaked almost to the foot of the stairs. Matt had his laptop backpack slung over one shoulder. We stepped over to the side to let others pass.

"It makes no sense that I'm going back to London and you're staying here," Matt said. "We're not nearly caught up."

"Matt, this isn't goodbye for another quarter-century. We're going to see each other again, often. I'm coming to London for

Christmas. That's only a couple of months away. Dad's going to try to come over here. And who knows how often you'll be back for meetings with Stephanie. I can zip down to New York or even San Francisco when that happens."

"I know, but it's still weird that you found me and now we're willingly separating again."

"Matt, I need to be back here for a bit. I need to get back to normal after Mom and after finding you and Dad. I need to lie low for a bit and figure it all out," I replied, still not sure if what I was saying was logical, either to Matt or to me. "But we have Skype and FaceTime and can talk as much as you like. Every day if we want."

Matt just stared at his shoes.

"Matthew, at the risk of getting maudlin, we've found each other. We're not losing each other again. We are together. We just won't always be together in the same city."

"I know. I know," he said. "Right then, bring it in."

We hugged.

"Thank you for yesterday's little field trip. It meant a lot to me, and I really believe it helped me," I said, holding both of his upper arms. "I'll Skype you tomorrow morning when I get in to the office – 7:30 Ottawa time would be 12:30 London time. Okay?"

"Good."

Then he turned and joined the line. I climbed the staircase but waited and watched over the railing. Matt looped into and out of sight as the line moved up and back through the cordoned path before emptying into the security screening area. When Matt made his last appearance below me, I suddenly understood. The pieces finally aligned in my mind. It shouldn't have taken so long.

"Matt. Hey Matthew, up here!" I shouted.

He looked up and eventually found me. I had to speak quite loudly to make myself heard.

"You never really had laryngitis, did you?" I called.

"What?" he replied, pointing to his ears, and shaking his head.

"You never really lost your voice," I said, more loudly this time.

"I was sick as a dog," he shouted back.

"You might have been sick, but you never lost your voice."

"I don't remember. I was sick!"

"Maybe, but you never really lost your voice, did you," I pushed.

"I lost mine, and you found yours."

He smiled, waved, and was gone.

Raise me up, please. But no. Lowered into too many waiting cold hands. A coat around me. "It's over," someone said. No, it's just begun.

CHAPTER 16

Abby was right. It happened the very day I returned to Facetech. I really hadn't noticed much going on beneath the surface, but Abby swore it was there and it was big. Then again, I already felt different in the wake of my trip, so I wasn't exactly in the best position to notice subtle shifts in the currents and eddies of office politics. I was dealing with my own eddies and currents.

It wasn't until I laid eyes on Abby again that first morning back that I realized just how much I'd missed her. I was in early, just to get myself ready to re-enter my working life. I was in my cubicle, leaning over trying to feed my laptop power cord down the hole cut in my desk to plug in to the power bar on the floor. I hadn't heard her approach but was made vaguely aware of her presence when she jumped on my back. Like some failed Olympic gymnast who clings to the vaulting horse rather than somersaulting off it and sticking the dismount, she simply stuck to me. Abby clearly thought the whole dismounting thing was overrated. She'd wrapped her arms around me tight and wasn't letting go.

"You're back! You're back!" she cried, still in full piggyback mode, her legs gripping my hips.

Yep, that's my back, all right.

"Um, hi Abby."

Like a dog chasing its tail, I turned around on instinct, hoping to greet her face to face. Normally this manoeuvre would have worked quite well. But with her essentially strapped to my back, it worked less well.

Eventually, she let go and dropped to the floor.

"And look at you in your funky hip new haircut!" she said, now holding my hands and giving my coif a pretty heavy once-over. "Seriously, dude, if you hadn't texted me that you'd be in this morning, I'd never have recognized you or jumped on your back. You're completely transformed. You look flickin' amazing! Seriously. It's like you've gone from playing bass in a '70s acid rock band, to the cover of *GQ*, in one shot, other than the clothes, I mean. Me likey. Me really likey."

Thanks. I figured it was time for a change.

"Thanks. I figured it was time for a change."

"Well, not really, Alex, the time for a change came and went years ago," she said. "But the important thing is, you're home!" She gave me a big hug. I squeezed back and, for the first time, felt natural doing it. "It's so good to have you back. It was weird not having you here where I could harass you at will."

What a coincidence, I missed your harassment. Why do you think I'm back?

"What a coincidence, I missed your harassment. Why do you think I'm back?" I replied, looking directly at her. "I practised my eye contact every single day and thought of you."

"Well, I'm glad because you sure weren't practising texting or emailing," she said. "Wringing flocking updates out of you was hard work. And as you know, I don't much like hard work."

"Yeah, I'm sorry I wasn't in touch more often. There was just so much going on that it was hard to find a moment to brief you on everything," I replied. "But now I can tell you the whole story in person."

"I want the full scoop, if not while we're working, then afterwards," she said. "Deal?"

"Deal."

She stared at me for a few more moments until it became a little awkward. Well, awkward for me. She seemed to be fine with the staring.

"Man, you look good. Now it's critical that we get you pants without pleats."

Good band name – Pants Without Pleats.

I just smiled at her. Naturally, Abby was wearing tight and not exactly office-appropriate jeans, along with – speaking of '70s acid rock bands – a black Deep Purple T-shirt.

Aren't you tempting termination with that outfit?

"Is Simone the Terrible away today, or is your wardrobe choice this morning an act of civil disobedience?" I asked.

"I think she's here today, but laundry did not get done last weekend," she said. "Besides, the Ashe heap has been weird and preoccupied lately, locked in her glass box. I don't think she'd notice if I wore my chainmail and hip-waders ensemble."

Do you sometimes rock the old fly-fishing-Lancelot motif?

"Do you sometimes rock the old fly-fishing Lancelot motif?" I asked. "I'd like to see that."

She lowered her head slightly and stared at me, her brow furrowed.

"Who are you and what have you done with my workmate, Alex?"

"What do you mean?" I replied. "I'm just making witty conversation."

"Yeah, and eye contact, too," she said. "I like it. And if you're interested, I picked up that one-of-a-kind outfit at an estate sale. The previous owner drowned one day while fishing. He tripped over a rock in the river, sank to the bottom, and couldn't get up."

I laughed. So did she. We caught up for the next forty minutes. It was nice. It was really nice.

Simone had called an all-staff meeting for 9:00 a.m. sharp. She arrived at 8:45. I popped my head in her office at 8:58. She appeared to be deeply engaged in her iPad.

"Hi, Simone," I said. "Just wanted to let you know that I'm back and on the job."

She looked up, squinted, and paused, a vacant expression on her face.

"Who are you?"

What do you mean, who am I? Even your attention span can't be that short.

"It's Alex, Alex MacAskill. Remember? I work here. I'm back now."

She squinted, stared some more, and eventually nodded.

"Right. But something's different. Did you gain weight?" she asked.

No, I gained a brother and lost some hair.

"No, but I did get a haircut while I was away," I replied. "That's probably it."

Simone apparently lost interest and returned to her iPad.

"Boardroom," she said.

"Right, on my way," I replied. "And thanks for the time off these last . . ."

"Boardroom!" she snapped.

I took a seat as far from the action end of the table as possible. I said hi to more of my colleagues than I usually did. Everyone was nice welcoming me back. They all seemed to like my buzz-cut, or so they said. They asked about my trip but clearly knew nothing about my successful search for a long-lost brother and father. I felt quite calm. I decided to test-drive Wendy's idea and act in the role of me, but as I'd like to be. Abby sat across from me and spent a good part of the time smiling at me. I smiled back and occasionally made a funny face or crossed my eyes to make her laugh. You know, classic grade six classroom fare, maybe grade seven.

By 8:59, the entire coding team from both floors had assembled in the boardroom. No one knew why Simone had called the meeting, but that was not unusual. Telling us why we were meeting would be surrendering some of her power over us. Simone was very, very good at protecting, preserving, and promoting her power. As usual, she could see from her desk that we were all present and accounted for by the nine o'clock starting time for the meeting. And we could all see she was still busy with her iPad. My money was on Candy Crush but it could have been plain old Facebook. She arrived right on time, at 9:09, and settled on her throne.

"All right, everyone. I needed to avoid another meeting at this time, so thanks for coming to this one, not that you had any choice in the matter," Simone said. "Okay, so since there really isn't an agenda for this meeting, just tell me where are we on Gold?"

She was looking directly at me for some reason. I decided just to wait her out in case she was actually looking at the person next to me.

"Alex? Update please," she said.

Why are you asking me? I've been gone for nearly four weeks.

"Well, Simone, I've been gone for nearly four weeks. This is my first day back. So I may not be in the best position to respond," I replied.

"I would have expected that having been gone for so long during a crucial time in the company's history, that your first priority, now that you're finally back, would be to figure out what the hell happened while you were sunning yourself on some beach."

Actually, I was in London and Moscow, you psycho-nutbar.

"Actually, I was in London and Moscow, you ssssee," I said. "I was dealing with pressing family matters in the wake of my mother's death. I was never on a beach. As for Gold, Design and UX did a fantastic job. I really like what they've come up with on the interface. I think it's clean and simple but still sophisticated. I hear the soft launch last week went well and that Gold has been quietly available for download by our beta testers since then. As far as I can tell, we can formally launch any time, at your imperial command."

Shit. I had really meant to leave that last phrase in my mind instead of dropping it on the boardroom table. All of my colleagues looked as if I'd just burped the alphabet in one go, which, incidentally, I successfully accomplished once back in 2001 with my mother as a witness.

"What did you just say?" Simone said.

I was about to fall on my sword and rethink the entire "act as the version of the person you want to become" thing when the glass door to the boardroom swung open. Carleen, Facetech's director of Human Resources, stood there. I'd never been happier to see someone from HR.

"We're in the middle of a meeting here," Simone said, annoyed.

"Simone, we have a call with Vancouver in my office at 9:15. It's about to start," Carleen replied.

"I can't do that call, it conflicts with this important all-hands-on-deck staff meeting. We're trying to build something and get it out the door. I don't have time for calls not directly related to my ability to bring Gold to market."

Carleen seemed to be barely holding on to the end of her rope.

"Trust me, this call *is* related to your ability to launch Gold. Please join me in my office," Carleen replied. "Stephen will be calling any minute now."

Carleen turned and hustled back to her office.

"Shit, shit, shit! I have no time for this," Simone snapped. "Don't anybody move!"

She stood up and stomped out of the room.

I watched, along with my colleagues, as Carleen lowered the blinds in her office as Simone arrived and dropped into a chair. Every HR director who inhabits a glass-walled office needs blinds.

It took about six minutes. We were still watching as the door to Carleen's office was flung open and Simone Ashe made a beeline for her own office with an expression on her face that nicely straddled the line between distraught and deranged. She carried a letter-sized manila envelope. Carleen followed but did not venture into Simone's office. Rather, she kind of hovered just outside the door. Inside, Simone was banging around, opening and slamming drawers, sometimes pulling out some items and stuffing them in her briefcase. Finally, she stood up from her desk, shoved her overflowing inbox onto the floor making quite an impressive noise that easily reached our ears in the boardroom, and walked past Carleen without a word.

Two security guards materialized from I don't know where and escorted Simone out the Facetech office door and presumably down to her car in the parking garage.

Carleen entered the boardroom.

"I'm sorry you all had to see that," she started. "In case it's not already clear, Simone Ashe is no longer an employee of Facetech. This is not a single, isolated move, but just one piece in a larger, longer-term reallocation of resources. You'll hear more about these changes in a company-wide town-hall conference call this afternoon. Until then, please just try to stay focused on your own roles, your own jobs, and let's concentrate on getting our work done. If any of you wish to talk about this, my door is always open."

We all returned to our workstations, a little shell-shocked, but thrilled that Simone Ashe was now officially an ex-employee.

"Well, that took a lot longer than it should have," Abby said. "She should have been toasted months ago."

"Ding-dong, the witch is dead," I replied.

"And what got into you in there?" Abby asked just as her phone rang.

She reached around to her side of the partition and picked up the receiver.

"Abby here," she said.

Her eyes widened as she listened.

"Sure, Carleen. I'll come right over."

She hung up and turned to me.

"Fuckitty fuck fuck."

"What did she say?" I asked.

"She told me not to worry, but that she wanted to see me."

"Well, that's good. She wouldn't have told you not to worry if there was any reason to, you know, worry," I said.

She grabbed her notebook and patted my shoulder as she headed over to Carleen's office.

"Godspeed," I said.

A casual observer would have said that I was busy working away for the next fifteen minutes, but I was just going through the motions, making my hands move over my keyboard, but doing absolutely nothing. I glanced periodically over my shoulder to monitor Carleen's office. The blinds were still lowered. Finally, Abby emerged and walked back to her chair. I couldn't tell from the look on her face whether it was good news or bad. I slid my chair around to her side.

"Well?" I asked. "Are you okay?"

"I don't really know. It hasn't sunk in yet," she said.

"What hasn't sunk in? I'm dying here," I said. "Did they hand you Simone's job?"

She contorted her face in an “Are you insane?” kind of way.

“No! Of course not. But I’ve been offered a promotion to the new London office that’s opening next week.”

“London! That’s amazing! Congratulations. You said yes, right? Please tell me you said yes.”

“I said yes before even thinking about it. But I have to get there, fast,” she replied.

“How come?”

“The office is opening sooner than they planned because we just landed a huge security contract with Heathrow. I’m going to help customize Gold to Heathrow’s specific needs. Holy shit, I’m going to London.”

My phone rang. It was Carleen. We spoke for just a few seconds, then I hung up.

“Maybe I’m going to London, too,” I said as I stood up.

I knocked on Carleen’s glass door.

“Come on in, Alex,” she said.

I entered and sat down.

“Alex, first of all, welcome back. How are you?”

“Thanks, Carleen. I’m quite well, in fact. It was a very good trip and I got done everything I hoped and needed to get done. And I’m back feeling very good, actually,” I replied.

“I’m glad. I like the new look. You seem, I don’t really know, but you seem somehow more present,” she said. “Anyway, I have a proposition for you, and this comes straight from Vancouver.”

“Okay,” I said.

"Alex, we'd like you to take over Simone's role managing the software team, on an acting basis to start, but with the full intention of moving you into the role permanently if it all goes well. And I think it will go well."

Holy shit.

"Wow" was all I could muster.

I don't remember much about the next three weeks. Four days after Simone Ashe flamed out, Abby packed up and moved to London. I went suitcase shopping with her one evening after work. I also took her plants off her hands. That was not good news for her plants. And I drove her to the airport. She held on to me for quite a long time before lining up to board. It felt nice. She was filled with excitement and trepidation about her new role, whereas I was firmly in the trepidation camp about mine.

I didn't have much time to miss Abby, but enough for it to register. I stuck with my acting exercise, trying my best to act how I wanted to be even if it was just acting. It seemed to help. I had to force myself to meet with the coding team. To make it easier, we met in small groups and one-on-one rather than the mass gatherings that Simone had always inflicted. It took more of my time, but less of everyone else's. But I think we achieved more in those smaller meetings than we would have in a larger gathering.

I'd been staying in close touch with Matthew and our father through various communications devices and apps. With Dad, it was mostly texts on his safe phone. But with Matt, FaceTime was our preferred method. Even though we were both swamped in our respective jobs, we never let more than two days slip by before we connected again. He was thrilled about my promotion. The funding from Stephanie Mosel arrived shortly after the paperwork was signed. Innovatengage was on its way to a whole new stage in its start-up journey.

The following Thursday, just before quitting time, Carleen called me in to her office. As I sat down in front of her, she activated her speakerphone and dialed.

"We're calling Stephen," she said as the phone rang in Vancouver.

I'd met Stephen Collinson, Facetech's CEO, when he'd come to Ottawa not long after I was hired. I'd avoided him ever since and had never had a real conversation with him.

"Collinson," said the voice on the speakerphone.

"Hi, Stephen, it's Carleen and I've got Alex MacAskill here with me. You're on speakerphone."

"Okay, great," Stephen said. "Hi, Alex. Thanks for making some time for us this afternoon."

Well, despite my instincts, I didn't think declining a call with the CEO was a very good idea.

"No problem," I replied.

"Listen, Alex, you've done a great job picking up the pieces after Simone left. By all accounts, the team has pulled together, you've all dug deep, and Gold is now out there and getting rave reviews from our beta testers. Plus, Carleen tells me the coding group is much happier with you at the helm."

Actually, they're happier simply because Simone is no longer at the helm. You could have put a three-toed sloth in charge and they would have been happier.

"It's a very good team. I'm just letting them do what they do best," I replied.

By then, I knew what was coming. What I suddenly didn't know was how I felt about it.

"Anyway, let's get down to it," Stephen said. "Alex, we'd like you to take on the role permanently. Carleen has been telling me for a couple of weeks now how you've really stepped up and become a leader. For us, promoting someone from within is always our preferred approach. So congratulations. We can officially remove the 'acting' from your title and etch what's left in stone."

Thanks so much, Stephen, but I'm feeling profoundly ambivalent about it all and I don't really know why. And by the way, I think "acting" will always be an appropriate word to associate with me and my working life.

"Thanks so much, Stephen, I'm feeling, um, good about what we've accomplished so far, and excited about what lies ahead."

"Good. Carleen is authorized to handle the negotiations with you, so I'll drop off now," said Facetech's CEO. "Thanks for your great work in a difficult time."

He hung up, leaving Carleen beaming at me.

"Well, after the Simone fiasco, it's nice to have some really good news to break to an outstanding employee," she said.

It's wonderful but why do I feel so unmoved by it all?

"Um, Carleen, I really do appreciate this opportunity. It's kind of what I've been working towards. But do you mind, before we negotiate and actually do the etching it in stone thing, if I mull it all over a bit? There's a lot going on and I'd just like to sleep on it for a night."

"Of course, Alex. We can talk in the morning," Carleen said. "But just to help with your deliberations, here are the compensation terms, base and bonus, we were hoping to agree on. And of course, Simone's office is yours, too."

She slid a sheet of paper over to me. I glanced at the numbers before rising to my feet. Wow.

I didn't sleep much that night. I tossed and turned, waffled and wavered, and finally fell asleep around 3:30 a.m. I woke up the next morning with a clear head, thinking about my mother. She'd raised me in that very apartment. It must have been so difficult at times. What an extraordinary sacrifice, made for me.

I went to the office, sat down with Carleen, and resigned.

As I walked out of the Facetech office for the last time, my personal possessions in a banker's box I found in the storeroom, I knew I'd made the right call. Five minutes before I broke the news to Carleen, I wasn't at all certain about my decision. Five minutes later, certainty arrived and that's what I etched in stone that morning.

I offered Malaya anything she wanted from the apartment. Anything at all. I insisted. Other than my bed, she took almost everything else – the living room couch and chair, the TV, the kitchen table and chairs, dishes, flatware, even the area rugs. She was almost overwhelmed. She claimed to be enjoying her new patient but said there would never be anyone like my mother. I agreed.

Save for one large suitcase holding my clothes, books, and some personal mementos by which to remember my mother, I drove the remaining contents of the apartment to a local women's shelter. They were very happy to take towels, two nightstands, my bed, and some framed artwork of dubious provenance. My landlord wasn't quite as understanding as Abby's. There were three months left on the lease until our annual renewal. I paid the three months without complaint. I also made arrangements with my bank so I could transact business remotely until I'd firmed up my plans. It only took about four days and I was free and clear. My final act before departure was to drive my car to Malaya's apartment. She met me outside. She looked puzzled when I gave her my car keys.

"The car is yours, Malaya. I'm going away for a while and have no need of it. It's yours," I said.

She shook her head and tried to hand the keys back. But I wouldn't take them.

"No, it's yours now. The insurance is paid up for two more years. I've already started the process of transferring the ownership and insurance over to you," I said. "You do have your driver's licence, don't you?"

She nodded, still holding the keys, looking bewildered.

"And this is for you," I said, handing her an envelope. "Just think of it as a bonus for all the extra time you spent with my mother and because of how much you did for both of us. My mother was very grateful you were there. I was too."

She opened the envelope and gasped when she saw the cheque for $10,000. She started to give it back to me, but I held my ground. By this stage, she was weeping. I hoped it might be enough to bring her family to Canada.

I decided on the same approach I'd adopted the first time. No heads-up. No warning. Just arrive and go with it. I stepped off the elevator wheeling my giant brand-new Mini Cooper–sized suitcase behind me. When I came through the door, Karen looked up, did a double take, but recovered quickly.

"Alex, you're back," she said. "Great to see you, again. Were we expecting you back so soon?"

"Hi, Karen. No, this is kind of a surprise. I see Matt is in his office." I looked to the far end where Matt was hunched over his desk, absorbed in whatever was on his laptop screen.

"Go on down," she replied. "He'll be thrilled to see you. He's been moping around ever since you left."

I left my suitcase in the closet and walked down to Matt's office.

His door was open. He was obviously fully focused and he did not look up from his screen.

"Still got an opening for an R&D lead?" I asked from the doorway.

Now Matt looked up.

"Are you serious?"

I nodded. Then he jumped up, came around his desk, and gave me a hug.

"Welcome back, brother," he said. "Did you just quit your job, pack up your troubles, pull a Dick Whittington, and move to London?"

Dick Whittington, whoever he is, was not involved in any way.

"I guess I did," I said.

"Yes!" he said with a fist pump. "I somehow knew you would."

"Well, I'm glad *you* did. I just figured it out," I replied. "Anyway, have you seen Dad lately?" I asked.

"At least once a week since you left," Matt replied. "It's really been wonderful. I really like him. Very, very smart. You know, he's moving up his retirement so that he and we can come out of the closet."

"I heard. He emailed me about it."

"Does he know you're back?" Matt asked.

"No. As I said, it was a pretty fast decision. Even I didn't know until a few days ago."

"I want to hear all the gory details. But in the meantime, let me show you your new office," he said, leading the way down the hall and into a slightly smaller, but still very nice office next door to Isabella's.

"I hope this will be satisfactory," Matt said.

"Anything more than a desk and a fraying fabric partition is a step up."

Matt gave me an extra key to his condo and I left him at the office. I unloaded my suitcase at Matt's. My plan was to squat in his condo only until I could find my own in the area. I took a quick nap at Matt's but woke up around seven.

Matt was tied up that night at an event. He'd asked if I wanted to go, but I declined. My initial plan had been to crash and try to catch up on my sleep. But by 7:30 or so, something else pushed its way to the top of my priority list. I pulled the address out of my wallet and plugged it into my iPhone map app. As luck would have it, it wasn't that far away, though it would have taken a longish Underground journey on three different lines. I called a cab instead.

It was about 8:15 p.m. when I arrived. It was a two-storey walk-up with two doors, one for the ground-floor apartment and the other for the second-floor flat. But before I did anything else, I slipped into the role of the Alex I really wanted to be. Then I rang the doorbell for the upstairs flat. After a moment, I heard footsteps coming down the stairs. The door opened and there she was. I was still tired and not at my most creative, so I regressed into cliché.

"Hello, stranger."

"Ack!" Abby cried. "Alex! It's you. You're here! What the flork!"

She wrapped me up in a bear hug and rocked me a little bit on the front porch. Then she took my hand and led me up the stairs to her flat.

"I can't believe you're here," she said. "Wait a minute. Why *are* you here?"

"It's a long story, but to cut it short, three days ago, I resigned from Facetech. They offered me Simone's job but I just realized there really wasn't anything keeping me in Ottawa any longer. So I'll be running R&D for my brother's company."

"Wait, you've moved here? You're living in London, now? Permanently?"

"Yep."

"WoooooFuckinHooooo!" she said, leaping to her feet and bouncing up and down for a bit. "That is so so great. I've been missing, um, hanging out together."

"I've missed it, too," I said. "I can't imagine anyone in the new Facetech London office is anywhere near as cool as we are."

"You got that right," she agreed. "But they're nice enough, and the work is cool. But now, you're here. That is fruckin' amazing."

"Well, that's what I was going for," I replied. "Fruckin' amazing."

Neither of us knew many people in London, so we ended up hanging out a lot together. She made me laugh, and I did my best to sustain eye contact with her. I really liked spending time with her even though we seemed to be keeping it all on the platonic plane. I introduced her to Matt and our father. They both really liked her wit and spirit.

Life at Innovatengage was wonderful. Matt would just talk to me about what the platform should be able to do in the future. He wanted it to be as versatile and flexible as possible so we could accommodate any organization's engagement needs. I started working with the existing platform running on its own server, for the exclusive use of the entire R&D team. In case I hadn't made it clear, I am the entire R&D team. I would then write the code to add new and different cool features. Then I'd show Matt what it would do.

About a week after I'd arrived back in London, Matt popped his head into my office.

"Hey, sorry to be the bearer of bad news, but Jackson Trent died yesterday in Ottawa."

"I know," I replied. "Cam Forster emailed me this morning."

"Me too," Matt said. "You may want to . . ."

"Send flowers," I interrupted. "I know. I already have, anonymously."

"Probably wise."

That night, I took Abby for dinner at the William Blake, not because the food is so wonderful, but so I could show her exactly where I'd first laid eyes on Matthew Paterson. We sat in the same booth. It was odd and wonderful being there with Abby.

She was loving her gig at Facetech-London, and doing well. After we'd finished dessert and were just enjoying our wine and one another, I thought the time was right.

"I've been thinking about this for a while now, and I want to tell you something about me," I opened. "It's something that happened to me almost ten years ago."

She raised her hand.

"Alex, I know. In 2005, you starred in a very short film known as ARCHangel that has enjoyed a good run on YouTube. It messed you up a bit for the last ten years but now you seem to be getting past it and getting on with your life. How'd I do?"

I just stared at her.

"Alex, your mouth is open. Do you want more dessert?"

I closed my mouth.

"How did you know that?" I asked.

"Alex, I've known for a long time. Lots of people know. Lots of people don't know. But it was a very, very long time ago," she said. "Now don't go thinking I'm minimizing what it was like, or even what it must still be like. I know it was capital F fucking horrific. I know it fucked up your life for a while, as it would anyone. How could it not? But it happened. That can't be changed."

Then she reached over and held my hand, using her thumb to massage the top.

"I know it's easy for me to say these things, but please do not let that event a decade ago define you. Do not wear it every day," she said. "A ten-year-old YouTube clip is not the boss of you."

That made me smile. In fact, it made me laugh. She laughed too. And she was still holding my hand.

"You made that very easy," I said. "And ever since I met you, you've been helping me get past what we always called in our household Gabriel."

"Gabriel," Abby repeated.

I scanned the rest of the pub and found what I needed. I stepped out of the booth and onto the patio area out front, where I snagged a stainless steel ashtray and brought it back to our booth.

"I wanted you to be here when I did this," I said.

I pulled a folded paper from my jacket pocket and flattened it out on the table.

"My mother put this away for me shortly after Gabriel went down, in more ways than one, on December 24, 2005."

"What's with the match?" Abby asked.

I said nothing, but peeled the tape away from the program to free the wooden match. I set the program in the ashtray, struck the match on the rough underside of the table, ignited the corner of the paper, and extinguished the match. We both leaned back in our seats to avoid the flames that rose a little higher than I'd expected. It burned bright, but quickly, and was smouldering ash in seconds.

"With you as my witness, I solemnly declare that officially, Gabriel is no longer the boss of me," I intoned.

Abby laughed and held both my hands. At that precise moment, the William Blake's acutely sensitive smoke alarm blared. We left money on the table, dumped the ashes in a garbage can by the door, and made good our escape. We walked, holding hands, all the way back to her flat. I didn't leave till morning.

THE END

ACKNOWLEDGEMENTS

It was perhaps just a matter of time before I would write about identical twins. There aren't many aspects, interests, or experiences of my life that have not somehow, obliquely or otherwise, made their way into one of my novels. I suspect that will always be the case, regardless of how many more books I have in me. So having been an identical twin for my entire life, this novel was inevitable.

My prenatal womb-mate and childhood roommate, Tim, and I remain as close and as much alike, in almost every way, as any two ever could. I am still mistaken for him, and he for me, almost daily, such is the physical resemblance that persists after nearly fifty-seven years. In the novel, the twins are shocked to discover they share identical physical mannerisms. This is a routine experience for Tim and me, though it's still a little unnerving to be at a social function and notice my brother on the other side of the room standing exactly as I am, our feet, legs, arms, and hands in precisely the same positions. When we both clue in to this, particularly if we're in close proximity, one of us immediately shifts our position. More than once I have shown up at an event to discover Tim is there wearing virtually the same colour combination of clothes. I even remember racing back home to change on at least one occasion to preempt lame Doublemint Twins jokes. (And if you don't know about the Doublemint Twins, you're younger than I am.)

Without getting gooey, it goes without saying that this novel would not have been written without my identical twin. He's been a loyal brother and friend through my entire life, but no more so than when I started writing. He was also an early reader of this manuscript and made important suggestions of what I should do with it – some of them even related to the novel.

I thank a great friend, Ian Hull, one of the nation's top estate lawyers, for his expertise. I'm so fortunate that Beverley Slopen, my indomitable literary agent, has been with me from the start. I am indebted to a wonderful team at McClelland & Stewart and Penguin Random House Canada. The editing/publishing legend Douglas Gibson has edited all of my novels, including this one. I'm thankful for his sharp eyes and insights, and his friendship. Bhavna Chauhan also brought her editing prowess to this manuscript, and the novel is better for it. Wendy Thomas, copyeditor extraordinaire, once again found issues and errors to which the rest of us were blind. Frances Bedford and Kaitlin Smith are my amazing publicists. They keep me on the road, and the books front and centre, and I thank them. Ellen Seligman was very supportive of this novel at a time when we now know she had more pressing matters on her mind. This will not surprise anyone who knew her. I will miss our conversations and her guidance.

Back to where it all begins and ends, my deep gratitude and love to Nancy, Calder, and Ben, who have always supported this often frenetic writerly life I now seem to have. I'm very lucky and very grateful.

Terry Fallis, Toronto, October 2016